RUNAWAY

SIXTH IN THE IMMORTALS OF INDRIELL SERIES

MELISSA A. CRAVEN

PRAISE FOR IMMORTALS OF INDRIELL

2016 RONE Award Winner – Best Book Cover
2016 YA Books Central Finalist for Best Indie
2015 Dante Rossetti YA Awards Finalist
2015 International Book Awards Finalist
2015 USA Best Book Awards Finalist

"I loved that Emerge wasn't the usual vampires, shape shifters and werewolves but an entirely new concept." Amazon reviewer ★★★★★

"Just when you think Allie's journey is coming to an end... Craven shows you just how wrong you were. You should NOT miss the end of this book." Amazon reviewer ★★★★★

"Craven has skillfully developed an Urban Fantasy set in a real life, believable context. I can almost believe this ancient race of Immortals actually lives among us." Hub Pages Reviewer ★★★★★

"Emerge is a story that begins as a single snowflake and ends in an avalanche. Craven has put together a story that unfolds again and again, revealing characters of unusual depth." Amazon Reviewer ★★★★★

"Craven has a talent for keeping her reader's attention as she reveals Allie's story, layer by interesting layer. And when you get to the last page, you're left wanting more!" Amazon Reviewer ★★★★★

"The immortal characters all have a special gift, but so does the author. Craven's is a superpower that we can all benefit from: storytelling." Amazon Reviewer ★★★★★

Runaway: Immortals of Indriell Book 6

By: Melissa A. Craven

Midnight Hour Studio INC

Atlanta, Georgia

For more information contact: Hello@Melissaacraven.com or visit the author's website at **Melissaacraven.com**

Cover design by: Daqri Combs: Covers by Combs

Edited by: Caitlin Haines

Interior design by: @BooklyStyle

ASIN: eBook

First Edition for Print by Midnight Hour Studio: June 3, 2021

Printed in the United States of America

In Runaway, find out what happened with Chloe and Graham after they went their separate ways. And then download your free copy of Scholar to discover everything there is to know about the Immortals of Indriell.

Visit **bit.ly/ScholarOffer** to download now

For the readers who have waited
so patiently for this book.
Your enthusiasm and support mean the world to me

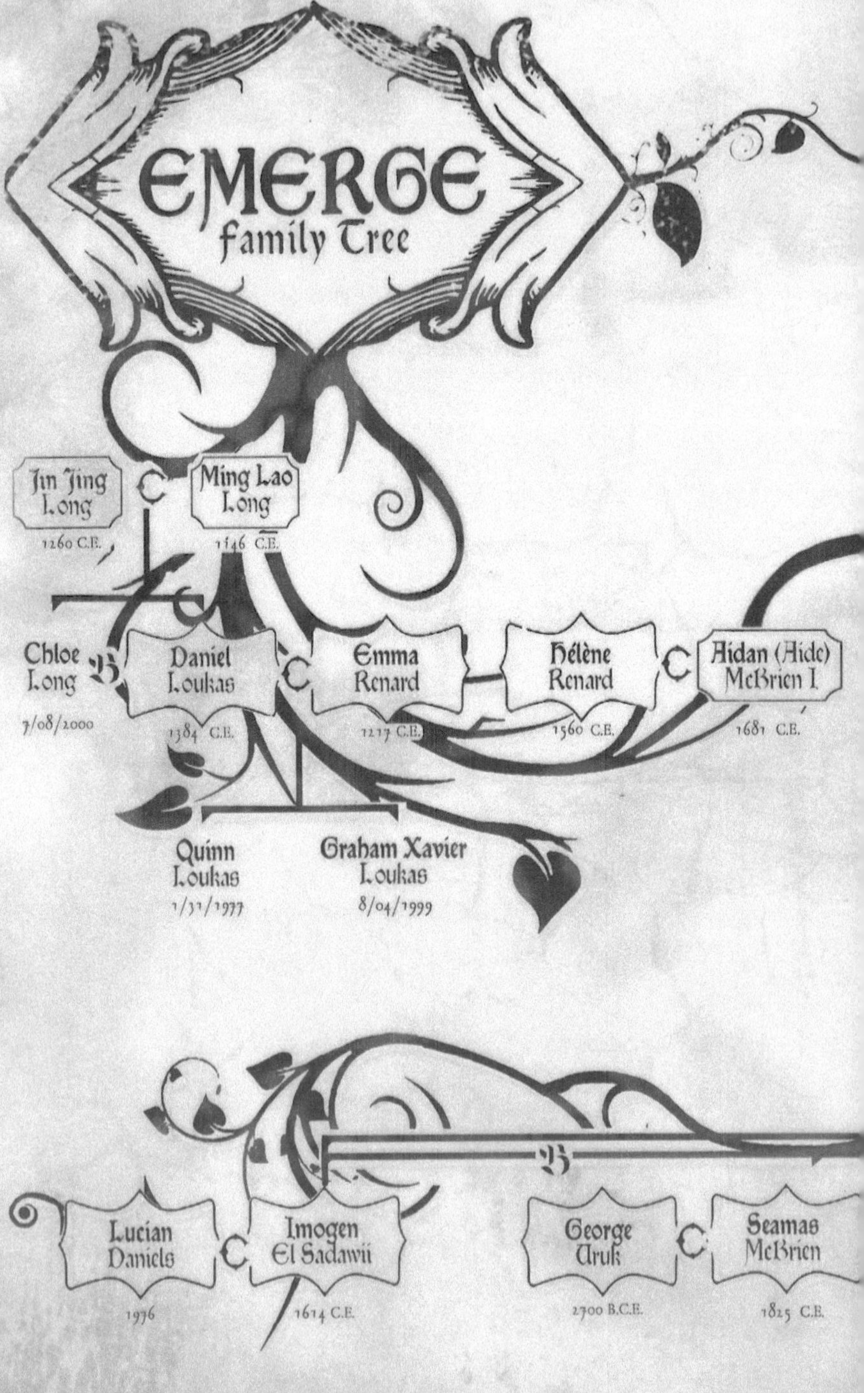

EMERGE
Family Tree
Jin Jing Long
1260 C.E.
C
Ming Lao Long
1146 C.E.
Chloe Long
7/08/2000
B
Daniel Loukas
1384 C.E.
C
Emma Renard
1217 C.E.
Hélène Renard
1560 C.E.
C
Aidan (Aide) McBrien I.
1681 C.E.
Quinn Loukas
1/31/1977
Graham Xavier Loukas
8/04/1999
B
Lucian Daniels
1976
C
Imogen El Sadawii
1614 C.E.
George Uruk
2700 B.C.E.
C
Seamas McBrien
1825 C.E.

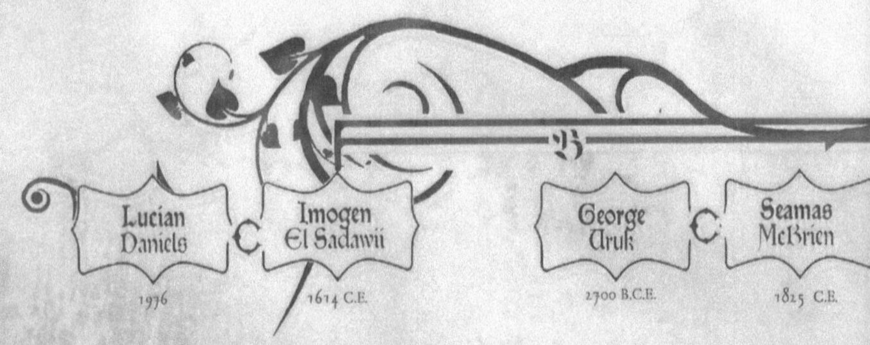

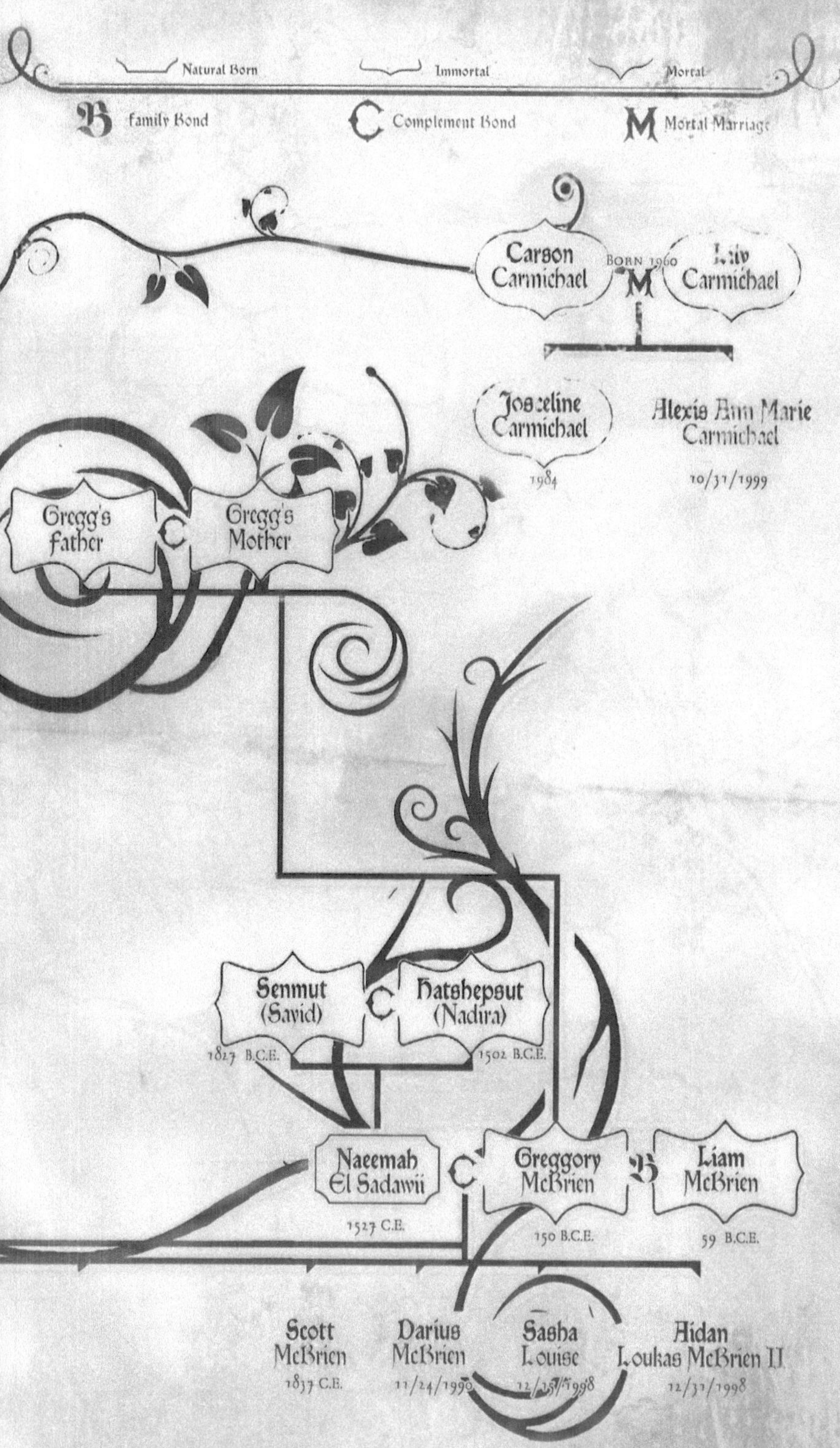

Natural Born
Immortal
Mortal
B family Bond
C Complement Bond
M Mortal Marriage
Carson Carmichael
Born 1960
M
Liv Carmichael
Josceline Carmichael
1984
Alexis Ann Marie Carmichael
10/31/1999
Gregg's Father
C
Gregg's Mother
Senmut (Sayid)
1827 B.C.E.
C
Hatshepsut (Nadira)
1502 B.C.E.
Naeemah El Sadawii
1527 C.E.
C
Greggory McBrien
150 B.C.E.
B
Liam McBrien
59 B.C.E.
Scott McBrien
1837 C.E.
Darius McBrien
11/24/1990
Sasha Louise
12/31/1998
Aidan Loukas McBrien II
12/31/1998

Immortals Of Indriell Series Timeline

June 2015

June 2015
Oct. 2015

Aug. 2015
April 2016

July 2016
Nov. 2016

Mar. 2016
April 2016

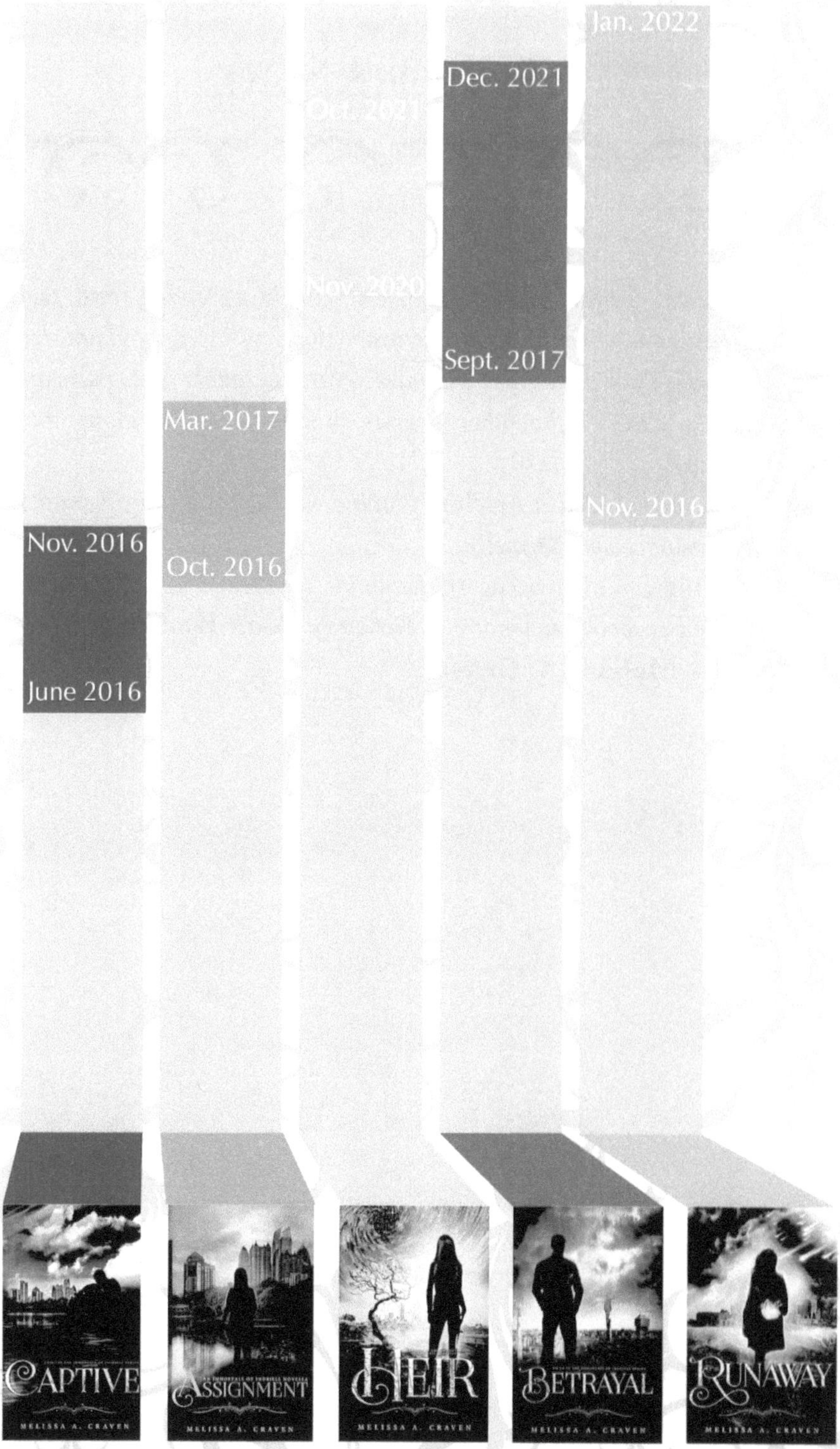

Nov. 2016
June 2016

Mar. 2017
Oct. 2016

Oct. 2021
Nov. 2020

Dec. 2021
Sept. 2017

Jan. 2022
Nov. 2016

Author's Note

Runaway begins where Judgment (Book 2) ended, and ends around the same time as Betrayal (Book 5). This is Chloe and Graham's story, but also includes several chapters with Allie and Aidan, and all the other friends they've collected along their journey.

I've included a timeline graphic to illustrate how Runaway falls into the series timeline.

And I'm always eagerly available to answer questions in my active Facebook reader group, ***Fantasy Book Warriors***

— **Melissa A. Craven**

Chapter 1

Chloe | Ming Lao's Funeral
After the New Moon | Kelleys Island, Ohio

Death was a new phenomenon for Chloe Long.

A week ago, she had everything. Friends. Parents and grandparents who loved her. Now, she had nothing.

Chloe walked aimlessly beside her shattered father. They'd hardly spoken since it happened. One night. One battle. A single moment had reduced her once proud father to a shuffling old man with white streaks through his jet-black hair.

And her mother?

Her powerful, fearless, *Immortal* mother now lay inside a box. Dead.

And she wouldn't be coming back.

Chloe couldn't wrap her mind around it. She'd seen the sword impale her mother's chest. The same sword that would have killed her father had her mother not stepped in front of him. All because that *woman*—Livia—had destroyed their Complement bond with her vile gift, leaving them vulnerable to death. She'd seen the life drain from her mother's face, and yet she still couldn't grasp the reality of it.

Chloe followed the funeral procession through the great hall of the underground where she'd grown up. Her mother was to be buried in the crypt in a special tomb their family had transformed into a garden. There, Ming Lao Long would lie with her parents —Chloe's grandparents—who also died that same day trying to avenge their daughter.

In one night, Chloe lost more than half her family. Something few Immortals would ever experience. Death wasn't supposed to come for them. It was unnatural, and Chloe didn't know how to deal with the kind of loss she'd never expected to experience. Death was so ... final. It happened sometimes when circumstances aligned just right. They were Immortal, but they weren't invincible. It just wasn't supposed to happen to her family.

Chloe kept waiting for her mother and grandparents to regenerate. It was what they did when severely injured. It took a while, but Immortals always came back from mortal wounds. Always.

This isn't fair!

Chloe was hardly aware of the procession as it came to a halt in the little garden they'd prepared for her family's final resting place.

Final? She gazed at the three coffins nestled in the center of the room. Each box held a piece of her soul, and she wondered if she would ever feel like herself again.

Trees lined the perimeter of the chamber, swaying in a soft breeze. Her family had been busy creating such a peaceful tomb. Bright sunshine blazed down on them, and puffy white clouds drifted high above. Her mother would have loved it.

Mourners circled around the coffins, but Chloe barely saw any of it. One by one, each person her mother had loved took a moment to say their final goodbyes and offer a gift for the departed. But Chloe watched with vacant eyes until it was her father's turn.

Jin Jing stepped up to offer his final gift to his Complement.

He reached into his pocket and brought out an ancient-looking fur slipper, crumbling with age.

Chloe's eyes filled with tears at the sight of it. Her father lost that shoe the day he met her mother. Cinderella style. Her mother had a gift for disguises; she could alter her appearance more than most Immortals. The day she'd met Jin Jing—then a Prince of China—Ming Lao was disguised as an Imperial guard. A man. Jin had taken one look at her and recognized his Complement. And then, he had a bit of a freak out moment when he thought he'd missed recognizing some vital part of himself. He ran from her, losing his shoe in the process. It had taken Ming Lao quite a while to find him and convince him she was in fact a woman. In the end, he'd said it wouldn't have mattered. She'd made a handsome man.

It was a funny story Chloe had loved hearing when she was a small child. Now, she'd never hear it again.

As her father knelt in front of her mother's casket, he touched the ground, bringing forth a babbling brook that circled the three coffins and flowed back into the trees, creating a little island oasis. He knelt there for a while, paying his last respects to the woman he'd shared his life with.

It wasn't right. They were supposed to be together. Always. Even in death. The only way to kill an Immortal was to murder their Complement at the same time. This ... this was torture for her father, sentenced to a life without his Complement. It was wrong. So wrong.

And then it was Chloe's turn. Silent tears streamed down her face as she knelt beside the new spring her father had created for her mother. She didn't know what she was going to do—what gift she would offer her mother and grandparents. The last days since their deaths had left Chloe in a turmoil of emotions. No one knew what she'd truly suffered the moment her mother died. She hadn't told a soul yet and wasn't sure she could explain what had happened on that battlefield—not that she even understood it herself.

For the last several days, Chloe hadn't slept at all. She didn't trust herself to sleep. She feared if she relaxed, even for a moment, she would lose control. The moment her mother took her last breath, something strange happened. Something so terrifying Chloe didn't want to think about it. A dark and powerful chaos churned inside her now. A power that wasn't hers. She could sense her mother in that power, and it frightened her. She didn't want to think about what it could mean.

Chloe placed her palms against the cool surface of the brook and began to sing in Chinese. A song her grandmother had taught her when she was little. Her voice shook at first. She was so tired; she still wasn't certain she could produce anything worthwhile. But as she sang, something snapped inside her, like a dam bursting, and that thing she'd been resisting—that thing she was almost certain was some sort of legacy of her mother's—came crashing out of her.

For the first time in her life, Chloe felt the pull of the earth and water around her. Both her parents had elemental gifts, and those elements spoke to her now. Chloe absently trailed her fingers through the water, her tears falling to mingle with the element. Unfamiliar power surged within her as her tears fell. She could feel the chaos of warring emotions that weren't completely her own. Her mother was *angry*.

The power tugged inside her, searching for a way out. She should be scared, but she wasn't. The more the power raged within her, the more connected she felt with her mother.

Fog gathered along the water's surface and began to swirl and undulate beneath her hands. A figure emerged from the vapor. As it mingled with her tears, it took shape and began to whirl around the caskets.

She heard the whispering, but Chloe ignored the startled

gasps. The vaporous fog snaked around her, and she could almost feel the warmth of her mother's embrace. Chloe continued to sing, letting the warring power inside her take control. She let the anger and anguish flood her as she cried, allowing herself to feel her loss for the first time. She could sense them all. Her fallen family embraced her in a comforting cloud. They were saying goodbye.

Chloe's shoulders fell as she finished her song. The angry surge of power had subsided for the moment. It was still inside her, but she didn't have to fight it for control. At least for now, it was quiet.

She'd made a mess of her final tribute to her family. While the others had given beautiful gifts of their power, Chloe had fallen apart at the foot of her mother's grave.

No one spoke as she sat, trying to catch her breath. Finally, she looked up, expecting to see nothing but pity in the eyes of her friends. But something else stared back at her. Three pairs of soulful dark eyes blinked at her.

Dragons. Made of the swirling vapor of her tears and her father's spring. Each were distinct, with familiar features. Two stood proudly beside Chloe, filling her with thoughts and good feelings from her grandparents. Eventually, they retreated to stand sentry beside their graves. The third one—the one with the familiar obsidian eyes of her mother—refused to leave her side.

"Mom?" Chloe whispered, peering into the dragon's eyes. Its scales of golden vapor glinted in the sunlight. The proud dragon bowed its head as if acknowledging her whispered words.

What have I done?

Fourteen Months Later

Winter | Kelleys Island, Ohio

Dear Dad,

I've tried. I've really tried, but I can't do this anymore.

We have to learn how to live without Mom, and I can't do that here with reminders of her everywhere I turn. I don't think you can either. It's not healthy. All we do is fight.

I talked to Allie, and she helped me see I need to be a little selfish right now. If I don't, I'm afraid I will never get past this grief, and I don't like the person I'm becoming.

I carry her with me every day, Dad. That won't change just because I'm gone. I'll carry her with me still, but it's time for me to take care of myself for a little while. I want you to do the same.

Promise me you'll try.

I love you. I'm not leaving because of you or anyone else. I'm leaving for me. I think she would want me to.

Please don't follow me.

Love,

Chloe.

PART I

ONE YEAR & EIGHT MONTHS LATER

CHAPTER 2

Graham | One Year and Eight Months Later
Early Fall | Salem, Massachusetts

Loneliness was a new experience for Graham Loukas. He'd grown up surrounded by friends and family. There was never a dull moment in his life ... until he went away to college.

"You excited for your sophomore year at MIT?" Uncle Lou asked for the third time on their awkward drive from the Boston Airport.

"Yeah, sure." Graham fiddled with his phone in his lap, watching the boats bobbing on the Broad Sound under the dreary September sky. It would be too cold for sailing soon. Not that Graham was anything close to resembling a sailor, but his aunt and uncle sure were.

"We should have at least a few more good days for sailing ahead of us. We'll get out on the water before you get too busy with classes."

"Sounds good," Graham muttered. Even after living with them during his freshman year at MIT, Graham still didn't really know his Aunt Gabrielle and Uncle Lou all that much, despite training with them every day. They weren't really his aunt and uncle. Lou

Fitzroy was his sister Hélène's father. Graham's mom and Lou were like fake-married a million years ago. Together, they adopted Hélène a few hundred years before his mom had met his dad.

Graham couldn't help but envy his friends from home who got to go to college together and train together. Allie, Darius, and Sasha all lived in a cottage by the lake. Their place was fun. But Graham's dream of going to MIT meant he had to go it alone since the others weren't as into technology and computer sciences as he was. But as a young Immortal, Graham had to have chaperones, so Uncle Lou and Aunt Gabrielle were it, and he was lucky to have them.

"Ah, only twelve more miles to Salem," Uncle Lou said in his stuffy British accent, his ever-present pipe tucked between his lips.

Graham was grateful his aunt and uncle were so eager to have him come live with them while he attended MIT, but he wondered how smart it was to choose Salem, Massachusetts as their home. Salem was known for burning witches at the stake. It seemed like a no brainer for Immortals with special powers to avoid such places. But Salem was a thirty-two-minute train ride to MIT. It should have been a perfect arrangement.

Graham just hadn't expected it to feel so awkward living with Lou and Gabrielle after hearing so much about them from his mom and sister all his life. Awkward didn't even begin to describe how uncomfortable the last year had been for Graham. Boring and lonely were close seconds.

"Oh! How were your online classes over the summer?" Uncle Lou asked, as if he'd finally thought of a decent question for his nephew.

"Great, actually." Graham smiled. "The classes were interesting, and I really liked the online platform. I kind of wish I could take a few more."

"Nothing can replace the classroom, though." Lou was a tried-and-true Ivy League academic type.

"True," Graham agreed. "Engineering classes would be difficult without in-person labs, but it was nice to get ahead." Graham was enrolled in an accelerated program to finish his Bachelor of Science in Electrical Engineering and Computer Science in just three years. He'd actually been a sophomore now for a few months already.

"Your aunt has been busy sprucing up your room since you left." Lou chuckled, taking an exit off the highway toward their Salem estate. "You've got a new bed and curtains and Lord knows what else."

"Awe, she didn't need to do that." Graham's face flushed. His aunt and uncle never had kids of their own, and he couldn't help but wonder if he was some sort of test drive for the future.

"She wants you to be comfortable, Graham. We both do."

"I appreciate all you guys have done for me." Graham clutched his phone, letting his power flood into his hands. Graham was a Tech. His abilities were all about technology. He could accomplish just about anything with a computer. Any gadget, really. He didn't need the computer engineering degree. But Graham wanted to learn the ways mortals managed to do the things they did with technology. If he could do it the hard way, then he could explain how he accomplished the things he did with his power in ways mortals could understand.

Graham: I'm going to need that escape text we talked about before.

Graham sent the message without typing it. It was just his way. The response came quicker than he'd anticipated.

. . .

Ezra: I'm free for the night, so I'll be ready for you :)

Graham smiled at his friend's reply. They'd met ages ago through Aidan, but they'd never actually met in person. Ezra was about the only reason he'd made it through his freshman year. A week into it and Graham had wanted to call it quits and go home, but Ezra helped him through it. They were about as close as two people could be who didn't know anything personal about each other.

They kept their secrets, but they talked about all the things that really mattered.

"Here we are." Uncle Lou pulled down the long drive to his estate just outside of Salem. The property bordered the harbor, and the massive house sat at the center of a wide sweeping lawn with cliff-side views of the sea. It looked like an old English manor house, which suited Uncle Lou and his wife. With it being just the two of them in such a huge house—three with Graham returning—the place struck him as a relic of a bygone era.

Keying in the code, Lou waited for the iron gates to swing open before he pulled his classic red Alpha Romeo through, leaving the windows down as they drove along the tree-lined drive to the house. The car belonged in a museum. There were only a handful of them ever made, but it was Uncle Lou's pride and joy.

"I'm sure your aunt is waiting impatiently for your arrival. She enjoys having you here, you know." Lou flashed his toothy smile, his wavy brown curls blowing in the cool September breeze.

"There she is." Graham had to smile at the sight of his feisty, red-headed aunt lingering at the front door of the mansion. She was French, like his mother. Gabrielle and Emma had been friends since the twelfth century. They were more like sisters than mere friends.

Dressed in jeans and riding boots, she was far more relaxed and modern than her staunchly British husband—but that wasn't saying a whole lot. Graham's aunt and uncle were horribly old fashioned.

"Graham!" Gabrielle called from her perch on the stone steps leading up to the front doors. "It's so good to see you, dear boy. I hope you've had a fun summer. You worked so hard last year in your studies."

"I did, Aunt Gabrielle. It was good to be home with my friends for a bit, but I'm excited to be back." Graham forced a smile for his aunt as she made a fuss over him. In truth, he was only happy to be back because it would mean he was that much closer to graduation and the next chapter of his life.

As much as Graham knew he needed to be here, he didn't *belong* here. Not that he knew where he belonged.

"Come, darling." Gabrielle draped an arm around him. "The valet will bring your luggage up later. I want to show you your new room." She guided him through the foyer to the right grand staircase—yes, there was also a left one—to his bedroom on the third floor.

"You didn't have to go to any trouble for me, Aunt Gabrielle. My room was fine before." He walked awkwardly down the wide hallway beside his aunt.

"Nonsense." She waved away his concerns. "I don't mind one bit, and truth be told, I rather enjoyed the chance to do some redecorating. I think you'll find the decor a little more masculine now. Perfectly suited for a young gentleman at University."

Graham really did love his aunt and uncle. He did. They were great people, but they lived in another age. It was the one thing that drove his mother crazy about her best friends. Both

Lou and Gabrielle stubbornly refused to move with the times. It was like they so enjoyed the nineteen-twenties they decided to stay there.

"Here we are." Gabrielle turned the corner at the end of the hall and up the two steps to another corridor of rooms. She stopped at the first door on the right. One that hadn't been there before.

"Wait, wasn't my room the one down the hall?" Graham pointed back the way they came.

"It still is." She winked. "We moved some things around while you were away. Go on in and get settled. I'm sure you're exhausted from all that traveling."

Yeah, the two-hour flight from Cleveland to Boston was grueling. Graham tried not to roll his eyes. "Thank you. I think I will lie down for a bit if you don't mind."

"Of course not, darling. Take the afternoon to rest. We will see you downstairs for dinner at seven sharp."

"Yes, ma'am." Graham reached for the sculpted brass doorknob, eager to escape into his room for a little while. Dinner was always an affair he'd rather skip. It took him exactly one night last year to learn that 'dressing for dinner' did not mean what he'd thought. One did not simply arrive at the dinner table in whatever attire they'd put on for the day. No, no, that was barbaric. In the Fitzroy household, one *dressed* for dinner. Graham had to ask his mom for more dress clothes last year. He'd left most of them here in his closet because he'd never wear them anywhere else.

It was absurd to think he had an entire wardrobe of clothes he only ever wore inside the house—er estate.

"Hope you like it," Gabrielle called over her shoulder as she disappeared around the corner.

With a deep breath, Graham stepped inside his room. It was nothing like he'd left it. His feet sank into the plush gray carpet that felt like little clouds under his feet. The ivory paneled walls were new. The whole room was new. Dark gray and espresso leather chairs stood under the windows with a pair of matching ottomans, studded in silver upholstery tacks shaped like horseshoes. The whole room had an equestrian theme. It was cute, but Graham wasn't a horse kind of guy.

The room was filled with rich navy, green, and ivory colors with gray and espresso leather accents everywhere. Pictures of horses hung on the walls. It looked like Ralph Lauren himself came over and decorated the room.

"I suppose it's better than the tug-boat theme from last year." He set his messenger bag on the wide wooden desk facing the leather chairs. Floor to ceiling ivory bookshelves filled the wall behind his desk. He had to admit, it would be nice to have such a big space to work in, but once he had his computers set up, it wouldn't look half as nice with wires and screens everywhere.

"She's knocked down walls." Graham shook his head with a grin as he stepped through the wide arched opening of his "study" down two steps into his bedroom. This was the room he'd used last year. Sort of. It was bigger now. A king size bed sat under the massive windows facing the ocean, and a gray leather love seat occupied the space in front of the gas fireplace that wasn't there just a few months ago.

She'd turned his simple bedroom into a master suite with a huge walk-in closet he would never fill and a bathroom with a jetted tub he would never use. There was one feature that had stayed the same. The wrap around balcony was his favorite spot in this enormous house. Last year, Graham had spent as much time out there as the weather would allow. It was his favorite place to study and read. Probably because the view reminded him of the cliffs and lake views of home.

Graham stepped outside and stared out across the expanse of manicured lawns and gardens stretching from the house to the cliffs in the distance. He could hear the roar of the waves and the scent of salt in the air.

"This year is going to be different." Graham took in a deep, cleansing breath of fresh ocean air and let it out before turning back to his room. He had a date with Ezra to keep.

Grabbing his phone from his bag, Graham flopped onto the cushy king size bed to text Ezra. "Ouch!" He pulled something sharp from under his back.

A pin. The kind worn on a lapel. Not that Graham often wore anything with a lapel to put it on.

He studied the thick silver pin shaped into an infinity symbol. It was smooth and polished and heavy. Something expensive his aunt had bought for him and forgotten about. Sighing, he set it on the nightstand and sat up to launch a game he'd designed. Calling Ezra wasn't as easy as texting a phone number he didn't even have.

Graham had never asked questions about his friend's situation. Once upon a time, Ezra was Aidan's student in some kind of Immortal community service program. That was before Aidan disappeared. They'd met more than a year ago when Aidan called to introduce Ezra to another gay Immortal—total straight guy thing to do—but Aidan's heart was in the right place. It turned out, Aidan was right, Ezra and Graham had hit it off—as friends—and had kept in touch as best they could. These days, Ezra was enrolled in some kind of hardcore training program that didn't give him much time or freedom. He didn't have access to things like cell phones with Wi-Fi, or even computers, but Graham had found a way around all that.

It was a work in progress. He'd managed to get Ezra to buy a cheap out-of-date cell phone without cell service of any kind. If anyone found it, they'd quickly see he could only use it to play offline games. But that was all Graham really needed. A piece of tech he could work with. He'd designed a couple of games for Ezra to download from a local Wi-Fi source and boom, he was in.

To anyone else, it was an old junk phone, but to Ezra and Graham, it was a lifeline. An untraceable one. They used the chat feature in one of Ezra's games to communicate without internet—one of Graham's more impressive inventions he was quite proud of.

Graham: What's up? Hit any high scores lately?

Graham typed their code message, preparing to wait for a while in case Ezra wasn't around.

Ezra: Same as always, mate. Can't get past level 42.

Graham smiled at his code response. They started nearly every conversation this way so they would know for certain they were talking to the right person.

Ezra: How was the flight?

Graham: Flight was fine, the drive to the estate was a bit awkward.

Ezra: You're the only person I know who can make the word estate sound like a bad thing.

Graham: She redesigned my room. It's a suite now with a study.

Ezra: You have first world problems, my friend.

. . .

Graham grinned, scooting down on his bed to get more comfortable.

Graham: Don't I know it. How's school for you?

Ezra: Boring and bloody awful training as usual. You?

Ezra always changed the subject the moment Graham tried to talk to him about his school and teachers. He'd learned to let his friend have his privacy and not pry.

Graham: Online classes were a breeze this summer. I'm hoping my in person classes will be better this year. Training with my uncle should be an exercise in futility once again.

Ezra: You need to make some friends this year.

Graham: I've never had to do that before. Turns out I'm really bad at it.

Ezra: Just be you.

Graham: Yeah, I'll get right on that.

Ezra: Don't over think it. It could be a lot worse.

Graham: I know, I know. I have everything I've ever wanted, and I'm an ungrateful jerk.

Ezra: You couldn't be a jerk if you tried. But I get it. The college thing didn't turn out quite like you dreamed it would. So, now's the time you get to adapt and find your new dream.

Graham: You might possibly have a point.

Ezra: When's your first class?

Graham: Tomorrow morning at eight. I have an advanced coding and infrastructure class.

Ezra: I have no idea what any of that means, but you will take note of all the cute boys you see—pictures would be nice if you can manage it without looking like a creeper. You know how I live vicariously through you.

Graham: That is a disturbing thought.

Ezra: It's sad that out of the two of us, you're the one with the most exciting life.

Graham: The most exciting thing on my agenda this evening is dressing for dinner with my aunt and uncle.

Ezra: Wear something smashing, just for me, please. You know how I love the fashions.

Graham: Yeah, yeah, I'll see what I can do.

Graham signed off and tossed his phone on the bed. He never asked what was so secretive about Ezra's training, but Graham could imagine he had very few privileges.

His situation sounded a lot like the kind of training Sasha had to do every summer for the Senate. Because of who her parents were, she got to keep her normal life when the Senate came snooping around a few years ago. She was a powerful girl. It was only a matter of time before they came to collect her. He imagined it was a similar situation for Ezra, except he didn't have the influential family to step in and advocate for him.

Talking to Ezra always reminded Graham of how much worse it could be. Sure, MIT wasn't anything like what he'd thought it would be. He didn't have any friends. The classes were difficult, the study workload was overwhelming, and the separation from his friends and family really got to him. But maybe he just got off to a bad start last year. Maybe Ezra was right. It was time to make a place for himself at MIT. Just because he was a thirty-minute train ride away from campus and didn't live in the dorms didn't make him any less of a student. He needed to make more of an effort this year.

Graham picked up the infinity pin his aunt had left on his pillow. Gripping it in his fist, he decided to embrace his circumstances. It was time to make the best of this.

Chloe | Early Fall | Long Island, New York

Chloe sat with her forehead pressed against the train window, her eyes closed and her music at top volume in her ears. AirPods were the only way to survive the train ride without succumbing to the migraines such proximity to mortals always gave her. Their indecision screamed so much louder than their Immortal counterparts.

Sometimes, Chloe wondered if it would be easier if she could just hear their thoughts clearly rather than the rushing white noise of their chaotic minds. She used to think she would eventually be able to decipher the thoughts and whispers she heard from those she interacted with, but after several years of listening, she'd made little to no progress with it. *I suppose that's what happens when you walk away from your trainers and mentor.*

Chloe ran a hand through her long dark hair streaked with purple highlights. Her dad would hate it, but Chloe liked to make frequent changes to her colorful hair. She also loved the eyebrow ring she'd gotten from a friend in Los Angeles last year. Immortal piercings were difficult to achieve. It wasn't a matter of just getting it pierced. She had to keep it from healing every night too.

It took nearly a year to get it to heal in a way that would allow for the permanent piercing.

Muting the volume of her music, Chloe took a deep breath and let her power well up within her. Using her gift, she searched for a familiar voice among the masses—those on the train with her as well as those in the towns and cities they passed through.

After weeks of running, trying to stay a step ahead of her father, he'd finally retreated. It happened now and then. Jin Jing would come looking for her and she'd have to run, using her gift to track his decisions before he made them, just as he used his gifts to track her movements based on the probabilities he could see as easily as she could see and hear his indecision. It was all very *Cats in the Cradle.* Whoever managed to get the upper hand would leave notes for the other. Hers begged him to go home and let her be. His demanded she stop acting like a child and return to Kelleys Island where she belonged. But that wasn't home anymore.

For the last few weeks, she'd traveled around New England and Canada, getting lost in the major cities of New York, Jersey, and Boston. But Chloe hadn't seen or heard a trace of her father in days.

Now, she was playing the game of did he actually leave or was he waiting for her to make a mistake? Or run out of money. But Chloe didn't need much money. She'd learned to do without a lot since leaving her sheltered life in Ohio behind.

As the train began to slow, thoughts of Justice had her leaning forward, eager to make a quick exit. She still had a long trek of ferryboats and trains ahead of her, but she couldn't wait to see her friends again. To see Justice. It was always difficult leaving him behind, knowing how much trouble—of the female sort—he could get himself into.

"End of the line," the attendant announced, pausing to give a wary look at Chloe's tattoos and general appearance. "Welcome to Montauk. End of the line." He moved on to the next car to announce their arrival at the very tip of Long Island. It would be the end of the trip for most on the train. This route took longer to get home, but it provided a great way for Chloe to be absolutely certain her father wasn't following.

Exiting the train station, Chloe walked along the busy street toward the bay until she found a restaurant she could afford. She lucked out with a local diner that had a cheap menu and waitresses who didn't ask questions. After a quick meal where Chloe didn't get to eat half as much as she needed, she ordered an Uber to take her to the Montauk Market across the street from the ferry docks.

At the market, she loaded up on snacks and drinks for the three-hour trip to New London, Connecticut, still not the end of her circuitous journey. She would probably have to spend the night at a shelter if she couldn't catch the last train out of New London.

The ferryboats were more expensive and slower than a bus would have been, but for someone trying to disappear, they were the best way to travel. Thoughts of seeing Justice soon kept her going, even when she was exhausted. Not that he was her boyfriend, or remotely interested in her. To him, she was just a roommate and his best friend, but to Chloe, he was so much more.

She watched the sun sink below the horizon as she paced the deck. Chloe wasn't the only passenger without a car, but she tried to avoid standing out—at least no more than her purple hair, tats, and piercing made her—so she kept to herself.

The ferry docked in New London with just enough time to spare for Chloe to make the last train out of town. By this time, she was confident her father had given up as he often did. Jin Jing's interest and enthusiasm for pursuing his daughter came and went as quickly as his energy. He would come for her again, but for now, it was safe to go home.

Home to Westbrook, her favorite place in the world. Barely a blip on the Connecticut coastline, Westbrook was a quaint little New England town straight out of a painting.

Just after midnight, Chloe waited at the Guilford, Connecticut train station for an Uber, trying not to nod off.

"You heading to Westbrook?" A young woman in a silver sedan pulled up to the curb.

Chloe tugged her AirPods from her ears. "Yep, that's me." She stood to gather her things. As she turned to the car, her vision went red with all the tiny threads of decisions her driver faced. With a sigh, Chloe slid into the backseat. "You should take the west route and avoid the highways." She closed the backdoor and leaned against the warm leather seat.

"The east route is faster."

It might be faster, but it would also likely end in an accident that could take the driver's life. "There's a twenty-dollar tip for you if you take the west route." Chloe absently flipped through her journal as if she didn't really care what the driver decided, though it was her last twenty.

"You got it," the girl murmured as she pulled away from the curb.

Chloe walked the last few blocks in the shadows, avoiding the cheery streetlights and intersections. Westbrook was an idyllic sort of New England town with brownstone townhouses and Revolutionary War relics on every corner. Chloe stared up at the old bank building towering over the town square. Unlike the other buildings, the leaky old Westbrook Savings and Loan was boarded up and in disrepair. She knew firsthand just how leaky it was since she and her closest friends called it home.

Chloe made her way up the stone steps, trusting in her best friend's ability to keep their home safe from prying eyes. No one knew just how many wayward kids called the bank home. Squatters they might be, but their Immortal gifts protected them from outsiders who only saw a derelict building in need of a good bulldozer—were it not for the landmark status that kept the building safe from such a fate. Every now and then, some historical preservation do-gooder came around, wanting to save the building from ruin. But the building itself sent them running. It didn't like strangers.

Pressing against the frosted glass doors, Chloe waited for the building to recognize her, warming beneath her touch. That was Dahlia's contribution. No one could enter the bank without her knowing. Chloe could feel the warm fuzzy greeting—like a favorite pet—as she stepped into the cold entry. The building took on a personality of its own, and she could sense it was happy to see her home again.

"And I'm happy to be home, old girl." Chloe ran a hand over the smooth milk-white brick, like glass under her palm. The dark first floor was cavernous and empty, as always. Huge cracked plaster columns towered above her, while intricate terrazzo tiled floors stretched out before her. She could just imagine how pretty the floors would be with the sunlight streaming in through the now boarded-up windows.

Her footsteps echoed down the wide hall as she made her way past the old tellers' desks to the stairwell leading to the upper floors. She couldn't wait to sleep in her own bed after all these weeks of crashing on cots and wherever else she could find to rest her weary body every few days.

"Is she home?" a familiar voice echoed off the concrete walls, and Chloe picked up her pace. "Was that her, old girl?"

"Yeah, Dahlia, slow down." Hudson's voice was drowned out by Dahlia's welcoming shrieks.

"Chloe! You're finally home!" Dahlia had her arms around Chloe before she stepped into the wide-open hallway they'd transformed into a common room. "I missed you so much." Her best friend tried to squeeze the life out of her. "You were gone way too long this time."

"I'm back now, Dahl." Chloe returned her squeeze, happy to be with her equal once again. "And I won't be leaving again any time soon. Now, tell me everything I've missed." Chloe dumped her things on the faded blue plaid couch at the center of the hall. It was one of many such couches they'd gathered from garage sales and dumpsters to furnish their non-traditional home. The result was a hodgepodge, eclectic, shabby sort of decor Chloe had come to love. It was home in a way Kelleys Island never was. She wasn't born into it; she chose this place. "How is everyone?"

"Same as always, really." Dahlia towed her into their makeshift kitchen that had at one time been some executive's posh corner office. Now, the room housed a mishmash of cabinetry they'd collected over the years.

Dahlia filled an electric tea kettle from the sink Justice had installed via some questionable plumbing hacks he'd found on YouTube and set about to make tea while they caught up.

"Hudson is busy with his research as usual. Noah and Jonah are off doing their techy thing in the computer room, and James is at work."

"Work?" Chloe sifted loose leaf tea into infusers, her brow arched in question. "He got a job? Like one that pays?"

"Right? Work is so unlike him." Dahlia shook her head, setting her blond curls bouncing. "We're placing bets on how long this will last."

None of them could keep a job for long. That was the downside for Immortals like them—the Scholars and Techs. Most of them experienced some level of ... side effects that made holding down a job in the mortal world very difficult. Chloe and Dahlia were the only ones who could manage a part-time job on a semi-regular basis.

Chloe would have to get back to work as soon as possible. She worked at the local library part time and made next to nothing doing it, but it was a consistent source of income. And her boss was great about letting her off when she needed to "focus on school," which was code for her time away from Westbrook when her father got a little too close for comfort.

The quiet library was a haven for Chloe because she could do her job without the constant headache of white noise since there were so few people present in the library on any given day.

And Dahlia made the big bucks working from home as a part-time telemarketer. She had a gift for selling things people didn't need over the phone. She also took online classes at the local community college.

"How's school?" Chloe leaned back in the red dining chair with the peeling pleather, trying not to ask what she really wanted to know.

"It's fine. Boring as usual and not at all what you want to hear about." Dahlia sipped her tea, eyeing Chloe with a smirk. "He's at it again." She heaved a big sigh. "No one can get him to come out of his room."

"How long's it been this time?" Chloe's foot bounced against her leg.

"Nearly a week, but he's not talking, and that's never a good sign. Before ... well, he hasn't been home much since you left. I don't know how to—"

"I better go see if I can get him to snap out of it." Chloe stood, leaving her steaming mug on the kitchen table and Dahlia looking like she had something she needed to tell her that Chloe didn't want to hear.

The house was quiet with everyone pursuing their own interests so late in the evening. Justice's room was on the top floor. It had once been an attic for storage, but he'd turned it into an open loft. He was an artist after all, and what was an artist without a loft?

"Hey, Justice?" Chloe called up the back stairs. It was never a good idea to sneak up on him when he was working. She made her way up the curved staircase, making as much racket as she could. "It's Chloe. I'm back." There was no door to Justice's loft, but he made his own kind of door. She met his resistance like a thick fog of chaos meant to send her scurrying for the common room. She was the only one who could resist his barrier long enough to reach him, and he could never keep her out for long. Even now, she could see him working in his fugue state, painting furiously along the back wall of his loft.

"Come in, I guess." His voice was distant and harsh—not like him at all, but she was used to his unpredictable moods.

He'd covered the mural wall he never let anyone see. A series of sheets hung from the ceiling like a patchwork curtain that blocked his deepest secrets from the world. Chloe longed to see what he painted when he retreated into his gift, but she wouldn't dream of invading his privacy.

His eyes still sparked with the fury of his power, like an ember burning in the darkness of night. He blinked at her, unseeing, and a moment later the darkness rolled away and his clear blue eyes emerged. He smiled, showing off his chin dimple she'd missed more than she cared to admit. "Chloe! When did you get back?" He raced across the room and swept her up in a warm hug, lifting her off her feet.

"Just now." She hugged him back, laughing as he whirled her around before he set her back down. The blond stubble along his chin scraping against her cheek. He smelled awful and he looked even worse, but her heart soared at the sight of him.

"I missed you, Chlo. You can't leave me for that long. You know how I get when I don't get my Chloe fix."

"So I heard. How long have you been up here? You stink." She frowned up at him, her heart thudding in her chest. She loved this boy, but after weeks away, she had to arm herself against his words. He treated her like gold, but he did not return her feelings.

"No idea, but I'm starving, so it's probably been a while." He grabbed her hand. "Let's go raid the fridge. I think Dahlia's been trying to get me to eat for a while now." He ran a careless hand through his shaggy, dirty blond hair.

"You really need to work on controlling your gift, Justice." Chloe squeezed his hand. "You have to take better care of yourself."

"I know, you're right."

He said the words, but she could see her concerns going in one ear and out the other. That was classic Justice.

"That was fast." Dahlia rolled her eyes when they joined her in the kitchen. "I've been trying to talk you down for four days. Chloe gets home and she has you down in less than five minutes."

"It's only because I can push through his barrier to get his attention." Chloe shrugged, taking a sip of her still hot tea.

"Yeah, that's it." Dahlia grinned, watching Justice rummage through the fridge.

"Did you leave that pizza for me on the landing, Dahl?" He emerged from the fridge with every kind of takeout carton available in Westbrook.

"Yeah, I was hoping you'd eat it, but that was a few days ago."

"I think I found it yesterday. I'm not sure I kept it down." He rubbed a hand over his face, scratching at the several days' beard growth on his chin—not that anyone would call his sparse blond stubble a beard.

"Well, I suggest you find it and clean it up." Dahlia fished out the bucket of cleaning supplies from under the sink. "Because I won't be cleaning up your post-fugue mess this time."

"Do we smell leftovers? And Chloe?" The twins emerged from their computer room looking like they hadn't seen sunlight or a decent meal in a few days either—not that the brothers were actual twins. Noah and Jonah reminded her so much of Graham in some ways. But they didn't communicate with the outside world so well. A bit awkward and smarter than most people, Noah and Jo kept to themselves, but they were still two of her favorite people.

"I do not smell." Chloe couldn't resist the smile that lit up her face at the sight of them.

"We didn't say you smelled bad." Noah wrapped his arms around her, Jo joined their hug huddle, and she felt like a twin sandwich. "You just smell like Chloe. Sweet and spicy, like cookies."

Noah always did the talking for both of them. Jonah rarely spoke. His power affected his voice, and he preferred using sign language.

"I missed you." Chloe signed and ran her hands over his hair, messing it up. "Both of you." But she leaned into Jo and whispered, "You're still my favorite."

"I heard that." Noah growled, reaching for a slice of cold pizza to add to his plate of reheated Pad Thai and jalapeño poppers.

"Hey, he's back." Hudson followed his nose to the food, pausing to clap Justice on the back and drop a kiss on Chloe's forehead. He was ridiculously tall and had to stoop to enter most rooms. "I like it when the family's all home. Chloe, don't leave us again anytime soon, okay?"

"I don't plan on it." Chloe smiled and helped herself to the buffet of takeout food, basking in the glow of the family that chose her. She loved these people just as much as her own family.

They were all Scholars and Techs. And Dahlia was the only other Immortal she'd ever known who was both a Scholar and a powerfully gifted Immortal. As her equal, she knew what it was like to straddle both worlds—and how difficult it was to try to be one or the other. With Dahlia, Chloe got to be both at the same time. And with the others, she got to explore the side of herself she'd never connected with among her more powerfully gifted family.

With them, she finally knew who she was.

Chapter 4

Graham | Early Fall | MIT Campus

Graham waited in line at the Eastman Court coffee kiosk, checking his phone for the time. He had a Design and Analysis of Algorithms class in fifteen minutes, and he didn't want to be late. Dr. McDermott refused to let students into the classroom after she'd arrived—no matter when that happened to be.

"What's up, Brooks, you *work* here?" one of the guys in line ahead of Graham spoke to the barista with a condescending laugh.

"My bad, I thought you were a student," one of the others chimed in.

Graham eyed the three boys. He was used to seeing them around campus. They were the legacy types. Loud, with too much money and zero gratitude for their privilege.

"Loukas." The third one gave Graham an approving nod before he turned back to their prey behind the counter. He got coffee at this kiosk nearly every morning, but this Brooks person was new and not very efficient at his job.

"Yeah." Brooks fumbled with the steamed milk. "I'm a student. It's called a work-study program. You know for people who don't have their great-grandfather's money paying for everything." He wiped the rim of a vanilla latte and handed it to the main bully.

"Bummer man. You know there are cheaper schools, right? For those whose parents didn't care enough to plan for college."

"Rude," Graham blurted before he could second guess himself. "Have some respect, man." He shook his head. There was nothing he hated more than a bully.

"No worries, Mr. Cutie-Cute." The boy behind the counter nodded with a good-natured grin. "These guys just don't know what it's like when MIT comes to recruit you—and gives you a scholarship—you don't say no." He turned to fill a cup with black coffee for another customer. "You work hard and pay your own way. But the legacy, I-bought-my-way-into-this-school-types wouldn't know anything about that kind of hard work, would you?" He turned back to the bullies with a heart-melting, dimpled smile.

"Whatever, man. I have a hall named after me." One of the boys snorted into his fancy latte.

"Well ... good for you." Brooks lifted a chocolaty mocha drink for one of the others.

"Seriously, man, if you're hard up for cash, let me hire you for one of my epic parties. We could always use a good bartender ... or stripper, depending on how desperate you are." He winked.

"You know, I think I'll be washing my hair that night." Brooks moved back to the register and waved Graham forward. "Can I help whoever is next?"

"Your loss, Brooksie." The lead bully dropped a twenty in the tip jar. "For your tuition. Wouldn't want you to have to drop out for being poor."

"You should keep that twenty," Graham said. "Sounds like you need it for lessons on how to not be a jerk for no reason. I'd be happy to teach you." He lifted his chin.

"Brooks, my man, you're right about one thing." The lead

bully clapped Graham on the shoulder. "This one's *adorable.*" He chuckled, sipping his coffee as he turned to leave with his bros.

Graham stepped aside, wishing he could get this guy on the mat for an afternoon of sparring. He watched them retreat, pushing and shoving each other like they'd accomplished some great feat for their social hierarchy.

"Did you want to order something?" Brooks pulled Graham's attention back to the menu, flashing his cute, dimpled smile again.

"Uh, black coffee. Large, please." Graham barely had time to choke back his startled reaction to Brooks' presence. His *Immortal* presence. He was just Graham's age and didn't give off a threatening vibe, but Graham's range for sensing another Immortal's presence was his biggest weakness. He often didn't know until they were staring him in the face like Brooks was now. Over the years, Graham spent a great deal of time learning to mask his surprise.

He looked up at the menu now, schooling his features into a practiced, bored expression, all but ignoring the barista's flirty gaze. Having never had a real boyfriend, Graham had yet to perfect the art of flirting.

"Sure thing, Mr. Cutie-Cute." Brooks winked and filled a large cup with fresh coffee. Graham's heart raced, and he could feel his face flushing scarlet. He hoped he could blame it on the cold weather and not his inexperience flirting with cute baristas before class.

"Hey, Brooks." Another barista stepped in through the back door, shedding her coat in a rush. "Sorry I'm running behind for my shift. You have class soon?" She moved to tie on her apron, talking a mile a minute.

"No worries, Peyton, I've got time." Brooks glanced at his phone. "Just enough to walk Mr. Cutie-Cute here to his next class." Brooks handed Graham his coffee, tossed his apron aside, and lifted the bar to exit the kiosk.

"Don't forget your Jacket." Peyton laid an expensive looking wool peacoat on the bar and bent to wash her hands at the sink. "See you tomorrow."

"Thanks, Callahan." Brooks moved away from the line at the kiosk, and Graham limped after him. The cold weather always made his limp more pronounced.

"Training accident?" Brooks glanced down at Graham's foot as they walked across the quad.

Graham followed his gaze. "Yeah, something like that." He shrugged it off. Most Immortals were confused by his lifelong limp, though Graham rarely thought about it. He was born with a twisted foot and had walked with a subtle limp all his life, though that never slowed him down. Of all his friends back home, he was the fastest.

"Bummer. I broke an ankle once, and it took forever to heal."

"Too bad we couldn't teach those idiots a real lesson." Graham glanced back over his shoulder.

"The way I see it, the mortal elite can do or say whatever they like. It's no skin off my back." Brooks reached to grab the door for him.

"True, but I have no time for bullies—no matter how long their lifelines happen to be."

"I appreciate the solidarity back there, though. You were very gallant." Brooks smiled, showing off his dimple. "I thought you were going to challenge him to a duel for my honor."

Graham blushed to the tips of his ears, shoving his free hand in his pocket. "Well, no one deserves to be treated like that."

"This is where I'd normally ask to buy you a cup of coffee and get your number, but you're going to be late for class and you already have my best brew."

"Okay." Graham nodded, not sure what he was agreeing with as he gulped the scalding hot coffee.

"So, how about your number instead?" Brooks asked.

"Oh, um, yeah, sure," Graham choked out, trying to ignore the burning pain in his throat. He glanced back at his feet. This was why he had no social life. He was so bad at it.

Taking a deep breath, he reached for Brooks' hand, resting his palm over the boy's phone. "You've got my number." He smiled. "Call me."

"Okay, Mr. Cutie-Cute, that was hot." Brooks grinned. "Did you leave me your name too?"

"Oh." Graham flushed again. "It's Graham."

"All right, Graham. I'll call you soon." He turned to leave, and something silver caught Graham's eye.

"Wait." He reached for Brooks' arm. "Your pin..." Graham stared at the silver loop of the infinity pin on Brooks' lapel. "I've seen that before."

"Have you?" He winked.

"What does it mean?" Graham's voice turned gruff as he lifted his gaze to search Brooks' face. It wasn't a coincidence that a pin just like that had showed up in his room upon his arrival.

"Oh, I have a feeling you'll soon find out."

With another dimpled smile, Brooks turned and left Graham in the hall.

Disoriented, Graham looked up at the classroom door to realize Brooks had indeed walked him to his next class, but Graham was positive he'd never actually said where his next class was.

CHAPTER 5

Chloe | Early Fall | Westbrook, Connecticut

Chloe loved her room. It was her favorite place in the whole building. Every morning, she woke to the sunrise over the town square, and every night, she got to fall asleep to the sound of the wind through the trees.

Chloe lay on her bed, gazing at the sunlight streaming in through the arched window trimmed with a riot of stained glass in reds, oranges, and yellows like a rainbow. Her room stretched across the front of the building, and over the years, she'd put in a lot of work to make it perfect. Her bedroom rested on a raised platform with a queen-sized mattress on the floor and two low bedside tables, each with a hanging pendant light suspended from the ceiling. She'd done the electrical work herself after studying an electrician's manual from cover to cover. Chloe learned things quickly, and she read even faster. And she never forgot the things she read.

Her desk sat at the center of the room, acting as a space divider. Facing the huge arched window, Chloe spent her days studying and watching the townspeople play out their lives below. Here, she'd learned what it meant to be a scholar.

Her ever-growing library stood opposite her bedroom, with

floor-to-ceiling bookshelves she'd managed to fill with her favorite books and her own scholarly recordings. Those, she never shared with anyone. She was still trying to figure out what all her aimless ramblings meant. Especially the dark and frightening ones that gave her nightmares.

Chloe shivered at the thought of what filled those journals, shaking off the fear that would consume her if she went down that path again. She would have to face it again soon, but not today.

A pair of couches flanked the bookshelves with a massive coffee table between them. Basking in the sunlight, reading, and writing, Chloe couldn't think of any other place she loved as much as her sanctuary here.

At home on Kelleys Island, her world was filled with endless training, fighting, sparring, and honing her powerful gifts, while neglecting the scholarly side of her heritage. Her grandparents were respected Scholars until they died defending Chloe's mother. At home, no one really knew how to train her scholarly side. But here, in her new home, she was teaching herself. Learning from her friends. And with Dahlia's help, they worked together to stay in shape. The two spent a great deal of time in the gym together, pushing each other to achieve their goals.

"Breakfast is ready!" Dahlia banged on Chloe's door. She and Hudson took turns with the twins, making breakfast for everyone. Chloe and Justice handled most of their evening meals when they didn't order out.

"Coming!" Chloe pulled a shawl over her shoulders, the blue fringe tickling her arms as she made her way to the common room in her PJs.

"Hey, Chlo." Dahlia intercepted her before she made it to the kitchen. "You know that thing I've been trying to tell you that you've been avoiding since you got home?"

Chloe rolled her eyes. It was impossible to hide from Dahlia.

She saw everything. "Yeah, what's her name? Or does he even know this time?" Chloe folded her arms over her chest. She could hear Justice in the kitchen, so it wasn't like he'd slept over with one of his many girlfriends. Not that they were ever long-term girlfriends.

"Scarlet." Dahlia moved to steer her back across the common room.

"Scarlet? Really?" Chloe snorted. "It's fine, Dahl. They never stick around long." She darted past her friend but paused at the center of the room when she heard a giggle from the kitchen. One she didn't recognize. "She's here?" She turned to Dahlia, her jaw dropping. "He brought her *here*?" He never brought his conquests home. No one brought outsiders home. Not without a vote from the group.

"I'm sorry, Chlo. He seems to like this one."

"Did you all ... vote on this? Is she ... living here?"

"There was no vote. But yeah, she's been staying here a lot."

Chloe sank to the brown leather chair nearest her, trying to hold the pieces of her heart together. "So, I ... we just have to accept her." She lifted her shoulders, steeling her resolve. "We're all here because of Justice, so it's pretty much his house, his rules, right?"

Dahlia crouched beside her. "He's a big giant jerk for not seeing it." She ducked her head to meet Chloe's sad eyes.

"It's not his fault he's not ready to see me yet." Chloe's stomach churned with nerves. She could not let Justice see how much it bothered her that he'd brought a woman into their home. A woman he had more than just a passing interest in.

"I can't imagine how difficult this is for you, Chlo." Dahlia squeezed her hands. "I don't think I could stand it, living with my Complement and her not knowing it? It's just awful to watch."

"It's not fun." Chloe stood. "Come on, let's get this over with." Chloe pulled her fringed shawl up around her shoulders, shivering in the drafty old room. She'd known Justice was her Complement after about a year of living with him. One day, she looked at him over her cereal bowl and she just knew it. But he still didn't see it, and she feared he would always look at her like the best friend he couldn't live without. Meanwhile, she watched him with an endless parade of women coming in and out of his life faster than she could learn their names—dying inside a little more each time. But he'd never brought one home before.

"There she is!" Justice dropped his enormous plate of eggs and toast on the counter to sweep her up in a big bear hug. "Scarlet, come meet my girl." He sat her down and moved to the table with his plate, scooting out a chair for Scarlet and Chloe. "My two best girls together at last." He spooned cheesy eggs over his jelly toast. No matter what was on his plate, if there was bread, Justice was going to make a sandwich.

Why did she have to be gorgeous? Scarlet was a curvy black woman with thick natural curls and golden brown eyes the color of warm topaz.

"Hi, Chloe, I've heard so much about you." Scarlet took her seat, beaming at her over the rim of her coffee cup. "Justice talks about you all the time."

"Does he?" Chloe sat beside Justice, helping herself to coffee and the box of donuts from the local bakery. "Funny, he didn't mention you."

"I feel like I already know you." Scarlet smiled, bumping shoulders with Justice, who wore a silly grin. Chloe had never seen him so crazy for a girl before.

"I'm sort of like you guys, but I've only just found out I have legit prophetic gifts."

"What? How?" Chloe scowled at her. She had to be in her early twenties, like the rest of them. There was no way she didn't know her gifts by now.

"I aged out of foster care about four years ago." Scarlet

shrugged, helping herself to the pile of slightly burnt bacon Dahlia had made for the twins. They couldn't get through the day without bacon. Chloe wanted to swat her hand away from the plate.

"I always thought I was a little psychic, you know. But never very powerful like other Immortals. I got by with Tarot cards and psychic readings for people, but I never stayed anywhere too long. People can get kind of obsessed with me after a while, even though I only see the small day-to-day things."

Chloe finished her donut and stood up to help Dahlia with the dishes. "So, I guess we won't be keeping you too long then?" She glanced back over her shoulder to see them holding hands under the table.

"Oh, I think I'll stay here for a while. It's good to be with people like me. I have a lot to learn. I've always known I was Immortal, of course. My parents told me when I was little—before they disappeared and I landed in mortal foster care. But Justice and the boys have really helped me understand my gifts."

"She has a gift for prophecy, like James." Justice draped an arm around her shoulders.

"Not as talented as he is, though. I just see things in the cards. Never anything important, but I read people pretty well." She eyed Chloe with a knowing nod. "It's not always useful what I do, but I'm learning to look deeper. To see what my gift is trying to reveal to me."

"Keep careful records and you'll eventually see the big picture." Chloe reached into the fridge for more bacon, busying herself with replenishing the table for the twins. They would be along shortly and were cranky until they had their morning coffee and bacon.

"What are you up to today, Chlo?" Justice asked. "I thought maybe you and Scarlet could work together. Get to know each other and help her out with all your Scholar know-how."

"Oh, um. I have work, actually." Chloe reached for her travel mug. She had planned to call her boss to let her know she'd be available again next week, but at the moment, she needed an excuse to get out of this house and away from freaking Scarlet.

"Too bad. Maybe we can hook up later tonight?" Scarlet smiled, her eyes soft and understanding. She could tell Chloe had a thing for Justice, and she was trying to be sympathetic. That was the really crappy part about living with a bunch of scholarly types. They could read Chloe better than she could herself. Hiding a broken heart from her friends was next to impossible. Except for Justice who was completely oblivious to what was right in front of him.

"Sure, I'll see you guys later." Chloe swallowed the lump in her throat and forced a smile for the two lovebirds planning their day together. It was fine, really. She was fine. Justice would be ready for her someday, and when he was, she would be there, and he'd never look at Scarlet or any other girl again.

Please God, don't let him take forever to see me.

Graham | Fall | Salem, Massachusetts

"Keep pushing, Graham, that's it," Uncle Lou said, guiding him through the exercise he'd attempted a million times without success.

"Now, search for the source of your gift. You're looking for any subtle division in the root of your power that you've yet to explore."

Sweat beaded his brow as Graham's legs began to shake. Still, he pushed himself to try again and again. Trying was the easiest way to get his uncle to move on from this exercise in futility.

"Think of your power as a mighty oak tree with dividing branches and deep roots hiding in the soil just waiting to be discovered."

Frustrated, Graham took a deep breath and reached for a tendril of his power, visualizing it as a tree branch with dozens of other branches. He only needed one. Finally, grasping hold as he'd done countless times before, he pulled the power into him.

"Yes, that's it! Keep pushing, you're almost there."

With quaking legs and the taste of copper in his mouth, Graham tried to hold on for the next part.

"Now that you have it, look for a rift in the root, a separation in this facet of your power you can grab hold of next."

And that was where all his previous teachers lost him. There was nothing of the sort to grab hold of. As Graham searched inward, exploring the source of his power, he never saw the variations—the splitting point of one of his abilities that might lead to a more powerful use of his gifts. A way to make it a weapon.

Like many before him, Uncle Lou was trying to turn Graham into something he just wasn't.

Sinking to his knees, a drop of blood oozed from his nose. "It's not there, Uncle Lou." His voice wavered as he shook his head. "You're not the first to try to get me there."

"It's okay, my boy. We will try again soon."

"No!" Graham punched the mat beneath him. "We're done with this. I'm twenty years old; if I was going to develop another gift or force a division into an existing one, it would have happened by now." Graham climbed to his feet, his breath coming quick and shallow.

"It's okay." Uncle Lou patted his shoulder. "You're young. You still have plenty of time to work hard at—"

"I am not broken!" Graham whirled on his uncle, eyes flashing with the fury of the power coursing through his veins.

"Of course not, I didn't mean to imply anything of the sort." Lou took a step back, a look of regret on his face.

Drawing a deep breath, Graham schooled his features, grasping at control before he said something he would regret. "There is nothing wrong with me." He dragged in another breath. "I am not the kind of warrior my parents are. Like you and Aunt Gabrielle. But that doesn't mean I'm somehow less because of it."

"I apologize, Graham." Uncle Lou's brilliant blue eyes filled with concern. "Never, for one minute, think that your aunt and I think of you as anything less than extraordinary."

Graham nodded, trying to believe his uncle's fine words, even when his actions said something else.

"You know we love you like a son. Having you here has been a blessing. If I have been overly enthusiastic in your training, it is only because I want the very best for you."

"I know, Uncle Lou." Graham forced a smile. It wasn't the first time he had to live with the fact that his aunt and uncle just didn't get him. They meant well, but they also didn't realize some of the things they said and did felt like thinly veiled criticism of what they perceived as his flaws.

"Let's call it a day, shall we? You've worked hard."

"Thanks." Graham moved to put his gear back on the shelves.

"So, how has it been since you've gotten back into the groove of things at school?" Uncle Lou asked as they headed upstairs to the main level. Graham spent a lot of time down in the dungeon-gym honing his fighting skills. He was a good fighter, more than capable of holding his own with his more powerful friends back home. From his point of view, Graham felt firmly grounded in his identity as a technologically-gifted Immortal, perfectly at ease in his own skin and capable of navigating his way through this world —until someone reminded him how different he was from his peers.

"It's been good." Graham followed his uncle up the winding staircase to the main drawing room—there were others—ones he probably hadn't even seen yet in this enormous house. "I like my classes better this year. They're more focused on what I want to be doing."

"Any new friends?"

"Some." Graham nodded before his uncle could offer to introduce him to another of their friends' Ivy League kids. He'd been down that road before and wasn't looking forward to a repeat. "In fact," Graham held open the door to the drawing room for his uncle, "I'd like to hang out at school some nights after training."

"You want to take the train back to Boston? At night?" Lou sounded like Graham had asked to take his infant brother skydiving.

"Yeah, just from time to time. You know, to take advantage of some of the social things going on at school."

"We will talk with your aunt about that, but I'm not sure I like the idea of you roaming around the city by yourself at night."

"Well, maybe we could talk to my parents about it too." *Being that I'm not twelve.*

"It's good to see you wanting to get out there, my boy." Uncle Lou clapped him on the shoulder. "Perhaps we could come with you to a football game some weekend."

"Uh, sure." Graham wasn't about to tell his uncle he was more interested in the cute barista he wanted to go out with. The one who still hadn't called him yet.

"Your aunt and I will be dining out tonight." Uncle Lou paused at the top of the stairs. "The cook has left you something for dinner in the kitchen. I'm sure it will be delicious."

"Sounds great; thank you." Graham sighed in relief as he headed up to his wing of the house. A night alone would be nice. He could only thank his lucky stars they didn't invite him to go out with them.

Flipping on the light in his study, Graham sat down on his comfy leather desk chair.

Graham: Hit any high scores lately?

He waited a moment to see if Ezra would reply, but he wasn't always available right away. Graham switched over to the latest texts from his mom. More new pictures of baby Parker. The kid was cute. Only a few months old and he had the entire family wrapped around his finger. Graham would do anything for that kid.

He was overjoyed when he found out he was going to be a big brother. It was the only thing he'd had to look forward to during his freshman year at MIT. He'd made it home just a few weeks before Parker Loukas arrived. Though thankfully, he'd missed all the gross stuff. According to Allie, she was traumatized for life after helping his mother through the difficult birth.

A wave of homesickness hit him as he watched a video of his exhausted mom sleeping beside the baby while his dad filmed them with commentary about his mother's state of mind. She was quick to threaten anyone who thought to wake the baby when he finally slept.

Was it even worth missing his little brother's infancy to be here at MIT? Sometimes, Graham wasn't sure why he was here at all. Parker was the main reason Graham enrolled in the accelerated program a couple semesters ago. If he graduated a year early, his brother would still be a toddler and Graham would get to be around for all the big moments.

Ezra: Now I'm stuck on level 43. It's a tough one.

Graham smiled as Ezra's message filled his mind through his gift. Reaching for his phone, he clicked over to Ezra's message, feeling a huge weight lift from his shoulders.

Graham: Training was brutal today. My uncle keeps pushing me, and it's not going well. He needs to back off and let me be what I am.

. . .

Ezra didn't respond right away, and Graham wondered if he got caught texting. He was about to start worrying when another message came through.

Ezra: Brutal, huh? That must be so hard for you. Seems like your uncle is just trying to help you be better, though. Have I ever told you about one of my trainers? Now she's brutal.

Graham winced at the underlying subtext of Ezra's text.

Graham: I'm sorry, I'm being a privileged brat again. Just ignore me.

Ezra: Well, let's just say I have an ability that can be enhanced by the life-force of the things around me. All I need is to shave off a bit here and there from plant life and the random cow or goat, and I'm good to go without really affecting my prey. But that's not good enough for my trainer. Did you know she makes me kill cute fluffy animals just about every day? Says it will help me when it really matters. She wants me to harden myself to the inevitable so I'll be ready. That's brutal.

Tears blurred Ezra's words on the screen. He rarely spoke of his training or anything specific about his life. Graham had no idea it was that bad.

. . .

Graham: You're right, I'm an ass. I'm so sorry you have real horrors to deal with and then you have to listen to me complaining about nothing. Forgive me?

He waited for several long minutes before Ezra's response arrived.

Ezra: I think I'm the one that needs to extend an apology. It's been a difficult week here. Things were getting better there for a while, but that's not saying much. I shouldn't take it out on you. You're the only friend I've got outside this place.

Graham: I am always here for you, Ez. I can't even begin to imagine what you're going through. I wish I could get you out of there. Wherever there is.

Ezra: How's that adorable little Parker doing? Is he walking and talking yet?

That was so Ezra. Graham sighed. He would do anything to help him, but any time he even hinted at it, Ezra changed the subject.

Graham: Well, he can't hold his head up by himself yet, but, sure, walking and talking should be happening any day now. But seriously, I can't wait till he's old enough to play. I'm going to spoil him rotten.

Ezra: Am I forgiven?

Graham: For what? Now, what do you know about cute boys who ask for your number and then never call you?

CHAPTER 7

Chloe | Fall | Westbrook, Connecticut

Chloe sorted through the books on her cart, arranging them according to the area where they belonged in the library. The bottom shelf of books stayed on the first floor, the middle went to the kid's section on the second floor, and the top shelf went to the third floor in the historical archives—her favorite place in the library. She always liked to end her day there.

Westbrook was a small community, but their library was the best in this part of the state. College students from all over came here to research their Revolutionary War histories. Chloe made quick work of the first-floor put backs, eager to get through the noisy kid's section next as quickly as possible. She didn't have much to return there.

Chloe made her way over to the ancient elevator, pulling the grate closed behind her. The library was busier today than usual, but the constant whispering of thoughts didn't consume her. She could decipher the familiar voices but still couldn't make out anything useful. Not with so many minds vying for her attention. If she focused, she could listen and record her findings, but she had a job to do. She would "study" later, after her shift was complete. The library was the perfect place for Chloe to hone her gift.

But for the task at hand, she needed to block out the noise. Shoving her AirPods in place, Chloe made her way along the aisles, returning books to the shelves. She enjoyed the rather mindless task. She scanned through each book before putting them back on the shelves, pulling out bits of information she stored in her vast memory. Sometimes, she would make a mental note of a book she wanted to check out. Though, she had to be careful not to take too many books home with her at a time. She read fast and slept little, so to keep anyone from questioning her abilities, she only allowed herself to check out two books a week.

Chloe loved learning. It came easy for her. In lieu of a formal college education, she read everything she could get her hands on. And she often followed along with Dahlia's online classes as a way to feed the thirst for knowledge she could never seem to assuage. Chloe desperately wanted to go to college, but she couldn't afford it, nor could she enroll under her own name for fear of her father showing up to drag her home. It was best if he never knew about her place here in Westbrook. So, she made a college of her own. Studying along with Dahlia made her feel like she was earning a degree, even though she'd never get the diploma for herself.

Chloe thumbed through a book of Longfellow poems. A first edition that included "The Midnight Ride of Paul Revere." The crumbling leather binding had been repaired numerous times, but it was still an elegant book.

One if by land, and two if by sea,
And I on the opposite shore will be,
Ready to ride and spread the alarm
Through every Middlesex village and farm,
For the country-folk to be up and to arm.

Ever since moving to this part of New England, Chloe had become obsessed with learning about the Revolutionary War. Living here and studying was like experiencing those days through the veil of time. It was so easy to look out her bedroom window across the aged town square and imagine Paul galloping along the quiet streets that night, warning the people of the impending arrival of the British soldiers.

Chloe shivered as she placed the book back on the shelf. A creeping dread had stolen over her while she was distracted with the book. She took a deep breath, preparing herself.

"You can come out, Grandpa Alex." She forced herself to shake off the cold fear his presence brought on. "I know you're there."

"Of course you do, dear one. I was just giving you a minute to adjust." Alexander stepped from the stacks, pausing at the end of the aisle to give her ample space. His was an intimidating presence. It always took her a few minutes to pull herself together whenever the Scholar made one of his unexpected visits.

"What brings you here this time?" She turned to place another book back on the shelf before she rolled her cart to the end of the aisle.

"What? I have to have a reason to visit my favorite young Scholar?"

"I'm not exactly a Scholar, Gramps." She pushed past him, perusing the aisles for her next returns. "Not that I'm not happy to see you." She couldn't resist her smile. She loved his visits, even when his arrival was more dramatic than it needed to be.

"Well, you're not exactly *not* a Scholar either." He followed close behind. His t-shirt emblazoned with the words "I cannot be held responsible for what my face does when you talk." He was the coolest grandpa ever. Not that he was *her* grandpa, but that didn't matter. She loved him no matter the family ties.

"I know, Gramps. I'm both, and that's cool and makes me a super special snowflake," she said in a bored tone.

"Why do you mock me? I am wounded."

"You're always wounded." She graced him with a smirk. "I suppose you want to come home with me?" She heaved a reluctant sigh. It wasn't that she didn't want to share him with her friends. It was just such an *ordeal*.

"Of course. You're my favorite, most special little group of up and coming bright minds."

"You're laying it on a bit thick, old man."

"I know no other way. Come on, sweet girl, I'll help you finish your work." He picked up a few volumes from her cart. "Oh, would you look at that; I wrote this one." He scratched his head with a frown. "Can't think of what it was about." He shrugged, putting it back where it belonged. "Must have been important way back when."

"So, what brings you to Westbrook?" She strolled along the aisle, quickly becoming comfortable with one of her most favorite people in the world.

"I'm not checking up on you for your father. Promise." He gave her a Boy Scout salute. "You and your friends are important, but you lack guidance. That's actually what makes you all so interesting to me. It's the ultimate nature verses nurture control group."

"So, you're watching us like a science experiment?"

"No. Yes, sort of. You know better than your friends what we're up against within the Scholar community."

"Yes." Chloe nodded. "They are less aware of what we face. I almost envy them really, the blissful ignorance." Chloe sighed. In the scholarly and prophetic community, they were fast approaching a dark time. A vast unknown period stretched before them. For a people who always knew more or less what to expect of the future, it was a frightening prospect.

"I've never known a time when I couldn't see what was coming." Alex stroked an aged hand across the leather-bound books on the shelf. "I see all that was and is, yet I cannot see what will be. It's maddening."

"Still nothing beyond the final prophecy?" Chloe asked, though she knew the answer. It just seemed so impossible that there was anything the Scholar didn't know.

There was little the prophetic community knew about the world beyond the final prophecy. The one about Allie. Chloe had seen the initial stirrings of that prophecy coming to fruition, but for the Immortal world, whatever came next was a giant question mark. She could see how that terrified Alexander and his wife Alísun—the last Queen of Indriell and one of the most powerful Prophets the world had ever known. Even she saw only darkness ahead.

But for Chloe, that darkness was even more alarming. She saw it in her studies. It was as if her gift could physically see it creeping along the horizon, ready to engulf her world and everything she'd ever known. The darkness plagued her scholarly gifts, but they would get through whatever it was, with or without the foreknowledge their predecessors once had to guide them. For her generation, uncertainty was all they knew.

"I don't know if you all need my guidance or not." Alexander patted her shoulder. "But I want to help however I can."

"It would help a ton if you'd let my friends remember you."

"That I can't afford to risk. But I can buy tacos for everyone." He grinned, settling his sunglasses on his face as he followed her back to the front desk and the end of her shift.

"Just ... be cool, Grandpa Alex." Chloe reached for the glass doors of the old Savings and Loan building, hefting a bag of tacos in her free hand.

"Me?" Alexander gaped at her over his sunglasses. "I am never not cool." He followed her across the dusty lobby, gazing up at the columns. "Looks familiar. I think I had an account here once." He turned toward the vacant teller booths behind the counter. "Yeah, I did have something here. A safe deposit box maybe." He frowned.

"They're all empty now." Chloe marched up the stairs. "We opened the vault and all the boxes, but all we found was a lot of dust."

"Oh, I had some jewels here for safekeeping." He followed her up the steps. "Or was it baseball cards?" He hummed to himself. "No matter, I know I sold whatever it was. Always admired the architecture here, though. Seems the building remembers me too. Remarkable how it greets you like an old friend, isn't it?" He stroked the banister as they shuffled up the stairwell.

"Yeah, Dahlia's gift is impressive," she said in a bored tone before she turned toward the Scholar on the first landing. "Okay, so can you rein it in, Gramps? Be less ... you?"

"No." He pursed his lips. "I cannot."

Chloe shrugged. "It was worth a shot." She turned back toward the stairs, but the Scholar stopped her.

"Before we greet the others, have you figured it out yet?" His silvery-blue eyes sparkled like moonstones with the light of his power, making her take a step back.

With a deep breath, Chloe sighed in frustration. "You ask me that every time you visit, and the answer hasn't changed. Unless you can give me *something* to go on, I have no idea what you're talking about."

Alexander nodded. "You are close." He placed a hand on her

shoulder. "But you must find your way."

"What does that mean?" A shiver snaked down her spine. It felt as if he were looking right through her.

"Forgiveness, sweet girl." He patted her back, urging her up the last few steps. "That is the key to everything."

"You speak in riddles, old man." She looped her arm through his, pulling him up beside her. "One of these days, I'll figure out what you're rambling about."

"Let it be someday soon." Alexander chuckled.

A shriek echoed down the stairwell, threatening to split Chloe's skull in two. "Every time, Dahl? Do you have to do that every single time?" Chloe rolled her eyes.

"It's you, isn't it?" Dahlia pushed past Chloe on the second floor landing. "You're the Scholar!"

"Yes, I am, dear sweet Dahlia, as beautiful as the flower you were named for." Alexander was a terrible flirt.

Dahlia's jaw dropped open. "You *know* me?" Tears stood out in her eyes, and she flushed pink with pleasure as she turned to Chloe. "The Scholar knows my name!" she hissed.

Chloe sighed. It was like bringing a rock star home.

"I do indeed. We've met on several occasions, dear girl. I'm afraid you just don't remember." The Scholar followed Dahlia into the common room.

"The legends are true then?" Hudson moved from his frozen stance by the kitchen door, shaking off his stunned expression. "You come and go among us, but no one ever remembers you?"

"It's for the best, young Hudson. How is your research going?" Alex moved into the kitchen, setting a bag of burritos on the table. "Last time I visited, you were struggling to understand your compulsion to write."

"I was." Hudson nodded, incredulous. "It's much better now that I've learned to trust it."

"I look forward to hearing about your findings, but let's eat first, shall we?" Grandpa Alex made himself at home, lifting plates from the cabinet and rummaging through the refrigerator for drinks.

"Sweet girl?" Alex peeked over the door. "Call the others down for Taco Tuesday. I'm starving."

Chloe shook her head, laughing. "You got it, Grandpa, but it's Wednesday."

"Whatever." He stuck his head back into the refrigerator.

"Seriously?" Dahlia smacked her shoulder. "You never told me the Scholar was your grandfather?"

"Ouch, Dahlia. That hurt. And I've told you a dozen times, he's my friend's grandpa, not actually mine. All my friends back home call him Grandpa Alex. You've met before."

Her eyes widened with shock. "He's *really* been here before?"

"A million times." Chloe rolled her eyes. It was always this way. Her friends freaked out that she knew the Scholar, never remembering that they'd met him before. But his visits were like a little piece of home.

Chapter 8

Graham | Fall | Salem, Massachusetts

After a long day of classes, Graham arrived in the main drawing room at seven sharp, wearing his best suit and his most convincing smile, but he wasn't in the mood for one of his aunt's exhausting dinner guests.

"There's our young man now," Aunt Gabrielle crowed from her high-backed chair that Graham always thought of as her throne.

"Good evening, Aunt Gabrielle." Graham crossed the room to kiss her cheek, eager to get this dinner behind him and get back to his studies.

"Come meet our guest, my boy." Uncle Lou gestured him over to the bar where a petite, slim woman stood sipping a tumbler of his uncle's favorite whiskey.

"Porcia?" Graham paused halfway across the room.

"That's right," Gabrielle said. "You must have met our dear friend when she visited Kelleys Island."

"Lovely to see you again, Graham." Porcia extended her hand to greet him, and Graham hesitated a moment before he took it.

It felt like a betrayal to exchange pleasantries with the

woman whose daughter had killed his grandmother. Thinking of Chloe, he dropped her hand as quickly as he could.

"Shall we adjourn to the dining room?" Gabrielle stood, leaving her half-empty glass on the side table. His aunt and uncle always had cocktails before dinner but refused to allow Graham to partake in such adult beverages.

"Something smells heavenly," Porcia said as they made their way into the grand dining room.

"Beef Wellington and new potatoes with roasted brussels sprouts and asparagus with hollandaise," Gabrielle announced. "And Baked Alaska for dessert."

"Sounds wonderful." Porcia smiled politely as Uncle Lou pulled her chair out for her.

These dinners were nothing short of luxurious and utterly pretentious—even when they didn't have guests to impress. Graham waited for the ladies to be seated before he took his seat opposite his uncle.

"Graham, you like beef Wellington, don't you?" Gabrielle asked as Uncle Lou stood to carve the enormous tenderloin.

"I've never had it," Graham replied. No matter how many times he explained to his aunt that he was a pescatarian, she just didn't get that he preferred to eat fish along with a vegan-style diet. For Graham, he just felt his best when maintaining a diet free of processed foods and red meat.

"Then, you're in for a treat, dear boy." Uncle Lou placed an oozing slab of rare beef wrapped in a crispy pastry and something that smelled strongly of liver pâté and mushrooms.

He was going to need to sneak in some takeout later tonight.

"Graham is a pasta-tarian," Gabrielle explained.

"Pescatarian," Graham corrected her—though, pasta would be better than what was currently on his plate.

"Oh dear." Porcia snorted into her glass of red wine. "I mean —I admire your dedication to your diet."

"What is it you don't eat again?" Uncle Lou asked.

"Oh, I like to keep a clean diet free of processed foods. Lots of fish, that sort of thing. But this looks delicious, Aunt Gabrielle." Not that she was responsible for actually cooking the meal.

Graham eagerly filled his plate with potatoes, asparagus, and brussels sprouts, already planning where he might find his source of protein later tonight. "How was your day with your ladies' group?" Graham tried to steer the conversation away from him.

"Oh, fine, fine." Gabrielle served herself last, making sure all at her table had whatever they desired. "We have a charity function we're planning next month, but nothing to report there yet." She eyed her husband carefully, communicating something in that way Complements often did without words.

Uncle Lou took a bite of his beef tenderloin, clearing his throat after he swallowed. "Yes, well, Porcia has joined us tonight for more than social reasons." He took a gulp of his wine.

Here we go. Graham chased his beef tenderloin around his plate to make it look like he was enjoying it.

"Yes, Graham." Porcia turned toward him, delicately cutting a brussels sprout in half. "Over the last few years, I've been working with students such as yourself. Young Immortals who have struggled in their training."

Graham set his fork down and reached for his glass of iced tea, trying to give his aunt and uncle the benefit of a doubt. Their hearts were in the right place, so he needed to give Porcia a chance to say what she came to say.

"She's done wonders with her growing group of students." Gabrielle reached for his hand. "We've asked her here to see if you might be a good fit for a mentorship of sorts."

"A mentorship?" Graham tried to keep the scowl from his face. "I suppose I do need a new mentor since mine was murdered a few years ago." He turned his sharp gaze on their *revered* guest.

"Oh dear." All the blood drained from his aunt's face as she folded her napkin in her lap. "I am so sorry."

"It's okay, Aunt Gabrielle, you probably didn't realize this woman—"

"I am apologizing to our guest, nephew." Gabrielle sat up straighter.

"No apology necessary, Gabrielle." Porcia turned toward him again. "Livia is my daughter, and her actions against your family are unforgivable, Graham. You have my deepest sympathies for the loss of your grandmother and mentor. Ming Lao's death was a tragedy."

"Of course it was," Uncle Lou chimed in.

"Hear me out, Graham," Porcia began again. "I work with students all over the country. Young Immortals with varying gifts. Scholars and—"

Graham threw his napkin on his plate and shoved his chair back from the table.

"Considering I am not a Scholar or a warrior, let me stop you right there." He stood. "I do not need to work with anyone who believes there is something wrong with me. I do not need the advice of anyone other than my parents and *trusted* teachers who understand my gifts and where my potential lies. I am young, but I have trained all my life. I know what I need. And this is not it. Please excuse me, Aunt, Uncle before I say something I will regret."

Anger coursed through Graham's veins as he charged up the stairs to his bedroom. He wanted to leave more than he ever had before. It was time he faced the truth: there was nothing for him here.

Graham: I'm going home. This isn't worth it.

. . .

Graham tossed his phone on his bed and went to retrieve his suitcase from the closet. Tonight's dinner was the last straw. He desperately wanted the MIT experience, but he also needed to train with people who understood him. His training would always supersede his education.

Graham: Oh yeah, hit any high levels lately? Graham sent the message through his gift as he sorted through his closet for all the things that actually belonged to him.

"Maybe I'll try MIT again in a few decades." He shoved clothes into his suitcase, leaving behind the fancier clothes Gabrielle had selected for him.

His phone chirped from the bed, and he snatched it up, launching the offline game he used to talk to Ezra.

Ezra: It can't be that bad. Tell me what happened. And level 44 was a breeze.

Graham climbed onto the bed to talk to his friend, grateful more than ever for Ezra's friendship. Not even bothering to type, Graham used his gift to send a rapid-fire message explaining the dinner.

Ezra: That's it? Your pseudo-parents don't get you? Isn't that like every kid's issue?

. . .

Graham felt a pang of regret for his complaints. At least he had parents and an aunt and uncle who cared for his wellbeing. Ezra had no one but his best friend, Wesley—and to an extent, Graham on the other side of the world.

Graham: You've got a point, but it's infuriating to constantly hear there's something wrong with you just because you don't meet someone's expectations of what you should be.

Silence followed and Graham set his phone down, wondering if he'd hurt Ezra's feelings again.

"Knock-knock?" Gabrielle's voice sounded at the door. "May I come in?"

"Of course." Graham kicked his bag off the bed and stood to greet his aunt.

"You know, this room could use a lighter paint color." She frowned as she gazed at the walls, absently reaching for Graham's suit jacket he'd discarded on his way into the room. She paced to the closet to retrieve a hanger, smoothing the fabric as she hung the jacket next to the others just like it.

"The room is perfect." Graham stood awkwardly, unable to think of anything to say.

"May I sit?" She gestured to the chair beside his bed.

"Please." Graham lunged to move his messenger bag from the chair.

"We never had kids, as you know." Gabrielle picked at the non-existent lint on her skirt. "We've thought about it of course, but the timing just never felt right, and truth be told, I'm more than a little afraid of messing up."

"Aunt Gabrielle." Graham sighed, feeling like the worst jerk on the planet as he sank to the side of the bed. "I apologize for my outburst."

"I didn't think." She shrugged. "It never occurred to me that Porcia was the absolute worst person to invite here tonight. She's such a wonderful woman and a great teacher. She trained your mother and I ages ago. Before she met her Complement and raised Livia. We were just girls back then—and so impressed with her independence."

"I appreciate the gesture." Graham hung his head. "But I'm fine. I know all the areas where I need to train—and trying to push me into a warrior's gift isn't going to work. I've tried it numerous times, but that doesn't mean I'm a Scholar when I have no scholarly tendencies. I'm not ashamed of my lack of talent."

Gabrielle reached for his hand. "You lack nothing, my dear, sweet boy, we never meant to imply such a thing. Porcia was here only to offer her assistance. She has trained with Scholars and those gifted with prophetic gifts—and those with more technologically-advanced gifts like yourself."

"I suppose I should have let her finish speaking." Graham's ears burned with shame. "I'm sorry I ruined your dinner, Aunt Gabrielle."

"Think nothing of it, dear." She smiled and rose to her feet. "You will consider her offer? I think she can help you far more than Lou or I could."

"Of course." Graham nodded. "I will think about it."

"I'll send up a plate with your dinner and some dessert. I flubbed your diet again, didn't I?" Her cheeks flushed with a rosy tint. "No beef from now on, I promise. You like eggs, right?"

"Eggs are perfect, thank you." Graham smiled.

"I'll make you a veggie omelet with lots of cheese—and toast."

Graham's stomach growled in response. "That sounds delicious, thank you." Graham walked her to the door, breathing a sigh of relief after she'd gone.

Racing to the bed, he grabbed his phone with several messages from Ezra.

Ezra: At least you have family who cares enough. It's just me and Wes now. I'd give anything to have my parents and my home back, but everyone's gone.

Ezra: Sorry, that was kind of heavy.

Ezra: And now I've lost you.

Ezra: Sorry.

Graham: That is heavy. But you'll never lose me. Promise. And now I'm going to go crawl under the bed and reconsider my definition of a problem. I'm truly sorry. You're going through way more than I can even imagine.

Ezra lost both of his parents just a little more than two years ago. Graham didn't know the details, but it couldn't have been easy.

He was such a jerk for complaining that his aunt and uncle cared too much about his future. They were products of another age, of course they didn't know what to do with a nephew with gifts they'd never even seen before. It wasn't worth running home. Graham stepped into his closet and shed the rest of his suit, replacing it with flannel pajama pants and a t-shirt.

Graham: I'm putting my suitcase back in the closet. I'm being a baby. Sorry.

Ezra: There's nothing to feel sorry about. Believe me, I know how family can get on your nerves sometimes. They worry because they care, they push because they care. It's their job to make you crazy.

Graham: How's training going? Any better?

Ezra: I see what you did there. You're pulling my tricks on me, changing the subject when it gets too real. You know I can't say much about my life here. Our training is bloody harsh, but there are some good things. We're a family of a sort. And at least I don't have a crazy aunt serving me pork roast and rare steaks. What'd she commission for tonight's dinner?

Graham laughed at the deliberate subject change, but he knew Ezra needed an escape. And their frivolous conversations were that escape. If that was the only thing he could do to help his friend, then he would be here whenever Ezra needed him.

Graham: Beef Wellington :(

He could almost hear Ezra's laughter.

Ezra: For real? That's like the carnivore's perfect meal. And so gross too, by the way. I have nothing against a good juicy cow, but that kind of pretentious food is too rich for my blood.

Graham smiled, sinking down into the blankets.

. . .

Graham: 😊 she's bringing me eggs and left-over Baked Alaska, whatever that is.

Ezra: I haven't had a real dessert in ages. Send me pics so I can live vicariously through you.

"Dinner's here!"

"Oh my God." Graham hopped up as his aunt barged in with a rolling cart in flames. "What's happening?" Graham ran for the bathroom to get a glass of water.

"Nothing, silly." Gabrielle giggled. "I'm toasting your meringue."

"The fire's on purpose?" Graham's shoulders slumped in relief.

"That's why they call it Baked Alaska."

"Oh." He grinned as she extinguished the flames with a silver domed lid and rolled the cart over to his chair.

"It'll be nice a gooey inside by the time you finish your omelet and toast."

"This looks amazing, thank you." Graham's stomach growled at the sight of food he could actually eat.

"May I ask ... why the strange diet?" Gabrielle stood by the door as Graham tucked into his plate.

"I feel my strongest when I keep a clean, vegan-friendly diet with high protein fish, shellfish, eggs, and cheese. Natural foods mostly." He shoveled a forkful of eggs with leftover asparagus and hollandaise sauce with mushrooms, spinach, and onions. It was delicious. "Whenever I eat beef or other dense meats, I feel sluggish, and I don't digest it well."

"Oh, you like shellfish?" Gabrielle brightened, like the lightbulb finally went off.

"I can eat my weight in shrimp and crab and clams and

anything else you put in front of me that comes from the ocean." Graham smiled.

"Good to know, I'll tell the cook to make some adjustments to our regular shopping. We'll get it right eventually." She moved to leave. "We just want you to be happy here, so in the future, if we mess up, and we will, just tell us. We won't break."

Graham nodded. "I'll do better communicating with you guys."

"Us too. Night, sweetheart. Just ring for the service when you're done."

"Good night."

Graham remembered to take a picture of his dessert before digging in to find out Baked Alaska was made of layers of chocolate cake and a thick wedge of gooey mint chocolate chip ice cream with a crunchy toasted meringue crust.

Ezra: I will be dreaming of this tonight.

Graham: One of these days, it's going to be you and me and all the sweets you can eat.

Ezra: It's a date, and I'm holding you to it.

Graham: Night, Ez. And remember, sometimes we find ourselves in less than ideal circumstances, but it's only for a time. You will get through this.

Ezra: 💔 Night, G.

Ezra: And ... thank you.

With a weary sigh, Graham went for a shower with thoughts of Ezra on his mind. Clearly his friend was in way over his head. Not for the first time, Graham wondered what he and his family could do to break him out of whatever twisted Senate training program he was in.

But without any specifics, Graham didn't even know where to begin searching, and Ezra was quick to shut him down whenever he brought up the subject of leaving his current situation. Aidan had trained with Ezra a few years ago, but the last time Graham had talked to him, he no longer knew where Ezra was. The Senate had likely moved him to some training facility for orphaned young Immortals. That was probably where Ezra had met his friend Wesley and wasn't likely to leave without him.

So, Graham did the only thing he could for Ezra. He was there whenever he needed someone to talk to, though it felt like far too little for a friend who was going through so much.

Walking back to his room, towel-drying his hair, Graham decided to refocus his efforts this semester. He wanted the education he was receiving at MIT, and it was only a few years of his life. He needed to follow his own advice. He would find a way to get through it and never complain again. There had to be something here worth staying for.

Graham crawled back into bed. He wasn't going to complain about his privilege again. It didn't make him any better than those bullies who'd gone after Brooks.

Brooks. The cute barista who'd never called him.

I'll just have to order more coffee. Graham reached for the bedside lamp and paused. The pin was back. The silver infinity loop. He'd moved it to his desk drawer so he wouldn't lose it. Had Gabrielle moved it back? There was a letter with it this time. Graham lifted the heavy linen envelope sealed with a navy wax blob imprinted with a strange emblem he couldn't quite make out. It was very snake like.

He broke the seal and pulled out an elegant card—like an invitation with fancy script and a black and gold ribbon down the center.

The note was short and confusing.

You will be hearing from the League of Ancients soon. You have been warned.

THE ALDERMAN

What was this insanity? He was certain that envelope had not been there when he'd left to take a shower. Who had been in his room? And who was the Alderman?

CHAPTER

Chloe | Fall | Westbrook, Connecticut

Chloe poured hot water into a glass teapot, watching the jasmine pearls bloom like fresh flower buds opening under the warmth of the sun's rays. The floral scent brought memories of her childhood with it.

Shoving those memories away, she placed the teapot on her coffee table to let it steep while she prepared for her morning studies. It was early, and the house was quiet as she curled up on her sofa under a warm blanket. She liked to record her thoughts in the early morning hours. She wasn't a Scholar in the way Justice and Hudson were. Their works were important documentation of the things they saw when they let their power take them to places she would never see. But she did have scholarly abilities. She just wasn't certain how useful those abilities would ever be, caught between the worlds as she was. Dahlia was the same—it was the thing that truly made them equals.

With a sigh, Chloe opened her journal. She'd filled dozens of them in the last year. Not that she ever expected what she wrote to mean anything. It was all darkness and bad vibes—none of it adding up to anything important. Smoothing a hand over the page, she noticed a familiar handwriting that wasn't her own.

"Alexander." She laughed, shaking her head and wondering when he'd had the opportunity to steal away into her room to leave his notes. He always managed to leave her bits of advice and thoughtful musings after his visits, but he'd never ventured into her personal journals before.

Sweet girl, you've progressed wonderfully here among your peers and I feel you are nearly there, though you may need a push. The future calls to you, my darling. It is all right here within these pages and I know it must be scary for you and your generation. The uncertainty scares even me, and I've seen it all. Your place within this future is a precarious one. You stand before a divided path. A literal representation of your remarkable gift. Which path will you take? Embrace her. She has much to teach you still.

And never forget, forgiveness is the key!

ALEXANDER

"Yeah? So, who is *she*, you crazy old geezer?" Chloe dropped her journal in her lap. Alexander's musings never made sense, but they always had a way of coming to light after the fact.

Forgiveness? Chloe wrote the word at the top of a fresh page. What did that even mean? Who did she have to forgive? Her father? She didn't hold any hard feelings toward him. If anything, thoughts of her dad just left her feeling sad.

Her mother? Now, that was a can of worms that didn't need to be opened. Chloe shoved the memory of her mother from her mind like she always did, reaching to pour hot jasmine tea into her mug.

Taking a careful fragrant sip, Chloe picked up her pen and

began to write her thoughts. She never went into a full-on fugue state or drifted so far into her writing that she wasn't aware of her surroundings the way the others did, but she did feel something come over her as she spilled her thoughts onto the page. Inevitably, her aimless writing would lead away from her thoughts and feelings and into subjects that were beyond her scope of understanding. That was when she felt most like a Scholar. She just hoped some day she could make heads or tails of what she wrote.

Forgiveness. She tilted her head back, gazing through the arched window to the town square below. Maybe the old man had a point. If she wanted to progress, she needed to break through whatever was blocking her. She took another sip of the jasmine tea her mother had loved so much and let her thoughts drift where she hadn't let them go in months. It was just too painful.

Did she blame her mother for her death? No. She scribbled a few notes in her journal. Her mother died fighting an enemy. Yes, Chloe was angry that her mother was no longer with her—outraged—but she didn't need to forgive her mother. Ming Lao had done nothing wrong.

Then, did she blame Naeemah and Gregg? They were supposed to be the ones who died that night in the orchard. That was what Allie had originally seen in her visions. She was the reason they were all there that night. But Chloe couldn't blame them for fighting for their lives. No one knew how it would end. If they had, she had no doubt Naeemah and Gregg would never have allowed Ming Lao to fight for them. Not if it meant her death.

Am I blaming Allie for meddling with a future she didn't understand? That wasn't it either. She couldn't blame Allie for any of it. That night, they'd all done the best they could given the circumstances.

Then, whose fault is it? Chloe wrote the question even as she knew the answer.

Livia. She nearly ripped through the page with the force of her pen as she wrote that dreadful name. *I will never forgive her for what she's done.* If Alexander expected her to forgive the woman who took her mother from her, then he would be waiting a very long time.

Anger and misery churned within her as she thought of that night. The vision of her mother's face when Livia's sword speared through her body was burned into her mind. The surprise. The agony of realization when she knew she would never recover from such a wound. Not after what that woman did to her Complement bond. Ming Lao knew in her final moments what lay ahead for her family. It had shattered her heart.

The churning burned within her core where her power lived. Chloe sat up, spilling the cooling remnants of her tea. "No. Please don't," she gasped. But it was too late. She would come. Just as she always did when Chloe let herself think about her mother.

"You can't keep doing this to me!" Tears welled in her eyes as the golden vaporous mist gathered in front of her. The dragon emerged, shimmering with the light of her power, concern shadowing the obsidian eyes that belonged to her mother.

"Why do you haunt me?" She hadn't allowed the dragon to form in months. Thoughts of her mother always led to this, and she couldn't bear it.

But the dragon didn't speak. She drifted to Chloe's side, curling on the rug in front of the couch like an oversized dog, her scales glinting in the sunlight.

"Forgiveness, huh?" She peered down at the form beside her. Maybe she did hold some hard feelings toward her mother. In a way. Chloe had nothing but respect and reverence for the memory of her mother, but this creature—the one with her eyes—

she hated this lifelike representation of her mother's spirit. Everything about the dragon reminded her of her mother's presence.

"Does Grandpa Alex think you have something to teach me?" She reached a trembling hand toward the beautiful dragon, so like the images from the ancient Chinese stories her mother told her as a child.

Closing her eyes, she sat back against the couch, resting her palm along the dragon's back. Her scales were warm and solid to the touch. Chloe still didn't understand how she'd created such a thing.

"I miss you, Mom." Her voice wavered as tears slid down her face. "If you still have something to teach me, I am listening."

Alexander had a point. He always did. Chloe followed her nose to the kitchen and the scent of something spicy and delicious calling her name. Her dragon padded along behind her, sniffing the air. The others knew about her, but they seldom saw her. If Chloe was going to let her hang around more often, she might need to give her a name.

The common room was empty this time of day as everyone pursued their individual interests, but someone had made lunch, and that would draw everyone out. "What do you think, girl?" Chloe eyed her dragon. "Should we give you a name?"

The gleaming golden dragon rose up to her full height, almost eye to eye with Chloe. She blinked her soulful dark eyes and bowed her head in agreement.

"I'll think on it. I can't exactly call you Mom. The others will think I've truly lost it."

The dragon snorted, and a puff of something that smelled like sulfur left her nose as she pushed past Chloe.

"Seriously, can you breathe fire?" Chloe trotted behind her. "Are you some kind of weapon?"

"Told ya we'd lure her out with good food." Scarlet's voice drifted from the kitchen, followed by an ear-splitting scream.

Chloe moved to put herself between the dragon and the stranger in her kitchen. She glowered at Justice, standing shirtless and barefoot in front of the stove. "You should have warned me she was here." Chloe reached for the fridge. There was no way she was eating whatever Scarlet had cooked. She didn't care how good it smelled.

"She lives here, Chloe." Justice, ever the oblivious male, spooned up a scoop of rice from the skillet. "You have to taste this." He moved toward her.

"I'm good, thanks." She shot a scowl at Scarlet, cowering in the corner. "She's mine." Chloe filled a bowel with leftover soup Dahlia had made and shoved it in the microwave. "I don't think she'll hurt you, but you should probably stay out of her way." She tried not to smile at the way the dragon sniffed at Scarlet with disdain.

"Sh—she sure is something," Scarlet breathed, inching closer to the door.

"Sorry," Justice whispered. "I should have warned you."

He knew Chloe only let those she trusted see her dragon.

"Maybe you'll remember to put it to a vote next time." She grabbed a seltzer water from the fridge and retrieved her soup from the microwave before she retreated to the common room. She smiled when she heard a terrifying hiss behind her. Maybe her own personal dragon-bodyguard wouldn't be such a bad thing.

Dahlia's eyes widened in surprise when she stepped back into the room. "I see you've had a busy morning." She glanced toward the kitchen, and Chloe shrugged, moving to sit beside Dahlia on the couch. She was going to have to get used to Scarlet's presence, but she didn't have to like it. Chloe just didn't care for the distance Justice's new girlfriend would inevitably force between them.

"We could all ask him to make her leave. You know we would." Dahlia's hands moved quickly, twisting and turning her knitting needles at a speed Chloe would never comprehend.

"No. This will pass." Chloe scooped noodles into mouth, watching her dragon investigate the room like a curious cat. If it didn't, and Scarlet stuck around, then she'd have to get used to it whether she liked it or not. She wasn't willing to give up her home or her friendship with Justice.

"What are you going to do?" Dahlia frowned, setting her nervous knitting aside.

"I'm going to go look up fierce dragon names. It's time this girl got a name."

Chapter 10

Graham | Fall | Salem, Massachusetts

A snake slithered up the bed. Its forked tongue flicked out to tickle the gooseflesh along Graham's calf. He tried to claw his way out of the blankets and from his dreams, but something gripped his ankle. Something hard and firm.

Something Immortal.

Graham's eyes flashed open in the darkness as the thing gave a vicious tug, pulling him from the bed. Hushed voices and footsteps echoed across the room. Their unfamiliar presence engulfed him, but it was too late. Before his eyes adjusted to the darkness, someone placed a hood over his head.

Graham's instincts kicked in, and he leapt to his feet before he could be further restrained. He grappled with his assailant, trying to get the hood off his head.

Crouching in a defensive pose, Graham focused on his other senses, listening intently to see how many intruders he was dealing with.

"We've got a fighter on our hands, brothers."

Graham couldn't place the amused chuckle.

"Let's get him to the van." The leader snapped his fingers and four pairs of hands grabbed Graham, lifting him like a sack of grain over their shoulders. He tried to cry out for help, but an oppressive weight settled over his mouth, stifling his protests as efficiently as a gag.

Graham struggled as they hurried down the steps and tossed him into the back of a waiting van.

How did this happen? Graham puzzled over his predicament as one of his captors secured his hands behind his back. This wasn't like what happened to his brother so many years ago. These captors were Immortals. And very young.

Can't be the Coalition. But what was this? How did they get past the gates?

Loud music blared through the van as they drove like maniacs along the highway. How had they gotten to his room without waking his aunt and uncle?

"What is the meaning of this?" Graham shouted over the music, but they quickly drowned him out, turning the volume up painfully high.

They drove for hours, stopping twice to throw two more captives into the back with Graham. Both were Immortal and terrified. A young girl sat pressed against him, shivering violently from the cold. The three captives leaned against each other for warmth and support.

When they finally stopped for the last time, Graham reached out with all his senses, trying to determine where they could be. They stumbled along an overgrown trail, the scent of pine and birch heavy in the damp air.

A forest in the middle of nowhere? This was not good. If only he had his phone, he could send a message asking for help. Without some form of tech, he was useless. Unless this came down to a fight. He could hold his own against just about anyone. At least in a fair fight.

"Circle around." Someone shoved him forward. An icy prickle of fear lanced down Graham's spine as a terrifying thought occurred to him. What if this was like Soma? Was he about to end up on an auction block like his brother once had?

A great creaking and groaning sound echoed around them. Metal against metal. Someone jerked Graham forward. "Climb down." His captor turned him around and cut the zip ties holding his hands secured. "Just for the climb." He moved Graham's hands to grasp the curved arc of a ladder. The top of a ladder leading down below the surface.

"No." Graham tried to move away from the opening in the ground.

"Move!" His captor shoved him forward. and Graham grasped the cool iron railing and carefully placed his feet on the first rung, moving one foot slowly down to the next one. It was a bunker of some sort. A very old one cast from iron. Or maybe it was an old sewer system.

This was someone's lair. As Graham left the surface behind, he wondered how long it would be before he breathed fresh air again.

The bunker was deep, and Graham moved slowly, making his way to the bottom blind. It reminded him a bit of the time he and his friends had played war games on the island near home. It hadn't been much fun for his friend Allie at the time, but the elaborate training exercise had prepared him for whatever he faced now.

"Hands behind your back," another gruff and unfamiliar voice sounded just below him. He'd reached the bottom. There was nothing to do but cooperate. Graham turned, placing his hands at his back for his captor to restrain him once again.

The zip ties were tighter this time.

"Follow me." The man took Graham's hand and placed it on his shoulder. "Keep up."

Graham turned back toward the others, not wanting to be separated from those he'd survived this ordeal with so far.

"Move." A meaty hand clamped down on his neck and shoved him forward.

"What's this about?" Graham asked, grappling for his guide's shoulder, grateful his voice came out strong and confident.

"Keep walking."

"Oh, I see, you're just the muscle. All right, take me to your leader then." Graham followed, the gaslights illuminated the way ahead, just barely visible through the fabric of the hood covering his face.

They walked along the dank tunnel for miles, back and forth through twists and turns and switchbacks until Graham could no longer keep track of the maze. Still, if given the opportunity, he would find his way out. Graham's technological gifts allowed him to collect and calculate data. His memory was capable of recalling what he needed when he needed it, and his captors seemed to know that about him. Which made him think this insane march through the tunnels was nothing more than a ruse to confuse him. The likeliest probability was that they'd traversed the same tunnels over and over, and there was a more direct route to the exit than they would have him believe.

"Wait here," the gruff voice ordered. There was another clanking noise and a groan as a heavy door moved on rusty hinges, swinging open with a screech. "Step down." His escort released his hands from the restraints, placing his hands to grip the stair railing. This railing was cool to the touch. Thinner than the ladder railing. More ornate and luxurious. They'd arrived at the lair of whomever was in charge, and now it was time for them to show off.

Graham made his way carefully down the wide steps, following the circular railing deeper into the structure. The light was brighter here, revealing a wide-open room he could make out through the hood. The gaslights burned at regular intervals, topping classic Ionic columns and supporting a barrel-vaulted ceiling.

Very impressive.

Shadows moved around the room, making little noise as Graham's escort guided him across the room to stand in front of an enormous fireplace, blazing with flames. Graham inched closer to the heat.

"Kneel." A heavy hand clamped down on his shoulders, forcing him to the cool tiled floor. His guard took a step back, and they waited in silence for the others to join them.

The girl choked back her fear beside Graham as they shoved her to the ground, and the other boy fairly vibrated with rage.

"Ladies and gentlemen," a smooth, cultured voice rang out across the cavernous room. "The season is upon us again. Welcome to the League of Ancients."

With a flourish, someone ripped off Graham's hood. Blinking in the glaring gaslights, he took in the room. Finely dressed men and women stood around, sipping champaign, beaming celebratory smiles at Graham and his companions. Yet, they all wore masks to hide their faces.

"Let us welcome this year's recruits." Applause and cheers erupted, and a quartet began to play a rousing rendition of *Flight of the Valkyries*.

It was a party, and Graham and his fellow captives were the guests of honor.

Chapter 11

Chloe | Fall | Westbrook, Connecticut

"Knock-knock."

Chloe looked up from her desk to find Scarlet peeking into her room.

"Can I help you?" Chloe forced a smile for her unwanted roommate.

"Wow, you have a beautiful room." Scarlet lingered at the open door.

"Er, thanks." Chloe couldn't blame her for wandering around the house. With Justice deep in another prophetic fugue, she didn't have anything to occupy her time.

"Justice is still busy with his work in our room, so I'm making rounds to all the roomies, taking the opportunity to get to know everyone. Mind if I join you for a bit?" Her gaze wandered across the room to Chloe's dragon laying curled up at her feet.

"I suppose." Chloe pushed back from her desk.

"I come bearing snacks." Scarlet stepped into the room with a tray of tea and scones. "Oh, my!" She stumbled back as the dragon stood, unfurling her wings and giving a wide yawn and snapping her jaws. "She has wings? Did she have wings the other day?" Scarlet's voice went up a few octaves. "And she looks bigger. Is she bigger?"

"Her name is Fei Long." Chloe patted her sun-warmed scales. "She seems to be changing the longer she stays out."

"Stays out?" Scarlet set the tray on the coffee table, and Chloe reluctantly went to join her.

"It's a long story." Chloe sat on the opposite couch, gesturing for Scarlet to have a seat. "I've resisted her in the past. Recently, we've come to an agreement. And it seems she's experimenting with her form. The wings showed up yesterday, and today she has all these colorful scales down her back."

"She is beautiful. What does her name mean?" Scarlet perched on the edge of her seat.

"Fei Long were the flying dragons of Chinese lore. They were considered Daoist creatures who had achieved Immortality. They were said to have the head of a dragon, the tail of a phoenix, and multicolored scales, so the name suits her."

"It does." Scarlet shook her head, unable to take her eyes off Fei Long. "I've never seen anything like her."

"Honestly, neither have I." Chloe scooted to the edge of her seat to pour tea for herself and her guest. Scarlet was nice enough. Chloe would have liked her a lot better if she had her own home to go to.

"I know I was a bit of a surprise." Scarlet offered her a scone. "And I can see how you would want to protect Fei Long from strangers. I'm sorry we invaded your privacy the other morning in the kitchen."

"It's okay." Darn it, why did she have to be so decent? "Sorry Fei Long hissed at you."

"I'll learn the house rules. I want to fit in here. I... don't really have anywhere else to go." She picked at a scone. "This is the first time I've lived with other Immortals like me. It's ... nice."

"It must be hard, getting such a late start." Chloe felt a wave of sympathy for her.

"It is. I have so much to learn from all of you. I don't quite get why Justice is keeping me out all of a sudden. I know he's working, but—"

"It's nothing against you." Chloe nibbled the scone—her favorite from the bakery on the corner. "He retreats into himself. He doesn't let anyone in when he's in touch with his power."

"Except you."

"It's not that he *lets* me in. I can just get through his barrier. I don't do it unless I have to, and I try to get his attention before I just barge in. He'll come out of it soon, and if he doesn't, I'll lure him out so he doesn't starve himself. He forgets to eat, so we leave food for him on the stairs, but most of the time he ignores it. And then, sometimes, he gets sick."

"That can't be good for him." Scarlet chewed her bottom lip. "Can you teach me how to get his attention?"

"I don't think that's something you can learn. It's about overpowering him, and I don't like doing it."

"I see." She sat back against the couch. "I'd never manage it. He's extremely powerful." She eyed Chloe warily. "And you're kind of intimidating."

Chloe snorted, thinking of Allie and Aidan and how powerful they were. She was nothing compared to the friends she grew up with.

"Seriously, Chloe, you have a freaking dragon." Scarlet laughed. "And you're the most important person in my boyfriend's life."

Chloe cringed at that word, wanting to scream at this lovely, kind girl that Justice was her Complement; that Scarlet would never have a claim on him, but she had better manners than that. It was her lot to bear the burden of knowing before Justice. To watch him with his girlfriends, knowing one day he would look at no other.

Fei Long turned baleful eyes on Chloe with a snort of sparks from her nose.

I wasn't going to say it out loud. Chloe rolled her eyes, wondering how the dragon always seemed to know what she was thinking.

"I know you have ... feelings for him," Scarlet said. "He always talked about his best friend, Chloe. I should have guessed there was more to it than just friendship. He's such an amazing guy, how could you not love him? And he's so crazy about you."

Chloe wasn't sure how to respond to that but there was no use denying it. "And he's crazy about you." She shrugged. "The heart wants what the heart wants."

"True story." Scarlet gave a rueful laugh. "Let's not hold it against each other? I hate it when girls fight over a guy."

Chloe smiled. She would totally love this girl in a different world. "Deal."

"Chlo?" Justice stumbled into the room, his eyes blazing like hot coals.

"Justice?" Scarlet shot to her feet, moving to meet him, but he shoved right past her like he didn't even see her.

"Come, I need you." He took Chloe's hand, pulling her into the common room.

"Is he still ... fugueing?" Hudson frowned from his seat on the couch as Justice steered Chloe across the common room to the loft stairs.

"Yep, he's not quite with us yet." Chloe went with it, stumbling to keep up with his longer stride.

"I'm coming, Justice." Scarlet charged up the stairs behind them. Chloe tried not to acknowledge the sense of satisfaction she got when he threw up his barrier behind them, leaving Scarlet struggling on the stairs. It was not a pleasant experience getting caught in Justice's barrier. From what the others told her anyway.

"Hey, buddy, can you hear me?" Chloe talked softly to him, hoping to pull him out of his fugue. He wouldn't be happy to find her here. She tried not to look at his private murals that he normally kept covered.

"Chloe?" He frowned as the light began to fade from his eyes. "Right, um." He shook his head. "I need you." He took her hand again, pulling her toward his mural wall.

"Wait, Justice." She tugged on his arm. "Are you sure?" She cast her eyes down at the floor. He was a private person when it came to his art.

"Oh." He turned toward the long wall covered in bright colors. "Yes. I'm sure." He shook off the last of his confusion, running his hands through his messy hair. He'd been at it for a few days this time. His blond scruff like a five o'clock shadow along his chiseled jawline, and his bare chest and worn jeans covered in paint splatters. "I need you to tell me what you see." He grabbed her shoulders and turned her to face the wall. "I trust you. I need you to see it, please? Chloe, what do you see?" His voice rose in a panicked whisper.

"Okay." She gripped his hand. "I'm looking, just take a few deep breaths for me." Chloe gazed up at the cracked plaster wall, searching the intricate weave of colors, light, and shadow for some clue to his anxiety. He'd seen something in his painting that frightened him. "It's beautiful," she whispered. And it was, though it looked like nothing to her. A riot of colors and textures filled the walls.

"You don't see it?" Justice trembled beside her.

"What am I supposed to see?" She turned to him, placing a hand on his shoulder. She tried to get him to look at her, but his eyes were moving rapidly across the wall like he was reading a page from a book.

"I don't know what it means, Chloe."

"It's okay. We'll figure it out." She took his hand, a wave of dread crashing over her. This was not the normal scholarly fugue. She studied the wall, letting her power fill her as she tried to see what he saw.

"You really don't see it?" He turned expectant eyes on her. She'd seen his paintings before. The ones he did on canvas. His sculptures too. They were always striking, and she knew they meant something more to him beyond the obvious. It was his way of recording his studies. He was a Scholar. Like the rest of them. Yet, his thoughts and feelings came out in colors and beautiful forms. But she and the others could "read" those.

"Give me a minute." She gripped his hand as she opened herself up to his work. She couldn't read it so much as feel it. Chloe closed her eyes as heat radiated from the wall, leaving her clammy and sweaty. Chaos and fear fought for supremacy. He'd used vibrant colors to mask the darkness and evil swarming in the background. It would be upon them before they were prepared. Before Justice was ready.

Chloe gasped and sank to the floor, pulling him down with her. He had to be ready for this.

"You see it, don't you?" He whispered.

She shook her head, unable to look away from the mural. "I feel it."

"Fear?" His voice cracked on the word.

"And ... madness." Chloe shook her head.

Justice closed his eyes, refusing to look at his work. "So much fear, Chloe. This thing ... it's coming for us ... for me. I can't get away from it. It's everywhere I go. I can't escape it. I can't go back, Chloe. It wants me to go back, but I can't do it." He leaned over, resting his elbows on his knees, sweat pouring down his face. "My gift sometimes shows me things others don't really see. That's why I keep my murals hidden, but that's normal for us, isn't it?" He gave her a pleading look.

"Oh, Justice," she whispered, staring up at the wall, rubbing her hand over his back in soothing circles. "No. It's not normal for Scholars to create things others can't see. Not like this."

He scrambled to his feet, his eyes filled with pain. "It's not?"

"You're not a Scholar, Justice. At least not just a Scholar." Chloe stood up. "I think you might be more like me and Dahl. A little of both."

"Both?" He frowned down at her.

"Like ... I think you're a Prophet. A Scholar and a Prophet."

"You think this is ... some kind of prophetic thing? Like Scarlet and her Tarot cards?" He moved to pull the drapes over the wall, shielding it from their eyes.

It was like he'd broken a spell that allowed her to look away.

"No. This is not just a one off prophetic gift, Justice." Chloe's gift still stirred within her, illuminating the myriad of pathways before Justice. "This is prophecy in the fullest sense of the word. I don't think you can escape whatever your gift has shown you today."

"How can it be Prophecy when I never know what any of it means?" Justice sank down on the edge of the bed and hung his head in his hands.

"Prophecy is often not understood without the one who created it. I think ... only *you* will truly know what this means in full, but it could take a lot of training and studying before that happens. The kind of training you can't get on your own." She turned toward him, letting her power flood her core. "You have a decision to make. I can see it like a divided path looming in front of you. It's something you've struggled with for some time. I think this is why you've gone into your fugue state more and more lately. You need help, Justice, you can't do this alone. You have to ... go back." She shook her head. "I don't know what that means. It's just what my gift is telling me you need to do."

Justice nodded, gripping her hands like they were a lifeline. "But what if I can't?"

Chapter 12

Graham | Fall | Unknown Location

"What is this?" Graham faced the expectant crowd, wishing he had a weapon in his hand. He spared a quick glance around the open chamber. It looked exactly like a castle dungeon with vaulted brick ceilings, gaslights, and a mosaic tiled floor with repeating patterns Graham couldn't identify. Creepy serpent and vine motifs covered every wall and architectural detail, and there wasn't a window in sight.

Graham checked on his two companions, each wearing a look of terror. Without another thought, he put himself between them and the champagne-sipping onlookers.

"Ladies and gentlemen, it appears we have a champion." The man addressing the room didn't give Graham the warm-fuzzies. He wore a menacing silver wolf's mask complete with fangs and concealing more than half his face.

The masks. The masks were not a good sign. Graham took a step back, his adrenaline pumping and ready for a fight. Everyone here was likely Immortal, wearing masks of varying degrees of concealment and creepiness. From fantastic gargoyles and dragons to fairies and foxes, every man and woman in the room gawked at Graham and his unfortunate companions. Yet, with his limited range, he couldn't sense a single familiar Immortal.

"Anyone care to fill us in, or are you all just going to stand there creeping us out?" Graham tried for a hint of bravado in his voice, but he was vastly outnumbered and his imagination was running away with him. This could be some sort of bored, rich Immortal catch and release situation. Or maybe he would have to fight—yeah, he'd probably have to fight before this was over.

Or someone was playing a terrible trick on him. His eyes were busy taking everything in. They all had one thing in common. The pin. Every visible lapel and bodice sported the silver loop of the infinity. Just like the one at home on his nightstand.

"Relax, my friends." The man spread his arms wide. "You are safe and welcome here among your peers. Tonight is an auspicious occasion for you three. Each of you has been selected by a fellow member to join the League of Ancients. If you can make it through the gauntlet, that is."

"And what, exactly, is this League about?" Graham asked. "Other than kidnapping people for no reason and freaking them out with your ugly masks and seriously disturbing dungeon? We'll circle back to that gauntlet thing in a minute."

"You know, it might be best not to piss them off," the girl next to him finally spoke, sidling up closer to Graham, for comfort or protection he wasn't sure.

"Didn't I tell you he was perfect?" Someone stepped from the crowd to join the host but kept his distance from Graham.

This guy seemed familiar, but with his face concealed behind an indigo and golden mask in the form of the jackal face of Anubis—and a golden Ankh painted on his brow—Graham couldn't place him.

"I'm sorry, have we met?" Graham wasn't in the mood for any of this.

"All will be revealed in time," the host said. "Please take your place with your fellow pledges."

"Pledges? Is this some kind of frat-sorority crap?" Graham folded his arms over his chest. "Because I didn't sign up for Greek Week for a reason."

"You don't *ask* to join the League." The host's voice grew menacing. "You are *invited* to compete for the honor of joining us."

"And if I don't care to join?" Graham pressed.

"Oh, you care." The host took a step toward Graham, but his Anubis friend stopped him.

"One moment?" Anubis mask asked and received a curt nod from the wolf-masked host.

The Jackal moved toward Graham; his hands held up in a gesture of good will. "You need to relax. I promise, this is important. You want the League on your side." His voice pitched low so only Graham could hear his warning.

"I'll be the one to decide that for myself, thanks. So far, I don't like your party. Or your idea of an invitation."

A chuckle of amusement echoed around the cavernous room.

"Have I ever steered you wrong, Mr. Cutie-Cute?" The Jackal lowered his head with a careful nod and a familiar wink.

Brooks. The sense of relief was fleeting. Something within him wanted to follow the Jackal, cling to anything familiar until this night started making sense, but the rational part of Graham's mind told him to remain on high alert. Nothing was as it seemed, and he didn't like it one bit.

"Shall we continue?" the host asked, his tone dry and unamused.

The Jackal nodded, stepping back into the crowd.

"Right then, where were we?" The silver wolf mask shone in the gaslight as the man made his way to the center of the room to stand before Graham and his fellow captives—because they were still captives until someone convinced him otherwise.

"The League of Ancients enjoys a long-standing fellowship with the Ivies and elite educators across the country. We seek out the best and brightest Immortals from the cream of the crop."

Yeah, I'm out. This smacked of the kind of elitism Graham despised. His mother had left her entire family behind in the twelfth century because of this very same elitism that would have seen her married to an old mortal man just to gain his wealth and titles. She'd taught her children different values.

"We come together as the brightest minds of our kind to collaborate and socialize with one another. You three have been chosen from your various schools because you each have the potential to bring something to the League that only you possess. That makes you special in ways far beyond your immortality. But are you worthy?" The host paused in his pacing to peer at them through his mask.

"Sounds really cool. Top notch. What if we still aren't interested?" Graham scratched at the scruff along his chin. "I see how all the secrecy, cloak and dagger stuff is important to you guys, but can I just put the bag back over my head and get a ride home? I promise, I'll forget everything by morning."

"You will each face the gauntlet in a few short moments," Wolf-mask continued as if Graham hadn't said a word. "Only one may be deemed worthy of us. Those who fail to impress us will be returned to their beds before dawn with no memory of this night."

"And what do we have to do?" the boy beside Graham spoke for the first time, his voice bright and eager. He clearly wanted to be the one accepted into the fold.

"Do?" Wolf-mask cocked his head in amusement. "Survive the gauntlet. Impress us with your skill, and perhaps we will let you join us. Perhaps not."

"What is your gauntlet?" the girl asked. "So that we may prepare for the trial." It seemed Graham was the only one who'd rather be home in bed tonight.

"This way, madam." The host bowed and the crowd parted to reveal a pathway of glowing fire.

"Hard pass." Graham shook his head and tried to leave, but four very large men blocked his way.

How did I get myself into this mess?

Graham watched as the girl stepped forward after volunteering to go first. The crowd swallowed her just as the four guards returned to place the black velvet hood over Graham's head. He heard her first screams just as the fabric shielded his sight.

Clearly, there was no way out of this. He would have to run the gauntlet and fail. That seemed to be the only path back to his warm bed and boring life of *never* flirting with cute baristas ever again.

"Stand aside, please. I need a moment with my recruit."

Brooks. Graham's fists clenched at his sides as Brooks approached.

"Keep the other one over there." He sounded nothing like the hard-working barista at MIT on scholarship, and more like the entitled jerks who'd taunted him just a few weeks ago.

Graham flinched at the touch of his hand on his shoulder.

"I am sorry about all of this secrecy, truly. The initiation is always rough." His murmured tone sounded more like the boy from school, but Graham didn't trust anything he said.

"How long have you been watching me?" Graham bit out.

"A while." Brooks sounded apologetic. "It wasn't just me. Others around campus decided to recruit you and asked me to get close to you before deciding if you were a right fit for the League. I'll be your second tonight."

"Look, Brooks, if that's even your name—"

"Of course it is."

"I just want to leave."

"Not an option."

"What happens when people are *recruited* and decide after they don't want to be part of this thing?"

"I don't know. It's never happened, but I suppose if you really want to leave—assuming you make it through tonight—you could petition the Alderman for permission to exit the League."

"Alderman?" Graham sighed. "You realize how utterly pretentious and ridiculous this all is, right?"

"We are a group steeped in tradition, and we value our heritage. I can imagine how crazy this all must seem from the outside looking in, but this is a good thing, Graham. A wonderful place where you can find friends and family who will embrace you for who you are."

"I already have that, thanks."

"Do you? Because I've never seen you with a single friend."

"I have friends. Ones who don't expect me to measure up to impossible elite standards." Graham took a step back from Brooks.

"An argument for another time." Brooks sighed impatiently. "I have to prepare you for the gauntlet."

"I saw the pathway of fire and brimstone. I assume I will walk over hot coals as you all pelt me with your power and your fists, and if I make it to the end, I'm one of you?"

"Something like that." Brooks took his arm to guide him.

"Do I at least get a weapon?"

"Only your power."

"Right." The only weapon Graham would have at his

disposal tonight were his fists because there was no way he was showing off his abilities to a room full of strangers.

"Do you want to go next? Or last?"

"I *want* to go home." Graham sighed. "But let's just get this over with."

"Strip."

"No thanks. I prefer it when my dates buy me dinner first."

"You're hilarious, Mr. Cutie-Cute, but if you want this over, then get on with it. You go into the gauntlet naked."

"And if I refuse?"

"Then, my big friends here will do the honors for you."

"Fine." Graham glared daggers at him through the veil of the fabric covering his head. He shrugged out of his t-shirt and hooked his thumbs into his waistband, shedding his pajama pants.

"What's wrong with your foot?"

"Nothing."

"They aren't going to like that," Brooks muttered. "Some kind of birth defect?"

"Yes. I was born with a twisted foot. Does that qualify me as defective?" Graham stood with his hands on his hips. "Can I go home now?"

"No. It's just highly unusual."

"It won't slow me down." A wave of humiliation swept over him, not for his twisted foot but for the way they had stripped him bare, literally and figuratively. He felt weak and exposed and angry all at once. He supposed that was the point.

A blood-chilling shriek brought his mind back to the gauntlet and the girl who'd approached it willingly.

"It seems Miss Tate has finished." Brooks shivered at the sound of her screams.

"How'd she do?"

"We will learn your fates once you've all made your attempts."

Rough hands removed the hood from Graham's head. He blinked in the gaslight, wondering what his mother might do to these people if she knew what was happening. That brought a grim smile to his face.

"That's more like it." Brooks gave him a look of approval. "I'd give just about anything to know what you're thinking right now."

"Just thinking about all the ways my mother would punish every last one of you for forcing me into this."

"Huh, that's adorable. You're a mama's boy."

"I'm not; she's just the feisty sort. Ex-pirate, you know."

Brooks snorted a laugh. "She sounds delightful. He turned to the guards, shedding his fancy robe and mask.

"I thought you were cute and all when I just thought you were a barista, but isn't this a bit much for a first date?" Graham eyed him from the waist up. Like Graham, he didn't have on a stitch of clothing.

"I told you, I'm your second."

"And what, precisely, does that mean?" Graham's eyes shot up.

"I'm running the gauntlet with you."

"What? Why? Why would you or anyone else do that?"

"It's not easy, what we're asking of you tonight. We wouldn't expect you to go into battle alone without a trusted partner at your side. Same for the gauntlet."

"No offense, but I don't trust you." Graham watched as a pair of burned and bleeding young women emerged from the cheering crowd. Someone threw a midnight blue silk robe over Miss Tate's shoulders, and another pressed a glass of champagne into her hand.

"I take it she did well?"

"We will find out soon enough. Are you ready?" Brooks laid a hand on his shoulder.

"You forget, I haven't been given a choice." Graham made his way over to the waiting crowd with Brooks at his back.

"Nor have I." Brooks came to a stop beside him. "But when this is over tonight, we shall be brothers."

"Or enemies." Graham shrugged.

A surprised gasp made its way around the chamber, and a hush fell over the crowd.

"I suppose they've caught on to my limp." Graham glanced down at his left foot. It twisted slightly inward, so when he stood straight, his weight rested on the side of his foot and not flat on the sole. Most people probably wouldn't notice if not for his subtle limp and the fact that he was stark naked.

"I'll follow you in and watch your back. Move as quickly as you can." Brooks' gaze wandered down to his foot.

"I should probably warn you I'm wicked fast, despite the imperfection, so try to keep up if you can." Graham leaned forward, eager to get this business behind him.

"I like your style, Loukas." A crooked smile lifted the corner of his mouth. "And here I thought you were sweet Mr. Cutie-Cute. Never would have pegged you for the arrogant type."

The crowd parted once again to reveal a long pathway, lit by torchlight and the fiery cobblestones set ablaze. Every few steps there seemed to be a cool spot where the stones didn't glow with the heat of the fire beneath.

"The rules are simple, Mr. Loukas." Wolf-mask returned to call the shots. "At the sound of the horn, run—and I suggest you don't stop until you reach the end."

Men and women, hiding behind their elegant masks, flanked the pathway, some bearing weapons, others their power. He wondered what they would do if, at the blast of the horn, he refused to run.

But it seemed they were one step ahead of him there. The four guards took up the rear, blazing hot shields in their hands.

As wolf-mask sounded the horn—an actual horn from a bull, like a freaking Viking raider—the guards moved forward, driving Brooks and Graham into the gauntlet. Whether he wanted this or not, it was happening.

The searing hot stones lit his feet on fire just as the guards' shields pushed him forward, setting his back ablaze.

Fine! They wanted a show, he'd give them one. Just not the one they wanted to see. Graham rushed forward, letting Brooks sink or swim behind him. Ducking to miss the strike of a sword, Graham rolled forward, leaping up and over a woman in his path, her scarlet red power building in her hands.

He didn't give her a chance to hit him with her powerful weapon before he charged into the fray, fists flying as he connected with those who would slow him down. Graham's power churned in his core, as hot as the coals at his feet, but he refused to reveal any ability he might possess that would help him along this nightmare highway—not that he had any such ability, but they didn't need to know that. Still, his power fueled him, lending him strength and the sharp focus he needed to see what he was up against.

Graham stumbled into darkness, everything vanishing except the agony at his feet and the near constant blows of fists and cudgels slamming against his back and legs, threatening to send him sprawling to the ground. He fought the oppressive darkness, a psychological trick meant to send his adrenaline into overdrive so he would panic and make mistakes.

But Graham kept his head, just as his father taught him. No matter what he faced, Graham had to keep a level head because he didn't have powerful gifts in his arsenal. Not like his warrior brother.

Graham pushed through the darkness, shaking it off like a

bad hangover, thinking he wouldn't mind running this gauntlet if Quinn was at his back, and not a stranger masquerading as a brother in solidarity.

A wave of fear hit him like a brick wall, and he knew it wasn't his. Graham pushed. Ducking and twisting away from the blows he saw coming and taking those he didn't as best he could. He moved slowly through the wall of terror, like crossing a swampy field.

Somehow, he ended up with a blunted mace in his hand, and he figured it was fair game. He elbowed through the Immortals coming at him with their mind games and dull weapons meant to cause injury but not incapacitate.

As he raced forward, his mind erupted in agony as an intrusive force threatened to tear him apart from the inside out. Clutching his head, Graham stumbled, forcing his feet to keep moving. It would all end the moment he reached the son of a bitch standing at the end of the gauntlet.

Graham brought his mace down, swinging it like a hammer, breaking the broadsword that threatened to run him through, and still his mind screamed with anguish, like a hot poker stirring his brain, leaving him confused and disoriented.

As he fought, his face slick with sweat and his feet blistered and burned, Graham refused to let the strong Immortal have free rein of his mind. They could force their gauntlet on him, but they would take nothing else from him tonight.

"Enough!" he roared, dragging his mace through the last of those blocking his pathway to freedom. As he stumbled toward a man wearing a golden lion mask that covered the top half of his face, Graham threw his fist back and landed a solid punch to the man's jaw before he fell at his feet. And just as suddenly as it started, it ended with a roaring cheer of approval from the crowd.

Brooks landed in a bloody heap next to him, his breath hot

and his body slick with sweat. "That ... was ... probably ... not the smartest decision. You just punched the Alderman."

"Well, he had it coming. And he shouldn't have been standing there if he didn't want to get hit." Graham rolled over onto his back, the cool stones were like a soothing balm to his burned and blistered body.

"Welcome to the League, brother." Brooks took his hand with a strong grip, and together they climbed to their feet to the applause of the captivated audience.

PART II

THREE MONTHS LATER

Chapter 13

Chloe | Three Months Later
Winter | Westbrook, Connecticut

Chloe turned down a side street, looking over her shoulder as she picked up her pace. She hated taking the long way home so late in the evening, but she couldn't shake the feeling that someone was watching her. It started at the library and grew stronger as she neared home.

Taking a deep breath, she focused on her surroundings, listening to the smallest sounds and sensations that might indicate an unknown Immortal presence nearby. That was one thing she was really good at. She smiled at the distant memory of Aidan teaching her how to listen like an Immortal even before her Awakening. She believed his patient lessons were the very reason she could sense other Immortals that would normally be out of range. She frequently used that particular gift to keep at least one step ahead of her father.

The only person she could sense now was James, heading home from his job as an assistant art teacher. He taught a children's pottery class at a local studio, and she was pretty sure he loved every minute of it. He was also taking the long route home tonight.

She turned the corner on the next street, standing with her hands in her coat pockets, waiting for James to join her. It was funny how they all came together here in such a random small town. James was from Kelleys Island too. Sort of. He'd joined the family about a year before Chloe left, living and training with Darius after his escape from Soma around the same time Quinn and Santi had also escaped. James brought Lennox with him. She'd found her forever home with her parents, Seamas and George McBrien.

Chloe didn't remember much about those days. She'd lived in a fog of anger and devastation in those first years after she lost her mother. But she'd connected with James. He was as lost as she was. He liked the family, and he'd benefited from the kind of training he desperately needed, but she wasn't sure he'd ever felt at home there.

One day, he'd just left, claiming he needed to find his way on his own. That was how James was used to operating. When Chloe arrived in Westbrook, the sense of aimless wandering that had been with her since she'd left home vanished and she knew she needed to stay. Eventually, she met Justice and Dahlia and moved into the old bank building with the others. She'd never expected to know one of her new roommates.

She watched James jogging to catch up to her, looking over his shoulder the way she had since she'd left the library.

"You feel it too?" The anxiety she'd been suppressing on her way home was out in full force now.

"What?" He glanced behind them along the tree-lined drive in the growing shadows.

"You've got the heebie jeebies too, don't you?"

"I don't know about that, but something is ... off." He frowned, falling in step beside her.

"Like someone's watching?" Chloe shot another glance over

her shoulder. Her gift told her no one was there, but she couldn't shake the feeling she was missing something.

"You don't sense anyone? Anyone unfamiliar?" James' eyes scanned the street and the sidewalk behind them.

"No, and I've been focusing on it all the way home. There's no one there." At least not in a physical way. She knew Grandpa Alex could see everything in an omniscient kind of way, and she wondered if that was what they were sensing. "If that's you, old man, stop it; you're creeping us out."

"Okay, that was weird. Who are you talking to?" James shoved his hands in his coat pockets, shivering in the cold.

"No one. Where are the mittens Dahlia knitted for you?" She looped her arm through his, sharing her warmth.

"I'd rather freeze than wear yellow pompoms on my mittens."

"She did go a little nuts." They all had new winter gear Dahlia had made during her latest fit of anxious knitting. It calmed her and helped her focus on her studies. Dahlia didn't journal like most Scholars; she knitted, cataloguing all her findings in her head. Last time, it was blankets and socks. The time before that was booties and sweaters.

James glanced back the way they'd come. "You really don't sense anyone following us?"

"No." Chloe tugged his arm, dragging him into the alley behind the bank. "It's safe—" Chloe halted, causing their shoulders to collide.

"What? What is it, Chlo?" James scanned the alley around them.

Joy filled Chloe's heart and mind as she looked up at the ugly rear facade of their home. "He's back!" She lunged for the basement door, waiting impatiently for the building to recognize her before the door would budge.

"Wait, Chloe." James charged down the stairs behind her. "Who's back? Wait, who is that?" James halted at the bottom of the stairs, grabbing her before she had a chance to dart across the basement gym.

"It's Justice!" Chloe couldn't contain her excitement. "He's home."

"Yeah, but who is that with him?" He scowled, turning his focus on the presence that had accompanied Justice home. "She feels familiar. And really old."

"Oh." Chloe frowned. "Yeah, she does." Her heart clenched at the familiar sensation. And not in a good way. She knew that presence but couldn't place it. Had Justice replaced Scarlet? Or was that just her wishful thinking?

Chloe and James walked quickly across the vacant gym floor. It was unusual for it to be deserted this time of day, but it seemed everyone was gathered in the common room, also very unusual.

"Justice?" Chloe called as she and James entered the common room. "You're back!" She charged across the room, eager for his embrace.

"There's my Chloe!" Justice rushed to meet her, his smile splitting his face as he swept her up in a big hug and whirled her around the room. He set her down next to the last person she wanted to see. Scarlet.

"You've been gone forever." She playfully punched him as she pulled back from his embrace. She couldn't let herself linger in his arms too long. It was too hard to let go.

"I'm so sorry we left you all hanging," Scarlet said, stepping closer to Justice. "But we're so happy to be home. She and Justice had left in the middle of the night after Chloe told him he was likely a Prophet and not just a Scholar as he'd always thought.

"You were so right, Chlo. I had to go home." Justice turned toward the woman he'd brought with him.

"I want you all to meet ... my mother."

Mother? Chloe stared at the familiar woman.

"Porcia?" she and James said at the same time. Chloe took a

step back, shaking her head. "Why are you here?" Her face flushed with anger. James moved to stand between Chloe and Porcia like the ally he was. He'd been there in the days after the orchard battle.

"Chloe, I'm so sorry, I didn't realize." Porcia took a step toward her, but James shook his head.

"Give her some space."

"Wait, how do you guys know my mother when I haven't even seen her in a decade?" Justice grabbed Chloe's hand, frowning at the woman he called mother.

"You said you never had parents." Chloe turned toward Justice, accusation in her eyes.

His lips pressed into a thin line. "It was easier than telling you a long, sad story I didn't want to dredge up. We don't have the best history, my mother and me. It's why I resisted going back, but you were right, my gift was telling me I needed her. She's helped me so much, Chloe. I think she can help all of us." His eyes filled with worry and concern.

Chloe shook her head. She wanted nothing more than an escape. To walk away and never see this woman again. Livia's mother was also Justices' mother?

Chloe's Complement. The man she would live out her life with was the brother of the woman who'd murdered her mother. How could she be expected to live with that knowledge when just the sight of Porcia brought it all back in a flood of memories she'd rather forget?

"I had the privilege of meeting Chloe and James when I visited their home on Kelleys Island a few years ago," Porcia said. "A dear friend of mine lives there."

"Yeah, your daughter," Chloe spat as a familiar churning welled up inside her. Fei Long was about to make an appearance, and for once, she didn't mind.

"Daughter?" Justice turned to his mother. "You know where Livia is?"

"That woman—" Chloe seethed, and James put his hand on her back to calm her, "—your *sister*, murdered my mother." Her entire body trembled with rage.

Justice moved to face his mother with a grim look, grasping her arm. "You lied to me?" His eyes smoldered with anger. "Where is she? Where's my sister if she's not with *him*?"

"Justice, darling, take a breath." Porcia extricated herself from his grip. She placed her hands on his face. "Breathe, son." She pressed her forehead to his. "We do not speak of him. You hear me? That man is dead to us."

"But Livia," he whispered. "She doesn't even know I exist." His voice broke when he spoke his sister's name.

"She doesn't know she has a brother because I couldn't trust her then. We can trust her now that she is beyond his influence."

"Trust her?" Chloe raged. "That woman is pure evil." Chloe lunged toward Porcia, but James held her back.

"Easy, Chlo. She's not worth it," James whispered.

"She's my sister." Justice pleaded with his eyes for her to understand, but he didn't know the horrors that woman brought into Chloe's life and the lives of everyone she held dear.

"I—I'm sorry, Justice, I can't do this." Chloe backed away, rushing into her room and slamming the door behind her before Fei Long burst forth and tried to devour Porcia. Fei Long didn't like it when Chloe was upset. They'd learned that the hard way after the golden dragon chased Scarlet around the common room just before she'd left with Justice.

With a wail of anger and frustration, Fei Long emerged in a fog of golden mist as she always had, but this time she breathed fire, her eyes blazing with fury.

And Chloe tasted sulfur as a puff of smoke left her own nostrils.

Chapter 14

Graham | Winter | Salem, Massachusetts

"Brooks, I'm hanging up." Graham closed the front door behind him, glancing across the brightly lit foyer before he charged up the stairs to his room. Gabrielle would freak if she saw his face. He ran a hand over his bruised jaw, catching his reflection in one of the many mirrors lining the corridor to his room. He looked like something that went through a meat grinder thanks to the League goons always looking for a fight whenever Graham refused the invitations to their events.

"It's not everything it seems," Brooks insisted. "Just meet with me and a friend of mine from the League, and we can explain."

"I've told you people a hundred times." Graham stopped at his bedroom door. "No matter how many times your people try to beat me up, I'm not interested in any of this. Can't we just leave it at that? I'm sure the League is amazing and wonderful and could do great things for me, but I just don't want that kind of elitism in my life."

"Says the boy who lives in a giant mansion by the sea," Brooks muttered.

"How do you know that?" Graham instinctively looked over

his shoulder. He'd had a lot of practice with that over the last months of the League watching his every move.

"I could explain everything if you'd just meet with me."

"Not interested." Graham stepped into his room. "I prefer things in my life to remain simple. I hope you can understand that." Graham didn't wait for his response before he ended the call and flipped on the light in his study.

After surviving the gauntlet, Graham had very little memory of the party that followed. He woke up the next afternoon, safe in his bed, with the last of his burns and blisters the only reminder of the previous night.

On his bedside table rested the infinity pin. The League of Ancients took great pride in their pins. Though, this one was slightly different. Before, the pin was smooth unblemished silver. The new infinity loop of his initiate's pin was more obviously a serpentine figure with textured scales and a nondescript head resting beside its tail. It came with a missive from the League. A wax sealed envelope containing a summons for Graham to attend his first official gathering of the League in three days' time. He'd been accepted into the League by a unanimous vote, but he wasn't going. If they insisted, they'd have to drag him in again.

Graham tossed his phone and messenger bag onto his desk chair and toed out of his boots before he realized he was not alone.

"What is the meaning of this?" His aunt's tone was direct and to the point—more decisive than he'd ever heard from her.

Graham stepped down into his bedroom to find her sitting in the chair beside his bed, the summons from the League in her hand. Uncle Lou sat on the bed beside her, studying the pin with a pained expression.

With a weary sigh, Graham sat down on the top step. "Just a bit of trouble I've been trying to get out of." He ran a hand through his hair, not in the mood for the third degree that was likely coming his way. His aunt and uncle would be all over this. They'd probably think it was the greatest thing ever.

Gabrielle snorted in disgust. "You do not simply walk away from the League, Graham. How long has this been going on?"

His head snapped up. "You know about this group?" That, he had not expected.

"Yes." Gabrielle shot up from her chair. "We have a great deal of experience with the League of Ancients." She began to pace.

"Then, you can help me get out of it?" Graham asked hopefully.

"Afraid not, my boy." Uncle Lou puffed on his pipe; his arm crossed over his chest with a faraway look in his eye. "Once they get their teeth into you, there's no getting out." They both looked at him with sorrow-filled eyes.

"You two need to use more words." Graham rubbed the back of his neck. "Because I am not going to this ... summons."

"If you don't, they'll send their guards to get you. You don't want that." Gabrielle tapped a finger against her lip. "We have no choice but to bring him in now." She turned to her husband.

"Bring me in? What are you talking about?" Graham rested his elbows on his knees, feeling the weight of a mountain on his back.

Uncle Lou shifted on the edge of the bed. "We will have to coach him before the next gathering."

"I'm not going, guys. I don't have time for this elite nonsense."

"It's not nonsense." They both turned toward him, fear and determination in their eyes. "These people do not play around, Graham." Aunt Gabrielle crossed her legs. "They've decided they want you, and they will collect you. It's what they do. That's why your face looks like that. It will only get worse the more you resist."

"What could they possibly want with me? If I really can't get out of this, then I need to know what I'm walking into. I'm going to need you two to be straight with me."

Uncle Lou moved to sit on the steps beside Graham, laying a hand on his shoulder as he spoke. "I promised your mother we'd keep you safe. I never suspected the League would come after you."

"It's strange." Gabrielle added. "They only seek the most skilled warriors. They want nothing more than absolute perfection." Her eyes drifted to Graham's not-so-perfect foot, and he scowled back at her.

"Oh, come off it, boy." She rolled her eyes, and he swore he could see some of the facade she'd worn for the last year begin to shatter. "We know just how wonderful you are, and we love you. You are sheer perfection. Those people couldn't ask for anyone more brave, more intelligent, or kind than you. But they do not appreciate those things unless they come in a package they believe is worthy. They do not have time for Scholars or Techs, or even Prophets. They can't see just how important such Immortals are to our longevity. To the League, the only thing that matters is power."

"How do you know so much about them?" Graham glanced at his uncle.

"We *are* them," Gabrielle said softly.

"We *used* to be," Lou added. "They just didn't notice when we turned against them."

"If you're still members, how did you not know about this?" Graham gestured at his face.

"Once you join the League, you're a member for life, but that doesn't mean you're always in the know." Lou stood with a groan. "Call the kids, darling. I believe it's time for a family meeting."

After fussing over his bruised and scraped face, Gabrielle brought Graham down to the gym in the dungeon, but instead of joining Uncle Lou, she guided him to a wall of shelves used to display weapons and artifacts from their life together.

Graham wasn't as shocked as he might have been if his own family hadn't had a similar secret passage into the underground back home. When the shelves moved aside to reveal a dark pathway underground, he just shrugged and followed his aunt.

He'd lived with them for more than a year, yet tonight was the first time he'd seen there was much more to them than their outward appearance. For the last hour, Graham even wondered if their carefully constructed facade was a clever disguise.

"Good, good, you're both here." Gabrielle stepped inside a torch-lit chamber at the end of the long pathway. It reminded Graham of the crypt at home, but with much less comfortable seating.

A great stone fire pit occupied the center of the round chamber. Several large boulders sat arranged around the glowing fire pit—three of which were occupied.

"Graham, I'd like you to meet Aria." Uncle Lou gestured to the young woman seated beside him.

Graham nodded at the girl, but he zeroed in on the other figure sitting on the cold stone boulder beside his uncle. "What's he doing here?" Graham stared at the very last person he'd expected to see tonight.

Brooks stood, his arm out in a gesture of peace. "I promise, I can explain everything."

"How do you know Brooks?" Uncle Lou asked.

"School," Graham muttered.

"Didn't we tell you to keep your distance?" Uncle Lou frowned at Brooks.

"He's the reason the League came after me in the first place, so obviously, he didn't listen." Graham crossed his arms over his chest.

"What?" Gabrielle turned on Brooks with a look of horror on her face. "Explain."

"No, Gabby, that's not quite how it went down," Brooks said in a relaxed tone.

"Gabby?" Graham glanced from his aunt to Brooks, second guessing everything he thought knew about his aunt and uncle. He'd never heard a single person address her as anything other than Gabrielle Fitzroy.

She took a deep breath before she sat down on one of the boulders. "I suggest you start at the beginning and don't leave anything out."

"He set me up," Graham interjected, moving to sit beside his aunt. "I was supposed to be his pledge."

Gabrielle turned toward Brooks for his explanation, but Graham couldn't see how he could talk his way out of this.

"That part is true." Brooks stared down at the faded blue of his jeans. "But the League already had their eye on him. They would have recruited Graham with or without me, so I thought it best if I did the recruiting. That way I could be his second in the gauntlet and also his guide through initiation. I just wasn't sure how you guys would react, so I didn't tell you." Brooks at least had the decency to look ashamed of his subterfuge.

"You want to use Graham to dig deeper?" Uncle Lou stared across the flames at Brooks, his pipe tucked between his teeth.

"We need new blood," Brooks said, shrugging. "We aren't getting anywhere with just us."

"Yes, but why Graham?" Gabrielle's shoulders fell. "My nephew is not the kind of young Immortal the Alderman likes to collect. He'll hardly have the opportunity to get close to him the way you can."

"I don't know yet, Gabby, but the Alderman already wants to collect Graham. That's why he's had you followed so closely." Brooks stared at Graham across the fire pit. "We need to know what he's after, but I've gotten as close to the inner circle as he's going to let me. My guess is Graham has some sort of knowledge or ability the Alderman—or the Grand Master—desperately wants."

"And I seriously can't just say no and walk away?" Graham asked. "How do they expect to keep me involved in a secret society I want no part of?"

"They will persist until they win you over. You can't walk away." Aria spoke for the first time. "Wherever you go from here, they will find you. But if you let them pull you into the fold, perhaps you can help us."

"And what would that entail?" Graham turned to his aunt. "Even more trouble I don't want?"

"We want to take them down," Uncle Lou said. "We've been working from the inside for decades and haven't been able to get close enough to remove the Grand Master of the League from his position of power. We still don't even know who he is."

"Lou, we promised Emma we'd keep him out of this," Gabrielle protested.

"I think even his mother would agree the only way out of this now is through it." Lou shared a look with his Complement. They decided something in that brief moment before Uncle Lou nodded and turned back to Graham. "When we first became involved in the League several years ago, they were a harmless social group. We were a family during a difficult time in this country. Back in '32, it was hard to get ahead and we helped each other."

"Lou, my man," Brooks interrupted, slapping him on the back. "That was nearly ninety years ago. We need to work on your definition of 'several years.'"

"Five, ninety, what's the difference when you're older than a thousand?" Lou flashed a toothy grin at Brooks.

Lou and Gabrielle were different down here. Graham looked from his uncle to his aunt. They were less proper and somehow not as refined. He liked them better this way.

"If that's what it takes to get out of this mess, then tell me more. Why do we need to take them down? What do they want from those they collect? Besides the obvious reach for more power?"

"They don't just want more power. They want control of everything," Aria said softly. "And they'll remove anyone standing in their way." She wore a hood to keep her face in shadows, but Graham was almost certain this young woman was the same one who had accompanied Miss Tate through the gauntlet. The girl who had failed to impress the League that night.

"And how do you fit into this group?" Graham arched a brow at her.

"My parents were in the League with Gabby and Lou until they disappeared nearly ten years ago. Your aunt and uncle practically raised me after I lost my parents. The Alderman believes I am a loyal legacy member, content with his explanation of their tragic deaths at the hands of the Coalition, but I know they are alive, and I will tear the League apart with my bare hands until I find them."

"But what do they actually want?" Graham scratched the back of his head. "If you want my help, I need specifics." Trouble seemed to follow him and his friends. If it wasn't the Senate taking Sasha away for secret training, it was illegal slave markets trying to sell his brother for profit. And now, an elite secret society wanted him for some unknown reason—just a regular Tuesday for Graham Loukas.

"The Alderman likes to collect certain elite of the elite Immortals," Gabrielle began. "Those with power, connections, money—whatever the Master dictates, the Alderman delivers. We believe the Master is using these people and the connections they bring to increase his own power. We just don't know what their ultimate goal is." Gabrielle looked to Lou for help.

"But?" Graham pressed.

"But ... in the last decade," Gabrielle's hands twisted in her lap, "young Immortals have gone missing from the League. Presumably into the service of the Grand Master, but we know some who have not gone willingly."

"And who is this Grand Master person?" Graham asked.

"No one knows," Aria said. "There is a reason we wear masks at League events. Many members hold positions of power throughout the world."

"So, this isn't just a local thing then?" Graham raked a hand through his hair in frustration.

Aria shifted in her seat. "The League gathers its members from the most elite colleges and universities across the globe, but the Ivies are its bread and butter, so they have headquarters here in New England."

"Our Alderman is Nicholas Ward," Uncle Lou said with a weary sigh.

"The Secretary of State? That Nick Ward?" Graham's mouth hung open in shock. "Of the United States? That Nick Ward? Are you sure? We're supposed to stay out of mortal politics. It's like a Senate mandate. How is he not in jail right now?"

"The Senate has lost their focus. In the absence of a full operating Chief Justice, they have become distracted and ineffective." Lou took an angry puff of his pipe. "I'm sure you can imagine the level of influence an Immortal like Nicholas has in such a position."

"He could be manipulating the President of the United States." Graham's stomach heaved at the idea. "How has our Senate allowed such a thing?"

"Nick is a persuasive," Aria interjected. "He gets what he wants. He can persuade the President and those closest to her to do almost anything he wants. Though, he has to keep his persuasion subtle."

"But over time..." Gabrielle trailed off.

"He could manipulate the U.S. Government to his agenda." Graham's heart sank to his toes. This was way bigger than him. He wanted out of this nonsense, but it just wasn't in him to walk away from such blatant abuse of power.

"And he's just the Alderman of the New England League," Brooks said sadly. "And he's also my father, so there's that too." He stared down at his hands in his lap.

"And you're working against him?" Graham couldn't fathom how that felt. His own father was the best man he knew.

"He doesn't have a clue. My brother either. He was the jerk in the wolf mask the night of the gauntlet. He's also a U.S. senator."

"So, if the Alderman of this one group, and his son, both hold positions of power within the U.S. Government, then it's safe to assume there are leaders across the world who are members of this League of Ancients."

"Correct assumption." Aunt Gabrielle laid a hand on his shoulder.

"Meaning we can't trust anyone, and we know nothing? That about sum it up?"

"More or less," Brooks replied, his dimpled smile making its first appearance of the night.

"We believe they are preparing for a major coup on the world stage," Gabrielle said. "We just don't know what it is or when it's happening."

Graham nodded, letting out a sigh of resignation. "All right then, how can I help?"

Chapter 15

Chloe | Winter | Westbrook, Connecticut

Hunger drove Chloe from her room on the third day after Porcia's arrival. She'd eaten every snack and protein bar she kept in her room, and there was only so much tea she could drink. Even Fei Long was extra cranky from the lack of sustenance. It seemed the dragon thrived on Chloe's energy, and when that was weak, so was Fei Long. This morning, she was nothing but a thin golden vapor, much like she was the day Chloe created her.

For days, Chloe had avoided Justice and his mother, who seemed to have made herself quite at home. Porcia's presence was everywhere. That feeling of being watched was a near constant state since her arrival.

"Morning, Hudson." Chloe shuffled into the common room, peering past him into the empty kitchen. Hudson ignored her, which wasn't unusual. He spent a great deal of time immersed in his studies that took him to some mental plane Chloe would never reach.

With his unseeing eyes nearly opaque, his hands flew across the pages of his journal. Hudson was ambidextrous, capable of writing on two different subjects at the same time. The left page seemed to be about recent events happening around the world, focused on young Immortals, while the right page focused on similar events from the past. Like a compare and contrast.

It was a mystifying sight to watch Hudson at work. Like all scholarly Immortals, his gift guided him to the information it sought. He didn't need books or other resources to "study" his endeavors. The information came to him through his power. That was how Scholars differed from those Immortals she'd grown up with.

"Chloe?" His voice rasped in his throat, grating like gravel as he emerged from his deep focus.

"Hey, Huds." She moved to take his hand. Sometimes he needed help finding his way back to this plane of existence.

"Thanks." He squeezed her hand, shaking off the last of his scholarly state. His eyes cleared, returning to their normal warm brown.

"What are you studying?" Chloe perched on the arm of the old leather chair that was his favorite.

"I don't know yet. I need to read through my last few days of journal entries to see what my gift is telling me." He smoothed an ink-stained hand over the pages of his neat handwriting. "There is something here I'm not grasping." He frowned at the book in his lap. "Something I'm not seeing."

Chloe's vision doubled as the words on the pages blurred, a few lines coming into sharp focus a moment later. She leaned forward, studying the lines more closely.

"What do you see, Chlo?" Hudson held the book up so she could get a better look.

On the left page, the line about the "power surpassing that of their ancestors" lifted off the page, shimmering in golden letters. On the right side, the line about how the "power will continue to fade with each passing generation, leading up to the darkness no prophecy can see beyond." Each line stood out to her in gold—the color of her power.

"Study this path." Chloe's voice sounded distant to her ears as she ran a fingertip over Hudson's writing. "Your historical findings talk about the corruption of power after the Great War in Indriell. The ancients did something to destroy the purity of our power."

Hudson nodded. "Yes, and it has diminished over time."

"But over here." Chloe pointed to a line about the youths of today "surpassing the strength of their ancestors." It contradicted the mention of the power fading. "This is important, Huds. This speaks of our generation. We are stronger and more capable than the generations before us. Time and again, our parents and grandparents struggle in their efforts to teach us because we defy the surety of what they know."

"It is coming. This darkness." He met her gaze, bright with the blaze of her own power.

Chloe nodded. "Our world is changing, and it's the Prophets' and Scholars' responsibility to see what's coming."

"We're all seeing it." Hudson ran a hand through his too long auburn hair. He hated getting haircuts. Sitting in a stylist's chair, chatting small talk with a mortal wielding scissors was about the worst sort of torture he could think of, so Chloe usually cut his hair for him.

"It's coming to us in these small, nonsensical pieces. It's hard to understand what our gifts are telling us. But you're a lifesaver, Chloe." He gave her a shy smile. "Your gift gives us direction when we're lost."

"I do what I can to help. My own studies aren't so useful."

Hudson squeezed her hand. "I know it must be confusing, caught between worlds. Scholars exist on a different plane most of the time. Your family and friends live on another. They are warriors. You are both."

"Neither here nor there." Chloe forced a smile.

"But that doesn't make you any less important to us or to your family." Hudson pulled her into a warm, slightly awkward hug.

"Thanks, Huds." She hugged him back, her stomach growling. Fei Long echoing the growl with a huff of her smoky breath.

"Go eat something and settle that dragon of yours. She's looking at me like I'm lunch."

"She doesn't actually eat food, you know." Chloe stood with a smile, feeling a lot better than she had in days.

"That you know of. She's looking a little waif-like today, let's not tempt her." Hudson returned to his journals, perusing his earlier studies.

Chloe rummaged in the fridge, retrieving eggs, cheese, and ham for a quick scramble to get something in her stomach. She'd stayed in her room too long, not eating nearly enough. Using her gift to help Hudson had pushed her over the edge, and she was light-headed now.

She cracked a dozen eggs and sprinkled cheese and ham into the skillet, stirring it quickly over high heat. Then she grabbed a loaf of bread, dipping a few slices into her famous French toast mixture. On second thought, she dipped a few more, the smell would lure Dahlia out of her room once it started cooking.

Sprinkling cinnamon over the soggy bread, she popped it into the oven, returning to her scramble just in time to flip it like a giant pancake.

"Do we smell cheesy eggs?" Noah asked, his silent twin following him into the kitchen. Jonah reached for two plates, turning to Chloe with an expectant smile he knew she couldn't resist. His hands moved quickly, spelling out the signs for bacon.

"We're out, sorry. There's ham in the scramble."

Jonah rarely spoke to any one other than his brother, but

occasionally, he spoke to her when they were alone. His voice was powerful and a little unsettling.

Chloe filled her plate and pointed to the stove where she'd left more than half of her scramble for them to split. She'd lived with the twins long enough to know they turned up whenever they smelled food, and breakfast in the afternoon was their favorite.

"It's hot, be careful," she warned Noah in her mom voice, rolling her eyes at herself that she even had a mom voice.

"You're the best, Chlo." Noah poured them each a glass of orange juice. "You always seem to know when we need a break."

"How are things in the Tech world?" She shoveled a bite of scalding hot eggs into her mouth, ignoring her own advice.

Jonah shook his head with a frown, salting his eggs to within an inch of their lives.

"Strange things are happening on the Immortal net," Noah explained. "We've been working with this group of jerks from CalTech."

"The ones who basically run the Immortal internet?" Chloe asked.

"They try to control it, but other Techs like us have made a home for ourselves online. They like to take credit for the things we do, but then they come running to us when they need something they can't figure out."

The twins reminded her so much of Graham. She missed her childhood best friend, but when she left home, she severed all ties. Even though he lived just a few hours away, she hadn't seen him in more than two years.

"So, what are you helping them with?" Chloe worried about them trusting the wrong people.

"They want to create a secure means of communicating offline and over long distances."

"Which isn't possible, right?"

"I'm sure it's *possible*." Noah shrugged, and Jonah snorted like she'd suggested they'd just learned their ABCs.

"But you're trying to beat them to the punch?"

"Not anymore. We don't know those guys or what they'd use our tech for. So, we're pretending to help them, hoping to find out more about their snooty little elite group. They think because we didn't go to college and we're basically homeless squatters that we're like, useless or something."

Chloe frowned at the twins. She didn't like the idea of anyone taking advantage of them. And she really didn't like the sound of this group. It tugged at something inside her, warming her power at her core.

"Find out more about them." Chloe stood to check her French toast. They needed flipping.

"Oh, can we have some?" Noah begged.

"I made the eggs for you; the toast is for Dahlia." Chloe tucked the cookie sheet back into the oven. "I don't like the sound of this group, guys. In my experience, any old snobbish group of Immortals is usually a front for something bad. You're right not to trust them."

"You think we should do some digging?" Noah asked, his bright blue eyes wide with interest.

"Yeah. Something tells me we need to know what they're really up to. Not just the CalTech people but the ones they're working for."

"You got it." Noah looked at his brother, frowning at something that passed between them before he nodded in agreement.

"What was that about?" Chloe asked.

"Nothing, we just know when you have that look on your face your gift is trying to tell us to pay attention. We'd be lost without you, Chlos."

Jonah kicked him under the table, nodding at his plate.

"Oh, right. Lost and hungry."

"Speaking of hungry, where's Dahlia? The French toast should have lured her out of her room by now."

"We haven't seen her since last night." Noah bent to peer into the oven.

"Leave it." Chloe pointed to his full plate of eggs on the table and retrieved her French toast before the twins talked her into giving it to them.

She made two huge plates of Dahlia's favorite meal and went to find her best friend.

"Knock-knock." Chloe tapped her foot against Dahlia's door. "I come bearing buttery-syrupy goodness."

Nothing.

Chloe could sense her in there, but she wasn't in a talking kind of mood. Steeling herself for what she might find inside, Chloe balanced both plates with one arm and opened the door to the dark and dismal room.

Great, she was in one of *those* moods. Dahlia's scholarly abilities were ... different. Where Chloe sat on the fringes of the Scholar world with her watered-down version of their abilities, Dahlia was in a league all by herself.

"Hey, friend," Chloe called softly.

"Hey, bestie," Dahlia's muffled voice came to her from the region of the bed. Her head somewhere near the footboard.

"Are you under the blankets or under the bed?" Chloe let a teasing note into her tone, hoping to gauge Dahlia's mood by her reaction.

"Blankets." She sighed. "All of them. Do I smell French Toast?"

"Yes, would you like some?"

"Maybe." She sighed again.

Whatever Dahlia saw or felt when she retreated into her studies, it always affected her mood. It was frustrating for her because she was often unable to express what she learned in terms the others could understand.

"Want to talk about it?" Chloe moved to sit on the edge of the bed piled high with multiple blankets. It was at least ten thousand degrees in the room.

"After." She shifted under the blankets until her face emerged.

"After food?" Chloe smiled and Dahlia nodded, shivering.

"Want me to get Fei Long to come snuggle you? She's super warm."

Dahlia managed a snort of a laugh, reaching for her plate. "Pass." She turned on her side and went to work on her stack of French toast. Syrup oozed off the plate and onto her sheets, but Chloe knew from experience, Dahlia probably wasn't coming out of that bed any time soon.

The others worried about her when she was like this. So did Chloe, but she let her friend do whatever made sense to her, and she made a point to be there for her until she felt like rejoining the world again.

Other times, Dahlia was exuberant and full of joy. But she inevitably came crashing down from that emotional high and Chloe was there for that too.

So, Chloe sat on the bed, leaning against the headboard, and waited in silence, enjoying her syrupy goodness, and not putting any pressure on Dahlia to talk until she was ready.

"This gift sucks sometimes." Dahlia finally spoke, setting her plate on the floor before she burrowed back under the covers. "But your French toast could cure cancer."

Chloe smiled at that. She was on the tail end of whatever sent her retreating into herself this time. "Glad to help."

"How can we stop it, Chlo?" Dahlia rolled onto her back and peered over the blankets at Chloe. Her eyes like burnished bronze, blazing with the strength of her power.

"Stop what?" Though Chloe could hazard a guess. It was all on their minds lately.

"The darkness. Isn't that what Grandpa Alex calls it?"

"Yes—wait, he let you remember him?" Chloe gaped at her.

Dahlia nodded. "He said I'm special because my gift affects me so severely, but I think he tells everyone that."

Chloe set her empty plate on the bedside table. "Honestly, I don't know if the dark time is something that needs to be stopped so much as ... survived. Our people are used to knowing what's ahead of us. Just because we can't see past a certain point doesn't automatically make it a bad thing. It's just an unknown thing."

"It's bad, Chloe." Dahlia's voice trembled. "I don't know anything for certain. You know I just get these feelings. It's going to be the hardest thing our world has had to face since the Great War."

Chloe nodded. "It won't be easy. But I think our generation is equipped to deal with whatever is coming in a way our parents and grandparents just aren't. They're so used to knowing what to expect. I think a lot of the fear and uncertainty we're sensing right now stems from them. They're putting so much nervous energy out into the universe. The closer we get to the dark time, the worse that's going to get."

"You're probably right. I just wish I could be of more use. It always feels like I'm on the cusp of figuring it out, like the answers we're looking for are right on the tip of my tongue, but I just can't get there. I'm such a useless Scholar." She burrowed back down into her covers. "And I'm a crap warrior too."

"You are not useless or crappy." Chloe moved to lie down beside her friend. "Though you might want to think about taking a shower." Chloe covered her nose.

"Ha-ha, funny girl."

"Seriously. Your abilities are just different and, in my book, different is a good thing. You're like a herald, Dahl." Chloe stared up at the ceiling. "Your strong emotions and feelings tell us what we should be looking for. You're always the first one of us to sense what's happening among the Scholars."

Dahlia pushed up onto her elbows. "Did you just call me a weathervane?" Her blond curls stuck up all over her head and Chloe couldn't help but laugh. When Dahlia cracked a smile, Chloe knew her friend would be okay.

CHAPTER 16

Graham | Winter | The Alderman's Manor

Graham tugged at his shirt collar.

"Stop fidgeting, you look as dashing as ever." Aunt Gabrielle pushed his hands back to his lap and handed him a seltzer water from the mini bar.

"You know me and suits, Aunt Gabrielle." He readjusted the League pin on his jacket lapel, watching the dark shadows drift past his window as the limo made its way up the long drive to wherever they were going.

"Comfort is overrated, dear. We must look our best tonight." Gabrielle was positively radiant in her ivory beaded evening gown.

"So, last time, with the whole gauntlet initiation thing, you guys couldn't come, but tonight you can?"

"Right." Uncle Lou sipped his glass of bourbon, also pensively staring out the window. Gabrielle seemed to be the only one excited about the evening ahead. "Last time was your initiation. Just because we are League members didn't mean our nephew would be chosen to join. There is very little nepotism within the League—in that regard anyway. The Alderman gave you the opportunity to make it in on your own merits without alerting us to the fact they were actively recruiting you. Now that you've survived the gauntlet, they've graciously sent us the happy announcement and an invitation to your ball this evening."

"My ball?" Graham stared across the limo at his uncle. "This thing tonight surely isn't just for my benefit?" The very thought horrified him.

"You are a new initiate. Tonight, you will meet all the local members," Gabrielle explained. "Be sure to spend plenty of time with Aria and Brooks so the League will get used to seeing you all together. We've managed to make it common knowledge that Brooks and Aria are best friends."

"Really? I got the impression they hated each other." Graham stared at his aunt, wondering if she was as oblivious as she sometimes seemed. He was beginning to think behind her trophy wife, lady-who-lunches facade, she was a shrewd woman more like his own mother than he could have dreamed.

Gabrielle turned toward him, blinking. "Within the League, appearances are all that matters. You will learn that quickly, nephew, or you will drown."

"She's right. You should continue to be wary, though not hostile." Uncle Lou paused to check his pocket watch for the time. Graham wasn't sure he'd ever seen anyone actually do that, and part of him wanted to capture it to post on TikTok, but that was probably not the smartest decision. "We were recently told of your less than gracious behavior the night of your initiation, and with your resistance for the last three months we'll need to do some damage control tonight to smooth things over with the Alderman. Did you really punch him?" Uncle Lou's lips twitched with amusement.

"The night I was abducted from my bed, kidnapped, and tortured? Yes, and he's lucky that's all I did." Graham clenched his fist in his lap, eager for another shot at the man who'd disrupted his nice, boring life.

Well, idiot, you wanted this year to be different. Graham sat back against the plush leather seat, studying the mask in his hands. Gabrielle had given it to him earlier. The skull leered back at him. In shades of ivory, black, and gold, it still managed to be beautiful. A play on a classic harlequin mask, the cheekbones were painted with black and gold diamond patterns while the remaining bones were painted a cracked ivory, with raised golden filigree patterns across the skull. The teeth were razor sharp and set with diamonds. Graham didn't want to even consider they might be real.

"The mask says a lot about the person underneath it." Aunt Gabrielle leaned toward him.

"And what does this say about me?" Graham lifted the beautiful, terrifying skull.

"It says 'don't mess with me, I bite.'" Gabrielle gave him an uncharacteristic smirk as she lifted her own golden and ivory deer mask to cover her face.

"Showtime." Uncle Lou placed his stark black horse mask over his head, concealing the top half of his face.

"What's the point of wearing this when they've already seen me without it?" Graham lowered the full skull mask over his face. The sensation of it was akin to being smothered with a very hard pillow.

"The League operates in complete secrecy," Gabrielle explained. "You ran the gauntlet with two other potential initiates, but they were not the only ones to run the gauntlet this season. Tonight, the League will welcome you, but they do not know which successful initiate you are."

"So, what will they call me if not by my name?"

"I am known as the Hind—hence the golden deer motif." Gabrielle pointed to her mask. "Lou is known as Pegasus—"

"Though, others of our ilk call me the Trojan." Uncle Lou

adjusted his tie as the limo rolled to a stop in front of a grand manor house.

"Then, just call me the Grim." Graham reached for the door handle. If he was going to do this, then he was going all in. The League of Ancients would rue the day they pulled him from his bed and put a mask on his face.

"Grim, dear? Shall I introduce you to Gaia's Ladies?" Madame M rounded on Graham near the bar. The busybody had cornered him once already this evening and he'd hoped to evade her. No such luck. She was determined to find him a girlfriend before the night was over.

"Gaia's Ladies?" Graham sipped his seltzer water, looking for a quick escape.

"Oh, it's a little club for the girls, you know." She playfully rapped his knuckles with her fine boned ivory fan. "All the *eligible* girls of the League." She beamed up at him with delight, her clear blue eyes shining through her feathered eye mask. "They're all in a dither over your performance in the gauntlet."

"I see." Graham nodded, taking another gulp of his drink. It had taken him all of five minutes inside the Alderman's manor home to realize the masks were nothing more than a symbol of the League's secrecy. They all made it a point to know who was under every mask. "Would it help matters if I said I'm very happily single?"

"Of course not." She waved to someone across the ballroom. "What was it that girl said in that book a few years back?"

"I-I couldn't venture to make a guess." Graham fidgeted with his collar.

"Oh, you know the book. The universal truth that any single man of status must be in want of a wife."

Graham narrowly managed to avoid shooting seltzer out of his nose. "Wife? I'm barely twenty, Madame M."

"Never too early to start, young Grim." She waved over a gaggle of young girls dressed like the fates, with varying degrees of ostentatious masks concealing their upper faces but not their nervous smiles.

"Oh, dear lord," Graham gasped as they rushed at him in a flurry of feathers and silk.

Thankfully, Madame M shooed them away after several moments of dull small talk. "Dreadfully boring girls." She shook her head. "We will find you a gem. A gallant boy like you deserves the belle of the ball."

"I've gone back in time," Graham muttered into his drink.

"What was that, dear?"

"I-er, always thought I'd just wait for my Complement."

"Nonsense." She snorted, turning to give him another once over. "My, you are modern, aren't you? Your parents must be absolute babies themselves. It's common among the ancient elites to arrange *acquaintances* with like-minded individuals. It's like a marriage in its advantages but more temporary. I suppose your mother is too young to be familiar with such practices."

"Um, well my mother predates the Crusades, so no." Graham smiled at the thought of his mother setting up *acquaintances* for her sons.

"Really? How ... interesting she would raise such a modern young man. I do hope you don't have one of those dreadful blue-collar gifts with computers and such. Oh, look, there's the Huntress. She's a good match for you."

"Ah, yes, she is quite lovely, but a little *girly* for my tastes." Graham leaned toward the Madame. "Would it deter you at all if I said I like men?"

"Not at all." Madame M turned without batting an eye. "The

Huntress has a brother just about your age. Quite tall and handsome."

"There you are." A slim arm wound through Graham's, clutching his bicep. "I've been looking all over for you."

Graham knew the voice behind the feathered bird mask. *Aria*.

"Yes, I was looking for you too, er..."

"They call me the Nightingale." Aria squeezed his arm. "And I believe you owe me a dance."

"That's right." Graham set his glass down at the bar. "If you'll excuse us, Madame M. It was lovely to meet you." Graham didn't wait for the lady to dismiss him before he grabbed Aria's hand and charged onto the dance floor.

"You're sweating." She laughed at his discomfort.

"She was trying to marry me off." Graham sucked in a deep breath.

"Madame M is short for Madame Matchmaker." Aria whirled gracefully around him, placing her hand on his shoulder.

"That does not surprise me." Graham took her hand. "But," he leaned in toward her, "you should know, I have no idea how to dance like this."

He moved awkwardly with the music.

"Here, follow my lead." Aria guided his steps until he began to relax.

"I knew I was going to a masked ball this evening, but no one told me it was also a trip back in time. I feel like I fell into an episode of *Bridgerton*." Graham looked over his shoulder at a line of waiting females watching from the sidelines.

"We should have warned you about Madame M. Don't let her distract you. You need to take advantage of your anonymity tonight. You have a golden opportunity to make important connections."

"Connections?" Graham frowned.

"Start building your network. Meet and greet and find those you can trust. That is why we are here."

"Right." Graham followed her to the edge of the dance floor as the music dwindled to a finish.

"You should probably get away from the ballroom while you can." Aria eyed the troop of girls heading toward them.

"Next time, I'm wearing a sign that says 'I like boys' because those ladies mean business."

CHAPTER 17

Chloe | Winter | Westbrook, Connecticut

"You did this when you were *fifteen*?" Dahlia blew a strand of sweaty blond hair from her face before she climbed back onto the elevated balance beam.

"Every *single* day of my life." Chloe crouched, her bo-staff at the ready. Dahlia might be her equal in power, but she was way behind in terms of her physical training.

"All right, I can keep up with fifteen-year-old Chloe." Dahlia found her footing again and crouched low. "Come at me."

Chloe skipped forward, taking the first advance. "Maybe sixteen-year-old Allie." She let Dahlia make her advance and retreat.

"And who is Allie?" Dahlia made a strike with her bo, nearly clipping Chloe's shoulder.

"Oh, just a friend from back home who got a late start at this too." Chloe danced back out of the way. In all the time since she'd left Kelleys Island, she'd trained with her friends and various others who'd come and gone, but few posed much of a challenge for Chloe. It gave her a new appreciation for her family and the kind of training they'd sacrificed everything to give her and her friends. She'd done a fair amount of complaining about how hard she'd had to work back then, but she appreciated it now.

After so much time away, and little to challenge her, Chloe had to work hard to stay in control of her power. She truly needed someone to push her, but Justice and Dahlia did the best they could.

"And remind me again why all of this crap is so important?" Dahlia huffed, lumbering across the beam with an unsteady gait. "We're just Scholars." She lifted her bo to deflect Chloe's strike, but at the last moment, Chloe whirled into a high round-house kick, striking her best friend in the face, sending her crashing down to the floor a good six feet below the beam.

"Ow! Chloe." Dahlia clutched her cheek. "What'd you do that for?"

Dahlia rolled onto her back on the mat, staring up at her with a wounded expression.

I've been too soft with her. Chloe took a leap, landing in a crouch over Dahlia, bo-staff at her throat. "Because you and I are more than the average Scholar." The warmth of her power churned in her core, spreading out to the tips of her fingers. Her gift rushed at her with an onslaught of too much information at once. Too many people in this house struggled with too many decisions. The noise was overwhelming. Chloe saw dozens of paths spreading out before her friend. So many directions Dahlia's life could take. With a single choice, her friend could change the course of her life forever. It was that way for most Immortals, but Dahlia was special. She was her equal, and Chloe had a vested interest in helping her friend seek out the right path. From what she could see of Dahlia's current direction, she needed to learn to defend herself and the others here who weren't as capable.

Chloe reached out a hand to help Dahlia up.

"Your eyes are freaky when you do that." Dahlia gripped her hand, climbing back to her feet.

"The others are going to count on us to protect them," Chloe said before releasing Dahlia's hand. "I'm ready for that, and I can teach you to be ready too."

"Ready for what, Chloe? What do you see for us?" Dahlia's bright hazel eyes gazed down at her. Dahlia was tall and built like a powerful, beautiful tree with long limbs and a strong physique. "I know the future is bleak, but will it really affect us here in our little Scholar bubble?"

"The darkness will directly affect all of us." The words slipped from her lips before she realized the magnitude of what she was saying. "You and I are more, Dahl. The others are Scholars. That doesn't mean they are weak or unimportant."

"It means they need a little extra help watching their backs while they do what they do." Dahlia nodded, taking up her staff again. "I know you're right. I need to do my part. Let's get back up there."

"Couldn't have said it better myself." The voice came from the stairs leading up to the vacant lobby.

Porcia. Chloe scowled at her least favorite person in the house. Justice—her second least favorite at the moment—was once again locked in his room, painting in his fugue state—a frequent occurrence these days.

"You're not welcome here." Chloe turned to place her bo-staff on the shelf at the back of the gym housing their training weapons.

"If you want to get technical about it, I own this building." Porcia stepped farther into the room, her slim figure casting a tall shadow on the blue mat. "Or did you all really think this little town wouldn't eventually figure out this building was full of squatters?" Porcia ran a finger across the top of an old shelf they'd found in the alley, wrinkling her proud Roman nose in disgust when it came away coated in a thick layer of dust. They stored their makeshift padded equipment on the shelf. Most of their equipment here was either found or made. They had little enough money for the bare necessities.

"I bought the building a few years ago when I realized my son was living here. We haven't always been close." She moved with graceful steps, like a ballerina gliding across a stage. "But I've done whatever I can to care for him from a distance."

"Then, what brings you two back together again?" Chloe stood with her arms crossed over her chest.

"You, actually." Porcia gave her a hesitant smile. "My son needs you, Chloe. You are a guide, and right now, he is lost. You all are." Porcia moved to sit on the mat, patting the ground beside her for Chloe and Dahlia to join her.

"I'm good here." Chloe refused to sit and talk to anyone who called Livia family.

"I'm with her." Dahlia draped her arm across Chloe's shoulders. "Solidarity and all."

"I am not my daughter," Porcia said in a small voice. "Though, I do love her more than words can express. I wish to explain something, Chloe. If you'll hear me out."

"I don't want to hear excuses. That daughter you love so much murdered my mother, and she broke my father." Tears sprang to Chloe's eyes, and Fei Long crept from the corner of the room where she'd laid curled up in the sunshine streaming in through the clerestory windows. A growling hiss rumbled in her chest.

"I don't wish to upset her." Porcia spoke directly to Fei Long, bowing her head in respect. "I only wish to help everyone who calls this place home."

"Fine." Chloe sat, folding her legs crisscross in front of her. "But make it quick; we are not done training for the day."

"We aren't?" Dahlia groaned as she joined them on the mat.

"Not by a long shot, Dahl."

"It is good to see you continuing your training here." Porcia smiled. "It is very important you all learn to hold your own against Immortals more powerful than you. If you work as a team, no one could touch you. And that is vital to your survival in the questionable future we're facing now."

"What do you know of the uncertain future?" Chloe scowled. She'd only ever heard Alexander speak of it that way.

"I'm getting ahead of myself." Porcia sighed. "To understand what is coming, you must understand what has been. My Complement is an evil, power-hungry man. He wasn't always that way, but since the height of the Roman Empire, he's craved more and more power. He believes he is righting ancient wrongs, and there is nothing more dangerous than a zealot who believes he is on the right side."

"So, you blame Livia's actions on her father?" Chloe snapped. She was so tired of the excuses.

"This isn't about Livia." Porcia pierced her with her dark blue gaze. "Livia was always her father's creature. But none of that matters right now. You look at me and you are reminded of what my daughter did to your family, but the one thing you must understand is that I have never called my Complement husband. We have never bonded. He sees the Complement bond as a weakness and believes he is above it."

"So? What does that have to do with me?"

"I loved Marcus Servius; the man once known as Lord Teigan of Indriell. I no longer hold such feelings. I love my daughter and always will, but as she grew older, Marcus came between us, and I couldn't trust her. Our bond is strong, but I see now that Livia did the things she did in some misguided notion that I needed protecting."

Porcia held up a hand to still Chloe's impatience. "When Marcus brought our son home and I bonded with him as mothers and their children do, I had an ally. Livia was always her father's, but Justice was *mine*. During those years, Marcus kept Livia from me. She never knew she had a brother because Marcus wouldn't allow the distraction.

"And then, when Justice was about ten years old, his father grew displeased with him. He would not be the powerfully gifted warrior his father expected. We knew he would likely be a Scholar, and Marcus holds no respect for the weaker and useless of our kind. He took my child from me." Porcia's voice cracked with emotion.

"That's how he ended up in foster care?" Dahlia gasped. "His father just ... gave him up?"

Porcia nodded. "Marcus claimed he wasn't much better than a mortal, so it was best for him to grow up among them. He dropped him off at a fire station and told him it was time to make his own way. I was to wash my hands of any lingering bond I held with my child. At the time, I was a captive in my own home. There was nothing I could do for him."

"What a monster," Dahlia whispered. "Poor Justice."

"I kept my eye on him. In my special way at least." Porcia gazed at Chloe through the veil of her lashes, unable or unwilling to meet her eyes. "My Complement will never again have my allegiance or my love. He believes I obeyed his wishes and let our child go, but there is a reason I named my son Justice. Marcus seeks to destroy the world as we know it. He seeks power and dominion over all. I will *never* let him succeed. I *will* have a world where my children are free of him, or I will die trying. I will have justice for the years Marcus stole from me and my children."

Porcia took a deep breath. "Marcus' hubris will be his undoing. I am on *your* side, Chloe. I do not condone what Livia did to your family, but she is no longer under his thumb. Her future will be one of her making, and she's never had that freedom before. I know my daughter. She will choose a better path."

Chloe shook her head, her mind reeling.

"I'm not asking you to forgive her, Chloe. That is none of my business. All I am asking is that you try to separate your feelings for Livia from your feelings about me. I only want to help you. Marcus will never look to the Scholar community as a threat. But we can stay a step ahead of him if we work together. Your generation is strong, stronger than he knows. This group, right here in this house, has the power to see what's coming and act on it. But they can't do it without you, Chloe. They need you. I've watched how they each seek you out for support and guidance."

"That *watching* you're doing; it needs to stop." Chloe scowled. "It's invasive and creepy." She was so tired of feeling like she was being watched, but she wasn't sure the others felt it as strongly as she did.

"It's not something I have much control over," Porcia admitted. "I see what I see."

Chloe bit her lip to keep it from trembling. "I can't do this. I look at you and I see ..." Tears burned her throat, and she shook her head.

"You have a choice to make, Chloe." Porcia stood. "I won't force you into anything you aren't ready for. I will leave if you decide it's too painful to have me here. My son needs you ... but you all need guidance. I just hope I've done everything I can to convince you how important this is. It's bigger than you and me. I will leave you with one promise. Though nothing will bring your mother back, Livia's gift will change and adapt to her new life. I've seen how she will grow once she learns to forgive herself for the things she's done. Forgiveness is always the key, Chloe. Forgiveness frees the soul."

Her words reminded Chloe of Alex's last message. *Forgiveness is the key to everything.* Had he meant she needed to forgive

Porcia? Was she the one who had much to teach her? *She's done nothing that needs forgiving.* Chloe met Fei Long's familiar gaze, seeking her opinion, but the snarky beast didn't seem inclined to offer one.

"With powerful Immortals like my daughter, gifts such as hers can sometimes have a mirror image. Where one side takes something, the other side can restore it. It won't bring your mother back, but perhaps one day, Livia will be able to restore your father to his former self. It's not exactly a promise as much as something to hope for. He misses you so." She shook her head sadly. "He just doesn't show it in the right way. I'm afraid parents don't always make the best decisions in their grief, but a good parent will fight for their child. That is all I am trying to do for Justice." Porcia nodded one last time before she left them to the rest of their workout.

CHAPTER 18

Graham | Mid-Winter | The Alderman's Manor

"Had enough dancing for one night?" Brooks stepped from the shadows of the balcony where Graham had escaped the ballroom. Already, he was so sick of the League and their constant need to celebrate every little thing with an elaborate party.

"More than enough." Graham turned to find Brooks in his Anubis mask once again. The sight of it bothered him more than he wanted to admit.

"It's just a facade." He leaned in, offering Graham a chilled glass of champagne. "I'm not actually the Son of Ra, you know." He elbowed Graham playfully. "And I'm the son of the Alderman in name only. He just hasn't figured that out yet." Brooks leaned against the bannister beside him.

Graham nodded, looking down at his shoes, trying to remember what he was doing here. He wasn't an elite. He didn't rub elbows with rich and powerful Immortals. How could he hope to make a difference?

Brooks laid a hand on his shoulder, and Graham met his aqua blue eyes behind the terrifying jackal mask. "We're here to stop the League from gaining too much power. To keep the aldermen and the Grand Master from succeeding in their plans."

"But do we really even know what their plans are?" Graham pushed away from the banister. "It just seems like we're chasing shadows."

"I've seen a map." Brooks pitched his voice lower. "In my father's office. It divides the United States into several kingdoms. They want to overthrow the Senate and resurrect the old ways. That map is the reason I've turned my back on my family and everything I've ever known."

Graham gripped the rough stone banister, staring off across the Alderman's gardens below. The man already had his castle and his court. This couldn't go any further. The League was heading for something big, and no one outside this group even knew who they were, much less what they were up to.

"I don't know what I can do, but I'm in this with you." Graham laid his hand over Brooks'. He tried not to show his flustered reaction when Brooks took his hand and gave it a squeeze. "I was hoping you would say that. My father would like to meet you."

Brooks stepped away from the balcony, gripping Graham's hand as he led him back inside and away from the chaos of the ball.

We're holding hands. Graham's heart threatened to beat out of his chest. *A cute boy is holding my hand. I can't wait to tell Ezra.* Graham shook his head, trying to get his mind back on what was actually happening.

They stopped outside a set of ornate double doors, and Brooks turned to face him, his lips only a few inches from Graham's. Not for the first time tonight, he cursed the stupid masks. "Tread carefully. He's interested in you, but I don't know why. Use it to your advantage, but don't ever trust him. Offer the Alderman whatever he wants within reason, especially if it gets you closer to him or the Master." Brooks lifted a hand to

Graham's throat, the only exposed part of his face. "And remember to breathe, Mr. Cutie-Cute."

Brooks knocked on the door and waited for it to open. "Oh and guard your thoughts. I'm pretty sure someone in his circle is a telepath, though I'm not certain how skilled they are."

"Oh, great, thanks for the tip."

Liveried servants—like actual footmen—opened the doors and announced the Jackal and the Grim to a room of VIP guests paying court to the Alderman in his inner sanctum.

"Ah, ladies and gentlemen, it seems my son has deemed us worthy of his presence." The Alderman in his golden lion's mask approached Brooks with the open arms of an adoring father.

"Good evening, Father." Brooks accepted his father's embrace like a loving son. "My friends and I were just enjoying your generous hospitality."

"And I see you've brought us a new friend." The Alderman turned his attention on Graham. Familiar aqua blue eyes peered back at him, but they lacked the warmth and kindness of Brooks'.

"May I present the Grim, sir." Brooks took a step back, his hands clasped behind his back.

"The Grim?" The Alderman circled him, sending Graham's nerves into overdrive. "A rather grim name, wouldn't you say so?" The man chuckled, looking to his followers for their response to his lame joke. Everyone around the Alderman erupted in peals of laughter.

What a— he stopped his train of thought and focused on the Alderman's mask. It was different from the last time Graham had seen it—right before he'd punched the Alderman at the end of the gauntlet. This time, the lion's mask covered his whole face.

"Tell us, young Grim, what do you think of our little club?" The Alderman's eyes wandered across the room to his VIPs.

"It's a great place to meet women," Graham blurted the only

thing he could think of that wouldn't reveal his true thoughts. "Er … sir," he added quickly as the room erupted in actual laughter—not the sycophantic twittering he'd heard since entering this room.

"Very true." The Alderman laughed, his eyes twinkling with merriment. "I take it you've fallen into Madam M's clutches this evening."

"Indeed, I have, sir. She seems to have taken a special interest in me." Graham shifted uncomfortably as a bead of sweat ran down his back. It was awfully hot in here.

"Well, it's a good thing the Jackal brought you to us then. Otherwise, Madam M might have you betrothed before the evening ends."

"I appreciate the escape. Er … and I'm honored to meet you, sir." Graham recovered himself enough to avoid saying anything utterly stupid again.

"As am I, Grim." The Alderman turned to his guests. "If you would all give us the room, I'd like to get to know our young initiate." The Alderman laid a hand on Graham's shoulder, and the room cleared faster than a Friday afternoon classroom at MIT.

Brooks was the last one out. Even the footmen had made themselves scarce.

"Have a drink with me, Grim." The Alderman stepped across the plush carpet to a drink cart laden with crystal decanters of expensive liquors. Graham wasn't much of a drinker. He could stomach the occasional glass of champagne or fruity wine, but the hard stuff tended to affect him more than most Immortals.

"Please." The Alderman offered him a seat. Graham sat down on the buttery smooth leather chair, not sure what to do with his hands until the Alderman placed a cool cut glass tumbler in them. Soft candlelight flickered around the room and his glass caught the light, making the liquid contents sparkle like fire.

"The League was very impressed with your performance in

the gauntlet." The Alderman sat in the chair opposite Graham's with his own drink in his hand.

"So much for anonymity." Graham forced a goodnatured tone.

"No worries, I won't share that knowledge with anyone ... if you'll do me one favor?"

Graham took a sip of his drink and swallowed, trying not to choke on the burn. "And what is that, sir?"

"Don't ever hit me with that right hook of yours again." The Alderman stroked his jaw beneath his golden mask. "You've got a hell of an arm."

"Sorry about that." Graham glanced down at his glass. "I think I would have hit anyone at the end of that gauntlet, sir. It wasn't personal."

"Of course, of course." The Alderman nodded. "You had a rough time of it, but you exceeded expectations."

"Really? Because I thought I botched it."

"Your peers that night likely performed better than you in terms of power and skill."

"Then, why did the League choose me?" Graham didn't expect an honest answer, but he was hoping for some indication of what they thought he could bring to the table.

"You didn't show off. You fought well. You kept your abilities close to the belt, and you didn't showcase everything you could do in hopes that it would impress us." The Alderman stood to pour himself another drink. "That shows us the one thing we seek above all else." He filled his glass with fresh ice and whisky.

"And what is that?" Graham asked, though he could hazard a guess.

"A shrewd mind, Grim. That is why you were selected to join us."

"May I ask what brought the League's initial interest in me?" Graham still couldn't fathom what they thought he could do.

"Your Aunt and Uncle are valued members of the community, so naturally we considered you, but we don't typically seek out those with gifts like yours. You're a Tech, much like a Scholar."

"I am technologically gifted, yes." Graham nodded.

"You don't like my comparison to the Scholars, do you?" The Alderman sat back and slowly crossed his legs.

"It's ... not an apt description, but I understand why many use the comparison."

"I like you already." The Alderman smiled. "You will fit in well among the elites. And you will be a valuable resource. We've never had a Tech among us before. Perhaps you will help bring some of us out of the last centuries." He leaned back in his chair, not offering to refill Graham's glass.

"I'm excited to be here, sir." Graham forced a smile, making an effort to keep his mind clear of incriminating thoughts. It was a lot harder than it seemed.

"Maybe not yet." The Alderman sipped from his fresh drink. "But you will be. We have a job for you."

"Me, sir?" Graham didn't have to force the tone of surprise into his voice.

"My sources tell me you have created a means of communicating across vast distances ... offline, which is something we've been seeking for some time."

Graham sputtered, playing it off like he'd choked on his drink. "How could you possibly know that?" Graham gaped at the Alderman. There was no way he could know about the system he'd built for Ezra. No one knew about that except for himself and Ezra, and he couldn't have anything to do with this.

"Grim, I know everything about my people, especially my newest initiates. The Grand Master could use a gift like yours. He is an important man, and he would pay handsomely for a communication system such as yours."

Graham nodded, trying to get his heart to stop jackhammering in his chest. "I see." He took a deep breath. "May I think about it, sir?"

"Of course." The Alderman nodded, his golden mask winking in the candlelight. "We have lots of activities coming up for our young members, and we want you to get settled and feel at home among us. I will be meeting with the Grand Master in a few weeks. I'd like to tell him about you then if that's okay with you, son."

He was good at this game, keeping Graham uncomfortable one moment and setting him at ease the next.

"Of course, sir, that would be excellent. May I talk to my aunt and uncle about the opportunity? I'd need their permission to work while I'm still in school."

"By all means, talk to them about it. I'm sure they'll be delighted to hear of it." The Alderman stood, and Graham scrambled to join him.

"We will meet again soon, young Grim. Until then, enjoy yourself tonight and in our upcoming events. You deserve it." He winked and escorted Graham to the door.

Ezra: Let me live vicariously through you. Tell me all about the party. Was there dancing? You know how I adore dancing. Was the food good? Tell me it wasn't just some sleazy college party with pizza and beer pong?

Graham paced across his room, trying to decide how to answer Ezra's text. He'd made several attempts already, but he'd deleted each one before sending. Part of him wanted to tell his friend about the League and the Alderman's offer. Maybe together, they could come up with a plan. But that wasn't the nature of their relationship.

Ezra dealt with enough. He didn't need Graham dumping all his baggage on him just because he desperately needed to unburden himself. The one thing Ezra seemed to need the most from Graham was an escape. He could do that much for his friend.

Graham: You would have loved it. Tonight was a fancy party at the Dean's house for all the top students. I wore a suite with one of those silk pocket squares my aunt is crazy about. I hated it.

Ezra: I bet you looked smashing, though. Were there any cute boys?

Graham smiled, rolling over on his bed to lay on his stomach.

Graham: Tons, but one in particular I've had my eye on for a while.

Ezra: Shut up! The barista was there? Tell me everything.

Graham: It was mostly boring. The food was excellent, but the music was old fashioned, and there was this crazy lady trying to play matchmaker with all the boys and girls.

Ezra: You avoided her, right?

Graham: So much. I think the evening actually turned into a date. Sort of. I don't really know.

Ezra: If you don't know, you're probably doing it wrong, mate.

Graham: It wasn't like that.

Ezra: Was there at least some good old-fashioned snogging?

Graham: There was handholding.

Ezra: Seriously? That's all I get? Handholding?

Graham: It was quite passionate.

Ezra: Passionate handholding? You're so adorable, but we might need to talk about that snail's pace you're moving at, mate. The cute barista probably doesn't even realize you're totally into him.

Graham: He does. There are just some underlying factors holding us back. You know how it is when you first meet another Immortal. We're building trust right now.

Ezra: Before you take it to the next level?

Graham: Exactly

Ezra: So ... what is the next level up from handholding? A play date at the park?

Graham: You're making fun of me.

Ezra: So much. You make it too easy sometimes. Just do me a favor the next time you think you might be on a date with Mr. Barista.

Graham: What's that?

Ezra: Kiss the boy and get it on video so I can see it!

Chapter 19

Chloe | Mid-Winter | Westbrook, Connecticut

Fire burned hot in Chloe's blood. She could feel the intensity of the heat, but it didn't burn her. It was like that night in the orchard, where the fires burned all around them.

Is my room on fire? She couldn't seem to make herself wake. Sleep lay like a thousand-pound weight on her chest, yet she couldn't remember ever resting so well in her life, and after a fitful night of horrifying dreams, Chloe was reluctant to give up such a sense of warmth and peace.

Finally cracking an eye open, her gaze landed on the fiery mystery of her heavy sleep. Fei Long—a much smaller version of her—lay curled on Chloe's chest, watching her sleep like the little creeper she was.

"How'd you get so tiny?" Chloe reached to scratch the dragon's chin. "You're like a cat this morning." Fei Long hummed deep in her throat, pushing her head against Chloe's hand for more scratches. The dragon appeared however she wanted most days. Today, she was long and small, without her usual wings and feisty temper.

"You usually vanish when I sleep."

Fei Long laid her head on Chloe's chest, blinking her

obsidian eyes in that knowing way that drove her crazy.

"I had bad dreams last night, so you came back to chase them away so I could sleep?" Chloe stroked the smooth scales of her back. "Thanks, old girl, I needed to wake with a clear head." Chloe sighed, dumping the snoozing inferno onto the bed beside her.

"Time to get up." Chloe scrambled from the bed. "We've got a lot to do today." She reached for her laundry basket full of carefully folded clothes, courtesy of Dahlia, who for some supremely strange reason, enjoyed doing everyone's laundry. Her girl was very domestic when she was broody.

The smallish Fei Long followed her around the room, sniffing her laundry basket and making a nuisance of herself.

"You must have been a cat in a former life." Chloe shooed her away from the laundry before she had a chance to set it on fire again.

A disgruntled harrumph sounded behind her, along with a crushing noise.

"Fei Long!" Chloe tried not to laugh at the now larger dragon perched on top of a wicker foot stool. "Get down before you break it." She rolled her eyes. "And pick a size for today and stay there. Personally, I like the small you, less of you to get in the way."

Fei Long puffed up, indignant, and was now roughly the size of a very large Golden Retriever.

"Don't give me that look." Chloe stuffed her favorite jeans into her pack. She traveled light whenever she left Westbrook, so the presence of her travel bag shouldn't raise too many questions from her roommates.

Fei Long grumbled, returning to her favorite spot under the arched window, the multicolored scales down her back sparkling in the sunlight.

"I'm serious, don't get too comfortable. We're leaving, so I need to see you turning back into golden mist, chop-chop because we don't need me freaking people out on the train, talking to my invisible, clumsy dragon friend." Chloe ignored the stubborn beast as she finished packing.

After sleeping on it—and dreaming of that awful night in the orchard—Chloe knew it was time to leave Westbrook. She couldn't deny that her friends desperately needed the benefit of someone like Porcia. They needed proper training much more than they needed Chloe, but she couldn't be part of it. The memories were just too painful.

Chloe moved to her blue painted dresser, searching through the drawers for anything she couldn't live without. This place had become her home and leaving it would be one of the hardest things she'd ever done. Harder even than leaving Kelleys Island. That would always be a home she could return to. But Westbrook was the first place she'd made it on her own.

She slammed the top dresser drawer shut, hanging her head as memories of better times flashed through her mind. Memories of her and Justice combing through antique stores and yard sales for furnishings they could afford. They'd come across this old dresser in a junk store. It was a chipped white back then, but he'd helped her drag it home, and they'd painted it together.

Fei Long snorted a stream of fire at her feet.

"Listen up, you overgrown lizard, I said we're leaving." Chloe zipped her bag, tossing it on the bed.

Fei Long snorted, shaking her head.

"You're wrong, I *have* thought about it." She marched across the room to gather the few journals she could take with her. Maybe once she'd severed ties with this place, she could text Dahlia and ask her to put her things in storage.

Fei Long let out a familiar roar of protest that sounded far too sassy for a regal dragon made of mist and golden power.

"Would you hush? You'll wake the whole town carrying on

like that." Chloe stared up at the shelves of books she'd collected during her time here. The dragon bumped into her from behind, snaking her long neck over Chloe's shoulder, nosing a picture on the shelf just out of reach.

"Right, we should take these." Chloe climbed up on the crate she kept near the shelves and gathered up the frames. "Just the pictures though." She lifted the one Fei Long knocked over with her clumsy snout, eliciting another impatient growl from her know-it-all companion.

Chloe stared at the picture of her mother. She rarely let herself look at her old family photos. Smoothing a hand over the glass frame, she nodded. "I know, you want to know what she would say about all this."

Fei Long huffed like it was the most obvious question.

"She'd tell me to get over myself and do what's right." Chloe managed a watery smile. She could almost hear her mom's voice telling her the only thing Chloe needed to focus on was herself, her happiness, and her training. Ming Lao was a warrior. A fierce mom with a spine of steel. She wouldn't want her daughter to mourn for her, but Chloe couldn't help how she felt. Staying here, training with someone so closely associated with her mother's murderer, felt like the ultimate betrayal.

Fei Long nudged her hand with her warm snout, her dark eyes staring right through her, like she could see Chloe's pain.

"I know, you're right, she was a lot like Porcia." Chloe held the frame clutched to her chest. "And a good teacher too. I wouldn't have made it this far without everything I learned from her and Dad. I can't deny my friends that kind of training, which is why we're leaving."

A loud thud crashed right above her and had Chloe cowering and Fei Long leaping onto the couch—which she was now roughly the size of—breathing fire and searching for the source of the attack.

"Close your mouth, Fei. It was something upstairs." Chloe rolled her eyes at the dragon who was far more coward than she'd have the others believe. "Do not singe my pillows again, and you'd better go back to your normal size if you expect to leave through the door any time soon." She set the picture frame down, but an ear-splitting wail sent an arrow right through her.

"Justice?" She raced to the door to find everyone gathered in the common room.

"What was that?" Hudson shouted, stumbling into the room in his boxers.

The shriek of pain echoed through the house, intensified this time.

Chloe darted for the stairs up to his loft, but his barrier was up in full force. He wasn't going to let her in this time.

"No!" Justice sobbed and it cut right through her.

"Justice!" She charged past Scarlet and tried to force her way up the stairs, but the invisible shield was like wading through mud, and it made her feel sick, like she might vomit if she didn't get as far away from this stairwell as possible.

"What's wrong?" Porcia scrambled up the stairs behind her. Scarlet, sobbing and near hysterical, had retreated to the common room with the others. "Help me break through." Porcia took Chloe's hand. "He grows stronger by the day."

Chloe gripped her hand, and fighting the overwhelming urge to flee, together, they moved up one step at a time.

"Don't fight us, Justice," Chloe whispered when he pushed them two steps back. "Let us help you through this because there is no way I'm leaving you alone up there."

"Listen to her, son. Let us through."

Sweating, Chloe pulled herself up one more step, her hand slipping in Porcia's clammy palm.

Finally, they broke through as Justice let out another mournful wail.

"No!" He stood staring up at his mural wall, blood dripping from his hands. His eyes blazed like embers with the fury of his prophetic power, sooty tears staining his pale face.

Chloe and Porcia rushed to his side, but she knew better than to touch him in this state. "Don't." Chloe reached to still Porcia's hands. "We have to talk him back."

"This can't happen." Justice slumped to the floor, trying to cover his head with his bloody hands. Porcia sank down beside him.

"Justice." Chloe called loudly. "We're here. I'm here. Follow my voice and find your way back." She kept murmuring comforting words as she finally looked at the mural.

"He painted it in his own blood." Porcia's voice was thick with tears as she twisted her hands in her lap, trying not to touch her son.

"So much pain and death." Justice shook his head, the fire in his eyes diminishing some.

"Justice, you're safe," Chloe called to him. "Come back to us, and we'll help you figure this out, so it doesn't have to happen."

"It's coming, Chloe." His voice scraped in his throat, like he'd screamed for hours. "We can't stop the darkness."

"And we will be ready for it." Chloe grasped his hand, watching carefully as the prophetic haze faded from his eyes.

Porcia took his other hand, searching for the source of his injuries, but he'd healed.

Scarlet shoved through the gathering crowd now that the barrier was down. "Justice?" She darted across the room, but Chloe held out her hand to stall her. "Don't touch him yet."

"We'll you're holding his hand." Scarlet snapped, reaching for Justice. "He'll want his girlfriend. Justice, I'm here." She laid a hand on his shoulder.

"No!" He recoiled from her. "Get away from me." He tugged Chloe forward, putting her between himself and Scarlet.

"What's wrong, baby." She crept closer and Justice trembled.

"Guys, get her out of here." Chloe shoved Scarlet toward Hudson and the twins.

"I'm not going anywhere." Scarlet struggled against Hudson's grip on her shoulders.

"You aren't helping him," Noah stepped in front of her. "The best thing you can do for him now is let Chloe talk him down. Give them some space."

Scarlet glared daggers at Chloe and burst into tears as she reluctantly went downstairs with Hudson and twins.

"Justice," Chloe whispered, squeezing his hand. "It's okay. You're okay," she murmured, sharing a worried look with his mother.

"Painted in his own blood." James stood staring at the mural, his eyes alight with the use of his power.

Chloe jerked her head toward James and then the painting on the wall. Like before, there were no recognizable forms. Just the deep red blood, splattered with other colors here and there.

"Cover it up. I can't look at it." Justice scrambled across the floor, away from the wall, his hands held in front of his face and his eyes wild with fright.

"Don't." James moved to stop Dahlia from pulling the sheets over the painting. "Just wait. I—I'll be right back." He ran toward the stairs, a strained look on his face.

Chloe and Porcia helped Justice move to sit on the edge of his bed, and Dahlia swooped in with a glass of cold water for him to sip.

"Thank you," Chloe murmured as she encouraged Justice to drink.

"What do you think it means?" Porcia whispered.

"Doesn't look like nothing to me." Dahlia said, stepping back toward the stairs. "I should leave you guys alone."

"Stay." Porcia waved a hand toward her. "He needs your

strength and friendship now more than he needs his privacy." She squeezed her son's shoulder as he gulped from the glass of water. "Can you tell us what you've seen, son?" Porcia pushed him to speak.

"No. He isn't ready," Chloe protested, grateful to see Fei Long swish her tail to get past Porcia. She rested her head on Justice's knee. The dragon would give him strength and a sense of peace.

"He will never be ready if we don't push him out of his comfort zone."

Chloe nodded. How many times had she heard her parents and teachers give that same advice? Justice's gift was a frightening one, but she knew all too well what would happen if he didn't continue to progress in his abilities. He was dangerously close to losing control now, and he needed his mother's expertise.

"There is one who will see beyond the darkness—" James burst back into the room, his voice thick with power as he flipped through his sketchbook to a sepia drawing of fire and dark charcoal shadows. *"—Beyond the future others of his kind cannot foretell. His prophecy will be written in the blood of his own hand."* James looked up from his prophetic drawing to study the mural as if he could see something the others couldn't.

Chloe moved to stand beside him. "What do you see?"

"Blood, fire, and so much death. So much unnecessary death." James walked along the wall like a viewer in an art museum. "You're the one we've been waiting for." He finally turned to Justice.

"It's the end," Justice rasped, his head resting in one hand while his other stroked Fei Long's smooth scales.

"The end of what?" Chloe asked.

Justice looked up, his bloodshot eyes seeking hers as he grasped her hand. "Everything. We won't survive."

CHAPTER 20

Graham | Early Spring | Salem, Massachusetts

Graham wiped the sweat from his brow as he bent over the raging hot forge. It felt good to get his hands into something creative again, and not for the first time, he was glad his dad had asked Uncle Lou to put in the forge when he first moved to Salem.

Down below the cliffs, his aunt and uncle had created an oasis along the beach with cabanas and an outdoor kitchen, much like the grottos at home. But hidden behind it all, lay the vast caverns and caves where Gabrielle and Lou worked with Aria and Brooks to take down the League. Graham's forge sat at the entryway into caverns, but he'd never realized what went on deep within the caves, right under his nose.

A cool ocean breeze brushed the hair from his face as he worked the bellows.

Like Aidan with his music and Allie with her painting, Graham thrived on creativity. His outlet was with metal working —more specifically, in creating new weapons. Weapons with a little more kick than a run-of-the-mill sword or knife. A few years ago, after studying Allie's crystalline sai blades that were imbued with the power of their maker, Graham learned he could create similar weapons—just not as powerful as hers.

His first was a knife that never missed its mark, but it only worked for him. He'd worked closely with Gregg over the years to hone this particular gift. It was his only weapon to mark him as a warrior like his family. And it was one he guarded carefully. Only a handful of people knew what he could do.

Graham retrieved the length of steel from the forge, checking the state of the metal before he returned it to the fire. He'd left his collection of unique weapons at home, opting for a more conspicuous arsenal of training weapons for his time in Salem. But with recent developments, he was feeling the need for an extra level of protection.

This would be his most ambitious project to date. A pair of blades forged from the same piece of steel infused with his power. He just wasn't sure yet how that power would manifest.

Lifting his rounding hammer, Graham placed the glowing hot metal on the anvil, smoothing his bare hand over the surface to check the malleability of the steel. The metal called to his gift, stirring within his core. Searing hot metal never hurt him, allowing him to work without the restraint of gloves or other protective gear.

"Let's see what you're going to look like." The first strike of his hammer against metal vibrated through his bones. It had been too long. The power burned hot in Graham's chest—as hot as the forge itself. As the metal began to take shape under his hands, Graham let his power guide him.

Setting his hammer aside, the metal moved and morphed as he murmured to it, coaxing it to form a razor-sharp edge that would draw the blood of his enemies and no other. The metal split into two fine blades so thin it would seem they would break the moment they cooled, but Graham whispered to them as he guided his own power to strengthen the steel.

For Graham, every weapon he forged took on a personality of

its own, like a living breathing thing. He murmured his concerns as his gift and instincts guided him.

He never set out to give a weapon a specific ability. That wasn't how his gift worked. Whatever power his weapons possessed in the end was a direct result of the creative process. His gift worked alongside his fears and emotions.

"That's it, old girl," Graham coaxed the flood of his power into the slim blades, giving them life. The weapons would be new, but the power within was an old soul. A little bit of himself and a little bit of whatever made Immortals what they were. He liked to think it was the power of time itself. A bit of the collective knowledge of all those who had come before him.

Just as he was about to submerge the blades in warm water, they revealed themselves to him. "Oh, I see how it's going to be." He smiled at the dim flicker of icy blue light at their core. "Thanks for the warning."

"Care to join me, Aunt Gabrielle?" Graham's ability to sense another Immortal's approach was laughable at best. This was a game changer for him.

"I didn't mean to spy." Gabrielle stepped into the cavern from the depths of the cliffs behind him. "I was in the gym and thought to come check on you. You've been out here for hours." She gave him a guilty smile.

"Have I?" Whenever he worked the forge, time seemed to speed up. He regretted never having enough time to push this ability.

"I couldn't help but watch you." Her eyes followed him as he plunged the fresh blades into a barrel of water. "It's interesting to see you at work with all your computers and modern gadgets and then see you at work here with all the old tools." She ran a hand over an array of hammers and chisels. "My father was a blacksmith, you know. He worked for your mother's father once upon a time. That's how your mother and I became friends."

"I prefer the old methods of traditional blacksmithing." Graham moved to the grinding stone to prepare for the next phase.

"It's astounding, what you can do, Graham. I don't know if you realize..." She trailed off.

Graham nodded. "Oh, I realize." He pulled the first blade from the water to let her rest. It would take a few days of hard work before the twin blades were complete and each set into a hilt of his design. His eyes blazed bright with the power of his gift at the thought of creating the hilts. The weapons would be longer than a traditional knife or dagger, made to fit his own measurements as Gregg had taught him.

"I've known only one other with such a gift." Gabrielle reached for his arm. "He was a great warrior, as are you, Graham. I am so sorry if we've underestimated you."

Graham shrugged and went to work with a chisel to remove any rough spots from the steel. "You know, there are all kinds of metal alloys, Aunt Gabrielle." His brow furrowed as he worked the blade. "Copper, titanium, steel, nickel, cobalt, aluminum, iron. Then, there's bronze, gold, silver, the list goes on and on. Some are cheap and their resistance to heat is low, some are hard and don't break easily, and others are pretentious expensive metals with shiny surfaces but are too soft for much use other than decoration."

Moving to the grinding stone, Graham ran the edge of the blade across the rough surface. "The thing is, Aunt Gabrielle, I like them all. Each serves a purpose, and none of those are more valuable than the others. It's what's inside that really matters. It's the same with us. Scholar, Warrior, Techie, or Prophet, it shouldn't matter. Those are just the kinds of shiny surfaces I'm not really interested in. If my gift changes the way you look at me, I think that's more of a you thing than a me thing."

"You're absolutely right." Gabrielle dropped her gaze to the ground.

Graham shook his head, clearing the last lingering effects of his gift from his mind. "Aunt Gabrielle, I'm so sorry. That was rude." He set his work aside, turning to focus on his aunt.

She held up her hands to stop him. "No, darling, it was the truth." She took his hands in hers. "Don't ever shy away from being truthful with me or your uncle. We can take it." She winked.

Graham turned back to his work. It was just beginning to sink in that Gabrielle now knew his secret. It wasn't that he didn't trust her. He did with absolute confidence. Graham just knew he had to keep the circle of those who knew what he could do as small as possible. He'd seen what the Senate had done to Sasha and her sister, Imogen. He would be right there with them if the Senate ever knew what he could do, and he always wanted to be the one who decided how and when he used his power to forge the kind of weapons that could wreak havoc in the wrong hands.

"The League will always underestimate you." Gabrielle laid a hand on his shoulder.

"Most Immortals do." Graham's shoulders fell. He wanted to live in a world where he just got to be himself without the pressure of living up to other people's expectations of what he should be.

"Let them, dear. They won't see you coming until it's too late."

"Thank you, Aunt Gabrielle." Graham squeezed her hand. "Want to know what she can do?" He gestured at the new daggers in progress.

"I'm dying to know. What was that light about?" She stepped up to the forge in her designer dress, unconcerned about the soot and ash everywhere.

"She will warn me when an enemy approaches, buying me a

little more time than my natural senses allow. And she will only cut deeply to those who mean me great harm."

"Impressive, Graham. Really." She admired the shining steel. "She ... er, thought of me as an enemy just now?"

Graham scratched his head. "She was only trying to protect our secret."

"Have you ever forged weapons for another?" Gabrielle lifted a brow.

"No, it's never felt right, but my dad has always wanted me to try it. Just so we know what kind of range my gift is capable of."

"Only you get to decide when and if you are ready for that. Just know the League would exploit your ability were they to find out. So, use that weapon as a last resort." She gestured at the blades.

"I will be very careful." Graham glanced back at his new weapons. He didn't need to tell Gabrielle that no one would ever be able to sense what his weapons could do. That was a secret he needed to keep.

"Have you ever tried other objects?" She lifted her brow at him. "Like say, a mask?" She gave him an evil grin.

Graham returned her grin. "That has a lot of potential. Do you think you could help me with something like that?" In his experience, most of his teachers didn't really know how to guide him.

"I can't, but your uncle is probably the only one who can truly help you hone this gift. We'll get started tomorrow." She turned back toward the caves. "Don't be late for dinner, and make sure you give yourself time to get cleaned up, we have another guest this evening."

Chapter 21

Chloe | Late Winter | Westbrook, Connecticut

"Drink this." Chloe poured Justice a steaming cup of strong dark tea while Dahlia scurried around the kitchen to get him something to eat. After the shock of his prophetic painting, he was still unsteady on his feet.

James and Porcia sat on the opposite side of the kitchen table murmuring over James' sketchbook, and Scarlet sat with them, nursing her hurt feelings.

The others had retreated to the common room to give Justice some space.

"What did you mean when you said I'm the one you've been waiting for?" Justice finally broke the silence, taking a fortifying sip of tea before he turned toward his prophetic friend.

James sighed, running a hand through his hair. "My brand of prophecy ... it's small potatoes compared to you and a few others I've met since I finally figured out what my drawings actually are. I grew up at Soma. You've all heard my sad story." He scratched the place on his arm where the Soma brand had faded over time. It was still faintly visible to those who had seen it before.

"I knew I prophetic gifts, and I hid it from everyone for a long time. But when I ended up with Chloe's family in Cleveland, for the first time, I had real training." He glanced to Chloe, and she knew he was uncertain how to tell everyone about the woman he'd trained with. A true Prophet and the last Queen of Indriell who was supposed to be dead.

"My teacher was ancient and wise." He stumbled over the words.

"You may speak of her as the last great Prophet of another age," Porcia interjected. "She taught you well."

"She did." James nodded. "I didn't stay under her wing long, but I learned a great deal from her. She saved my life, teaching me what it means to be a Prophet." He pushed his sketchbook to the center of the table. "I drew this just before I left my teacher. The sketch itself doesn't say much, but the meaning behind it is as clear to me as words written on a page." He glanced at Justice. *"The darkness is coming, but there is one who will see beyond it. This untested Prophet will spell out our doom in the blood of his own hand. Only then will we be prepared for what will come."*

James leaned back and studied Justice's clean hands as if he could still see the blood there. His eyes pulsed with the light of his power. "My gift tells me you are a fulfillment of that prophecy."

"What, because I cut myself and some blood got mixed into the paint?" Justice moved so Dahlia could place a plate of eggs and toast in front of him.

"He knows because he's the Prophet who delivered this prophecy," Chloe said, feeling useless in her desire to help him. This was why he needed his mother, but Chloe wondered how much even Porcia could help him with this. "Any Prophet will know without a doubt when they witness the fulfilment of their own prophecies."

"Exactly, my power might not be anything special, but it doesn't lie," James said. "You are the one we've been waiting for, Justice. You can see what's coming where no one else can."

"Tell us what you've seen so we can help you." Porcia laid a hand over his. "The weight of prophecy is too much of a burden for one man to bear alone."

"Listen to your mother. Holding on to it will only hurt you." James took a bite of toast, and for a moment, everyone focused on the simple breakfast Dahlia had prepared.

Chloe reached for his hand under the table, giving it a gentle squeeze. "We're all family here," she reminded him.

"Events are already in motion," Justice began in a quiet voice. "I don't know how or if they can be stopped. I don't really even know what it all means."

"Do you need to look at your painting again?" Scarlet asked, sniffing back her tears. "So you can ... read it to us and we can help you through this." She moved her chair closer to his, her hands fluttering uselessly as she reached to touch his shoulder.

Chloe tried not to roll her eyes. For as much as Scarlet hovered over him like a clucking hen, she knew next to nothing about his gifts.

"I don't ever want to see it again. I'm painting over it tomorrow." Justice shook his head, as if to dispel the images from his mind. "I don't need to see it again. I'll never forget the words." Justice leaned back, his eyes smoldering with the rise of his power.

"It has begun. The child of prophecy walks among us, gathering her equals, while the darkness surges like a storm on the horizon. She is at war with those who refuse to move forward. What was once lost will return as a swarm of locusts on the land. The yin and yang that both created and destroyed them will vanish forever, leaving the children of Indriell to fade into their final twilight."

Justice's grating voice echoed in the kitchen for a moment before Dahlia whispered, "What the crap does that mean?"

"It means..." Porcia stood up, rummaging through the cabinets, retrieving a dusty bottle of brandy she poured into her tea and then passed the bottle around. "... We are finally getting somewhere."

"Who are the children of Indriell?" Scarlet asked as she poured a healthy portion of brandy into her cup. Chloe watched as she glanced at Justice, her face a storm of confusion, hurt, and fear.

"The ancient royal Immortals." Dahlia moved around her to set a stack of fluffy pancakes on the table. "But that makes no sense. They've all vanished from existence."

"It's not them." Chloe reached for a pancake before they could disappear. "The reference probably means all Immortals." Which meant Justice's prophecy was a dire warning. Not for the first time, she wished she could call her dad for advice. But he wasn't that man anymore.

"That's rather ominous." Scarlet glanced at her boyfriend for confirmation, but Justice sat quietly eating pancakes and eggs. He was still too shaken to be fully back in the conversation. It always took him a while after coming out of a fugue, but it was a good sign to see him going through the motions.

"The part about the yin and yang doesn't make sense." Porcia sipped her hot toddy. "Both created and destroyed makes me think of the cyclical nature of life and death."

Chloe nodded. "I thought that too, but does it mean that cycle will end for everyone?" She glanced at Justice. He was in his own world, but Scarlet insisted on fussing over him, murmuring questions and running her hands through his hair in a helpless gesture. Chloe resisted the desire to break her fingers. He wanted to be left alone. Not physically. He liked being around his friends, on the fringe of the conversation while he worked his way back. But he didn't like it when they fussed over him. It was best to let him eat and move at his own pace as he regained his strength.

"—don't you think, Chloe?" Porcia looked at her.

"I'm sorry, what was that?" She turned her attention back to the conversation.

"The storm of locusts could be a reference to a plague on the land."

"Possibly." She leaned back, shaking her head. The power of her gift pulsed in her head like an angry drum. Thin red lines zigzagged across the room, bouncing from one person to the next as the white noise of her friends' thoughts and indecision demanded her attention.

"Chloe?" Porcia leaned forward with a concerned frown. "What are you seeing?"

"It's okay. I'm okay, it's just a lot of noise all at once." Chloe waved her hand at all the red lines no one else could see. Her head throbbed and her visions blurred. It was too much.

"Could it be like ... the end of the world?" Dahlia folded her arms across her chest. "Like in the traditional mortal Armageddon kind of way? Asteroids, plagues, famine, aliens? Some threat to the world as we know it?"

Chloe tapped her fork against her plate, trying to focus on the conversation. "No." She shook her head, ignoring the invisible red lines that connected everyone in the room. "It's bigger than that. This thing has thousands of moving parts." She wasn't sure where the thought came from, but right now her gift was guiding her, and she could almost see all those moving parts.

"What do you mean by that?" Porcia leaned in eagerly.

Red light exploded in Chloe's mind, and she cried out with the pain of it.

"That's enough." Justice stood up, knocking his chair over and grabbing Chloe's hand. "Just back off." He draped an arm around Chloe's shaking shoulders and guided her out of the room with all its chaos and confusion.

"Justice, wait!" Scarlet called behind them, but he ignored her, taking the steps up to his loft two at a time.

Chloe struggled to keep up with him. "What are you doing?" She rubbed the back of her head.

"Buying us some time away from the Spanish Inquisition." He guided her to the huge ladder on the landing outside his room. It led up to the roof.

Without a word Chloe nodded and followed him up.

"Sit." Justice pointed to the blacktop of the roof.

Still shaking, Chloe sank down onto the sun-warmed surface.

"Thanks for the quick escape." Chloe fidgeted with her hands in her lap.

"It's bad enough when they do it to me, but I can't stand it when they gang up on you like that."

"They aren't ganging up." Chloe laughed. "They just want to help. Even your mother," she grudgingly admitted.

"I never realized how much pressure comes with an ability like yours. Not until recently." Justice sat opposite her, hugging his knees to his chest. He was still in a vulnerable state from the use of his prophetic gift. "It's hard being the center of all that." He waved his hand back toward the kitchen.

"They mean well." Chloe picked at a paint stain on her jeans. Her power still churned in her chest, but the overwhelming onslaught of information had faded the moment she left the kitchen with Justice.

"You know that's why I came back sooner than Mom wanted." Justice rested his forehead against his arms.

"You were gone for three whole months." Chloe sighed. "It felt like years."

"Right? It was awful without you, Chlo. I had to argue with

Mom to get her to come back with me. She wanted me to train with her for at least a year before we came home."

"You need it," Chloe said.

"I needed to be here more. Scarlet is great. And things are going really good with Mom, but the two of them together ... it was too much fussing. Too many questions. You know how I hate that."

"I wondered if that was getting to you." Chloe's heart skipped a beat at this casual criticism of his girlfriend.

"She means well. Both of them." He gave a rueful smile. "But you never expect anything from me. You don't need me the way they do."

"I beg to differ," Chloe was quick to interrupt him. "I need you, Justice. You and Dahlia are my best friends. I don't function well without either of you."

"But you don't rely on me to make you ... happy. I love that about our friendship. I can be myself with you and not worry about how you'll respond or what you need from me." He shrugged. "It turned out I didn't function so well without you either."

"And now? With everyone here?"

"It's better with you and Dahl."

"Then we'll figure out a way to get through the training you need, and we'll deal with all the unwanted attention that comes with it."

"Thanks, Chlo." Justice laid back on his elbows, looking up at the sky.

Chloe smiled, admiring his profile. She would do anything for him. Even be his friend when she wanted so much more. That was what being a Complement meant. She would be whatever he needed her to be, for as long as he needed it. That she loved him more than anyone in this world ever would was enough to sustain her ... for now.

"Chloe?" Noah called as she and Justice returned to the kitchen.

"What's up?" Chloe pinched the bridge of her nose. Her head still throbbed with a dull ache.

"Right. Um." He tugged on his ear. "You remember that project you were helping us with a while back?"

"That thing you were working on with the CalTech students?" Chloe sank down onto her seat at the crowded kitchen table. Everyone was still discussing Justice's prophecy.

"Not with." He ran a hand through his short brown curls. "I think you guys need to come see this." He waved for everyone to follow him. "I think this might need all our eyes."

Chloe didn't often go into the computer room where Noah and Jonah worked. It was usually a mess, the likes of which no amount of scrubbing could clean. Jonah looked up with excitement in his eyes as they entered the room.

The twins had one wall dedicated to their computers and multiple screens. A thread bare couch sat against another wall, but the entire front half of the room was normally covered in cork board. Every inch of it was now covered in photographs, news clippings, charts, and sticky notes, with various colors of twine connecting the important elements of their investigation.

"What have you found?" Chloe walked to the front of the room, trying to make heads or tails of their findings. The twins were Techs like Graham. Most of their work happened in the digital world of technology. This tangible research was something very different for the twins.

"We've been experiencing some developments in our abilities. Some things that have had us second guessing what we've been working on." Noah followed Chloe to the investigation board. "But that's not important right now. We're focusing on our research." He moved to clear the sofa so the others could sit.

"A few months ago, we fell into a situation with some other Techs online. Students at CalTech. They were all in a dither about some elite project they'd been tasked with. They were all like, *you two couldn't possibly know what you're doing because we go to CalTech and you're homeless losers."*

"Get to the point, Noah." Chloe couldn't take her eyes off their investigation wall. Her gift lit up with all the alarm bells, though she still had no idea what she was looking at.

"Right. So, these geeks were all in some kind of competition to develop a new form of communication. *Offline* communication, as in no internet. So, naturally, that piqued our interest."

"I remember you were offended by the project." Chloe turned, following the thin red lines of her gift leading from Noah and Jonah to their board, where it split into a thousand new pathways. Much like it had just moments ago in the kitchen after discussing Justice and his prophecy.

"Exactly, and you led us in the right direction. At first, we were going to try to shut them all down. That kind of tech could lead to anarchy in the wrong hands. But you helped us see our best path was to follow the competition and find out who was behind it."

"Did you?" Porcia asked, turning from the board to the twins. Her mouth was set in a firm line, like she might not approve of their project.

"No." Noah sighed. "But we did discover this." He gestured at the board. "That part of J's prophecy about *those who refuse to move forward*—and yes we were eavesdropping—reminded us of what we found here. And what Chloe said about a thousand moving parts."

"And what exactly is this?" Dahlia asked from her perch on the couch. "Help us see what you see because that wall just looks like a snarled mess of information I can't begin to pick apart."

"Oh, right. Sorry." He scratched his head in confusion for a moment. The twins absorbed massive amounts of information at a glance. They could make sense out of chaos and often struggled to communicate with those who couldn't see the big picture as quickly as they could. "All of these people are connected. They're all super rich, or the children of the super rich. Most of the adults are hundreds if not thousands of years old. Some of them are the oldest people we've ever encountered."

"What do they have in common?" Porcia asked.

"They hate technology. There's very little information about any of them online. No social media accounts, nothing. They turn their elite noses up at anything modern—though most of them can navigate the modern world without issue. We believe they are some kind of club or fraternity, but we don't know what they want. At least not yet. We've had to resort to old fashioned physical research."

"And you think they are behind this search for a way to communicate offline?" Chloe clutched the sides of her head, trying to focus on the twins and ignore the demands of her gift.

"This group, whoever they are, they don't like Immortals like us. They don't have much respect for the Scholars, Prophets, and Techs. They've been around for a long time, but they've never shown an interest in our community. Until recently." He moved to the board to show a list of students from various high-profile colleges and universities. "A few years ago, they would never deign to invite these Immortals into their club, but that's the shortlist of the recruits they've considered—at least the ones we know of."

Chloe snatched the paper from the wall, scanning the names. "Are you sure about this?" She took a breath that sank like a stone into the pit of her stomach.

"Positive. We don't put anything on the wall unless it's validated information."

"Why is Graham Loukas from MIT on this list?" Chloe demanded, her hands shaking.

"Graham?" Porcia moved to take the list from Chloe.

"Because the society—that's what we call them—has a vested interest in him. Why, do you know him?"

"Yeah." Her eyes burned, and her head throbbed. "He's my best friend from back home. Is he okay?"

"Last we knew, he was on the Dean's List at MIT in some accelerated program to graduate a year early."

"Chloe." Hudson burst into the room. "There you are. Do you remember that research you were helping me with? The one about all the old prophecies?"

Chloe scanned the room for Justice, locking eyes with him. Taking a deep breath, she choked back her fear for Graham and whatever he might have gotten himself into. "Yes, vaguely." She ran a clammy hand through her hair, trying to maintain control of her power.

"Right, so all these bits of old prophecies kept surfacing in my writing, and I was frustrated that I didn't know what they meant. You helped me research them ..." His face went blank for a moment. "I just don't seem to remember how."

Grandpa Alex's books helped with that project. "I borrowed some books, remember?"

His face screwed up with that vacant look people got when they were actively forgetting the Scholar. "Right, right. Anyway, all of this made me think of what I found after researching." He thumbed through one of his journals filled with his messy scrawl.

"We made a list of all the ancient prophecies that mentioned the coming darkness."

Porcia leaned over the book. "Where did you get these?" She ran her hand over the page filled with prophecies.

"A Scholar friend of mine from back home helped out, but

Hudson's been working on filling in the missing bits from his own studies."

"Oh, I see." Her eyebrows shot up at that. "He doesn't give out this kind of information often."

It was Chloe's turn for surprise. "He doesn't make you forget him?" she blurted.

"Who?" Hudson glance up at her.

"Nothing, never mind." Chloe turned her attention back to Hudson's journals. It shocked her that Grandpa Alex would trust Porcia enough to let her retain her memories of him.

"This is valuable information, Hudson." Porcia laid a hand on his shoulder. "We will need to study these to see what they might reveal about Justice's prophecy. Keep these well guarded. It could be the key to guiding us all forward."

"It's all connected," Chloe whispered as she perused the confusing and often contradicting lines of prophecy given by various Prophets across time. The invisible lines of her gift pulled information from the page, leading to articles and photographs on the wall, filling in the gaps in the twins' research. She couldn't begin to decipher all of what her gift was trying to tell her. But she would in time.

Porcia stood beside her as the others fell into a chaotic conversation about their individual pursuits that might connect to all of this in some way. "They'd be lost without you, you know."

"I didn't do anything except listen."

"No, you've done so much more, Chloe." Porcia took her hands in her firm grip, and Chloe tried to fight the impulse to pull away from her. "You are a guide." Porcia dropped her hands. "You see what they struggle with, and you guide them through it. They need you, Chloe. I know my daughter has hurt you. She stole something precious from you. If my being here is too much for you, I will leave. They need you more than they need me."

"No." Chloe shook her head. "They need you too."

"Then, you will stay?" Porcia asked.

"Who said I wasn't?" Chloe's bag was packed and ready to go back in her room, but after the events of this day, she knew it wasn't the right time to leave. She lifted her chin in defiance, but Porcia just gave her a crooked smirk.

"Then, we will find a way to work together?" Porcia asked.

Chloe gazed around the room before she nodded. "For their sake. But I have something I need to do first."

"So do I." Porcia turned a worried gaze back to Noah and Jonah's wall.

Chapter 22

Graham | Early Spring | Salem, Massachusetts

"Good job today, kids." Gabrielle returned their practice weapons to the display shelf in the vast cavern they used as a private gym. It was located behind a secret wall that led to the proper gym where Graham had trained until recently.

Since joining the League and his aunt and uncle's efforts to bring it down from the inside, Graham trained with Brooks and Aria in the cavern where they could be certain of their privacy as they worked on their plans.

"Thanks, Aunt Gabrielle." Graham held a white handkerchief to his nose to stop the bleeding. They were pushing him out of his comfort zones, but in a more positive way than before. Now, they were focusing on his strengths as a fighter, using his power to increase his natural skill.

He was making progress across the board since they finally started trusting him to know his own strengths. When he wasn't sparring with Brooks and Aria, he was working with Gabrielle, learning to decipher an enormous amount of information at once. It was a lot harder than it should have been. Graham's vision was beginning to go wonky whenever he used his gift.

"Tilt your head back, darling. It will stop." Gabrielle absently waved a hand at him as she turned to Aria and Brooks, both sporting signs of overtraining. "Poor dears, you must all be starving. We're having lobster and stuffed crab for dinner; you should stay and eat until you're feeling stronger."

"That sounds great, thanks." Graham eagerly accepted the invitation for his friends.

"Actually, we have plans tonight," Brooks said, and Graham's shoulders fell. He was hoping to get to spend some time with Brooks outside of the League and training, but it never seemed to work out.

"That's too bad," Graham murmured his reply.

"Don't you remember, Graham?" Brooks turned his dimpled smile on him and gave a sly wink. "We were going to go to that thing at school tonight."

"Well, I'll stay and eat their share. You two have fun on your date." Aria, ever the blunt one, clapped them each on the back and went to make herself at home upstairs.

Date? Graham's face flushed at the idea.

"You're still up for it, right?" Brooks grabbed his gym bag and tossed it over his shoulder.

"Uh, sure?" Graham tried not to make it sound like a question. "I'll, uh, just go get changed."

"Okay then, you boys have fun," Gabrielle called. "Just be careful."

"Sure thing. Later, Gabs, Lou." Brooks waved and followed Graham through the secret door into the manor basement Graham had dubbed the dungeon when he first moved to Salem.

"You're adorable when you're flustered, Mr. Cutie-Cute." Brooks grabbed Graham's hand to stop him mid-way up the stairs up to the main floor. "I thought maybe you could use a night out on the town and away from the olds. But I didn't exactly ask." He gave a confident smirk. "We've been busy with the League, but that doesn't change the fact that I'd really like to ask you out on a real date. If you're interested."

"I'm interested." Graham turned three shades of red, but he didn't care. Brooks finally asked him out. "I've been interested since the day we met at the coffee kiosk, but then you never called me."

"I didn't call? That was rude of me." Brooks slipped his arm around Graham's waist as they continued up the stairs. "Oh wait, that's right. I knew I was going to have to let the League kidnap you, and I didn't want to be *that* guy. I wanted to wait for you to make your choice about the League before I did this." They came to a stop at the top of the stairs, and Brooks pulled him close. His eyes studied Graham's, their lips just inches apart, before he kissed him. It ended too soon, but Graham took a deep breath before he spoke.

"That was a good choice."

"What, the kiss? Or waiting until I could be honest with you?"

"Can I say both?" Graham smiled and guided Brooks up to his room.

Brooks whistled when he stepped into Graham's room. "And people say I'm the silver spoon type." He made himself at home in the plush leather chair beside Graham's bed. "I've said it for years: I wish Lou and Gabby were my parents. And not just because they have more money than Fort Knox."

"They're the best." Graham ducked into his closet to grab date clothes. If he even had any date clothes.

"Can I use your bathroom to freshen up while you freak out about your outfit?"

"Yes, and I'm not freaking out," Graham called from the depths of his closet, totally freaking out about what to wear. "Brooks?" Graham tossed his shirt on the floor and stuck his head out of the walk-in, his hair standing on end. "Where are we going?"

"I made reservations at this amazing steakhouse. Casual dress though, so don't come out in a suit."

"Oh, okay." Graham didn't want to remind him he didn't eat red meat. Maybe they'd have some kind of fish there.

"They have a specialized all beef menu. The steak tartare is fantastic."

Gross. Graham's shoulders fell.

"I'm kidding, Mr. Cutie-Cute." Brooks laughed. "I know what you like. We're going to my favorite sushi restaurant. You can totally wear whatever. It's not fancy."

"Perfect." Graham darted back into his closet to find something suitable for a sushi date. "You enjoy teasing me, don't you?" Graham called out as Brooks opened the bathroom door.

"Very much. It's probably going to get worse the more you blush."

"Noted." Graham hunted for his blue checkered shirt. The one that made his eyes look even bluer than their normal cornflower.

He'd been on dates before. Some way back in high school with girls he'd liked but never wanted more than friendship. And after he came out, he'd dated a few random guys—mostly mortals —but none that made his heart beat fast and his face flush red just thinking about them. This date was special. He just wished there was time to talk to Ezra first. He could use one of his pep talks.

Graham finished gathering his things and went to check on Brooks. "You need anything in there?" He knocked on the door.

"I can't do anything with this hair." Brooks opened the door and blew his errant curls out of his face. "I need a haircut, but there's never time."

"Sit." Graham pointed to the bench in front of the vanity he never used. "I'll fix it." He ran his hands through Brooks' silky dark curls, thinking he should have probably put a shirt on before he came in here.

"Who knew you had a six pack?" Brooks stared at his abs. "You think you know a cute, nerdy Tech guy, but then he takes his shirt off and he's all ripped."

"I have never in my life been a nerd, thank you. I was on the football team in high school." Graham worked a small amount of hair gel into Brooks' wavy dark hair, styling it without making it too fussy. That wasn't his style. Graham stepped back. "How's that?"

Brooks stood next to him, staring at their reflection in the big mirror. "Looks great. And also, we look hot together." He elbowed Graham.

"Okay, my turn to freshen up. I still smell like a gym rat." Graham shooed him out of the bathroom. "Make yourself at home." Graham closed the door and leaned against it. This was going to be a fun but stressful-in-all-the-best-ways kind of night. He couldn't wait.

Graham: No doubt about it this time. That was totally a date.

Graham sat on his corner balcony at three am, grinning at the full moon shining down on him. It was the perfect first real date with Brooks. They even managed to avoid all talk of the League and other heavy topics of conversation. It was a perfect night.

Ezra: Yes! Is there video? I need to see some proof. I'm not sure you can be trusted to know what counts as a date.

Graham: I'm not recording my dates, Ez. But I will say he was a perfect gentleman, and it was a PG-13 good night kiss with another date next weekend.

Ezra: Scandalous. Someone might have to hose you two down with some ice water.

Graham: Jealous?

Ezra: Insanely. But I'm happy for you.

Graham: Thanks. You're the first person I wanted to tell. You're the one I want to talk to whenever anything interesting happens.

"Easy, Graham," Uncle Lou cautioned. "Let my gift guide yours."

"That's easier said than done when I really don't know what your gift is going to do." Graham took a deep breath, trying to focus on the hunk of metal beneath his hands and not the intensity of his uncle's powerful gift.

"You have to trust it, my boy." Uncle Lou rubbed a hand over his sweaty face. The forge was hot, though it never affected Graham as much as it did others. His gift protected him from the blazing heat. "Trust in me to guide you."

Graham nodded. In theory, he trusted his uncle without fail. In practice, it was a little harder to yield to his power. "Let's go again."

"Relax this time, Graham," Aunt Gabrielle called from her seat on the sidelines. "Just let it wash over you, like a comforting wave of serenity."

That was so not what it felt like. Graham's shoulders tensed, preparing for the onslaught of his uncle's power that felt more like an aggressive attack than anything remotely serene.

"Wait, Lou." Gabrielle left her seat and came to Graham's side. "It's going to feel violent if you don't relax." Aunt Gabrielle squeezed his shoulders, reminding him to stay calm. "Take a deep breath and exhale, counting to three, and then reach for your power. Try to ignore Lou's invasive presence. It will only last as long as you resist him. Trust your uncle and let it happen. The hard part will be over in an instant."

Graham forced a smile, returning his cooling steel to the forge to buy another moment to prepare himself. A cold sense of dread washed over him. He didn't like using his ability in front of others. It was different last time when Gabrielle happened upon him, but now they felt like voyeurs, preying on his creative gifts.

In the past, Graham had followed his instincts and let his creative ability evolve naturally. This felt too much like pushing his limits. He shoved those uneasy thoughts to the back of his mind. His aunt and uncle were the best people Graham knew. They wouldn't push him further than he was willing to go. For the sake of what they faced with the League, he was willing to try anything that might help.

"Okay, lets do this." Graham willed himself to relax. To focus on the glowing hot metal beneath his hammer. Whatever Uncle Lou's gift was, it was going to help Graham control what his untested gift could do. If he could find a way to create with purpose, it would only help them fight against the League. He'd never had that kind of motivation before.

Graham hammered the hot metal into a long rectangular sheet as the silvery light of Uncle Lou's gift swirled around them. Graham fought the urge to resist the pull of his uncle's forceful guidance. The onslaught of his power was like a storm threatening to rip him apart from the inside out, and something within Graham's power did not like it. At all.

Trust him. The words formed in Graham's mind as a reminder to let this happen. The assault on his senses lasted only a moment this time. He could still sense the surge of the storm swirling around him, but Graham now stood in the eye of that storm with his uncle.

His arms felt light, like someone else controlled them. Still, he hammered the thinning metal into a sheet he would form into a new mask.

"Very good, Graham." Uncle Lou's voice sounded distant, though they stood shoulder to shoulder. "Let my gift guide yours."

Graham still wasn't sure what that was supposed to accomplish, but he gave in to the silvery light, letting it pull his own gift out of him. The icy blue light of Graham's gift entwined with Lou's, clearing his mind so he now worked with purpose.

Discarding the hammer, Graham used his bare hands to shape the hot metal over a mold of his eyes and nose he'd made from sandstone. It wouldn't yield a smooth, beautiful finish like a casting might have, but they weren't after beauty today. Today was all about function. About using his gift with intent to give his creations a specific ability.

I need protection. The thought came unbidden to his mind, like he was disconnected from his mind as well as his body now.

So much power surrounds us...

That thought wasn't his ... not entirely.

Graham fumbled with the tongs, the assault of his uncle's storm hit him like a bolt of lightening, sending a scorching hot streak of pain through his body before he regained control and returned to the eye of the storm where it was safe.

"Easy now, my boy. You're doing great."

Graham wasn't sure who spoke. His focus was on carefully moving the mold of his face to the cooling rack. The metal was still hot, but it glowed with the blue and silver streaks of power Graham had crafted into the metal.

Releasing the tongs, Graham let out a breath and took a step away from the newly forged mask. The movement swept him into the storm again, lighting up his nerve endings. Graham's mind went blank as he fell into the storm.

"Graham? Are you okay, darling?" Gabrielle looked down on him, her warm hazel eyes filled with concern.

Graham groaned as he sat up. "How did I get on the ground?"

"You fell, and I'm afraid my power knocked you for a loop." Uncle Lou stood behind his wife, his face showing equal signs of concern.

"Did it work?" Graham pushed himself up on shaky legs.

"I think we're definitely getting somewhere." Gabrielle moved back over to the forge to examine the roughly hewn mask.

The steel still swirled with blue and silver currents of power. "It needs to cool." Graham's palms itched to pick up the mask, but it wasn't ready yet.

As the light began to fade from the cooling metal, the mask revealed its power.

We protect. No one shall draw his blood.

"Well, that was new." Graham frowned down at his latest creation.

"What will it do?" Lou asked eagerly. It was the first time he'd witnessed his nephew's ability for himself.

"As long as I wear this, no blade will cut me." It was one of the most remarkable weapons he'd ever made. No, not a weapon. Armor.

"That's impressive, my boy." Uncle Lou stood beside him, admiring their work.

"I couldn't have done it without you, though I'm still not sure what your gift does."

"Think of me as your muse." Uncle Lou winked. "My gift bolsters creativity, though it only works when there is trust and mutual respect. It shouldn't be as difficult from now on."

Graham wilted with relief. Here was a piece of armor that

could protect his body. At his age, it could be the difference between capture and escape, should the League ever discover what he was up to.

"Again." Gabrielle shook her head. "This is not the weapon we need. It's certainly useful, but we need something ... more. Something that will protect you from notice long before any real harm could come for you."

"Now? Like today?" Graham wanted to seek his bed. He'd been up for more than two days, and his body was stressed to the breaking point from such hard training.

"Yes, now." Gabrielle retrieved a fresh bar of steel and handed it to him.

With a groan, Graham placed the bar into a pair of tongs and slipped it into the fire.

It was easier the second time, easier still the third time. Within a few hours, Graham had lost track of how many masks he'd created. Each one cast aside as Gabrielle demanded they try again and again.

"No. No, that's still not it." Gabrielle shook her head at the mask that would allow Graham to hear all conversations in English. "These are all perfectly useful." She gestured at the growing pile of utilitarian masks. "But it's not what we need."

"I don't know how to make it if you won't tell me what it's supposed to do." Graham sank down to sit on the cool stone floor. "Maybe we should try again tomorrow."

"One more time, Graham. I want to try something a little different this time." Gabrielle shared a glance with her Complement.

Graham nodded. He'd do whatever she asked if it would get him out of this forge faster.

Gabrielle helped him to his feet. "Do you know why they call me the Golden Hind?" Her eyes sparked with the warmth of her power.

"Because you wear a golden deer mask?" Graham shrugged, knowing there was much more to the name than that.

"In Greek mythology, the hind was a sacred beast, revered by the gods. She was said to be impossible to catch, that was why Zeus set the task to Hercules to capture her. It was said that those who came in contact with the hind felt an overwhelming urge to protect her."

"Okay, but what does that have to do with you?" Graham was exhausted and wished she would speak in plain English.

"That is how my gift works, darling. They call me the hind because my power exudes the same urge to trust and protect me from harm." Her eyes filled with warmth and sunshine.

Graham could feel it now as she turned her gift on him. A powerful surge of trust welled within him, along with an urge to protect his aunt at any cost. She was a precious jewel not to be harmed.

"They call me the golden hind because I am impossible to capture." Gabrielle smoothed a cool hand across his brow. "But most Immortals can sense when I'm using my gift against them. Some can fight the influence, others can't resist. But a mask imbibed with my gift..."

"It's brilliant." Uncle Lou came to stand behind her. "Do you think it could work?" They shared another one of those looks that communicated something vital between them.

"Care to share with the guinea pig?" Graham stared up at them from his comfy spot on the floor.

"I know you're so tired." Gabrielle bent down to his level. "But while your gift is primed, do you think you could try once more?"

"You want to funnel your power into mine to give my creation a version of your protection?" Graham furrowed his brow in confusion.

"You see, Graham, it would be exactly what we need to keep you safe."

"How?"

"You've created nearly a dozen masks today, and we've tried each one of them, but your uncle and I can't sense when you're using the power of the mask. Your gift provides a level of undetectable protection that our enemies won't sense. You're shielding your creations' abilities. No one would ever suspect you."

Graham had known that fact about his gift, but his eyes widened at the realization of what it meant for his role within the League. "Do you think I can do it?" He struggled to his feet.

"It's worth a try." Gabrielle moved to stand behind him at the forge.

"Whenever you're ready." Uncle Lou nodded as Graham pulled a fresh bar of steel from the flames.

With a deep breath, Graham reached for his power one last time. Lifting his hammer, he gave himself over to his power, coupled with his uncle's guiding hand.

He barely felt it when Gabrielle placed her hands on his shoulders.

The malleable metal thinned into a long rectangular sheet under his hammer. Streaks of silver and blue power ran like electrical currents through it as he worked.

She is powerful... a distant voice whispered.

Golden streaks of light seeped into the metal beneath his hands, swirling around his blue power like a protective shield.

She can protect the boy.

Graham's chest burned with the smoldering of his power.

"Keep going, Graham," Gabrielle shouted in his ear. "Keep a tight hold on your power."

He had full control. Graham held the root of his creative gift firmly in his grasp. Blue light erupted from his chest, swirling around all three of them like a cage.

This was different from any experience he'd ever had using his power. Suddenly, he had more control. He felt stronger and more energized.

And then, he saw it. Finally. After so many years of searching for a variation in his gift, the root of his power split into a new branch. It was hardly more than a handhold, but Graham reached for it now, grasping it firmly in hand. It was so simple, this thing that had eluded him for years.

Power raged through him, but he controlled it. He owned it.

Twin spheres of blue light rose in front of him, undulating and rippling in the heat of the forge.

We are here to serve. The voice did not belong to Graham or his thoughts. It was decidedly female. *The lady wishes to protect the boy, as do we.* The balls of light swayed and flickered in a mesmerizing way, pulling Graham into a daze as he worked.

Her power will keep him safe. The shimmering light of his power moved from the twin spheres to encase his hands and arms like gloves, caressing him in a loving embrace. *We shall serve him well.*

"Graham, rein it in! You're draining her!" Uncle Lou's terrified tone finally broke through the barrier that stood between him and sound reason.

Gabrielle's sobs cut through him. *You're hurting her!* He recoiled from the obtrusive light of his power. The voices murmured in confusion.

We wish only to serve. To protect our master. The spheres bobbed and blinked back at him in innocence. *We will do what is best.*

Fear and regret swept through Graham as he tried to rein in his power, but the control he thought he wielded vanished. The disembodied voice was in control now.

Graham jerked and thrashed, trying to move away from the

forge and the power that was torturing his aunt and terrifying his uncle, but the light of his power held him rooted.

Stop! Graham ordered. *I am your master.*

The orbs blinked back at him.

But we know what is best. They moved to perch on his shoulders, forcing him to continue his work on the mask that glowed golden under his hands. *It is our duty to serve.*

Gabrielle shrieked, and Uncle Lou tried to pry the hammer out of Graham's grasp. But he was too strong.

No! Graham refused to relinquish control to his gift. He shook his head. This was just an odd manifestation of his gift he had to overcome. "It is your duty to obey me." Graham's voice grated in his throat.

The master is strong. The blue spheres danced in glee. *But is he certain?*

"You will not harm this woman." Graham set his hammer aside, gripping the edge of his workspace to keep his hands still.

But we must finish the master's creation. They blinked at him, as if waiting for permission.

"I will finish it." Graham lay his hands over the hot metal as if to protect it from these creatures.

If you are certain.

"Leave me," Graham ordered.

As you command. The balls of light rippled and faded into nothing.

As his power left him, Graham and Gabrielle fell into a heap on the stone floor.

"Gabrielle?" Uncle Lou gathered her up in his arms and moved her far away from the blistering forge, laying her among the cool shadows of the cavern.

Graham rose to his feet on shaky limbs.

"Graham?" Uncle Lou put himself between his nephew and

his Complement, arms raised as if ready for a fight if it came to that. "Talk to me, my boy, are you well?"

"No." Graham's shoulders shook with silent sobs. "I don't know what just happened, but I've finally done the thing everyone has been trying to get me to do since I was sixteen years old." He turned toward his uncle, anger, regret, and a great deal of fear warring inside him. "I am a weapon now."

Chapter 23

Graham | Early Spring | Salem, Massachusetts

Have we displeased you, master?

Graham charged up the stairs to his room. Slamming the door behind him, he sank to the floor, closing his hands over his ears to block out the voices.

We know what is best. The orbs of light danced in his mind, seeking his approval.

"Shut up!" Graham lurched to his feet and fled to his bedroom as if he could escape the torment of his mind. What had he done to Gabrielle?

After he'd finally regained control, Aunt Gabrielle lay unconscious but breathing. White as a ghost and shaking with anger, Uncle Lou sent him away. This was probably the end of Graham's welcome here.

Maybe he could move to the dorms with Brooks or get a place with Aria.

Groping for his phone on the nightstand, Graham curled into a ball and did the only thing that would calm him. He called his mom.

"Hey there, sweet kiddo," Emma answered the FaceTime call with her usual greeting. "This little boy is just about to go down for a nap, and then I'm all yours."

Graham wiped his eyes as he watched his mom move carefully to the corner of her office in the underground, placing Parker like a stick of dynamite about to explode into the crib.

"This brother of yours is a little troll. He only likes to sleep down here." Emma grabbed her phone and tiptoed into her gym, letting Parker have her office for his nap.

"Now, what do I owe the pleasure of a mid-day call from my genius child? Though, I can't take credit for your intelligence, that's all your father." Emma sat down in a corner chair and finally looked at the screen.

"What's wrong?" Her tone made the instant transition into worried-mom-I'll-fix-it-or-kill-whomever-harmed-my-child mode.

Graham sat up against his headboard. "I think I need to come home."

"What happened? Is it school?"

"Training went ... really bad today. I hurt Aunt Gabrielle."

"Well, that happens, hon. She's not going to hold that against you."

"It was bad. Uncle Lou couldn't pull me back." Graham's eyes burned with the threat of tears again. "I did it. I found the division in my creative gift, and it's not good."

"Tell me everything. We'll figure this out, and if we have to talk to Lou and Gabrielle, then we'll have a family meeting."

With a sigh Graham launched into a detailed explanation of what happened. "The voices." He shook his head. "I've never heard anything like it. They lured me into a trance, like they were their own entity and not a manifestation of my power. It's like they manipulated me. I know that sounds insane."

"It doesn't." Emma wiped her eyes. "You are not to blame, Graham. Strange things can happen when you push your limits like that. Gabrielle knows that better than anyone."

Graham shook his head, dancing spheres of light rippled in

his peripheral vision, and he could hear their indistinct murmurs of conversation as if they spoke just over his shoulder. "I can still hear them."

"You are my son." Emma shrugged, tears bright in her diamond clear eyes. "And this is my legacy to you. To both of my eldest sons, it seems. I can only hope Parker takes after your father more."

"What do you mean? Quinn has this too? Why would he never tell me?"

"Our gifts are seductive. Your brother's have manifested in ways he's battled to control every single day since his Awakening. His self control is admirable. But I did not fare so well when I was young."

"What are you saying?" Graham ran a hand through his sweaty hair.

"You've heard my stories of my life as a pirate and pillager. I made those days seem like great adventures when you were a little boy, but I was a madwoman, a slave to my power."

"The voices?"

Emma nodded. "I hear them too. So does Quinn."

"So, I haven't lost my mind then?" Graham breathed a sigh of relief. If there was precedent for this, he could manage it.

"No, but I'm afraid you have a long road ahead of you. You will have to resist the temptation of your power. The voices will do everything they can to manipulate you. You have to be the master of your power, not them."

"Will you talk to Uncle Lou and Aunt Gabrielle, help them understand what happened?"

"I will, but they already know, hon. I would come get you in a heartbeat if I thought I was the best person to help you through this, but I'm not."

"How do they know?"

"Who do you think helped me through it?" She smiled. "You're in the best place you could be."

"What do I do now?" Graham felt helpless.

"First, you're going to go take a shower, and then you're going to go to sleep. And when you wake up, your aunt and uncle will be there for you, and I want you to trust them to guide you."

"I miss you, Mom." Graham wanted nothing more than to go home to his family and forget any of this happened.

"You've been faced with a challenge. I wouldn't wish it on you for anything in the world, but I know you can conquer it, and in the end you will be stronger for it."

"Thanks, Mom."

"Graham, darling, wake up," the familiar voice called to him through the fog of sleep. Too much sleep.

"Wha's happening?" he muttered into the pillows he'd burrowed under.

"Up and at 'em, my boy, we've got work to do." Uncle Lou dragged the blankets off the bed. "You've slept most of the day away."

"Time's it?" Graham stared up at his aunt and uncle with bleary eyes.

"Nearly two o'clock. We've got just enough time for some training before the League event this evening."

"Which tie do you like?" Gabrielle held up five options for him. But as Graham locked eyes with his aunt, everything came crashing down on him.

"Aunt Gabrielle?" He struggled to sit up, his legs twisting in the sheets. "Are you okay?"

"Me? Oh, I'm just fine, darling." She moved to sit beside him, letting the array of ties fall to her lap. "Don't you worry one bit about yesterday." She waved it away like it was nothing.

"But ... but I tortured you. You should be kicking me out right now." Graham glanced around his bedroom and the boxes of new clothes scattered around. "Not buying me new clothes I don't even need."

"Nonsense, you can never have too many good suits."

"And the torture?" Graham's lips twitched with the hint of a smile. "Are we ignoring that?"

Gabrielle shrugged her delicate shoulders. "It's already forgotten. Things happen in training. It's not a predictable science, and as your family and your guardians during your time here in Salem, it's our duty and pleasure to guide you through these things. It's nothing."

"What about you, Uncle Lou? Is it nothing?" Graham moved to sit on the side of the bed, his muscles screaming in agony from the intensity of yesterday's events.

"I like the blue tie. It brings out your eyes." Uncle Lou smiled, resting a hand on Graham's shoulder. "I'm proud of you, you know." He moved to sit on Graham's other side. "We pushed you yesterday, and you rose to the challenge. I'm just so sorry it went the way it did, but that's no fault of yours."

"I'm so sorry I hurt you, Aunt Gabrielle." Graham turned toward her. "I won't let it happen again."

"Graham," Uncle Lou said. "Our gifts manifest in ways we often can't understand, but they're still part of us. We helped your mother, and we'll help you the same way. In time, you'll come to terms with this ability, and you'll learn how to manage it and those cheeky balls of light."

"You could hear them too?" Graham's eyes widened in surprise.

"Our gifts were linked at the time, so I heard all of it. And your constant attempts to keep control. You did well."

"How about we grab some lunch and then go see if it works?" Gabrielle asked with a grin.

"See if what works?" Graham scratched his head.

"The mask, darling. Aren't you dying to try it out?"

"Oh, right. Yeah." Graham grinned. "You think it might have worked?"

"Only one way to find out."

Chloe | Spring | MIT Campus

Chloe sat at a table under an umbrella across the campus quad. Hiding behind her sunglasses and a large iced coffee from the coffee shop down the street, she waited, watching the young college students come and go from their classes. In so many ways, she envied them. She'd missed out on going to college when she left home not long after her high school graduation.

She'd worked hard to graduate early so she could catch up with her friends back home. They used to be everything to her, and she still missed them every day. It hurt a little less now than it used to.

Chloe had to resort to her old trick, using her headphones to block out the white noise of so much chaos around her. Mortals were an indecisive bunch. Yet, she couldn't block out the visual aspects of her gift. Thin red lines connected various groups and individuals, changing almost as fast as she could track them. It was impossible to keep up with. It was beginning to worry her that she might miss some vital clue because there was just too much information for her gift to process. She'd reached a point where she wasn't sure she could go on without help. She just didn't have anyone to turn to.

Chloe watched the Immortal boy behind the counter at the coffee kiosk. A cloud of indecision hung over him, and red lines zoomed in and out of focus. She couldn't get a clear read on him, but he seemed to be at the center of some monumental decisions.

"Hey, Mr. Cutie-Cute!" The boy lifted his hand in greeting. "I got your usual right here."

Chloe shrank back into the shadows, just far enough away that she knew Graham wouldn't sense her, but close enough to hear the boys' conversation.

She smiled when Graham's face lit up at the sight of the boy. She wanted him to be happy. To enjoy the college experience he'd wanted just as much as she once had. But she had to make sure he was making his best decisions, or if he was in over his head. She studied him. He looked tired and stressed. A cloud of red threads snarled between the boys. Whatever Graham was caught up in, this boy was right there in it with him.

"Can you take a break?" Graham leaned over the counter, sharing a quick kiss with the cute boy.

"For you, yes." The boy lifted the counter to exit the kiosk and the two headed her way to sit at a nearby table. Chloe moved her seat back, staying well out of Graham's limited range among the shadows of the cherry trees lining the courtyard.

"You know, after I met you at the League, I thought the barista thing was a ruse to get close to me," Graham said.

"It was." The boy smiled again, reaching across the table to take Graham's hand.

Chloe hoped this guy was for real because if he hurt Graham, he was going to have to answer to her.

"So, you just kept the job?" Graham frowned.

The boy laughed. "I really am a scholarship work-study student. I used to work at the kiosk on the other side of campus before I met you. I switched with the guy who used to work at this location so I could keep seeing you."

Chloe followed their conversation, focusing on the signals her gift gave her.

"But why? It's not like you need the money."

"Who says I don't? My father cut me off ages ago when I refused to become a lawyer and pursue a future in American politics. My mom helps me a lot, but I'm not actually the silver spoon type my father wishes I was. I'd much rather make it on my own and decide for myself which path is for me than take the legacy route to a life I never wanted."

"You continually surprise me." Graham sipped his coffee.

"I'm a lot more than I seem. Granted, I sold the Mercedes my dad got me for my eighteenth birthday. I've been living on that for years. It makes him crazy." The boy gazed over Graham's shoulder, meeting Chloe's eyes. She nodded at the recognition.

"I think someone's here to see you." The boy returned her nod.

Graham turned in his seat, and Chloe lowered her sunglasses, offering her childhood best friend a genuine smile and a wave.

"Chloe?" Graham shot out of his chair and across the cobblestone patio. The years melted away as she flung herself into his arms.

"I've missed you." She held on tight. He was taller, broader, and a lot happier than the last time she'd seen him. This Graham was thriving with the weight of past trials finally off his shoulders. But that didn't mean he didn't have new trials.

"We've all been so worried about you." He wrapped his arms around her. "How are you here right now? Last I heard, you were in L.A."

"Oh, that was ages ago." She pulled back, studying the red lines that wound around Graham and his boyfriend. "Let me look at you." She took a step back, the warmth of her gift welling within.

"I'll leave you two to catch up." The boy moved to leave.

"Wait. Brooks, this is my best friend from home. Chloe, this is my boyfriend, Brooks."

Chloe didn't miss the flash of surprise that crossed Brooks' face. She suspected that was probably the first time the "B" word was used, and she was glad she got to see it.

"Nice to meet you." Chloe gave him a nod. As happy as she was for them, she was here for a reason, and she needed to get to the bottom of it.

"You too. I've got to get back to work, but you should join us for dinner if you're still around later."

"Thanks, but I won't be staying long." Chloe took Graham's hand as they walked across the quad.

"Do you have classes soon?" she asked.

"In a bit, but I have some time." Graham turned to her. "Out with it. I can see it on your face, you have something to say."

"What have you gotten yourself into?" She scowled up at him. She remembered a time not so long ago when they met each other eye to eye.

"What? With Brooks?" He glanced back at his boyfriend. "You don't approve?" He frowned.

"Of course, he's wonderful. You two are all sorts of adorable. I'm talking about the other things I've seen. You've gotten involved with the wrong kind of people, haven't you?" She studied the murmurings of his indecision. The lines connecting him with Brooks and other far away things and people she couldn't see. He was dealing with a lot, but everything her gift told her said he was making all the best choices.

"Your eyes are smoldering, Chlo." Graham led them to a quiet corner in the shade at the edge of the quad. "What have you seen?"

She frowned, still studying him with her gift. "You're making your best decisions. That's all I needed to see."

"Oh, no. You're not getting away that easy. What do you know about the League?"

"Is that what they call themselves?" She folded her arms across her chest.

Graham glanced over his shoulder and pitched his voice lower. "The League of Ancients. I can't go into it in detail, but I'm working with Gabrielle and Lou and Brooks to find out more about what this group has planned. Now, it's your turn to tell me what you know."

"I have friends." She lifted her chin. "They're like me and you. It's been a whole different world being around other Scholars and Techs. It's freeing in a way I never suspected. There are things happening in our world, Graham. So many things don't make sense yet." She shook her head. "But we're working to understand. Two of my friends are Techs, and they're investigating this League. It's not good. I'm worried about you getting involved with them."

"I know what I'm doing." He squeezed her hand. "Just like I trust you to know what you're doing."

"You're right." She sighed. "I just needed to see for myself that you were okay." She studied the threads connecting him to Books and this place. It was good. He was good. Safe enough ... for now.

"And what do you see?" He knew her gift as well as she did.

She let out a breath. "You're on the right track. Keep doing what you're doing and call me if you ever get in over your head."

Graham looked back over his shoulder at Brooks. "Oh, I'm pretty sure it's too late for that."

Chapter 25

Graham | Spring | Unknown Forest

The mask worked like a dream, but *the girls* were making Graham's life miserable. The dancing balls of power bickered and whispered wherever he went, trying to sway him to follow their lead—which was never a good idea. Thankfully, no one else could hear them.

For the last few weeks, Graham had worked with his aunt and uncle to control this new aspect of his gift. Most of the time it felt like an exercise in futility to resist the temptation of the girls. They liked to catch him unawares, luring him in with their subtle and persistent whispering.

Currently, they were not happy with him. He'd made them promise to leave him alone tonight. He wasn't ready for dealing with them in public, and he needed to be laser focused tonight. They'd reluctantly agreed to keep their thoughts to themselves. He was willing to bet that promise wouldn't last more than fifteen minutes into the evening.

"You ready for this?" Brooks squeezed Graham's hand. He knew nothing about the mask or the girls, but Graham was still grateful for his boyfriend's support. It wasn't that he didn't trust

Brooks with his secrets. He just wasn't ready to burden him with all his baggage just yet.

League events were beginning to take over Graham's life. He found himself more invested in helping his aunt and uncle investigate the illegal activities of key League members than in his daily classes.

He would never have chosen this path for himself, but now that he was in it, Graham was determined to make a difference. And for as long he was still on the Alderman's radar, he intended to use his interest in Graham's technological skills to get closer to the Grand Master. If they could discover who he was, then they would be one step closer to revealing the League's plans for the Immortal world.

Graham needed to know what the Master's end game was. With his new mask carefully hidden under his decorative skull mask, Graham might just pull off a serious coup tonight—as long as he could get an audience with the Alderman.

"You look worried." Aria stepped between Graham and Brooks in the growing twilight of the forest.

"My face is hidden behind this thing, how can you tell?" Tonight's skull was made of pewter and obsidian. It covered most of his face, leaving his cheeks exposed. It also weighed a ton with the added layer of steel under it.

"You look stiff as a board. Relax, this is a party, not an execution." She patted his arm, scanning the crowd for her spies. She had them everywhere, gathering bits of information on key members of the League. Aria worked closely with Gabrielle and Lou, but she had her own agendas. Graham pitied those who were involved with the disappearance of her family. They would pay dearly for it whenever Aria was ready to strike. They called her the Nightingale, but to Graham, she was more like a viper.

"The League has too many parties." Graham sighed. "Don't they ever get bored with it?"

"This is not just a party," Brooks said. "On the surface, it's all fun and games, a harmless mixer for the youngest members. But underneath it all, the Alderman is working behind the scenes like a puppet master. All the while Madam M is out there playing matchmaker, putting the families together like strategic pieces on a chessboard."

"And you ask why I'm tense." Graham shook his head. Standing on the sidelines with his two friends was the quickest way to get Madam M's attention, and he'd like to have one night where that did not happen.

"Let's get out of here." Aria linked her arms through each of theirs, leading them along the dark forest path with the other young League members following.

This time, they weren't at the Alderman's home or the dungeon headquarters of the League of Ancients. Tonight was all about spoiling the youngest generation with fun and games designed to show off their abilities and congratulate themselves on how wonderful they all were. Graham and his friends steered clear of the games, preferring to rub elbows with the older League members in attendance.

"I've heard whispers that the Lady Gray herself is here tonight." Aria glanced over her shoulder into the shadows of the birch wood forest.

"Who is she?" Graham asked. It was hard to keep up with all the code names and lack of faces to go with them. He could hear the girls whispering and buzzing just out of his line of sight. They murmured something insane about capturing the Lady Gray to question her for *the boy*.

You will do no such thing. Graham tried to return his focus on the conversation, but the girls were determined to mesmerize him with their plans. *What did you promise, girls?*

Sorry, they chorused in his mind.

"She's one of the Ancients my father panders to," Brooks said.

"Who?" Graham shook his head, trying to shove the girls' chatter to the back of his mind.

"The Lady Gray. They call her that because she's important, but no one knows where her loyalties lie. They say she has the Master's ear."

"The Alderman has arrived." Aria nodded toward the massive tent erected for the occasion. "Go do your schmoozing, boys. I'm going to hunt down the Huntress and see what news she has for me." Aria slipped into the shadows of the forest before Graham could ask her how the Huntress was connected with their little group.

"We all have our networks of spies. You will too, in time." Brooks leaned in closer, his breath warm on Graham's throat, though they had agreed not to flaunt their growing relationship for the League to see. "Be careful tonight, Graham. You seem distracted."

"I'll be fine." He smiled. It was best if everyone thought of them as nothing more than friends, in case things went badly for them in the future, then they couldn't be used against each other.

Graham watched the Alderman move among his guests. "What should I do?"

"Put yourself in his line of sight. He will want to speak with you again, but try to get him to nail down a time and date to meet with the Master."

"You really think the Master will want to meet me?" Graham still didn't think it was likely.

"If your communication system works like you explained it to me, he's going to want to bring you into the fold, and that's what we need."

Graham nodded. "We're never going to get anywhere if we don't have someone inside the Alderman's inner circle. Might as well be me."

"Let's meet back here at dawn." Brooks set off into the crowd of young college students. As the Jackal, he had a high-profile part to play. He had to be seen, where the Grim could fly under the radar, trusted and guileless, but mostly ignored. He was just a harmless blue-collar Tech after all.

Graham made his way toward the tent where a growing crowd of League sycophants swarmed the Alderman. He refused to be one of them. It was best to let the Alderman call for him first.

"Come with me." A firm hand gripped his arm, leading him away from the Alderman and his League.

Graham pulled back. "Who are you?" He studied the tall slim woman wearing a feathered peacock mask. Her presence was a familiar one he couldn't quite place.

"They call me Lady Gray. Now, come with me before anyone sees us." She gripped his arm again, pulling him behind a copse of birch trees.

"Do I know you?" He stumbled after her.

"You know very well who I am." She lifted her mask for a brief moment, but it was enough.

"Porcia?" Graham blinked in disbelief. He hadn't seen her since he'd walked out on his aunt's dinner party months ago. "I didn't realize you were in the League."

"Well, I'm here and wearing a mask. You do the math." Porcia gave him a curious look. "There's something different about you tonight." She searched his eyes.

"You're the Lady Gray?" Graham looked over his shoulder, hoping no one saw them slip away. It wouldn't do for the Grim to be caught with anyone of questionable loyalty.

"Yes, but I serve the League under a different Alderman on the west coast. I travel frequently among the League communities."

"Your reputation precedes you."

"From your lips to the Grand Master's ears," she muttered. "I don't have a lot of time. I try to make my appearances quick and mysterious. Enough to get the Grand Master's attention, but never long enough to get swept up into his web."

"Was there a reason you sought me out?"

"Yes. Now that you've been initiated, I take it you are working with Gabrielle and Lou?"

Graham nodded.

"They really wanted to keep you out of all this, but now that you're here, I need you to take advantage of the opportunity the Alderman has given you. He will hesitate and drag his feet on the matter, but you need to push him to get an audience with the Master." She studied his face again—what little of it she could see. "I think he will trust you, though he moves at a glacial pace. They all do." She waved an irritable hand at the tent where all the oldest members gathered.

Graham leaned forward to whisper. "Do you know *everything*?"

Porcia chuckled. "When it comes to dealing with the Grand Master, I have to stay five steps ahead of him. I know he is interested in you and your abilities, but I'm not sure why. We need to get you on the inside."

"Do you know who he is?" Graham asked, hardly believing it could be that easy.

She nodded. "He was once my husband and dearest friend, but that was another age and none of it matters anymore."

"But we need to know who he is. If you can tell me—"

Porcia shook her head. "His name doesn't matter. He will evade you like water draining from a sieve. You'll never capture him, but you can spy on him. If you're very smart about it."

Let's take her, the girls whispered, their flickering light bobbing along Graham's peripheral vision. *She has much knowledge.*

You two need to chill. We're not abducting anyone. Ever. Now, zip it.

"Can you play this role, Graham?" She searched his eyes. "I know you are young, but he already wants to collect your skills. That is all we need to get close to him in a way he will never suspect. He will underestimate you." She studied his eyes through his mask. "I don't know why, but I think he will trust you. You have such a non-threatening manner about you."

That was the mask at work. "I can do it." Graham took a deep breath, grateful even Porcia didn't seem to realize his power was at play, shielded behind his creation. "I just worry that the kind of technology I've developed could be dangerous in the wrong hands."

"Then, don't let it out of your control." She took his hands in hers.

"How do you mean?" Graham frowned.

"Find a way to make yourself and your ability the center element of your communication system so there is no way he could cut you out of the system."

"Well, I kind of already am. It would never work without me as the conduit. Everything has to pass through me to be delivered to the recipients. It's not a matter of delivering a couple of fancy phones that work offline and then checking out. The devices will never work without me. My gift is essentially the router that makes it all work."

A smile lit Porcia's face. "So, you can access all the information that passes through your gift to the recipient?"

"In a way. It's comes through me in code, and it's a lot of information all at once. It would be difficult to decipher the information if I am not the recipient on the other end of a piece of tech."

"Could it be done in time?"

"It's likely, in time, I could find a way to process the information that passes through my gift. At the moment, the best I can do is keep a record of everything my gift processes. Translating it to useful information will have to come later, if ever."

Porcia laid a hand on his shoulder. "That is excellent news, Graham. I will do my best to get you whatever help and support you need so you can learn to develop this aspect of your gift."

"I will have to explain the way it works to the Alderman if not the Grand Master himself."

"I will speak with Gabrielle. She will teach you how to guard your thoughts so whenever you are with any of the aldermen or the Master, you will be able to conceal this aspect of your gift. To them, your communication system must be absolutely confidential. Their own hubris and ignorance of modern things will make that easy. They'll never suspect the young man with the honest eyes. Though, the Grand Master is cunning. Do not lump him in with the others."

"What is he planning? If I'm going to stick my neck out, I need to know what this is all for."

Porcia looped her arm through his, pulling him farther into the shadows of the dark forest. "That is why we need you, Graham. I don't know what his next move is, but I know we are running out of time. My son is a Prophet. He sees beyond the final prophecy. The Grand Master will destroy us all if we don't stop him now while we still have a chance."

"Then, I will do what I can." Graham squeezed her hand tucked into his elbow. "I need to put myself in front of the Alderman this evening."

"I have to go make an appearance elsewhere. Good luck, Graham. And thank you. You have no idea what this means for us."

"I have a feeling I will understand that very soon." Graham set off across the forest to the tent glowing with lantern light. He had one shot at this. He needed to make it a bullseye.

"That's not quite how we operate, young Grim, but I like your ambition." The Alderman clapped Graham on the shoulder. They stood on the edge of a cliff, observing the vicious game of capture the flag playing out below.

Graham winced at a particularly brutal attack that cast two young members out of the game and probably straight to a Senate hospital facility. This was nothing like the training games they had at home that were meant to teach them something. This was just about the biggest show of power, and he wanted nothing to do with it.

"I'd be happy to show you how my tech works, sir, but I fear it might lose something in the translation if I'm not able to work directly with the Grand Master."

"I'm afraid he won't be available to meet with you. Though all the aldermen and the Master could benefit greatly from your communication system, we would need you to set it up in a way that can be easily managed between you and I, at least for the moment.

"I have a good feeling about you, young Grim. Let me take you under my wing, and the League will protect you as one of our greatest assets. There's no rush to make any decision tonight. We have all the time in the world to talk business."

"Thank you, sir, that sounds like an incredible opportunity." Graham tried to put just the right amount of "awe shucks" into his voice, playing into the guileless persona his mask provided him.

"Excellent. Now, you mentioned your system works through a series of games and applications that don't need a WiFi connection to function, is that correct?"

"Yes sir." Graham nodded eagerly. The situation wasn't going quite as he planned. The Alderman wasn't in a hurry to make anything happen, but there was a chance Graham could steer him onto a path he and the Master could be more comfortable with. One that just might limit the risk Graham had to take.

"You will teach me how to use this tech of yours, and then I will pass on your instructions to the interested parties. There's no real need to involve you any further unless we run into issues down the road. I'd like to set you up with a home office where we could contact you when necessary. You'll be generously compensated for your work of course. Think of it as an internship that could lead to letters of recommendation from several high-profile world leaders such as myself."

"Of course, that would be excellent, sir." This could work out better for Graham in the long run. Once he set up the system and programed the aldermen's devices to work with his gift, they would forget all about the Tech guy who made it happen. He was willing to bet the Grand Master would never even know his name. And they were all old enough and clueless enough about technology to never suspect he was at home learning to monitor their communications.

"May I meet with you sometime next week?" Graham asked. "I can have a phone programed for your use and one for the Master as well. You can be assured the phones will only work with each other and any future devices linked to the offline network. Your communication with each other will be more secure than any mortal technology could ever hope to be."

"That's what I like to hear." The Alderman gave Graham another slap on the back. "I'll send a car for you on Monday. The Master will be pleased with your hard work."

"I am at your disposal, sir." Graham shook his hand, hoping this didn't end in a disaster for him.

PART III

FIFTEEN MONTHS LATER

CHAPTER 26

Allie | The Following Summer | Atlanta

Allie writhed in her sleep, familiar faces swarming like bees all around her. Faces she despised for their stubborn refusal to work with her.

A bead of sweat rolled down her back from the oppressive heat of the night. Her legs tangled in the sheets. Summer in Atlanta was just too hot. At least at home they had Lake Erie breezes to keep the evenings cool.

The mass of Senate officials moved to her peripheral vision, but she was still restless in her sleep. Her hands moved and her eyes rolled as she sat up, more aware of her dreams than ever before. This was new territory for the First Princess of Indriell.

Strange places flashed before her eyes, faster than she could register them. Her powerful mind worked to sort them into boxes for perusal later. Deserts, vast tundras, wastelands, jungles, cities, rural forests. None of it made any sense, but that was okay. It would come together eventually. She'd learned to accept that about her clairvoyance.

Something slender slipped into her hand. She gripped the pencil tight as a sketchbook grazed her lap. Her hands flew across the pages, making notes and scribbles that made perfect sense to her now but wouldn't later.

A torrent of information flooded her mind, and she reached out her left hand, grasping until a second pencil slipped between her fingers. A moment later, a cool breeze swept through the room, and a comforting hand lifted the damp hair at her nape, securing it back in a messy bun.

He was really here, watching over her in her sleep. Too bad he wouldn't be there when she woke. Aidan preferred to sleep on the couch these days, but when her clairvoyant dreams plagued her, he came to her aid.

Allie pushed those confusing emotions to the back of her mind, focusing on her gift as it guided her to something new and probably terrifying. Everything was terrifying for Allie when she was supposed to be this great, amazing leader, and everyone looked to her for guidance when they just hadn't realized she was a walking disaster.

Familiar laughter filled her ears and warmed her heart. "You're not a walking disaster, Lex." The bed dipped beside her as Aidan's heft joined hers. She wanted to wake from this vision, but she was locked in it and needed to focus.

The disapproving faces of the Immortal Senate still scowled at her from the sidelines as landscapes and derelict buildings swam before her eyes. Gabe would help her decipher this vast amount of information during their training sessions later, but she had to be present within her vision. Not thinking about Aidan and time alone in their room.

Well, she called it their room, though he insisted on sleeping opposite days from her, and even when they did overlap, he slept on the couch—the noble son of—

"Focus, Allie." Aidan moved from her side to sit in the chair beside her bed, not that she could see him, locked in her dreams as she was. She felt him whenever he came to watch over her dreams. They weren't as scary as they were when they were just kids, but sometimes Allie wished they could get back to that level of intimacy.

"I'll leave if I'm distracting you."

Allie was pretty sure she stuck her tongue out at him because he laughed again.

Her hands moved over the pages of her sketchbook, scribbling shapes and forms as her gift guided her.

Sometime toward dawn, Allie fell asleep, worn out from the deluge of information on a night when she'd desperately needed rest. Her job was so demanding of her time, she seemed to live in a constant state of exhaustion.

"That was definitely new." Aidan stared down at her.

Allie blinked up at him resting on his side, looking refreshed and ready for another long day of helping her run Soma. She, on the other hand, felt like something the cat puked up.

"But you don't have a cat." Aidan's mouth lifted in a crooked smile.

"How do you keep doing that?" Allie rolled over to face him, covering her face with the sheets to shield her morning breath. "Are you reading my mind? I thought we weren't doing that anymore."

"I'm not invading your thoughts, Lex. I'm just answering when you speak out loud, not that you've said much that makes sense in the last hours." Aidan draped an arm around her, and Allie took advantage of his nearness to snuggle close.

She yawned into her sheets, closing her eyes to enjoy the moment. "Wait." Her eyes snapped open again. "What's new?"

"Did you know you were ambidextrous in your sleep?" Aidan reached behind him for her sketchbook. "You can draw two different things at the same time on two different sides of your sketchbook. It was an impressive thing to watch."

"Yes, but does it make a lick of sense?" Allie flipped

through the book she'd nearly filled in one night. "Jeez, no wonder my hands ache this morning. I must have been at it for hours."

"Look at this." Aidan flipped to the center page where Allie had drawn a map of the continents, each labeled with their various terrains, though she hadn't bothered to name any specific locations.

"Any idea what it means?" She looked to him, hoping he was more observant than she was.

"Not a clue, but these locations need to be researched. They may prove important at some later date."

"I'll get Colin Creevey to work on it and see what he comes up with."

"You know that's not his name." Aidan's wide shoulders shook with laughter.

"I know, but he's always asking for my autograph." Allie yawned and snuggled down in the blankets, the cool morning breeze swept through the room from the balcony. "Thanks for opening the doors. I was roasting alive in here."

"You're welcome, baby." Aidan pulled her close against his chest. "I'll always be here to check on you and your dreams, but I'm glad you're able to handle them on your own. You've gotten so strong, Lex."

Allie ran her palm along his shoulder. "I'm just glad you're back." Though, if she were honest, he wasn't fully back. Not yet. Something still stood between them.

"I should leave you to get ready for your day." Aidan pulled away, like he always did these days.

"No." Allie rolled on top of him. "Stay." She let her weight pin him to the bed. "You're always leaving too soon." She peppered his face with kisses. "You should stay."

Aidan grabbed her hands, laughing at her antics as he rolled her off him. "Alexis Ann, you know I am powerless to resist you.

I'll stay as long as you want, but we have work to do." He dragged her sketchbook between them.

"Work-schmirk." Allie groaned. "You know I can't function before coffee."

"I'm amazed my mother hasn't beat you into submission on that yet." Aidan reached behind him to produce two steaming cups of coffee from the dining hall.

"I won that war." Allie pounced on the coffee. "But I suppose we do need to put our heads together to stop the one looming on the horizon."

Chapter 27

Graham | One Month Later
Summer | Salem, Massachusetts

We must wake him. Twin spheres of light danced around Graham's head.

The boy needs his rest.

We will see to his rest soon. He must wake for this.

Graham nearly jumped out of his skin at the blaring tone of a call coming in. He'd fallen asleep at his desk again, the weight of his skull mask leaving him with a throbbing headache.

We interrupted master's rest!

It's your fault.

"Girls, stop arguing." Graham shoved the voices to the back of his mind, letting them bicker amongst themselves.

Reaching for one of a dozen phones scattered across his desk, he made sure his mask was in place. "This is Grim." He answered the phone labeled with a green sticker. One of his spies calling in to report.

"It's the Siren," a familiar voice filled his ears, though he had no face or proper name to go along with it.

"What did you find?" Graham launched a series of computer programs to make a record of this call. His spies trusted him implicitly, but that was mostly due to the mask he wore even when conversing via audio calls.

"The Northwestern Alderman is on the move again."

"Same as last time?" Graham reached for the world map he kept on his desk. The aldermen tended to stay within their regions, but over the last eight months, his spies reported patterns of movement among their ranks.

"I have the coordinates this time," the Siren said, breathless in her excitement. "Are you ready for this?"

"Shoot." Graham entered the numbers as she read them off.

"Wait, are you sure about that? Twenty-five degrees north, seventy-one degrees west?"

"Positive."

"That's right in the middle of the Bermuda Triangle." Graham scratched his head and scribbled the location on his map.

"There's something there, Grim. I know it. It could be the key to all the secretive activity among the aldermen in recent months. They are up to something huge."

"We need to find out if any of the other aldermen are traveling to this location."

"I'll get my people on it, sir."

"I've told you to stop calling me that, Siren."

"Sorry, sir, it's ingrained in me after a lifetime in the League."

"Don't give away details like that."

"I normally don't, but I trust you, sir."

Graham sighed, wishing he didn't feel such guilt for manipulating the people who were so loyal to him. Not that he would ever betray them. "Keep me posted."

"Will do, Grim ... sir."

With a groan, Graham removed his mask, thanking the girls once again for its protection.

You honor us, sir. The twin spheres of his gift returned from sulking behind him, eager to be close to him as always.

"Knock it off, girls, I'm going to bed." Graham stood with a stretch, smiling at the way they zoomed ahead of him to the bedroom like they intended to prepare the way.

They were annoying in the extreme, but they'd come to terms with their role over the last year. In no uncertain terms, Graham was in charge. Not them. He'd fought them tooth and nail for the upper hand, and they now seemed to respect him for it.

Another phone rang, and Graham wanted to throw it through a window, but this phone was special. It was his direct line to the Master. Retrieving the mask, Graham returned to his desk and grabbed the basic smartphone with the blue sticker.

"This is Grim, sir, what can I do for you this evening?" Graham quickly launched his customized tracking system to determine where the Master was calling from this time. He liked to get around, but for the last few months, he'd spent a lot of time between Spain and Italy—and he was in an awful mood.

"Grim, glad to catch you so late. I hope I haven't interrupted your rest."

"Of course not, sir. You know me, I'm always up late working." That was one thing he'd learned about the Master. He was almost always polite and had a way of showing he cared about the people who worked for him. If Graham didn't know any better, he'd really like the guy. "I'm happy to help, sir."

"I know I can always count on you. I have a rather large favor, and I'm afraid I'll need it done quickly."

"I'll do my best, sir." Graham continued to work his programs, pinpointing the Master's location and recording the conversation for his records.

"I need at least one hundred new devices."

Graham nearly dropped the phone. "One hundred, sir?"

"And I'll need them quickly, so I'm happy to provide a fifteen percent bonus for the rush job, on top of your usual fee of course."

That would net Graham well over a million dollars.

"I can do that, sir. I'll just need the usual information to program the devices."

"I'll send you the basic location information, but each device will need to be programed to have a direct line to me and to each other, and I'll need them by next Friday. I'm leaving for the tropics to meet with my aldermen."

Make that more than two million dollars, and more work than Graham could reasonably do in such a short time. Each device would need to be keyed into the offline network Graham had built from nothing.

"Sir, I graduate from MIT next Friday. I still have a few exams to prepare for too."

"Congratulations, dear Grim, that is excellent news! I'm so proud of the work you've done for my team all while staying at the top of your class. Very impressive. I would offer to write you a letter of recommendation, but I don't want to lose you to another opportunity. With your graduation on the horizon, I think it's time you officially join my team."

"Th-thank you, sir. I would be honored." Graham's heart thudded in his chest. He'd worried this day would come eventually. "I—Do you mean in person, sir? Like, full time?" Graham paced behind his desk, uncertain how to talk his way out of this. He was trapped. He couldn't turn down the Master's offer, but there was no way Graham could actually join him. He would never escape the League if that happened.

"Absolutely. You enjoy your last week as a student. You will join me in Barcelona on Monday." It wasn't a question. "We have to deal with a certain young woman who calls herself a princess."

"Y-yes sir. I've heard all about her." Graham gripped the edge of his desk. That Allie was on his radar was no real surprise. With her recent clash with the Senate and the takeover at Soma, she was likely on everyone's radar.

"Good, good. I look forward to seeing you soon."

"Of course, sir. Thank you. And I'll have the devices delivered to your usual pick-up site by Friday."

"I appreciate your loyalty, Grim. There are so few one can truly trust these days."

"You can always count on me, sir." Graham almost fainted as he ended the call and tossed his mask aside.

The girls were back, hanging over his shoulder, as they liked to do.

What is he worried about? Is he okay?

He's always worried about those phone things he makes.

"We have to program a hundred devices, girls." Graham wiped a weary hand over his face. "It's going to be a long week."

We can help. The girls flickered and blinked in their eagerness to be of use.

"Perhaps you can help with the phones. But we'll deal with those later." Graham put his feet up on the desk and leaned back in his chair. "Bring up all the records of the Master's communications over the last eighteen months."

The girls bobbed and weaved, transforming from their usual spherical shapes into lines of data that hung before him like augmented reality—without the special glasses.

What does the boy wish to see?

"Scan all the Master's communications for these coordinates." Graham rattled off the location of the Bermuda Triangle. "Also search for any references to the tropics."

As you wish.

It had taken most of the last year and a half to hone this newest aspect of his gifts—the girls didn't just affect his creative gifts, but every other aspect of Graham's power as well. They were always there, eager to lend their assistance, and he'd had to come to terms with their constant presence.

Streams of data and code swam before his eyes, pulled directly from the immense storage of his mind. The numbers and letters flickered with the blue light of his power. "Stop. Go back to the line containing the coordinates." The girls scrolled back to the line of code Graham wanted to translate.

Leaning forward, he scribbled notes on a scrap of paper. "It's an island." He leaned back. "Pull up a map of the Caribbean and the North Atlantic Ocean."

The girls readily complied, morphing their shape from basic lines of code into an intricate map of the Caribbean, complete with topographical details.

"Show me all the islands on record in this area." He pointed to the center of the Bermuda Triangle.

They zoomed in, but there was nothing there. San Salvador seemed to be the only island between Bermuda and the rest of the Caribbean islands. At least from what was on record.

He's almost there. Should we take control? It's all stored in his mind, but he's not gathering the right information.

"No, you should not take control. Show me what's in this region that might not be on official records. Something that wouldn't show up on mortal satellite imagery."

He figured it out all on his own. We are so proud.

"I'm not an idiot, you know." Graham ignored the girls' banter and studied the map they showed him now. "Zoom in here." He pointed to a dot at the center of the coordinates. "That's what we're looking for. Now, what's the Master want with an island no one knows exists?"

Graham sketched the location of the island on his map, adding it to the growing number of locations in remote areas of the world the Master had shown interest in over the last several months. He and his aldermen were preparing to make a big move. Graham just didn't know what that could be.

Should we show him?

"Do you have something to add to the information I've requested? Something you've gathered from our intel on the Master's communications?"

Yes, master. We do, but we fear you must ask the right question first.

Graham sighed with impatience. They took him so literally, but it was the best way to keep them in line.

"Can you show me what's on this island?"

We can. The girls practically beamed at him.

The map image vanished, replaced with photographs of the location. Drone images. Graham studied the blue-tinged photographs, wishing he had hard copies to study in detail, but he'd yet to figure out how to move the information his gift processed into print.

"What's that?" Graham leaned closer, his nose almost touching the flickering image of the tiny island. "Girls." Graham sat back, grinning. "What's probably the biggest myth about the supposed disappearances in the Bermuda Triangle?"

It's reported that there may have been unusual magnetic anomalies in the area that could explain the issues with compass activity around the triangle.

"And who uses such powerful, natural magnetic phenomenon in our world?"

The Coalition, the girls chorused.

"Exactly. I'd bet my life on it there's a Coalition prison on that island." Graham studied his map marked with other remote locations the Master had shown an interest in. The Yukon, Madagascar, the Sandwich Islands, and other islands along the Ring of Fire in the South Pacific. Tasmania, the Sahara Desert, rural China, Death Valley. Were these all Coalition prisons? And why would the Grand Master of the League of Ancients focus on these locations if they were?

"Run through the Master's text messages with his three closest aldermen for the last six months." Graham stood up behind his desk, letting his power burn low in his chest as he focused on the jumbled lines of code his gift collected whenever a message or phone call passed through him. "Look for any mention of prisons or the Coalition."

His gift collected an enormous amount of information and Graham was only beginning to crack the surface. He'd often worried it would take him too long to search through the information to find anything useful in time to do anything about it.

Staring at the endless pages of results from the search, it seemed he was right. With the Master's job offer, Graham was out of time. He needed to disappear.

"You look tired, little brother." Quinn made himself at home on Graham's bed. The entire family had arrived for his graduation, and Graham was happy to see them, but he'd spent the last week walking a dangerous tightrope.

The devices were programed and delivered to the Master. The payment had made its way to Graham's secret bank account and then transferred to another, more secret bank account with all the other millions he'd made during his time with the League.

"It's been a stressful week." Graham leaned back against his headboard, his laptop balanced on his lap.

"Yeah, I'm sure all the tests and projects you've been busy with have been taxing." Quinn rolled onto his side to face Graham.

"Oh, school stuff? That's no trouble." Graham yawned, waving away his brother's concern. Though he did wonder if there was any way Quinn could help him out of the jam he was in.

"What's your next step, little man?" Quinn asked. "Any job offers?"

"One." Graham set his computer aside and paced to his closet to check that his bag was packed just in case he found a way out later tonight.

"You don't seem too happy about it." Quinn moved to sit on the edge of the bed as Graham shifted through his closet checking to make sure he had everything he would need. Maybe he could catch up with Chloe. She had lots of practice flying under the radar.

"Well, I'd have to be in Spain on Monday if I take the job."

"Don't," Quinn's voice sounded oddly serious. "Come home for a while. It's not safe to be out in the world right now. You've been so focused on school for the last few years, but it's a volatile time in our world. Take some time before you make any big decisions."

"I can't." Graham shook his head. He refused to take his troubles to his family. They'd had enough of that in recent months. And Graham was well aware of how volatile their world was. Probable even more than his brother.

"You have to, little man." Quinn smiled. "Who else is going to stand up with me?"

"Stand up?" Graham shot his brother skeptical look. "What are you saying Quinnton Greggory Loukas?"

"It's Santi." Quinn grinned. "We're bonding, and I want you there for the ceremony."

"She's your Complement?" Graham moved to sit beside his brother on the bed. "I'm thrilled for you, man. Santi is great."

"She is. She and Sasha are like sisters at this point too."

"How does all of that work? It seems so complicated. A Complement *and* a Syntrophos, and you're right there in the middle of two very stubborn, smart women. Sounds like hell to me, bro."

Quinn laughed. "It's not. We've found a way to make it work, and we're comfortable with our unconventional relationship."

"It's not like having two wives, is it?" Graham wrinkled his nose. "Not that I'm judging."

"It's nothing like that. Sasha is head over heels for Jayesh. She is my best friend, and Santi will be my wife."

"Wife?" Graham shook his head. "You're way, way too young for this." But he really wasn't. Quinn's time as a captive of Soma had aged him in a way that made him seem far more mature than his twenty-four years.

"What can I say? When it happens there's no reason to wait." Quinn clapped him on the shoulder. "So, you'll be there to stand with me? I can't do this without you."

Graham shook his head, his voice strangled in his throat. "I'm sorry, I can't be there."

"Your new job can't wait a few weeks?" Quinn sounded crushed.

"It's not that." Graham stood to pace across the room. The girls came bursting out of him, chattering away with their concerns, but Graham waved them away, grateful his brother couldn't see them.

"Spill it." Quinn's big brother voice nearly had Graham spilling his guts.

He hung his head. He was so tired. Tired of everything. "I'm in trouble." And then, he did spill his guts, letting it all out, hoping his big brother could fix everything for him like he used to when they were just kids.

"Why have you kept all of this from us?" Quinn guided Graham back to sit on the bed.

"I didn't want to drag you all into the League with me. Once they get their hands on you, they don't let go."

"You think we don't know how to deal with threats like them?" Quinn laughed. "Little man, we are so out of touch with what's going on with each other."

"I think I have to be in Barcelona on Monday. I don't see a way around it." Graham rested his head in his hands.

"No way." Quinn shook his head like it was no big deal. "I'm the master of the dream world. I've got this."

"I don't know how the dream world can help. The League will come after me no matter where I go. If I take the job, at least I won't blow my cover."

"What about all those freaky masks?" Quinn gestured at the wall of masks hanging in his closet. "They don't know who you are, so how can they find you?"

"Don't think for a second that the Master doesn't know exactly who I am by now."

"First, you're going to stop calling him Master. Graham Xavier Loukas calls no one master."

"Fine." Graham cracked a smile. "Then what?"

"Then you're going to go graduate because I'm dying to see my little brother walk across that MIT stage to get his diploma."

"And then what, you're just going to walk me out under the cloak of your gift?"

"That's exactly what I'm going to do. And then, Dad's going to fly us all to Atlanta, where I'm going to walk you through my dreamworld barrier surrounding Sterling Tower, and you're going to live there, completely safe from this League of Ancients and their creepy masks."

"It can't be as easy as that." Graham didn't want to hope it could be as simple as walking away. "What about my friends?"

"Allie and Aidan have issued an invitation to all young Immortals to come to Soma to train and live in safety. Bring your friends with you."

"And what about Aunt Gabrielle and Uncle Lou? The League will retaliate against them if I escape."

"They're family. They can come too."

"That's it? I can just walk away from it all? Is Allie really that powerful?"

"She will be our queen, Graham. She's the real thing."

"But I have research. Important things that could have a huge impact on our world. I can't abandon that. I have theories I still need to prove." Graham ran an unsteady hand through his hair. He couldn't abandon his work after all the blood, sweat, and tears he'd put into it.

"Bring your research with you. Soma is the place to be for all young Immortals. Whatever you're dealing with, it doesn't need to rest all on your shoulders. I guarantee there is someone at Soma who can help you."

"I just ... I don't know." Graham felt so trapped.

"Why don't you call this dude and tell him you just can't take the job in Barcelona. At least not right now. Blame it on your age and your family obligations. Then offer to keep working for him remotely. See what happens."

It wouldn't work. People didn't turn down job offers from the Master, and Graham couldn't just call him up like they were buds. But maybe it was worth the risk. If it worked, he could keep up his work. If it didn't, he'd be safe inside Soma. "All right." Graham nodded. "Let's do it. I mean, I can't miss my brother's wedding."

"Excellent. You get ready for your graduation and let me take care of the rest. Before you know it, my walkers will be escorting you into Sterling Tower."

Graham gave his brother a sad smile. "I hate to say it, Quinn, but we're going to need to get to know each other again. I have a feeling we've both been through so much we're hardly the same boys who grew up together."

"Nah." Quinn waved off his concern. "We just need a little time to catch up. I'll always know my little brother right here." Quinn thumped Graham's chest. "Right where it matters most."

"Graham Xavier Loukas. Bachelor of Science in Electrical Engineering and Computer Science."

Graham rose from his seat, his red stole fluttering in the breeze as he walked the stage. A surge of pride swelled within him. He did it. He graduated from one of the most difficult programs in the country in only three years.

We are so proud. The girls fluttered and flickered with excitement as they followed, invisible to all but Graham.

"Congratulations, young man." Dr. McDermott shook his hand as she handed him his diploma and sent him on his way to have his picture taken at the edge of the stage.

Graham spotted his brother at the bottom of the stairs. They waited for Dr. McDermott to announce the next graduate before they joined hands and faded from notice of all those in attendance.

"Let's get out of here, little man." Quinn guided them through the crowd of unseeing eyes to where their parents waited with Parker. Graham was looking forward to spending more time with his baby brother. He just hoped he would be as good a big brother to Parker as Quinn had been to him.

With a last look at the campus Graham had grown to love, all five Loukases joined hands and walked away. Away from MIT and the League of Ancients ... and Brooks.

CHAPTER 28

Graham | Summer | Atlanta, Georgia

Graham closed the door to his new apartment on the fourteenth floor of Sterling Tower. The last thirty-six hours had been intense. He'd left without saying goodbye to Brooks. There wasn't time, but he'd asked Aunt Gabrielle to give him a letter.

It was a difficult letter to write. He'd loved his time with Brooks, but he knew they didn't have a future together. Graham had seen random glimpses of his Complement more and more throughout the last year. He wasn't ready for that yet, but he didn't want to stay in a relationship that wasn't going anywhere. Breaking up with him in a letter was the coward's way out, but Graham hoped to see Brooks again soon. He desperately wanted to salvage their friendship.

Graham's mom had invited Lou and Gabrielle to come to Soma as soon as they were ready. She'd extended the invitation to Brooks and Aria as well. If the phone call he was about to make didn't go his way, then it wouldn't be safe for them to stay within the League much longer.

The studio apartment was built for roommates with one wide open space and a wall of bookshelves at the center to divide the space. A sectional sofa sat on one side of the shelves and a full-sized bed on the other. A small kitchen occupied the wall beside the entrance with an enormous bathroom on the other. The second bed sat just beyond the sofa, raised on a platform near a wall of windows. Right now, it was all Graham's, but with Soma filling up, his mom warned him it probably wouldn't stay that way.

Graham set his messenger bag on the sofa and sifted through the contents, retrieving the phone with the blue sticker and his mask. He'd never called the Master before, and his hands trembled at the prospect of what he would say.

Before he could talk himself out of it, he settled the mask over his face, hit send and waited, fully expecting to get the Master's voicemail.

"Grim?" the familiar voice echoed in his ear, not sounding the least bit annoyed by the unexpected call.

"Yes, sir." Graham shot up from the sofa to pace the length of the room. "So sorry to bother you, sir."

"Not at all, son. You caught me with a rare free moment. How was the graduation?"

"Wonderful, thank you for asking." Graham's pulse pounded in his head.

"Was there something you needed?"

"Yes, sir. My brother is getting married," he blurted.

"Well, then congratulations are in order." A note of annoyance crept into the Master's voice. Graham needed to get to the point.

"You see, sir, I'm only twenty-one. Quite young to be heading out on my own."

"I see. Might I venture to guess your mother had an absolute fit when you told her about the job offer?"

Graham sighed with relief. "Yes, sir. She's reluctant to let me travel so far on my own when I don't have family who can accompany me. I would love to accept the job offer, sir, but it might not be possible right now." Graham held his breath, waiting for the Master's response.

"Not to worry, young Grim," he finally responded. "I am a father, after all. I know how difficult it can be for a young man to earn his wings, so to speak. You may continue to work remotely for the time being. Perhaps we could arrange a meeting the next time I'm in the Boston area. I would be happy to set your mother's worries to rest."

"Thank you, sir." Graham pumped a fist in the air. "That would be ideal. I really appreciate you taking my call, I know you're a busy man."

"Well, I am always happy to help those who are loyal to me."

"Of course. You can count on me."

"In the meantime, do try to cut those apron strings. Your youth excuses you now, but I'll have precious little patience for that in the future."

"Yes, sir. I understand."

Graham took a shaky breath as the Master ended the call. It wouldn't last long, but he'd bought some time for himself and those he'd left behind in Salem.

Graham followed the concierge assigned to him upon his arrival. The endless corridors all looked the same as he followed his guide to the dining hall. It was his first full day as a Soma ... resident? Student? He wasn't quite sure what his role would be here. Or if he would even be expected to have one.

"Here is your ID card." The concierge handed him a badge with Graham's picture on it. "Use it to unlock doors, buy food in the dining hall, or clothes from the tailor shop. You'll use this for everything so don't lose it."

Graham nodded, eager to be on his own. "Where could I find Quinn Loukas?"

"Quinn?" The boy arched an incredulous brow at Graham. "Oh, he's a busy man, I'm afraid you'll have to set your sights a little lower. As a new student, you'll need to meet with your advisors to find out what your schedule will be. They'll get you settled with everything you need."

"Well, I'm not so sure I'll be taking any classes. Quinn is my brother, so if you could point me in the direction of his apartment or office, that would be great."

"Brother?" The boy stared at Graham like he had three heads. "Oh wow. I'm so sorry, I didn't realize. Yes, you can find his office on the seventeenth floor."

"Thanks." Graham took his ID badge and headed into the cafeteria. He'd go look for his brother after food. The stress of the last two days had left him exhausted and starving.

Graham made his way through the breakfast line, loading up on pancakes, eggs, and plenty of fruit. No one paid him any attention as he wandered across the dining room, looking for a free table.

Taking a seat, Graham sighed. This felt too much like the college life he'd left behind. He hoped they would let him stay here, even if he had no intention of taking classes or participating in life at Soma. Graham just needed a safe place to keep up his work.

"Graham!" A familiar flash of red hair caught his attention mid-bite. Then the entire dining hall lost their minds as students leapt from their seats to get a closer look. Some standing on their chairs with their phones out.

"Allie?" Graham dropped his fork and shot out of his seat. It was so good to see a familiar face. Allie collided with him, her arms wrapping around him. He hugged her back, trying to ignore the attention they were getting.

"What's with all the staring?" Graham asked, pulling away to get a good look at her. She was the same old Allie. He could see that right away. She was older and stronger, and he knew she'd been through a lot since high school, but she was still Allie.

"I missed you!" Allie pulled him back into an exuberant hug. "Don't mind the staring. You'll get used to it eventually."

"So, you're some kind of princess now?" Graham tried to ignore the onlookers, but they'd grown silent. It was creepy.

"Finish your breakfast and come up to the seventeenth floor." Allie started to back away. "Don't mind me everyone, just greeting an old friend." Allie waved at the crowd. "Er ... as you were."

"I'll come with you." Graham grabbed his tray. "I think I lost my appetite." He eyed the onlookers, dropping his tray off at the return on the way out.

"Sorry about that." Allie cringed. "They think I'm some kind of celebrity, so you'll probably get some of the weirdness by association. I apologize in advance." She skipped ahead of him to push the call button for the elevator. "But I'm so glad you're here!"

"Me too. It's good to be back with family." Graham forced a smile for his old friend.

"Oh no, what's that look for?" Allie frowned. "You don't like it? I can get you a better room if it's too small."

"No, Allie, it's great." Graham rubbed the back of his head. "It's only ... I just graduated MIT. I'm not sure the whole class thing, eating in the dining hall is for me."

"Oh." Allie laughed. "I'll set your concierge straight. You're family. You take whatever classes you want—if you want. Just make yourself at home. No obligations. Though, even I take a few training classes. I could recommend some once you get settled. And you're officially invited to come up to the office level for private meals, or come over to my place on any night when we have food in the house."

"Thanks, Allie." Graham breathed a sigh of relief as the elevator doors opened and a flood of students exited the car, all smiles for their resident princess.

"Anytime, Graham." Allie held the door for him.

"Graham? Who's Graham? Where's..." the frantic voice trailed off as Graham turned toward the one calling his name.

"It's you." The boy fought against the retreating crowd, elbowing his way through.

Graham's brow furrowed as he tried to place him. Then his eyes widened in surprise. "Ezra?" It couldn't be.

The tall, slim young man bounced on the balls of his feet. "Hit any high scores lately?"

Graham's face lit up with a grin he couldn't contain. "I'm on level 76 and it's a tough one." Ezra slammed into him. "How are you here?" He pulled Graham into a hug.

"It's a long story." Graham couldn't believe he was really here. "Shouldn't you be in some crappy Senate training program in Europe?" Graham asked. "How did you get away?"

"It's a long story, mate. I'll tell you all about it over dinner and movie, which needs to happen as soon as possible." Ezra stepped back, looking over his shoulder. "Wes! Come meet Graham."

"What going on here?" Aidan stepped off a second elevator, drifting over to Allie's side.

"Graham?" Aidan grinned. "I heard you finally made it."

"Seems one of your soldiers knows Graham," Allie said.

"Soldiers?" Graham looked from Aidan to Ezra and his best friend, Wes.

"We have a lot of catching up to do, little man." Aidan pulled him into a back slapping hug. "I was right, then, you two did hit it off as friends?"

"We kept in touch." Graham shook his head in confusion.

"Wes is my Syntrophos," Ezra explained. "We've been training with Aidan and Naomi for years."

"I've heard a lot about you." Wes extended his hand. "Probably more than strictly necessary, but if you know Ez, you know how he likes to talk."

Graham smiled, shaking Wes's hand. Maybe this place wouldn't be so bad.

Chapter 29

Chloe | Late Summer | Westbrook, Connecticut

Chloe studied the journal resting in her lap, her eyes drooping from the gentle sway of the train taking her home at last. She'd spent the last four months traveling the west coast, evading her father's attempts to find her. He'd been more persistent this time.

His last note pleaded with her to meet with him just to talk. It was the most reasonable he'd been in years. He almost sounded like the father she remembered. But Chloe had a home she was eager to get back to. She'd been away far too long this time.

She missed her runaways. The rag-tag group of misfits who'd come together to create a loving family. They were the ones she needed now.

Her gift pulled bits of information from her journal. Pieces she'd written and some from Hudson's studies on the old prophecies. She was still trying to figure out why his gift was pointing him toward the past prophecies when he was surrounded by those creating new foretellings about their immediate future.

The future of the Immortal world was dire. That much was certain to Chloe, though she didn't have the gift of prophecy. Things were changing rapidly, and she felt an overwhelming need to understand what her own gifts were trying to tell her.

But her stupid girl brain was focused on one thing only. Seeing Justice again. Four months was a long time to spend alone, missing him, and thinking of him building a life with Scarlet.

As the train slowed, Chloe's heart started to race. In just a short half hour, she would see him again. Maybe this was the time her homecoming would be different. Maybe this time, after months apart, Justice would finally see her.

Maybe he and Scarlet had ended things. Maybe he was ready for something more permanent.

Chloe gathered her things and was the first one off the train and into her waiting Uber. Summer was fading and the New England fall colors were just beginning to make an appearance. Chloe gazed out the window, trying to appreciate the scenery when all she wanted to see was the idyllic little town square of Westbrook.

When the driver let her off at the corner opposite the Westbrook Savings and Loan, Chloe jogged around to the back of the building, waiting impatiently for the old girl to recognize her and let her in.

Finally, she charged up the stairs to the common room. "Hey, guys! I'm home!" She rounded the corner at the top of the stairs and ran right into Dahlia.

"Next time, I'm coming with you." Dahlia wrapped her arms around Chloe, her powerful frame nearly engulfed Chloe's smaller one. "Four months, Chlo. That's way too long."

"I'm so glad to be back." She returned her best friend's hug. "I feel so far out of the loop. How's everyone doing?"

"She's back!" Scarlet came tearing down the stairs from Justice's loft.

So, she's still here. Chloe tried not to sigh with impatience for the perfectly kind-hearted young woman she'd probably adore if she were anyone's girlfriend but Justice's.

Recently, Chloe had let her thoughts turn to Justice more

frequently than she did when at home. To him and the future they would one day have together. Coming home, it was hard to set those dreams aside again.

"Scarlet. Hi." Chloe accepted the tall, slim girl's embrace.

"We were just making some cookies this morning. Can I get you some coffee or tea to go with them? We have so much catching up to do." She bounced eagerly on her feet.

Chloe caught Dahlia's reflection in the mirror hanging over the couch. She was furiously shaking her head, trying to get Scarlet's attention.

"You're not going to believe this. I have huge news!" Scarlet beamed, holding her left hand in Chloe's face. The hand now sporting a tiny diamond ring. "We're engaged!" Scarlet clapped her hands in glee.

"Engaged?" Chloe mouthed the word. "To who?" She managed to get the words out over the lump in her throat.

"To Justice, silly." Scarlet nudged her playfully. "We're going to be like sisters! You know Justice loves you to pieces, so I was hoping you'd be my maid of honor."

Thankfully, Dahlia stepped between Scarlet and Chloe before Fei Long made an unscheduled appearance to tear out Scarlet's stupid throat.

"Hey, Scarlet, why don't you go make us a big pot of *calming* herbal tea?" Dahlia steered her toward the kitchen. "We have so much to talk about. Let's get some snacks, and we'll all get comfy on the sofa and talk all things wedding." Dahlia practically shoved her into the kitchen.

"Eek! I can't wait." Scarlet squealed, disappearing into the kitchen.

"I'm so sorry, Chlo," Dahlia whisper shouted, turning just in time to catch Chloe before she stumbled. "I tried to stop her."

"H-he's mine." Chloe choked, blinking back the tears burning her eyes.

"The idiot still hasn't figured that out yet." Dahlia guided Chloe up the stairs to Justice's loft.

"No." Chloe shook her head, grabbing onto the wall for support. "I'm not ready to see him."

"Oh, Lord, no. You're not ready to see anyone yet, much less the clueless wedding planner back there making a plate of her god-awful cookies. No, we're going to the roof." Dahlia kept them moving past Justice's room to the wide ladder that led up to the roof.

Chloe climbed in a daze, wondering what just happened. How could her Complement be marrying someone else? She lifted her eyes to the bright blue sky, feeling like she might burst.

"Okay." Dahlia shoved her toward the back of the building. "Scream. Let it out, let Fei Long out, breathe fire, whatever you need to do to get through the shock." Dahlia stood back, her bouncy blond curls dancing in the wind.

"Is he *stupid*?" Chloe shouted. "Who gets married like ... like a mortal?" Fei Long came bursting out of her in a vaporous cloud of golden mist and fire. If Chloe was heartbroken, Fei Long was pissed. The angry dragon reared her head back and roared, belching fire and smoke.

"Scream, Chloe! Let it out." Dahlia leaned back and shouted along with Fei Long's snarls of outrage.

Chloe shrieked, and the tears came. She couldn't stay here and watch him get *married.* "He's ruined everything!" Chloe threw her head back and roared, letting all her anger and heartbreak out in a single wail of agony that seared her throat. A wave of lethargy hit her, and she collapsed on the blacktop roof.

She felt empty and emotionless as she stared up at her best friend.

"You know, I was just joking." Dahlia sank down to her knees beside Chloe. "Trying to lighten the mood."

"What?" Chloe's voice sounded like gravel in her raw throat.

"You ... just breathed fire, Chlo." Dahlia gaped at her. "And the sound you made." She shook her head, tears in her own eyes. "I've never heard anything so heartbreaking."

"How can he marry her?" Chloe wiped her face, coming away with streaks of soot on her hands. She'd have to think about the whole breathing-fire thing later. "It doesn't make any sense. Immortals get married once. To their Complements."

"Both Justice and Scarlet have spent a lot of time in the mortal world. They were in foster care, so they have that in common. It makes sense to them. But I don't think he's going to go through with it."

"Whether he does or not, I can't stay here and watch them play house together."

"Where will we go?" Dahlia reached for her hand. "I'm not staying here if you're leaving. Whatever comes next, we do it together."

Chloe clutched her hand, unable to express how much her support meant to her. Though, there was no way Chloe would take Dahlia away from her family. No matter how much Justice had ruined it for her.

"I thought I heard my Chloe up here." Justice came jogging across the blacktop, a huge smile on his stupid perfect face. "You were gone way too long this time." He pulled her up and wrapped his arms around her. "Did you hear my big news?" He leaned back, holding her at arm's length.

Chloe took one look at him and knew he just wasn't ready. He wouldn't be ready until he was. And that was okay. She burst out laughing. "Oh my God, what's wrong with your face?" She grasped onto the one thing that would keep her sane through this difficult conversation.

"I'm going to leave you two to catch up." Dahlia backed away. "Chloe, make him shave that thing off; he's freaking everyone out."

Chloe shook her head. "Is that supposed to be a soul patch on your face? Or is it a fuzzy blond caterpillar curled up under your lip?"

"Ha, ha, funny girl." He grabbed her and tickled her relentlessly.

"Justice, stop!" She laughed. "You have to shave that thing off, seriously."

"Eh, Scarlet likes it." He shrugged, letting her go. "She says it covers my chin butt."

"She wants to change your face?" Chloe stared at him in horror. She loved his little chin dimple. "That's not cool, man. Your face is fine the way it is."

Fei Long hissed at him, sending a puff of smoke and sulfur his way, along with a menacing growl.

"What's your problem, you overgrown lizard?" Justice reached for Fei Long and scratched behind her ears. "You know you missed me."

The traitorous beast leaned into his scratching, her eyes rolling back in her head.

"That's what I thought."

With the mention of his new fiancée, Chloe backed away and sat on the brick parapet at the rear of the building, letting her legs dangle over the side. Fei Long curled up behind her, resting her head on Chloe's lap.

Justice took the space beside the dragon, leaving her head between them.

"Married, huh?" Chloe stared across the forest dotted with roofs and chimneys. She couldn't look at him for fear she might start breathing fire again.

"What can I say? I love her." He shrugged. "It just makes sense for us, you know?"

"No. I can't say I do." Chloe sighed. "She's not the one for you."

"How do you know?" He turned toward her, pulling his knee up to his chest. "She could be."

"Have you bonded with her?"

"No. Not that I know all that much about the Complement bond. It's always felt like this abstract thing, so far ahead of me I can't even imagine it."

"But there's someone else for you, Justice. You could meet her at any given moment."

"It's easy with Scarlet. I've never been good with girlfriends before her. I know it's not forever with us, but who knows when I'll find my Complement? Why can't I have a life with someone I care about while I'm waiting?

"Good point." Chloe nodded, staring at her hands in her lap. She didn't know why she'd never realized it before, but Justice was never going to see her as long as she was right there in front of him. She needed to let him find his own path to her. However long that might take.

"Besides, there is no way I'm ready for my Complement, now or any time soon. I'm a mess and she's ... God, Chloe, she's perfect." He smiled and Chloe's heart nearly stopped in her chest.

"I get these super strong glimpses of her all the time."

"Right." Chloe nodded. She used to get those little insights about him. They stopped when she came to the realization he was right there with her all along. "So ... what's she like?"

"She's powerful and so strong—not just physically, but in every way that really matters. She's got it together too. And I get this feeling she's absolutely smoking hot." He grinned, and Chloe shoved him.

"Seriously, though, I'm so not ready for that kind of woman. I can sense she's waiting patiently for me to get my life together."

"So, what, you're practicing on Scarlet?" Chloe didn't want to admit to herself how much his words had lifted her spirits. She still couldn't stay and watch him marry another woman, but the ache in her chest had lessened some.

"I do love her, Chlo." He gave her a pleading look, begging with his eyes for her to understand and give him her blessing. "We both know it's not forever, but it just ... it feels like the right next step for us. Like if I can make it work with Scarlet, it will help me be ready for something more permanent when the time comes."

He had no idea he was asking his Complement to step aside for another woman. That he was tearing her to shreds right there on the rooftop. And he would never see it if Chloe didn't give him the space he needed.

"Married?" Chloe shook her head, forcing a smile. "Such a big step."

"A grown-up step." Justice grinned. "I'm scared to death. You gotta be there for me. Be my best man or whatever the mortals call it."

"I don't know if I can be the maid of honor and the best man."

"You're mine. I saw you first." He moved to stand, offering her his hand. "Come with me. I have to show you something."

Chloe took his hand, a wave of sadness hitting her at the feel of his palm against her skin. He wasn't hers. Not yet. Right now, he belonged with Scarlet. But someday, he would be hers forever. She would have to be okay with that.

Chloe followed him back to his room, trying not to think about how much everything was about to change.

"There you two are." Scarlet bent over the sofa, fluffing a bright red pillow that hadn't been there the last time Chloe ventured into Justice's room. She supposed it really wasn't just his domain anymore. She gazed around the room at all the brightly colored decor Scarlet had brought to the space. It so wasn't Justice. He preferred muted colors and minimal clutter.

Chloe arched a brow at him as if to ask, is this what you really want? He just smiled and shrugged in response.

"I thought we could all hang out in the common room this afternoon and do some wedding planning now that the maid of honor is back." Scarlet beamed at them both.

"Oh, no, Scarlet, Chlo's my best man. You're going to have to fight me for her." Justice pulled Chloe against his side.

"Oh, you don't think I will?" She stood, grinning with her hands on her hips. "I'm so glad you're finally home. It's weird when one of us is missing."

One of us? Chloe needed to start thinking of Scarlet as part of the family if this was really happening.

"Could you give us a minute, Scarlet?" Justice nodded toward the end of the room.

"Oh, right. Yes, I'll just be downstairs if you need me. Dahlia's planning a huge welcome home dinner tonight. I'll go help her in the kitchen." Scarlet was all smiles as she made her way down to the kitchen to bother Dahlia. Seriously, Scarlet was not so great in the kitchen.

"What's up, J?" Chloe pulled away from him, needing some distance.

"I have something to show you." He turned toward his mural wall, reaching for the curtain of sheets covering it from prying eyes.

"This probably won't make any sense to you. I've come to terms with the fact that no one will ever see exactly what I see. I'll do my best to translate it accurately." He pulled the cord, sliding the sheet-curtain to reveal half of the wall covered with his latest work.

Chloe gasped, stumbling back onto the chair behind her. Staring back at her was her. An enormous portrait of Chloe covered the wall, but it wasn't the Chloe she saw when she looked in the mirror. This version of her was a bit older and much more beautiful than she'd ever hoped to be.

Justice scratched his head. "I think you can see I missed you something awful." He laughed, giving Chloe a moment to view his work.

"It's beautiful." Chloe choked back the tears that threatened to spill. "Way more beautiful than I am in real life, that's for sure." There was something of her mother staring back at her.

"I think this is how my gift sees you. It's like my soul's interpretation of yours." He crouched beside her, taking her hand.

He was so close to seeing it. Chloe closed her eyes. What he just said reminded her of something her mother once said about the way Complements see each other. That they most often will see things about the other that no one else could understand. That's what Justice brought out in his painting of his Complement. Yet, he still didn't recognize her.

"There's a lot more here than a portrait." Justice squeezed her hand. "Bear with me while I try to interpret this prophecy."

"About me?" Chloe tore her eyes from his painting.

"Yes. You're on the wrong path, Chlo." Justice blurted. "You're caught somewhere in the middle of where you set out to go and where you need to go from here. I think we're holding you back." He moved to sit on the arm of the chair. "Does any of this make sense to you?" He peered down at her. "I don't want to you to lose yourself, but I'm afraid you're nearing the point of no return."

"What does that mean?"

Justice sighed and moved back to the wall to pull the curtain again, revealing the other side of the wall. It was a second portrait of Chloe. This one was dark and ugly. A twisted mirror image of the other Chloe. She stared down at them with a disdainful sneer, her dark smoky eyes smoldering with hate.

"What does it mean?" Chloe covered her mouth with her

hands. She couldn't take her eyes off the evil version of herself because that was exactly how this painting felt. Evil. Her eyes filled with tears, and her heart skipped a few beats. She didn't want to look at it anymore. "Cover it up, please," her voice cracked with the weight of her emotions.

"I don't know when or how it will happen, but you are headed toward becoming that Chloe." He pointed at the dark portrait. "A power-hungry, anger-filled version of yourself you won't like." He moved to cover his work.

Chloe scrubbed at her tears. His words reminded her of something Allie once said. Back then, Allie gave her the nudge she'd needed to leave Kelleys Island behind. Now, it seemed Justice was doing the same.

"My prophecy says if you don't make a significant change now, you will embrace the coming darkness and the one who will bring it, destroying the Immortal world as we know it."

Chloe shook her head. "I can't have that much sway in the future of our world. I'm just Chloe." She turned wide eyes on him.

"And I'm just a Prophet who paints what he sees." Justice took her hand again. "I don't know how to help you, but I guess sometimes even the guide needs a little guidance. Do whatever you feel you need to do and don't feel bad about it."

Chloe gave one more glance at the paintings. "Paint over it." Chloe stood. "Consider the message gratefully received." She squeezed his hand one last time and turned to join the others downstairs.

Chloe had a lot to think about. Where could she go if not here?

"Knock-knock?" Hudson stuck his head into Chloe's room.

"What's up, Huds?" Chloe sat curled up on her couch, staring out the arched window over the town square. For the last few days, she'd stayed in her room on the pretense of all the studying she had to catch up on when really, she was trying to decide her next move. And avoid Scarlet and her incessant wedding planning.

Whoever heard of a couple of Immortal kids getting fake-married like foolish idiots. She shook her head in annoyance. It would be an entirely different story if they were Complements, but they weren't.

"I can come back later if you want." Hudson stood stooped in her doorway.

"No, come on in. I could use a welcome distraction."

"Would you look over these old prophecies with me again? I've gathered a few more bits and pieces, but I still can't make heads or tails of it, and my gift just won't let me leave it alone." He perched on the edge of the couch beside her, nudging the cat-sized Fei Long out of the way.

"She's decided she likes belly rubs, so you're probably not getting out of here without a good half-hour of scratching her belly." Chloe helped him move the sun-drowsed dragon to the other end of the couch.

"You have the strangest pet." Hudson chuckled, shaking his head at the lazy dragon.

"Let me take a look at what you've got." Chloe pulled his journal onto her lap. "Wow, you have been busy." She flipped through the pages, seeing more of the prophecies filled out from his translations and the hodgepodge he'd collected over the last months.

"Tell me this speaks to you?" Hudson rubbed a weary hand over his face.

"When was the last time you slept?" Chloe examined his bleary eyes.

"A few days, I think." He shrugged. "Whenever I lay down, all I see are these stupid prophecies that don't mean anything." He sat back with a sigh. "I'm exhausted and so sick of studying this, but my gift is like a dog with a bone."

Fei Long lifted her head, sniffing at Hudson's hands.

"She likes bones now." Chloe gestured toward the plush doggy bed she'd put in front of the window. It looked like a bone yard now, covered in half-eaten bits of charred bone.

"You do know she's terrifying, right?"

"What? Oh, she likes to cook them first." Chloe smoothed a hand over the page with Hudson's neat scrawl. "This is impressive, Huds." Chloe's gift pulled bits of information from the pages, rearranging them and fixing some of the translation errors.

"This is really interesting." Chloe tucked her feet under her and pointed to a line of text. "I think this is speaking of the rise of the Syntrophos."

Hudson wrinkled his brow. "I thought those were a myth from the Indriell legends."

"Oh no, they're very real. My nephew Quinn is Syntrophos to one of my best friends from back home." Chloe ran her finger down the page, trying to see what the old Prophets said about those like Sasha and Quinn, and Allie and Darius. Back when those bonds had formed for her friends, Chloe wondered if Graham might have been her Syntrophos, but it never happened for them, and they were both secretly jealous of the bonds the others shared.

"This reference here about an army of bonded *beloved*, though but a mere handful, will change the world—is that speaking of the Syntrophos?" Hudson looked to her for guidance.

"I think so. I don't know all that much about them. I didn't pay much attention to anything beyond my own grief after my mother was killed."

"I'm sorry if this brings all that up for you." Hudson reached for his journal as if to leave.

"No, it's okay." Chloe held onto the book, glancing at Fei Long. "It's odd, you know. I don't feel that overwhelming grief anymore. I haven't for a long time."

"I just don't understand what these things have in common. There are references to armies and what sounds to me like a roving mass of insane zombies. Then, there are assassins, spies, and queens. It's just a mess." He leaned back, resting his head against the couch cushions.

"Well, first of all, you need to rest. You're not going to get anywhere with this until you take care of yourself." Chloe set the book aside and went over to her bookshelf, sorting through the tins of tea and dried herbs.

"Make a pot of tea with this tonight. Let it steep until it's as strong as you can stand it. It will help ease your mind." She handed him the tin of tea.

"What's in it?" Hudson frowned, a doubtful look on his face.

"Lavender, chamomile, and magnolia bark, with valerian root, skull cap, and ashwagandha root." Her mother's recipe for a good night's rest when the mind just wouldn't allow it. "Brew it strong so it's potent enough to do the job. It tastes pretty bad though, so you'll want to chug it."

"Gotcha. Then what?"

"Then, we'll keep working at it." Chloe nudged him toward the door. "Can I make a copy of this?" She clutched his journal.

"Keep it. I have other copies." Hudson leaned down to give her a hug. "Not sure what we'd do without you."

"Love you too, Huds. Now go get some sleep." Chloe managed to get the door shut behind him before the tears came. She was going to miss them all so much. But like Allie once told her, sometimes self-care needed to come first.

Justice's vision of the evil Chloe would haunt her forever. She had to act now. They would be okay for a little while under Porcia's guidance. Chloe would see them all again soon. At least she hoped.

She moved back to the couch, her eyes darting across the pages of Hudson's journal. Her gift pulled her toward the words, rearranging and sorting the prophecies that had likely been lost to the world for ages. With the guidance of his gift, Hudson had managed to pull them back together through his studies. It still wasn't quite there yet. But maybe she could finish what he'd started.

She pulled a stack of letters from the gap between the couch cushions where she'd sat most of the day, writing her goodbyes, leaving careful instructions and reminders to each of her family. For the twins, she reminded them to eat something green and leafy at least once a day and to keep working on their investigation of the League of Ancients. There was something going on there that was vital they understand. That Graham was caught up in it all still worried her.

But she was going to find out exactly what he was up to very soon.

For Hudson, she reminded him to sleep so he could keep his mind sharp and to get out of the house every once in a while before he turned into a legit hermit.

For Justice, she'd thanked him for pushing her and wished him all the best in his life with Scarlet. His letter had been the most difficult to write because she wasn't certain when she would see him again. It could be months. Years. A lifetime.

For Dahlia, she left the longest letter with instructions on what needed to come next. She trusted her best friend to carry out her wishes to the finest detail and to protect their little family of Scholars and Prophets.

Now, there was nothing left to do but leave the home she'd come to love more than any other.

Chapter 30

Chloe | Early Fall | Sterling Tower

Chloe sat on the park bench, staring up at Sterling Tower. Everything within her screamed to run away. That she couldn't possibly go back to being everyone's little sister. The overlooked and often forgotten little Chloe. Not quite warrior, not quite Scholar.

But the haunting image of Justice's portrait refused to leave her mind. For the girl who knew everyone else's best choice, she had no idea which path would lead her away from the doom and gloom version of herself Justice foretold. She only knew she needed to make a big change and hoped for the best outcome.

Would they even take her back after the way she left? The way she'd cut them all out of her life, never looking back, never checking in?

Chloe chewed her bottom lip. Grandpa Alex claimed it would be as easy as walking across the street. He and Navid had tried to get her to come inside with them, but she had something she needed to do first. A question she needed to ask.

"Chloe?"

Chloe turned toward the familiar voice. She'd changed since

the last time Chloe saw her. Allie was strong, confident. A warrior through and through.

Chloe immediately second guessed her decision to come here. She didn't belong in the past with her old friends. But had nowhere else to go.

"Allie." Chloe stood, her chest tightening with anxiety. White noise rushed over her. Indecision engulfed Allie like a dense fog. The thin red lines of Chloe's gift shot off in a thousand different directions. Soma sent Chloe's gifts into overdrive, and she wasn't sure she could survive the noise.

"It's good to see you." Allie came to stand in front of her.

"It's been a while." Chloe shifted nervously on her feet. "I hear you're some kind of princess now." One way too busy for the likes of Chloe Long and her silly dragon.

"Something like that," Allie said dryly, and Chloe heard a hint of her old friend in her tone. "Would you like to come inside? See what we're about?"

Chloe had thought a lot about what she might say to Allie. What excuse she could give for coming. One that didn't start with, *I can't watch my Complement marry his girlfriend, but I don't have anywhere else to go, can I crash on your couch?*

"You train people here? People with modern gifts?" Chloe blurted the partial lie she'd concocted on the train ride south.

"We do. And we guarantee your safety while you are here. The only way in and out is through Quinn's barrier." She gestured over her shoulder at the entrance to the building.

"Yeah. I forgot he's a dream walker, right?" Chloe flushed. She'd failed miserably in keeping up with her childhood friends.

"Right." Allie nodded. "Why don't we just sit here? You can tell me about whatever you're struggling with." She gestured at the bench where Chloe had met with Alex and Navid just minutes ago. She hadn't expected Allie to drop everything to come out here right away.

"It's too much," Chloe said, dropping down onto the bench. "I can't handle it anymore."

"What is it? Your path of least resistance?"

Chloe gave a halfhearted smile. "Yes. I forgot you called it that. It was always more of an intuition when I was a kid. Now, it's evolving into a physical manifestation of my gift, where I can actually see all the decisions the people around me struggle with and how all those decisions are connected. And the sheer volume of the voices is more than I can handle. I used to be able to silence them, but I can't seem to control it anymore. I'm back to wearing headphones all the time now." It was mostly true. She did resort to wearing her headphones more often lately. It just wasn't the real reason she was here.

"So, it's more information than you can possibly process at once?" Allie asked.

"Yes. That's it exactly." She hadn't even thought about it that way before. But it was so often an information overload—had been for a long time now. Maybe there was something she could learn here. "I haven't had a mentor in a long time, but I've always been able to handle my progress on my own. Until now."

"Graham and I are in a class that would probably help you." Allie sat relaxed and at ease beside her. It was like all the years melted away and they were just two friends again.

"Graham's here?" Her voice shook with emotion. He was safe? She breathed a sigh of relief that he'd found his way out of the trouble he'd been headed for the last time she saw him.

"He just arrived a few weeks ago after his graduation from MIT. We're all here, actually. Right where we need to be. And we'd love to have you join us. Graham and I are both struggling with the same thing you are. Our gifts are overloading us with too much information that's made it almost impossible to function. My visions are constant. I see them everywhere I go. Even now, they are swarming all around you, demanding my attention.

Some days, I can hardly handle it. But I'm coping. We have a new teacher who is helping us learn to process what our gifts are trying to tell us faster, so we aren't crippled by what we see and hear."

"That sounds like exactly what I need." Chloe leaned forward, her elbows on her knees. It was strange to feel like she had something in common with her more powerfully gifted friends. "But can I really come back? To the family?" Chloe managed to get the question out before she changed her mind.

"Of course, you can. But here, it is mostly just old friends. The family comes and goes frequently, but Soma is a place for the young."

"Dad's going to come find me here if I stay too long." Chloe wasn't at all ready for that reunion.

"And we would let him in with open arms. But you don't have to see him if you don't want to." Allie leaned in, her earnest eyes filled with so much love and concern Chloe wasn't sure she could handle it. She didn't deserve it.

"It's too hard. Seeing him without Mom."

"I actually understand how difficult that is for you. The man who greeted you is my natural father, Navid. My mother was killed the same way your mother was. I never knew her the way you knew and loved Ming Lao, but knowing I won't ever have that chance is painful."

"It still hurts, Allie. So much," Chloe whispered, choking back the fears and grief that would have Fei Long returning in a ball of flame any moment. She didn't need to freak Allie out with that just yet.

"I know. But maybe we can offer you a respite from the pain." Allie took her hand. "And if Jin shows up, then maybe my father could help him too. Will you come inside with me?"

Chloe nodded and stood. "I can't promise I'll stay." Part of her wanted to leave now, before she even asked the questions she came here to ask. The book of prophecies sat in her messenger bag, waiting for someone to figure out what they all meant.

Allie draped her arm around Chloe. "You can leave whenever you want. All you have to do is ask."

They turned toward the front of the building, and Chloe gasped when Navid appeared through a rent in the atmosphere.

"Don't worry, it's just the dreamworld protecting us." Allie grasped her hand. "Quinn and my father are dream walkers. They've surrounded Sterling Tower with a layer of the dreamworld. No one can enter without a walker to escort them in."

"Impressive." Chloe followed Allie to the strange opening. "Just ... before I go in there." Chloe paused, playing with the cord of her headphones.

"Spit it out, Chlo. It's just me. They might call me First Princess now, and I'm sure I've changed over the years, but I'm still me."

Chloe smiled at that. She really did sound like the old Allie. "My friends. I don't know if they're really safe where they are right now."

"Bring them here." Allie shrugged as if it were that easy. Maybe it was.

"They're mostly Scholars. A few have prophetic gifts." Prophets were rare. She didn't want to out Justice. If he chose to come here, she wanted him to be able to keep his gift for prophecy a secret if he chose.

"We have lots of Scholars here. Lots of Techs too. We don't discriminate, Chlo. All are welcome." Allie took a deep breath. "But you should know, I've managed to tick off the entire Immortal Senate. They're not too happy with me or my position here at Soma."

"You wouldn't be you if you weren't ticking someone off." Chloe smiled and followed Allie into the dreamworld.

They said you can never go home. Soma wasn't home. But

maybe it could be.

Chloe followed Allie down the endless corridors, cringing at all the whispering and staring that came with being seen with the First Princess.

Allie seemed to take it in stride. Awkwardly waving and smiling at those they passed. She was the same old goofball she was when they were kids.

"We're packed like sardines in here," Allie called over her shoulder, tapping away on her phone. "We don't have any private rooms left, but how do you feel about rooming with Graham?"

Chloe breathed a sigh of relief. "That could work." She felt confident they could reconnect, especially after her last conversation with Graham nearly a year and a half ago. It had been easy then and she really hoped it could be that way again.

"He's probably in his room working." Allie turned a corner and held a door open for Chloe. "He keeps to himself most days, but he comes up to the penthouse in the evenings to hang out."

Chloe followed her up a short flight of stairs. "It's *almost* been like old times." Allie shot her a wink. "We've been hardcore missing Chloe lately. I can't wait for us all to be together again at Quinn and Santi's wedding."

"Wedding?" Chloe halted on the landing.

"Sorry, *bonding* ceremony." Allie rolled her eyes and pointed to her head. "I'm afraid the mortal brain is here to stay."

"He and Santi are Complements?" Chloe barely remembered the girl her nephew had brought home when he escaped Soma.

"Crazy, right? They're way too young to get married." Allie stepped into a quiet hallway.

"For real." Chloe muttered. But at least they were Complements and not just playing house like some people.

"Here we are." Allie stopped at a door near the end of the hall. "He doesn't know you're here yet. I thought we could surprise him."

"Okay." Chloe nodded. She'd been inside Soma for maybe twenty minutes. Her mind was reeling with how much her life was about to change.

"It's okay, Chlo." Allie draped an arm across her shoulders. "It's weird coming home after all this time. No one's going to push you. That's why I brought you here to get settled with Graham first. Just take small steps from day to day. Before you know it, Soma will feel like home."

Chloe took her first small step and knocked on the door herself. But Graham didn't answer.

"Hi, Allie." An unfamiliar boy opened the door with a pair of dogs dancing at his feet. "Come on in, he's just too lazy to get off his bum and answer the door," the boy spoke with a British accent.

"I heard that." Graham's familiar voice set Chloe's nerves at ease.

"Wait a second." The boy smiled. "You must be Chloe." He held the door open, waving for them to step inside. "I've heard so much about you."

"Chloe?" Graham jumped up from the couch and leaped over the back of it as Allie and Chloe stepped into the foyer of the small apartment. "Are you here, here?" He pulled her into a warm, familiar hug, running his hands up and down her arms as if to make sure she was real.

"As opposed to astral projection?" The boy shared a laugh with Allie.

"Turns out I need to crash on your couch." Chloe glanced at the cute boy who seemed very at home in Graham's apartment. "At least for a few days."

"No way, roomie." Graham hugged her close. "You live here now."

"Are you sure? I don't want to impose."

"Come in, come in." Graham tugged her bag off her shoulder and moved to set it on a bed behind the massive bookshelf in the center of the space. "This is your room back here. Mine is over there." He pointed to the bed in the corner along a bank of windows overlooking the city. "There's not much privacy, but we'll be fine. I can't believe you're here." He turned, grinning at Allie. "How did you talk her into coming?"

"I didn't. She just showed up and I brought her straight up here. You'll help her get settled into whole Soma thing?"

"Sure. It's not so bad once you get used to the staring and whispering."

"We'll leave you two to get reacquainted." The boy called his dogs to heel.

"Oh, I'm sorry." Graham shook his head. "This is my friend, Ezra. Ezra, Chloe."

"You and I will bond later." Ezra leaned in to hug Chloe. "Don't worry, you'll love me."

"He's an acquired taste," Allie whisper-shouted. "Call me if you need anything. Graham has my number."

"Okay, bye." Graham shooed them both through the door along with Ezra's dogs. With a deep breath, he turned around. "Are you okay?" He grabbed Chloe's hands and towed her over to the couch.

"I don't know. Yes." She shook her head. "I'm fine, I promise. Just overwhelmed. It was time to move on and I didn't have anywhere else to go." She shrugged, unbidden tears welled in her eyes and for a horrified moment she thought she might lose it right here in the new studio apartment she couldn't pay for.

"Shake it off, Chlo. It's just me." Graham paced to the kitchen. "Relax and I'll make some tea. We'll watch a movie and if you feel like talking at some point, then cool. If not, I totally get it."

Tears streamed down her face, and she let out a stifled sob. She couldn't hold it in any longer. As her power churned within, Fei Long came out in a burst of golden mist.

"Holy shit, what the Sam-Hell?" Graham dropped a stainless-steel mug on the floor. It bounced on the marble tile, but he couldn't seem to take his eyes off Fei Long.

"Rein it in Fei," Chloe murmured, wiping her eyes. "You're too big and clumsy for such a small room."

"She's Ahh ... she's changed a bit since the last time I saw her." Graham leaned down to pick up the mug and went back to making tea.

Chloe loved him for pretending like having a giant golden dragon appear in his living room was no big deal.

"What's her name?"

"Fei Long. She's kind of a brat."

The dragon hissed at her, but she shifted her form into a smaller one and hopped up on the couch to make herself at home. Turning in a circle, she sniffed the air, curled up in the corner of the sectional and stuck her tongue out at Chloe.

"Wow." Graham's shoulders shook with laughter. "Did she just tell you off?"

"Pretty much." Chloe laughed. "I'm just really glad she can't actually speak."

Graham carried a tray from the kitchen into the living room, taking the seat farthest from Fei Long, leaving Chloe between them.

"So ... what's new?" Graham poured hot water over Jasmine pearls, adding a bit of honey just the way she liked it.

That small gesture said he still knew her like he always had. The dam broke inside her, and Chloe spilled her guts to her childhood best friend.

CHAPTER 31

Graham | Early Fall | Sterling Tower

Graham lay on the grass, staring up at the puffy white clouds of the idyllic afternoon. The terrarium warehouse was Graham's favorite place in all of Soma. That and the studio apartment he shared with Chloe. When it was just him, the apartment was his least favorite place. But with Chloe there now, it felt like home.

He turned to watch her lying beside him, her eyes closed in peaceful contemplation of her gift. That was what they were supposed to be doing right now. Focusing on the sheer volume of information their gifts delivered to them, sorting through the bulk of it as Gabe had taught them. Look at the big picture first and then break it down into manageable parts for closer examination later when they were ready for the next stage.

Gabe was a great teacher. Apparently, he had worked for Soma back in the days when it wasn't a safe place. He was all too happy to stay on once he'd proven himself to the First Princess. Allie had talked Graham into taking Gabe's class and he was glad he'd agreed—despite his heavy workload working for the Grand Master.

Now, with Gabe's guidance and the surety of Graham's safety behind his brother's dreamworld barrier, he was free to sort, translate, and examine the Master's communications without hindrance or worry of being found out. And with Gabe's help, he was getting through more data than he ever had before.

Of course, the League would eventually realize he'd abandoned them. There was only so long the Alderman would give him for his "trip home" for his brother's bonding ceremony. He just hoped Uncle Lou and Aunt Gabrielle could buy enough time to get their affairs in order and make the move to Sterling Tower before the Alderman discovered Graham wasn't returning. And he really hoped Brooks would come with them.

Brooks. Graham sighed. He really missed their friendship, and he hated the way he'd left things, but a lot had changed for Graham in the months since his move to Atlanta.

A hesitant hand reached for his, and Graham smiled, turning to the boy who occupied his thoughts more than he was ready to admit.

Ezra. He still couldn't believe he was here at Soma. Graham wasn't sure he would ever truly grasp all Ezra and his Syntrophos family had been through during their time with the Milan initiative, but having him here in person was ... everything. It was like finding family.

"What are you thinking about?" Ezra lay close to his side, his warm fingers wrapped around Graham's. "You know, even though our entire friendship existed in the digital world until recently, I can still read you like a book. You're cracked about something, mate."

"Cracked?" Graham laughed. He loved Ezra's Britishisms.

"I'm sorry." Ezra cleared his throat and went into a horrible American accent. "You're bothered about something, my friend. What gives?"

"Ez, we've talked about your terrible accents." Wes gave his Syntrophos a lazy shove from his spot on the grass on Ezra's other side. "Stick to the one you're good at."

"I wasn't talking to you. You know I have other friends now. Ones who happen to appreciate my accents and my fashion sense, thank you." He turned back to Graham with a smile Graham struggled to resist. "Seriously, what's bothering you?"

"Oh, just the usual, too many things on my mind at once." Graham scowled up at the sky, trying to remind himself he'd only sort of ended his last relationship. It wouldn't be over until he talked to Brooks in person, but he wasn't taking Graham's calls. "Do you guys know how annoying it is to have a mind that can't seem to settle on a single thought?"

"I do." Chloe raised her hand, her eyes still closed with a contented look on her face. "It's super annoying." She and Graham both threw their hands up at the same time, slapping a high five like they did when they were little kids. Both dissolved into a fit of giggles. It was good to be home.

Home wasn't the house where he'd grown up. Home was with the people he loved. He glanced back at Ezra, ever the cool, fashionable Brit in his dark sunglasses and Hawaiian shirt.

"You two are adorable." Ezra smiled, turning toward Graham. "You sure you're not Syntrophos?"

"Definitely," Chloe chimed in. "We will leave that complicated crap to Wez."

"Wez?" Wes burst out laughing. "I love it. I'm going to make everyone start calling us that."

"I think my name should come first." Ezra frowned. "Ez-resly. Or maybe Ez-res. I like that one."

"It's totally Wez, Ez." Chloe shot him a smirk.

"Yeah, you can't make up your own ship name," Graham added. "It's not how it's done."

"I don't know." Ezra smirked at them over the rim of his sunglasses. "You two act like Syntrophos. We'll call you Gram-oloe."

"You're really bad at that." Chloe snorted.

"We're not Syntrophos. We're just two old besties, who manage to pick up where they left off no matter what they've been through. Right, Chlo?" Graham nudged her. It was weird being back with their old friends, but from the moment Chloe knocked on his door, all the years vanished between them.

"Right." She forced a smile, something she didn't think he knew she was doing whenever she felt out of place here. "Oh look, it's Parker." Chloe sat up, watching Emma and Daniel walking toward them with his baby brother stumbling between them.

"Hey, buddy." Graham sat up, holding his hands out when Parker screeched at the sight of him. He loved that kid more than anything in the world, and so did Ezra.

"Bubba." The little boy ran across the grassy hill, a little unsteady on his feet as he flung himself into Graham's arms.

"I missed you, little bubba." Graham hugged him tight. "Where did you come from?"

"D' sky. Daddy flew." Parker danced a little jig and fell on his rear end.

"Dad uses just about any excuse to fly that plane of his down here."

"Hey now, we were due for a visit." Daniel came to sit with them on the grass. "We missed our boys."

"Parker, look at mommy," Emma called, her camera at the ready. "Give big bubba a hug. We need more family photos with your brothers."

Parker ignored their mom in favor of making funny faces at Ezra who was already reaching for him.

"Hi, Parker. Come to Uncle Ezra." Ezra beamed a smile at the baby.

"Ra!" Parker squealed and reached for Ezra's nose. Ezra scooped him up and buried his face in the baby's hair.

"Oh, sorry. I forgot to warn you guys about the nose grabbing." Emma sighed as she came to join them. "He thinks he's collecting them."

"Did you steal Uncle Ezra's nose? Oh, he still has that sweet baby smell." Ezra hugged him close. "One of these days, I'm going to have a least six babies just like you, and I'm going to spend all day spoiling them rotten."

Emma laughed. "He's sweet smelling now, but give him a minute and you'll change your mind about that." Emma sat between Daniel and Chloe who was sporting one of her fake smiles. Even here among her family, she was still pining for her Complement. The one who was too thick to see how great she was.

Graham couldn't imagine how hard that must be for her. He was so ready for it himself; he just knew in his soul that the moment he laid eyes on his Complement he was going to be a goner.

Brooks would understand.

He glanced back at Ezra, his heart coming to a complete stop for a brief moment. The girls erupted out of him, zooming around him with their excited babble.

Graham sat up straighter, blinking at the glare from the sun off the lake. Something warm and tingly rocketed up his arm and through his chest.

"You okay, Graham?" Chloe frowned at him. "You look like you've seen a ghost."

Ezra shot up from his spot on the grass beside Graham. "What's happening?" His eyes filled with hope.

"It's you." Graham reached for him. "It's always been you." He shook his head, his heart in his throat.

"Oh my God, you figured it out? You know?" Ezra launched at him, pulling Graham into his arms, tears in his eyes.

He pulled away, searching Graham's face. "You better not be having a go at me, mate."

"How long have you known?" Graham managed to get the words out. He was having an epic moment he never wanted to forget. His entire world shifted on its axis. Ezra was his Complement. The girls exploded into a cloud of glittering blue light that rained down on Ezra and Graham, enveloping them in a cocoon of warmth.

"I've known since I saw you waiting for that elevator with Allie. I think I always knew." Ezra reached to touch his face, like he wanted to make sure Graham was real. "You created that magic phone that pretty much saved my life. How could you not be meant for me?"

"Let's give these two some space, shall we?" Emma gathered Parker up in her arms, trying to hide the tears in her eyes. Graham hardly noticed his family. He was lost inside his own world that now and forever would include Ezra.

"No!" Chloe gasped. "No! It's not fair. They hardly had to wait at all. They literally *just* met in person."

Graham was too caught up in the most profound moment of his life to notice his best friend's distress. He lifted his hand to touch Ezra's face, in complete awe of what was happening.

"It's just us now," Ezra whispered. "For the rest of our lives together, you are all I will ever need, Graham Loukas."

Graham pulled him close, their lips meeting in an electrifying kiss that promised so much more when the time was right for their bonding. It was unlike anything Graham had ever felt before.

"I should have known." Graham shook his head. "It shouldn't have taken me this long to see it. You've been there with me through it all. Whenever something happened, good or bad, even the silly inconsequential things, you've been the one I've wanted to share it with." Graham grasped his hands, never wanting to let go.

"Now you know, that's all that matters." Ezra beamed the

most beautiful smile at him, and Graham vowed right there that he would try to put that same smile on his future husband's face every day of their lives together.

"Wait." Graham pulled back to peer at Ezra's face. "You want how many babies?"

Chapter 32

Chloe | Early Fall | Sterling Tower

"No, Daniel, put me down!" Chloe shouted at her older brother. Her eyes rolled back in her head as a jealous rage flooded her body. "It's not fair!"

Power churned in her chest, hot and furious. She didn't even have time to warn Daniel before Fei Long came bursting out of her in a blaze of fire and golden scales.

White-hot fire spewed from Chloe's mouth in a roar of fury, smoke, and sulfur. Rage filled her senses until she saw red.

Children ran screaming up the grassy slope from the lake, but Chloe couldn't see anything beyond her anger. All the pent-up emotions she'd bottled up since her return came rushing out of her.

"Chloe!" Daniel called to her through the wall of flames she'd brought forth.

Tilting her head back to the sky, she let out an otherworldly snarl. The echo of Fei Long's roar bounced off the mountain in the distance, testing the boundaries of the warehouse.

Chloe and her dragon stood within a ring of fire where no one could reach them. For once, she didn't have to plaster on a fake smile. She didn't have to pretend that her heart hadn't broken into a thousand pieces when she left Justice behind to marry another woman.

She didn't have to hide her pain from the others who would never understand what it felt like walking away from her Complement, not knowing when she'd see him again.

Chloe collapsed on the charred ground, tears and soot streaking her face.

"Well, this is a new one," a familiar voice sounded behind her. "A fire-breathing, dragon-wielding Immortal is definitely one for the books."

She looked up just as Aidan stepped through the ring of fire, completely unharmed. He crouched beside her, wiping the tears from her face with his thumbs.

"Oh, how well I know this pain." He held out his hand. "Come with me."

"Leave me alone, Aidan." She hung her head. "This isn't the kind of thing you can just use your gift to make me all better."

"Believe me, I know. There's only one thing that will help this." He took her hand and pulled her up from the ground she and Fei Long torched. Most everyone had seen her dragon by now, but the fire show was probably not going to go over well.

"I swear, Aidan McBrien, if you try to take me out for ice cream right now, I will set my dragon on you so fast, even you won't be able to outrun her."

Aidan threw his head back and laughed. "I always knew you were going to be a force to be reckoned with."

Chloe stared around the wide circle of fire. "You know, you might be able to walk through fire and not get burned, but I'm not so sure I can."

"No worries." Aidan lifted his hand and snuffed out the fire.

The warehouse was deserted. Except for the two lovebirds lost in their own little world down by the lake. An earthquake wouldn't get their attention now.

"Let's get you away from here." Aidan steered her toward the doors to the tower. "We don't need a repeat."

Chloe couldn't take her eyes off Graham and Ezra, and to her horror, she started to cry again. Not silent sad tears, but blubbering, ugly sobs.

"You need to hit something, Chlo. We both do." Aidan gave a lingering look at the happy couple, and she swore she saw a bit of her own rage and fury reflected in his eyes.

"You *know*." She stumbled after him down the long concrete hall leading away from the warehouse. "You know what this feels like, don't you?"

"Like you'd relish the opportunity to murder every happy couple you've ever seen? Yeah, I'm familiar with the feeling."

"Who?" She stepped onto the elevator behind him, Fei Long stuffing herself in with them.

"Not here." He shook his head, punching the button for the gymnasium.

Allie insisted on closing the gym in the late afternoons to give everyone a chance to enjoy some downtime after training and classes.

Aidan typed in a code at the door and held it open for her. The place was empty. "Punching bag." He pointed to a row of them. "Trust me, it will help."

Chloe set off across the gym, the anger still coursing through her veins.

"Let it all out, Chlo." Aidan hopped up on a low half-wall to watch her. Fei Long paced anxiously behind her.

"It's not fair!" She threw a bare-knuckled punch at the bag, sending it swinging wildly. She could still taste the sulfur in her mouth, and a puff of smoke curled from her nose as she threw another punch, and another. Her dragon let out a mournful roar of solidarity.

"Stupid, clueless *Prophet*!" She kicked the bag, shaking her head. "He's never going to see it." Chloe flew into a series of high kicks, sending the bag slamming into the one beside it. "Justice is an idiot. I love him, but he's slow ... and so ... un-self-aware."

Chloe met the swinging bag with her fists, taking out all her frustrations on the harmless bag. "He's also brilliant, talented, and one of the kindest human beings I've ever met." Smoke puffed from her mouth with every breath.

"Yell, Chloe. Just scream until you can't stand it," Aidan called from his seat on the low wall. "You too, Fei Long, help her get it all out."

Chloe screamed, letting it tear her throat. Fei Long echoed her pain, and it somehow made her feel better. The more Fei Long raged, the more the pressure loosened in her chest.

"And those two, back there." Chloe sobbed. "It's just not fair. They didn't even have to try."

"I have to admit, when I saw what was happening, I thought about throwing them both in the lake." Aidan rubbed a weary hand over his jaw. "It's not fair, Chlo. It's not, but Justice will come around."

Chloe sank down to the floor. "He's getting married." She sniffed.

"Married?" Aidan hopped down off the wall to sit beside her. "Why?"

"Because he's stupid." She gave a watery smile. "He thinks he has a lifetime of waiting ahead of him, so why not be happy now?"

"Well, clearly he is an idiot." Aidan scoffed.

"He's in love." Chloe shrugged. "It's not unheard of. We've all been in love before. Look at how crazy you were about Allie when we were kids."

"Were?" Aidan smiled.

"Still?"

"Always."

Chloe gasped. "It's really her? How long have you known?"

"I don't think I ever had a chance of loving anyone else, Chloe. I've known since the night we lost your mother."

"*That's* why you left?"

Aidan nodded. "She'd just bonded with Darius. They needed time to focus on each other, and I was just ready to burst with the knowledge that she was my Complement. It's Allie; I knew it was going to be a long wait. But once I was gone, it got easier. And after I bonded with Naomi and got involved with the other Syntrophos, it hurt a little less."

"But you're together now." Chloe's eyes widened. "And she *still* doesn't see it?"

Aidan scrubbed both hands across his face. "It's going to take her as long as it takes. I have to be patient."

"But if you're *together* together, how has it not happened? Surely it would have hit her by now."

"We are not together like that. We can't be." A haunted shadow crossed his face. "Though, she doesn't understand why. I won't force her to recognize our bond. It sucks, but it's up to us to wait as patiently as they need us to be."

"But this is Allie we're talking about, Aidan. It's going to take a sledgehammer to her head to get her to see it."

Aidan smiled. "I'm aware. It took her mother more than a thousand years to finally recognize her father."

"Oh my God, I will kill Justice if he takes that long." Chloe couldn't imagine all the lonely years she might have ahead of her. Of loving someone she couldn't have, yet never wanting anyone else.

"Leaving was the right thing to do for yourself. You need distance and time to get used to the idea that it might not happen for Justice any time soon. The Complement bond happens for us only when we are ready for it. Sometimes, people like Graham and Ezra are lucky. And some are like Quinn and Santi. It took them a few years, but they slowly came to the realization together. And then, others are like you and me. Unlucky in love."

"It kills you a little bit more every day when you know they still aren't ready. How do you stand it, Aidan? Staying so close?"

"Well, I was always a bit of the self-sabotaging sort." He shrugged.

"Thanks for this." Chloe reached for his hand. "It's been a long time since the old days, but it's good to know some things never change."

"Well, here's a bit of unconventional advice for you. You know what gets me through it?" Aidan gave her a devilish grin. "Thinking about all the ways I'm going to get back at her for putting me through this torture."

Chapter 33

Chloe | Four Months Later
Winter | Sterling Tower

Chloe watched the group of girls ahead of her in line at the cafeteria. Living at Soma was like experiencing high school all over again. Not that the girls were bullies. Chloe never had trouble with that in school. It just reminded her of her last year of high school when most of her friends had graduated and she found herself isolated and alone. She was so grateful to have Graham and the others back in her life, but Chloe missed her people, her family.

Shoving her tray through the line, Chloe tried not to think of Dahlia, but these days she even missed Scarlet. And the boys too. She hoped they were doing well without her.

"Over here, Chlo!" Graham waved her over to the table he shared with Ezra and Wes and some of their friends. She liked them all, they were great people, but they weren't *her* people.

Chloe shook her head, heading out through the double doors. She'd eat her lunch back at the apartment. Glancing down at her newly acquired Soma attire, Chloe hardly recognized herself. The black athletic leggings and jacket were comfortable, but they weren't her style at all. The purple streaks had faded from her hair, and she hadn't had the opportunity to dye it something new. She just didn't feel like herself here. Every night, Chloe vowed she would leave and go home, but every morning she remembered the look on Justice's face when he'd told her he loved Scarlet. She couldn't go back to that.

Chloe turned the corner to her hall, fishing her keycard from her pocket.

"Oh, sorry." She made a quick sidestep to avoid colliding with the only other person in the hall.

"Chloe?"

"Dad?" She dropped her tray, splattering soup all over the walls. This was it. She couldn't stay here. She'd have to go back to living the nomadic life until she found somewhere else to settle down. Chloe started to turn, ready to run.

"Chloe, wait." He grabbed her arm to stop her.

"No!" She jerked away. "You don't get to drag me home like an errant teenager!" She was so sick of this cat-and-mouse game they'd played for too many years.

"No, Chloe. I'm not here to ambush you." He dropped her arm.

She stared up at his startled face, not sure what to do next. He sounded different.

"I-it's good to see you." He took a step back, as uncertain as she was.

She studied his familiar face. "You're different." He looked ... good. Really good. Much better than he had the last time she'd seen him more than a year ago. Some of the white had faded from his hair, so it was no longer snow white but peppered with white and black.

"It's okay. I'm better now." He gave a weary sigh. "I won't keep you. I just ... I owe you an apology for my behavior the last few years. It's been ... hard without your mother. I still don't know who I am without our bond. I'm not whole, Chloe." He shoved his hands into his jacket pockets. "But I'm trying. I'm getting help."

Chloe nodded, still wary. "Well, we aren't the same people who lost her." Her heart broke for her father. That was the hardest part about seeing him. So often over the years since Ming Lao died, Chloe had searched for a glimmer of the loving father she'd once known, only to see nothing of him reflected in Jin Jing's cold eyes. She could see it now, though. The warmth and love was back. He might not be whole, but he was healing as best he could.

"No, we aren't. But I'm also not quite the monster I became when you needed me most." His voice broke, and he shifted nervously on his feet.

"Dad. I don't—"

He held up his hand to stop her. "It's on me, sweetheart. I messed up. You've only done what you needed. You ran away because I gave you no other choice."

"I don't blame you, Dad. I haven't been running *from* you. I've been running toward ... a future I still don't see." She sighed, letting her shoulders drop as if an enormous weight dragged her down.

"Still, I'm the parent." Jin Jing took a hesitant step forward. "It's my job to help you spread your wings and fly. I know you don't really need me anymore, Chloe. You've done an amazing job all on your own. I didn't make that easy for you, but if you think we could maybe start over, I'd love to give that a try."

Chloe flung herself into her dad's arms. Neither of them would ever get over the loss of Ming Lao, but maybe they could pick up the pieces of their broken family and try to move forward together.

"I hear that dragon of yours is really something to see." Jin held her close, and she laughed. Really laughed.

"She's something all right." Chloe snorted. "I'll have to re-introduce you to her. She's changed a lot in recent years."

"That will have to wait for my next visit. I'm only here for a quick meeting with Allie and her council to discuss the recent law changes the Senate is trying to force on us."

"The ones about the Senate monitoring all Awakenings and Provings? Yeah, that's not happening when it's my turn to Prove —though I can't imagine that will happen any time soon."

"I'll be back for Quinn and Santi's bonding ceremony in a few weeks, and we'll spend some quality time together." Jin Jing draped his arm around Chloe, and she tried not to show how much that small gesture affected her. It had been too long since she'd seen this version of her father.

"It looks like Graham's wedding will probably happen soon after Quinn's."

"Really?" Jin's eyes widened in surprise. "Is there something in the water around here? You guys are way too young for this."

"Don't get me started," Chloe muttered. She didn't blame Graham and Ezra for not waiting. If Justice caught up to her tomorrow and they could be together, she wouldn't want to wait either. They were just so *young*.

"Well, then, I guess my next visit will be a long one." Jin pulled her close to his side, and Chloe melted into her father's arms, marveling at how well she still fit there. "We have a lot of catching up to do, kiddo."

Chloe wrinkled her nose up at him. "I'm so not a kid, Dad."

"I don't care how old you are, you'll always be *my* kid."

"That's a comforting thought."

Chloe scribbled a line of prophecy from Hudson's journal into her own, rearranging a portion of the garbled translation with the guidance of her gift. "This just doesn't add up to *anything*." She tossed the notebook onto the coffee table.

"What're you working on, Chlo?" Graham lifted his feet off the table, startling her with his presence.

"Where did you come from?"

"I got back from lunch like an hour ago, but you ..." he waved at her with the half-eaten apple he was munching on, "you haven't really been here if you know what I mean." He sat with his computer on his lap, staring at her.

"I was just studying." She gathered up her pile of journals, a little embarrassed to be caught in such a state. For too long, she'd lived with Scholars who understood. She shouldn't let her guard down so easily here.

"It's so cool how you do that." Graham set his computer aside and leaned forward to look at her scribbling. "It's like you're on some other mental plane the rest of us will never achieve."

She laughed at that. "You should see some of my friends who are real Scholars."

"You're a real Scholar. You might be a bit of both, but I don't think that makes you any less of a warrior or any less of a Scholar."

Chloe shook her head, smiling at her childhood best friend. "I love you, Graham."

"I love you too, Chlo. You know you have to be my witness, right? Wes and Quinn are going to stand up with us, but I want you there too."

"I'd be honored." Chloe reached for his hand. "And if I haven't said it yet, I'm really happy for you two. Insanely jealous, but happy."

"Thanks. You know Justice will come around. He's yours. That won't change just because he's not ready for you right now."

"I know." Chloe sighed, setting her journals aside. There was no real need to hide this part of herself from Graham. He was family. "He's just so *slow* about it."

"We'll be picking out china patterns for you before you know it." Graham grinned.

"Gross. I'm not doing the big to-do Santi and Quinn are throwing."

"Us either. I thought Ezra was going to want all the flowers and doves and whatever else he could think of, but he said the sweetest thing the other day." Graham blushed. "He just wants to get to the marriage part. All the other stuff is just a delay to what's important."

"Babies." Chloe snorted.

"What?" Graham frowned.

"That boy wants children as soon as possible."

"Don't remind me. I'm kind of freaking out about that part. I'm all for a big family, but I'm so not ready to be anyone's parent."

"He just wants a family, Graham. He lost his parents, and he's been through hell with the Milan Initiative. Give that sweet husband-to-be of yours whatever he wants."

"Oh, I will. I'm just terrified about the whole six kids thing." Graham chuckled. "You think if I get him a couple of puppies as a wedding present, it'll buy me some time?"

"Probably not." Chloe grinned. "But I'm down for babysitting."

"Seriously, what is this?" Graham eyes pulsed with the light of his power as he pulled her journal across the table. Something there caught the girls' attention. Though she couldn't see or hear them, she knew they were always buzzing around his head.

"It's a list of old prophecies my friend Hudson has been working on for ages. We've been trying to piece them back together from bits of research we've pulled from various sources."

"Sources ... like your gifts?"

"Yeah. The information just comes to Hudson. For me, it's a little more subtle. My gift is useful in a general guidance sort of way. I just can't figure out what's so important about these old ramblings."

"Maybe you just need some fresh eyes on it." Graham leaned forward.

"The Scholar gift is strange. Sometimes, these things are compulsive. Hudson's gift won't let it go, and it seems like yours is catching the fever too."

"Maybe," Graham murmured as he studied the prophecy she'd just revised. "This one seems to be about Allie and maybe Darius and Aidan too. The child of prophecy bit usually refers to them. But what does this part about soldiers battling an unseen enemy with their ... heart's blade mean?" Graham lowered the journal to peer over it at her. "That makes no sense."

"The translations are rough. That's been our biggest hurdle, but I *think* it might be a reference to the Syntrophos. I just can't decide who their unseen enemy would be."

"Oh, yeah." Graham scratched his head. "That could work." He moved to sit beside her on the floor. "Show me what else you've got."

"Really? You're interested in all this?" In her experience, the warrior types were never interested in a Scholar's work. But then, Graham was always more empathetic than most.

"Yeah, I think this could be important, Chloe."

"Okay." Chloe opened Hudson's journal, flipping to the two prophecies that seemed to go together, but they stumped her.

"What do you make of this one?" She slid the book over to him.

The infiltrator will speak with honeyed words, luring his foes into his labyrinthine trap. The unseen enemy will trust the spy and those who call him master. Without the spy we are doomed.

Graham shivered beside her, his eyes widened with shock.

"Graham, does this mean something to you?"

He shook his head. "You think this next one goes along with it?"

"It doesn't fit at all, but then my gift tells me it does. And even Hudson agrees, though we can't make sense of it." Chloe studied the line of text. *There is one who shall speak with his gift and forestall the escape that will lead to a bloody annihilation and send the children of Indriell into their final twilight.*

"My friend Jonah speaks with his gift in a literal sense," she said. "His power affects his voice, so he doesn't speak often. He communicates through his brother and with sign language. If this prophecy is about anyone, it's likely Jonah, but I can't find a connection with him and the spy from the other line of prophecy. It's like a puzzle I just don't have all the pieces to."

"Maybe it's not about him." Graham moved his hands to his lap under the table, but Chloe didn't miss the fact that they were shaking. "Are you sure this translates as *escape*?"

"Positive, but that is the word that has really stumped me. Do you know what it could mean?" Chloe studied him with her gift. Threads of indecision lit up around him.

"But this one over here, it could be about you." Graham pointed to a page in another journal spread out across the table.

"Me? Definitely not." Chloe looked over his shoulder.

"Not much of it makes sense, but this line about the *one with the opposing natures, who will cultivate those with the gift of foresight and wisdom while destroying those who are doomed to repeat the past*—that could be you, Chlo."

"It's so not, though." She pulled the book from him, shaking her head. "Tell me what freaked you out about the other one, Graham. It means something to you."

Graham reached for his computer. "I have a hunch, so just go with me on this. I need to see if a piece of your puzzle fits into mine." He started pecking away on his computer, bringing up a series of maps and notes Chloe couldn't make heads or tails of. "Girls, I need Chloe to see this."

It was strange how the girls appeared in such a similar way as Fei Long. Graham had only recently learned how to let other's see his amazing gift.

"Bring up all the data we have on the Grand Master's communication concerning the location we've been watching."

Chloe watched the girls as they exploded into millions of tiny blue lights, reforming as pieces of code. Graham scanned the information, scribbling translations into his notebook. She smiled, shaking her head as she watched him disappear into his own little world. He wasn't a Scholar, but his gift behaved so much like hers, it was impressive to witness.

Graham pulled pieces of code from the endless stream of data, setting certain bits aside for translation. Chloe sat quietly watching as his gift guided him. Graham soon gathered a long list of potential nuggets of information that might be useful to the puzzle he was trying to piece together.

"Escape?" He murmured to himself, bringing up a map of a series of islands Chloe didn't recognize.

"Oh, dear God." Graham finally sat back against the couch as the light of his power left his eyes. "He can't do this." Graham ran a hand through his hair. "It will turn our world upside down." He turned to Chloe, reaching for her hand.

"What is it, what have you found out?"

"We have to stop him." Graham closed his computer and started stacking her journals on top of is.

"Stop who? Use more words, Graham."

"The Grand Master. It all fits, Chlo. We need to take this to Allie. Like right now."

"Why would she need to see a bunch of old jumbled prophecies that don't make sense?"

"Because I'm pretty sure all these old prophecies are about us. And they're being fulfilled right now."

Chapter 34

Allie | Winter | Sterling Tower

"You can't go in there! The First Princess is in a council meeting!" Allie looked up from her notes to see Graham come charging through the double doors to her conference room, dragging Chloe behind him.

"Sherbet Lemon! Sherbet Lemon!" Graham shouted the secret password to her secretary before she had a chance to throw them out.

"Honestly, Ms. Carmichael? It's not a secret password if *everyone* knows it." Mrs. Mitchell stood with her hands on her hips.

"It's okay, Graham and Chloe are family. If they have an urgent need to speak with me, let them in." Allie tried not to laugh at the scowl on her secretary's face. Mrs. Mitchell was her fourth secretary, and her favorite. She didn't fuss over Allie and wasn't afraid to tell her off. She needed someone like that in her corner. But her secretary hated these kinds of interruptions.

"You have a very large *family*, Ms. Carmichael." The older woman glowered at her, as if she didn't believe for a second that Chloe and Graham qualified as immediate family.

"You can never have too much family." Allie stood to greet

her friends, ignoring the amused murmurings from her council. "Now, what's the matter, you two? Come sit. You both look freaked out." Graham was white as a ghost.

"Sorry to interrupt, Allie ... er ... Ms. Carmichael ... princess lady," Chloe rambled, looking uncomfortable in the room full of all her old friends.

"Chloe, you were my first sparring partner." Allie laughed. "You knocked me off that old balance beam a million times. If anyone gets to bypass ridiculous formalities, it's you." And honestly, Allie was just giving them some time to get settled before inviting them to join her council anyway.

"So, we were just looking over some of Chloe's scholarly journals." Graham stepped forward and set a stack of journals on the table, taking a seat beside Quinn and kicking out a chair for Chloe to sit beside him. Graham had never once been intimidated by Allie's power or her new position.

"I'm sorry to interrupt." Chloe gingerly took her seat. "Graham seems to have discovered something in my research, but I'm still not sure what he's rambling about."

Allie returned to her seat at the head of the table. There were empty seats all around. The older adults weren't always in residence, but her permanent council members were all present today. That was a good thing because Allie was certain something major was about to come to light, and she was going to need her closest friends to get through this.

"Tell me what you've been working on, Chlo. Then, we'll see what Graham has figured out."

"Oh, I've just been working with a Scholar friend of mine on some old prophecies." Chloe waved her hand at her journals, like her work wasn't important. "We've been pulling together everything the ancient Prophets foretold of the days leading up to the final prophecy. We've had to do a lot of translating ... and it's really just a big mess of random bits of translations at this point."

"You're stuck in the middle of it," Graham said. "You and Hudson have been working on this for over a year. You see a bunch of random puzzle pieces, but I think they belong in the puzzle I've been working on. I think this could be big." He turned to meet Allie's gaze. "Really big."

"What did you see, Graham?" Chloe reached for one of her journals, studying his face. Allie watched as her eyes smoldered with the smoky swirling light of her gift. "You've decided something. Something big." Chloe's eyes widened, and she clutched her ears with a groan.

"What is it, Chlo?" Sasha reached for her hand, moving to sit closer.

"It affects everyone here." Chloe rocked in her chair, sucking in deep breaths. "Everyone in this building."

Allie slid her chair over to Aidan's, rummaging in his pocket for his phone and AirPods.

"Can I help you with something?" Aidan gave her a smirk. "We've been over this, babe, my pockets are not your backup purse."

"Got it." She walked over to Chloe and slipped the AirPods into her ears, setting the music on a soft, calming playlist. "That should help some, right?" Allie crouched beside her.

Chloe nodded, clutching the AirPods to her ears. "Yes, that's perfect, thank you." She took a deep breath and nodded for Graham to continue.

The room fell silent as Graham flipped through the journals, his eyes scanning the pages for the information he sought.

"Don't freak out, I'm going to use my gift here." Graham leaned back in his chair. "Girls, I need the others to see the information I'm going to ask you to display."

Allie grinned as a brilliant blue light burst from Graham's chest, swirling like twin spheres around the room. She'd only heard him speak of the girls before in their classes with Gabe.

"I'm sure," Graham responded to their unspoken question.

"*But the boy never let's us speak to others*," a creepy chorus of disembodied female voices filled the room, emanating from the flickering blue spheres of power.

"That is so cool!" Allie leaned forward.

"Girls, can you show my friends here the information I've just gathered?"

"*Can they be trusted, master?*"

"Yes, and we've been over this. Don't call me master. You know my name, use it."

"*Yes, Graham, sir*." The blue balls of light burst into a rainstorm of tiny dancing spheres, coming back together to form words and phrases.

"Allie, can you gather anything from this list of subjects?" Graham sat back, his eyes still roving the pages before him.

Allie studied the list floating before her eyes, trying not to geek out about how cool her friend's gift was.

"Child of Prophecy

"Soldiers bearing their heart's blade

"Roving armies of the crazed and addicted

"One who bears the assassin's mark

"The one with opposing natures

"The infiltrator who speaks with his gift."

Dread filled Allie to the core. Graham was right. This was huge. "We need to see the rest of these prophecies. Chloe, you're a genius! You've revived history we've likely lost to the ages."

"What is it, Allie?" Darius caught onto her sense of urgency before anyone else.

"It's us." She leaned forward, watching as Graham's girls filled in the missing pieces from the larger prophecies. "It's all of us. I think we can all agree by now that references to the child of prophecy sometimes refers to me, Aidan, and Darius, and other times, it means all of our generation. Here, I think it means the former."

"And the rest?" Graham asked, leaning forward as eager as she was to get to the bottom of this.

"Soldiers bearing their heart's blade refers to the Syntrophos. The roving armies of the crazed and addicted are the dream walkers. The Assassin is Sasha and Jayesh, and their special ops team. The one with opposing natures is likely Chloe—and probably a reference to her Scholar and Prophet friends too, and the infiltrator is you, Graham, right?" She turned her attention back to Graham.

"My thoughts exactly." Graham's voice cracked nervously.

"But what does it all mean?" Quinn stared at the glittering lines of prophecy.

"I don't know what they all mean yet, but let's look at the one about the infiltrator for now." Graham stood up to pace. "I think we might be running out of time for this one."

"The infiltrator will speak with honeyed words, luring his foes into his labyrinthine trap. The unseen enemy will trust the spy and those who call him master. He speaks with his gift and will forestall the escape that will lead to a bloody annihilation and send the children of Indriell into their final twilight.

"That's about you, bro?" Quinn asked, sounding as impressed as Allie felt.

"You tell me. For the last two years, I've been working with Aunt Gabrielle and Uncle Lou to investigate the League of Ancients. With the help of the Alderman's son, I've managed to infiltrate the inner circle, providing all the aldermen and the Grand Master a sophisticated tech system that allows them to communicate offline. I've used my gift to foster a false sense of trust between me and the Grand Master of the League. All the while, I've been using my Tech gifts to monitor the Master's communications with his aldermen. During my time with the

League, I've built a network of spies who trust me implicitly—and they've nicknamed me the master spy. I regularly speak with my gift as you can see, and they refuse to use my name, preferring to call me master instead." Graham folded his arms over his chest, staring at Allie. "If this isn't about me, I'd like to meet this guy because we have a lot in common."

"Escape?" Allie shook her head. "That word bothers me almost as much as this bloody annihilation part." Allie shifted in her seat, trying to rein in the surge of power that shot right through her. With her hair standing on end and goose bumps running down her arms, she agreed with Graham. This was big, and this particular prophecy needed their immediate attention.

"That single word brought everything together for me. It was the missing piece of a puzzle I've been trying to assemble for years." Graham turned to speak with the floating orbs of his gift. "Girls, can you show us the map of the aldermen's recent activity?"

Allie marveled at his ability to process the information his gift absorbed. It was so fascinating to see how different gifts manifested in others.

"I've been monitoring their activity for some time now, and I can tell you the aldermen and the Grand Master have been searching out some of the most remote locations across the globe." Graham pointed to several places Allie recognized. Locations along the Ring of Fire in the South Pacific, the Sahara Desert, Antarctica, Siberia, and the Yukon in North America. But there were other locations she hadn't dreamed of. Madagascar, the Sandwich Islands, Easter Island, remote China, even Death Valley.

Allie shared a look with Aidan and Darius.

"What do these places mean, Graham?" Darius asked. "And who are these aldermen?"

"I have a list of their names and general locations. Each one of them holds a significant role in the mortal political systems across the world. I've been so focused on that, I failed to see what was coming for us first." Graham leaned against the conference table, pointing at the Bermuda Triangle. "There's an island here at the center of the triangle. One not on mortal records." The girls zoomed in closer to the island. "I believe the island has a strong natural magnetic field, and that is the source of all the legends regarding shipwrecks and those lost there."

Allie shot out of her seat, fumbling with her messenger bag draped over her chair. "Prisons!" She could barely get the word out as she snatched up her sketchbook and laid it out on the table. "They're all prisons." Allie met Aidan's gaze, willing him and Darius to get there faster.

"How do you know?" Graham crossed the room to her side. "That was my initial suspicion too, but I didn't think much of it at the time. Why would he bother with carefully guarded prisons?"

"Do any of these locations mean anything to you?" Allie flipped through pages of maps she'd sketched in her sleep.

"Some are the same." Graham glanced between her drawings and his maps.

"Not all," Allie whispered. "But together we might have a complete listing of every known Coalition prison."

"Wait, why would this Grand Master person bother with Coalition prisons?" Santi asked. "What aren't we seeing that has the two of you so freaked?"

"He's not just the Grand Master, Santi," Allie said, stepping away from her sketchbook to study Graham's map as the girls updated it to include the locations from Allie's drawings. "He is the Grand Master of the League of Ancients. He's also the ancient, Marcus Severus, and Robert Sinclair, the elected Senator to the International Senate. Lord Teigan of Indriell, and the current Marches, Marius Von Essen III or maybe IV, Master of the Coalition."

"Okay ... but how is the leader of the Coalition an Immortal?" Chloe asked. "They'd never allow it."

"It's a long story, Chlo. Marcus is also the man who raised Livia after he took her from our family. She's divulged all his secrets, and he and I have had some issues recently." Allie's mind whirred with all the things that needed to happen to stop the thing she knew was probably happening right this minute.

"Mrs. Mitchell!" she shouted, forgetting about the intercom she was supposed to use to be more professional in such instances.

"Yes, Ms. Carmichael?" her voice crackled over the intercom in response. "Is there something you need?"

"I need to speak with Vince as soon as possible. His contact number is in my cell phone."

"The mortal ex-boyfriend, ma'am?"

"Yes, now, Martha. It's important."

"Right away, ma'am."

"What are you thinking, Allie?" Aidan gave her that look that said she was acting impulsively.

"I'm thinking we're in deep crap." Allie paced around the marble conference table, studying Graham's map. He was on the same page with her, and he was trying not to freak out.

"Where do you think they'll strike first?" Allie ignored the others and fired her questions at Graham. They would catch everyone up to speed later.

"The Caribbean." Graham pointed to the small island that didn't exist on any other map she'd ever seen. "They've been meeting there for months. My guess is the aldermen are already in control of the island."

"Who do you think they have imprisoned there?"

Graham shuddered. "Probably the oldest and most dangerous of our kind. Ones who probably haven't seen the light of day in thousands of years."

"And he's just going to let them out? Just like that?" Allie shook her head, trying to wrap her mind around what Marcus could be thinking. It would be the end of the world as they knew it. Immortal prisoners at large with no notion of what the mainstream modern world was like?

She shivered as her mind flashed with memories of Isebeau the night Greyson betrayed Allie, attempting to trade her for his wife who had spent more than a thousand years in a Coalition prison. Isebeau was half-insane and weakened from her time under the powerful magnetic influence. Allie could only imagine hundreds more just like her, wandering the modern world and trying to tap into their power again. It would be anarchy. And the perfect distraction to keep her and the Senate busy, allowing Marcus just enough time to tear their world apart and build it back up to his liking.

"Allie, even if he is the Master of the Coalition, they aren't just going to let him ... liberate the prisons. They will fight him on that, won't they?" Graham turned pleading eyes on her.

"What about the bloody annihilation part? The one that will lead to the end of all Immortals?" She leaned against the table for support. The other members of her council whispered among themselves, trying to keep up with her conversation with Graham.

"That could mean a million different things."

Allie shook her head. "He's going to murder them. All of them."

"What? No, Allie." Aidan moved to get her attention. "What would be the purpose of that?"

"It's why he took over the Coalition in the sixteenth century." Allie moved to the door to meet Mrs. Mitchell. "He's been working toward this for centuries, and all his little chess pieces are in place. He's got a League of puppets out there, poised to bring our world out of hiding. What do you think is going to happen when he unleashes thousands of ancient Immortals in a modern world they'll never understand?" Allie's core grew molten hot with the churning of her power. She could see a swirling mass of new visions moving in her peripheral sight. Her gift processed this new information faster than ever before. She knew it in her soul that Marcus was about to make his first big move that would lead them into the darkness her grandmother foretold of thousands of years ago. It was time, and she had to act before it was too late.

"I have the boy on hold, dear." Mrs. Mitchell stood in the doorway. "Shall I have him call back when you aren't dealing with important matters?"

"No, I need his help." Allie took her cell phone from her secretary. "Vince?" she barked into the phone.

"Hey, Allie, I was in an interview, but your assistant is persistent. Is this urgent?"

"It's life or death. I need you to listen carefully, Vince. Warn your people." She paced along a worn section of carpet. She seemed to do a lot of pacing in here.

"You know they aren't really *my* people. Never really were."

"No, I know, but you're my only contact who can get inside the Coalition."

"Okay, wow. It must be dire if we're speaking plainly. How can we help?"

"You have to get them all out." Allie threw up her free hand in frustration, letting her fingers run through her tangled curls. "Out of their homes, out of their offices. Tell everyone who will listen that it's time to take a vacation. The Immortals are coming for them." Allie shifted anxiously. There was still so much to do. "They're going to remove the Coalition and seize control of the prisons.

"Why are you coming for them?"

"No, not us." She clenched her fists, frustrated that her mind moved faster than everyone around her. "Just trust me, Vince." Her voice cracked with anxiety. "Their leader is an Immortal, and he's been planning a coup for a few hundred years! He's going to wipe them out, and you know what that means for us."

"Kahlynn?" His voice dropped a few octaves. With the mention of her adopted niece, he was finally taking her seriously.

"Exactly, and if you want her to have any kind of future, you and Kayla need to get your friends together and start warning people. I don't know how much time you're going to have, but we have to save the ones we can while we still have time."

"Okay, okay. I'll handle it."

"I'm so sorry to dump this all on you guys, but you're all I've got."

"We'll do our best, Allie, but take care of yourself too. It's not your job to save the world."

"I'm afraid it just might be." Allie ended the call and speed dialed her parents.

"Hey sweetheart," Lily answered on the second ring. "I'll get your father, one second."

Allie waited impatiently for her parents to come back on the line.

"What's up, kiddo?" Her dad's cheery voice calmed her, just like it always had. She knew she could count on them.

"You know that thing I've been worrying about lately?" She told her parents just about everything these days. It was just too hard to keep her lives separate.

"The dreams?" Lily asked. "Have you figured it out?"

"Prisons," Allie blurted. "Your people are in danger. Both sides, I think. I need you to warn whoever you can while there's time."

"Okay," Carson said. "We'll handle ours, you handle yours."

"Thanks, guys." She loved that she didn't have to spell it out for them. She could always count on them to never ask questions.

"What's happening, Allie?" Aidan came to stand in front of her, placing his hands on her shoulders. "I know you're like fifty steps ahead of the rest of us, but take a moment to help us catch up so you don't have to do this alone. Can we take a step back to the murdering people thing?"

Aidan was so good to her. He never failed to support her, even when he didn't understand.

"You're right." Allie grasped his hands on her shoulders and took a deep breath. Returning to her chair, she winced at the sea of confused and worried faces staring back at her. Her most trusted friends were in session with her today. Aidan and Darius were always with her, but even Naomi sat quietly beside her Syntrophos, trying to understand what was happening. The same for Sasha, Quinn and Santi, Dean and Tessa, and Chloe and Graham. All her youngest council members. That had to be luck on her side. They would move quicker than the olds would.

Allie leaned back in her chair, trying to still her racing heart. "Over the last few years, I think we've all been trying to assemble our own little puzzles, not realizing we've all been working on one big puzzle."

"That's what finally clicked for me," Graham said. "It's all relative."

"Graham and I are seeing the big picture, and in a second you're all about to get there with us. This is scary, guys. But we need to keep a level head and make our best choices." Allie gave a nod to Chloe. "You'll keep us on track as we make decisions?"

"I'll do my best." Chloe returned her nod.

"That's all any of us can do." Allie sighed. "Marcus is going to massacre the Coalition. That's the piece of the puzzle I've been missing."

"But how do you know so certainly?" Darius asked, his midnight blue eyes filled with confusion.

"The prophecies." Allie gestured at the pages of notes Chloe and her Scholar friend had meticulously gathered. "They speak to me." Allie scratched her head, trying to find the words to explain what she meant. "I just know. I knew the minute I read the last phrase of Graham's prophecy. *He will forestall the escape that will lead to a bloody annihilation and send the children of Indriell into their final twilight.* It's as clear to me as my own name."

"Maybe I'm just jaded," Naomi finally spoke up, "but do we really care if he does annihilate the Coalition? I mean, clearly, we can't allow him to liberate the prisons. But couldn't we just stop Marcus from doing that? We have the locations of the prisons right here. I hate to say let's let him kill a bunch of people, but they kind of deserve it, don't they?"

"She's right," Tessa said. "We should focus our retaliation on keeping the prisons under our control—protecting our people who have been tortured by theirs. Then, we could search records to see what prisoners can be released right away, which ones need to stay behind bars and those who need rehabilitation first."

"We will get there, but that is not our immediate concern." Allie ran a weary hand over her face. This was where she might lose them. "If the Coalition is massacred, it will be the end of us. It says it right there in the prophecy."

"Okay, but how?" Sasha asked, turning to share a look with her Syntrophos. Even Quinn wasn't with Allie and he was always quick to catch up.

"Where do you people think babies come from?" Allie asked the room at large. "Not the ones like Parker or Chloe and me who were born of an Immortal mother. Where do you think you came from, Sasha? Your origins are probably the most complicated of anyone here. You were adopted when you were five. You remember the orphanage in Haiti where you lived before Naeemah found you. How'd you get there?"

"I don't know." Sasha blinked at her like it was a silly question. "It's a mystery, and there are many theories. I guess I never really thought about it."

That was where Immortal traditions and values separated Allie from her friends. Mortals had a pathological need to know where they came from. Immortals never seemed to think that was important.

"I'm going to need you all to think about it. Where do Immortals come from because it's not the stork?"

"I've always assumed we came from a mortal mother in the usual way," Dean offered. "I mean, the simplest of answers is usually the most accurate."

"Exactly." Allie slammed her hand down on the table. "We're going to have a super quick lesson on Immortal birds and the bees, and then we're going to take action, okay?"

Heads nodded, but she wasn't sure they didn't think she'd lost her mind.

"You all know my niece, Kahlynn. Liam found her when she was just a baby. Not long after her mortal mother left her for him to find. Her birth parents are Vince and Kayla. She looks just like them."

"That's ... kind of an opinion, not a fact," Naomi said.

"Some of you already know that Vince's father was once a member of the Coalition," Allie continued. "He got out of that world when Vince was a baby, but Vince still grew up on the fringe of their world. He has friends and family who are still active members of the Coalition in Cleveland. That's how he's been able to help every time I find myself in a desperate situation with the Coalition."

"I know they had a baby together in high school," Aidan offered. "But are you really so certain it was Kahlynn?"

"Positive. It takes a son of the Coalition—Vince—and a Banished Daughter—Kayla—to make an immortal child—

Kahlynn. Both Vince and Kayla are direct descendants of the mortals banished from Indriell after the Great War."

"Don't take this the wrong way," Graham said, "but how do you, of all people, know this?"

"You all know the Coalition was born during the expulsion of the mortal children from Indriell. Those who hated us for the actions that led to their mortality came together to keep their hate alive. They became the Coalition. On the flipside of their hate came the Banished Daughters. They believed the last Queen of Indriell did the best she could for them given the circumstances. They believe she saved them every bit as much as she saved her own kind.

"The Coalition and the Banished Daughters are our mortal ancestors. They came from us. The same blood that runs through our veins, runs through theirs. The only difference is in our longevity." Allie leaned forward. "They live very long and healthy lives—for mortals. They carry a small spark of the pure power within them. The power that makes us Immortal.

"Where we are thrown into an Awakening on our sixteenth year, they experience an Awakening of their own, though most of the Coalition don't understand what it means. The Banished Daughters do. During their "Awakening," a Daughter will seek out her Complement, and when the conditions are right, the result of their union is a new Immortal child—though it can only happen that one time. Sometimes, they stay together and sometimes they drift apart only to come together again years later. Any child they have then will always be a Banished Daughter—and again, only the one."

"And what, they just give up their first child?" Sasha asked.

"Yes. In most cases, the Banished Daughter has been trained all her life for the possibility that she might become the surrogate for an Immortal child. Kayla was adopted, so she never knew what to expect. In many ways, she is the opposite of me. She didn't know what she was until after she'd given up her child to Liam. She was driven by the power of her instincts to find him. She once told me it was a compulsion she couldn't control. The closer she came to giving birth, the more she was driven to find the child's father. She couldn't understand how she could just leave her baby with a total stranger, but everything in her screamed that Kahlynn was Liam and Livia's child. Not hers."

Allie took a deep breath, carefully watching the stunned faces of her closest friends. "Kayla didn't understand any of it, so she never told Vince she was pregnant. She lived with her secret for more than a year when my mother, also a Banished Daughter, explained it to her. And later to me."

"How ..." Quinn shook his head. "How have we not discovered this before?"

"The Banished Daughters hide their secrets well." Allie sighed.

"And they have Complements?" Darius asked. "Within the Coalition?"

"Yes, though in most cases, the son of the Coalition usually leaves to join the Daughters. That is how Vince's father came to leave the Coalition behind. His wife gave birth to Darius."

"Wait, I'm your ex-boyfriend's ... brother?" Darius scowled at her. "I think my head just exploded."

"Want me to really blow your mind?" She shot him a grin. "I'm Graham's sort-of aunt."

"What?" Graham gaped at her.

"My older sister—my mortal sister, Josceline, was your biological surrogate. It's why my parents like you more than me. You're kind of their first grandchild. You have Joss's eyes."

"Holy crap." Graham leaned back against his chair. "Is that why I've never been super intimidated by you like I always was with Aidan? Because we're family?"

"Probably," Allie said.

"Can I ... meet your sister sometime? Is that weird?" Graham glanced at his brother in uncertainty.

"She'd love to see you again." Allie smiled. "Oh, and while we're spilling all the secrets, Imogen's husband, Lucien, is my adoptive brother. He looks just like my dad."

"Okay, so our world just got way more complicated." Aidan sighed. "We can't let Marcus destroy the Coalition. Clearly, he doesn't know what will happen if he succeeds."

"Or he just doesn't care." Allie shuddered. "If he wipes out the men of the Coalition, no more Immortal babies will be born outside the few natural births every few hundred years. Which means eventually, our numbers will dwindle to nothing. And before you know it, we'll all fade into the ether."

"But how are we going to protect the prisons *and* the Coalition at the same time?" Darius asked.

Chapter 35

Allie | Winter | Kelleys Island

Allie paced across the common room. It was so strange to be back home on Kelleys Island after living in Atlanta for so long. It was more than a little unsettling to venture beyond the protective bubble of the Dreamworld surrounding Soma. It was like going into battle without armor.

And she had more battles on her plate than she could handle. With everything happening at lightning speed, they all decided to move their headquarters back to Kelleys Island to keep Sterling Tower from becoming a bigger target than it already was. And they needed the guidance of their elders in this venture.

"I hate not knowing if everyone is safe." Naeemah twisted her hands in her lap.

"I hate asking my friends to do dangerous jobs I should be doing in their place." Allie moved to sit between Naeemah and her grandmother.

Alísun took her hand and gave a gentle squeeze. "That's the hardest part about our job, dear. As First Princess, you're too important to risk."

Allie snorted at that, but she never got the chance to argue that point with her grandmother.

"Quinn!" Santi shot across the common room to greet her soon-to-be-husband. "I was so worried. How did it go?"

Grandpa Alex entered the common room behind Quinn.

"I'm not going to lie, I was worried they'd keep you, Gramps." Allie stood, wringing her hands and feeling utterly useless. She hadn't wanted to send her grandfather with Quinn, but it was the best way to make them forget they'd ever seen an Immortal in their midst, and the safest way to get them out of there if things went bad.

"It was touch and go there for a while." Quinn sighed as he moved to sit on the floor with Santi. There weren't any vacant seats in the common room. Everyone was home and eagerly waiting for updates on more than one front.

"They didn't like what we had to say," Alexander began, "but Vince and Kayla convinced them to listen to us before they tried to arrest us."

Allie had thought her grandfather had lost his mind when he suggested they try to parlay with the Cleveland Coalition. But they needed to reach as many members as possible in the shortest time frame.

"And?" Aidan pressed.

"And they agreed to spread the warning quietly among their families and friends, avoiding all mention of the coming massacre in emails and text messages," Quinn explained. "Some didn't believe us. Others seemed to respect our willingness to help them. None of them wanted to let us walk out of there. Only time will tell how this will affect our relationship with the Coalition."

"Let's hope if we save them, they'll stop hunting us," Graham said. "Did you have to make a vanishing getaway?"

"Yeah, we gave them a double whammy of our abilities," Alexander said. "I made them forget us, and Quinn made us disappear so we could walk out in one piece."

"Have we heard from Sasha and her team yet?" Quinn asked,

looking worried for his Syntrophos. Allie felt bad for sending them on separate missions, but Sasha's gifts were needed elsewhere.

"Not yet." Naeemah crossed her arms over her chest. "Last we heard, they were nearing the location. We might not hear from them again until tomorrow."

"So, we're in for a long night of waiting then." Quinn turned to Santi, taking her hand in his.

"There was a moment while we spoke with the Coalition today where I thought it was going to go very badly for us. I haven't felt that helpless since the night I showed up at Soma with a collar around my neck." He gazed at her like she was the sun and he was starved for the light of day. "The thought that I might not get to come home to you nearly destroyed me. I don't want to wait any longer."

"What about Sasha?" Santi traced the lines of his palm with her fingertips. "It will break her heart not to get to stand up with us."

Quinn shook his head. "She will understand. We may not have another chance, Santi. Our world could shatter any minute if we don't succeed in stopping Marcus and his aldermen. In a matter of hours, he's going to know what we did today. The Coalition might not remember we were there, but they will remember the message we brought. It will get back to him."

"Which means we've shown our hand," Allie said softly, not wanting to sway their decision, but Quinn was right. They made their first moves today. Marcus would be quick to make his. "It's only a matter of a day, maybe two if we're lucky, before he retaliates."

"But we planned the wedding to happen on the rooftop at Soma. Everything is there."

"We can still have the celebration when we get back," Allie offered.

"We have almost everything we need here." Quinn gazed around the room at their family. Even Santi's parents and grandparents had come with the others. It was the perfect opportunity for an impromptu bonding ceremony. "Sasha will forgive us for not waiting. If I know my Syntrophos at all, she'd be madder if we waited for her, given the dire circumstances."

"And the sleepless, nerve-wracking night we have before us," Emma added.

Santi took a deep breath and nodded, beaming her beautiful smile at her Complement. "Let's do it."

Epilogue

Allie | Winter | Kelleys Island

"Allie, we have to go." Aidan tugged her hand. "We have a ceremony to get through—to get to, I mean." He smiled sheepishly at his slip.

"Just a minute. I have a couple of texts from Martha I need to reply to first." She sat on the bed in Aidan's studio in the underground. They hadn't been here in ages, and it brought such happy memories of an easier time—though she'd never have thought of those days as easy when she was in the middle of them.

"Wait, what?" Allie stood up, her feet sinking into the suede mattress that made up the floor of his bedroom. "I have to call her." Allie dialed her assistant and set it on speakerphone.

"Ms. Carmichael, don't you have a ceremony you should be witnessing?" Mrs. Mitchell's voice echoed across the room.

"Your last text, Martha. Tell me it was a typo. There are how many new students asking for entry into Soma?" Allie stared at her screen shaking her head. They were at full capacity already; if they took on any more students, they were going to have to make some major changes to the way Soma functioned.

"At least a hundred, ma'am. They started lining up across the street early this morning. They all say they're friends of your closest friends. I have a list here, one moment."

"We can't take in another dozen students." Aidan shook his head, trying to fasten his cufflinks. "What are we going to do with a hundred?"

"We'll have to figure something out." Allie felt that suffocating feeling she got more and more lately. Where she couldn't breathe, and her eye started twitching.

"Breathe, babe." Aidan came to stand behind her, rubbing her shoulders to help her relax. "No one expects you to do everything."

"I expect me to do everything. That's the problem." Allie sighed.

"Here we are," Mrs. Mitchell came back on the line. "I have several friends of Chloe Long's. A rather adamant young lady named Dahlia and her friend Justice have made a nuisance of themselves. And quite a few friends of Graham's from New England as well. One says he's his boyfriend, but didn't he recently find his Complement? That could get messy. Oh, and some friends of Livia's have requested an audience with her. When should I say she'll be back? And Briggs has brought at least a dozen young dream walkers wanting to train with Quinn. And we also have a group of young friends of Aidan's who said they studied with him at the Milan Initiative."

Aidan grabbed the phone from Allie's hand. "Who are they Martha?"

"An Ace and Lola, along with some of their friends."

"We have to let them in, Allie. They need us." Aidan turned his dark eyes on her. She couldn't deny him anything. And she couldn't deny any of these kids access to Soma.

"Let them all in, Martha. After the usual screening of course."

"Where are we going to put them all?"

"Put them in the warehouse for now. They can bunk in the cabins there until we find better accommodations."

"We're already using several of the cabins, dear."

Allie took the phone back from Aidan. "Then, pitch some tents and find some sleeping bags. We'll turn one of the gyms into a big slumber party for the little ones. Just put a Band Aid on it for the time being and get them off the street."

"We'll handle it, ma'am," Martha replied. "But we're going to need to increase our supplies if we're going to be feeding and housing all these people."

"Get the kitchens to implement the rations we've discussed, and I'll be back in a few days."

"All right. Don't worry about a thing, we'll take care of it. You enjoy your break."

"Thank you, Martha." Allie ended the call.

"Don't think about it now, Allie." Aidan took her phone from her. "We can't do anything from here, and you know Mrs. Mitchell is a miracle worker."

"You're right. She'll do a better job of it than me anyway." Allie sighed.

"If I failed to mention it, I love the dress. You look beautiful in lavender." Aidan stood behind her, his long arms pulling her against his chest.

"I'd rather be in jeans and a t-shirt."

"Same." Aidan tugged at his collar.

"But you look handsome in your fancy suit."

"Let's go watch our friends get married so we can ditch the fancy clothes as soon as possible." He grabbed her hand and led them out to the common room to meet the others.

Allie held Aidan's hand as they stood with their friends in Naeemah's terrarium garden where they'd spent so much time as kids. Those days felt like a million years ago now. Quinn was getting married! Allie shook her head in disbelief. They were so young. Allie couldn't wrap her mortal brain around getting married when their world would still consider them adolescents for several more decades. It was crazy. But it worked for her friends. Santi and Quinn had been through so much together, and their time at Soma had matured them in ways Allie hoped they would never experience again.

Santi and Quinn stood facing each other as Graham, Chloe, Allie and Aidan held hands in a protective circle around them. They faced away from the happy couple. Their job tonight was to protect them during the most vulnerable moments of their lives and bear witness to their bonding—no matter how long it took.

Allie had witnessed only one bonding ceremony, and that was through a memory Gregg once shared with her of his own bonding with Naeemah. It had taken them days to complete the bond. It was a difficult thing for some to come to terms with, particularly when the parties were as old as Gregg had been when they married. Gregg had lived for centuries without his Complement. To relinquish his power to Naeemah was an extremely difficult thing to do. Allie sincerely hoped it would be easier for Santi and Quinn because they were so young. They did not have several days to complete this important ritual. Time was of the essence.

Allie glanced at Aidan, squeezing his hand to get his attention. He gave her a hesitant smile before he returned his gaze to the fountain at the end of the garden.

He was so distant since his return from the Milan Initiative. Even after seven months, he was still so closed off, refusing to share the telepathic bond they'd once lived with every day of their lives. She missed the intimacy of that bond. She knew in her soul he still loved her just as much as he always had, but something stood between them and it broke her heart a little more each day.

Aidan's thumb stroked the pad of her palm, and she smiled. He could convey so much through a simple, calming touch. She could almost hear the voice of his thoughts telling her not to overthink it. She was trying to be patient. To give him all the time he needed to deal with everything he'd experienced at the hands of Marcus Servius.

If she could ever get her hands on that man, she wasn't sure she could contain her judgment gift. If anyone deserved that end, it was him. And she wouldn't feel bad about it.

A wave of fear hit her, and she tried to push it back down. She was so scared ... of everything. Of making one wrong decision that could affect everyone she loved. So many things were coming at her at once; she wasn't sure she was equipped to handle any of it, least of all her Proving she was supposed to be preparing for.

Allie glanced to her other side where she held Chloe's cold and clammy hand. She studied Chloe's familiar face, struggling to get through this ceremony. It was hard for her, witnessing the one thing she wanted more than anything. This Justice guy must be something special. She could hardly wait to tell Chloe he was waiting for her at Soma.

Chloe stood ramrod straight, her gaze zeroed in on the fountain Aidan also stared at. Allie squeezed her hand, and Chloe turned toward her with a frown. She stared at something over Allie's head for a moment and then smiled, nodding as if she agreed with Allie's decisions. It was a huge relief to have Chloe back home. Not just because her gift helped Allie know she was making her best decisions, but because Allie trusted her and valued her opinion.

And she'd missed her so much. She'd missed all of them. Her closest friends were finally returning, bringing with them a host of new friends, Syntrophos, walkers, Scholars, Prophets, and equals they sorely needed in the fight to come.

A gasp of surprise sounded behind her as a cage of blue and golden light fell around them, curling in on the couple at their center. It was happening! Allie's heart swelled at the thought of two of her favorite people coming together. It really was a miracle they ever found each other. And now, they would have their whole lives together. For Santi and Quinn, they would come together as one entity, the time before would fade from their memories until they could no longer remember a time when they weren't together. They were so lucky.

Allie met Aidan's dark gaze, her heart so full of joy and the love she had for him. She couldn't imagine ever loving anyone as much as she loved him. The idea of bonding with her Complement hit her hard in that moment. With her mortal brain, she often forgot it would happen to her someday too. For now, she wanted to enjoy every moment she had with Aidan. That was all that mattered.

Allie bowed her head, listening to the murmurs of Santi and Quinn's voices as they each relinquished their power to the other. In the few precious moments before they completed the bond, they were essentially mortal. Santi held Quinn's power within her as he held hers. Their power would merge as they became one at the completion of the bond. That was why it was so very important for them to be guarded by those who loved them. They would never again be as vulnerable to death as they were right now.

Allie moved with the others as they locked arms, her hands grasping Aidan and Chloe's forearms. They began to circle the couple, their eyes watching for anything that could harm them in this moment.

The joyful laughter that came from Santi and Quinn brought tears to Allie's eyes. She watched as the light of their power shot into the sky to fall in sparks like fireworks as the ritual came to an end.

She would never forget how beautiful this moment was. How perfect these two were together. For the very first time, Allie truly understood what the Complement bond meant. It wasn't something to dread. It wasn't a decision that was taken from her. It was ... everything.

"Allie!" Sasha's voice rang across the garden. She turned to see Jayesh and Sasha running onto the lawn, hands clutched and trembling.

"What's happened?" Allie and Aidan moved together to meet them. Santi and Quinn right behind with Chloe and Graham.

"Are you okay, Sasha?" Quinn asked in a worried tone.

"We're fine." She nodded. "The navigation through the Bermuda Triangle was confusing. It took too long to get there."

"What about the prisoners? Were the aldermen there?" Graham asked.

"Did your team find a way into the prison?" Allie asked.

Sasha shook her head. "The prison was deserted. We were too late. The only thing they left were the prison records. The worst of our kind were kept there, and now hundreds of dangerous Immortals are at large."

Are you ready for the final book in the Immortals of Indriell Series? This multi-point of view novel is releasing later this year. Sign up here to receive the first ten chapters before anyone else.

Chapters will be sent weekly, beginning ten weeks before the release date

DON'T FORGET YOUR FREE BOOK!

In Runaway, find out what happened with Chloe and Graham after they went their separate ways. And then download your free copy of Scholar to discover everything there is to know about the Immortals of Indriell.

Click to download now

Also by Melissa A. Craven

Immortals of Indriell Series:

Emerge (Book 1) | Catalyst (An Immortals of Indriell Short Story) | Edge (Book 0) | Judgment (Book 2) | Scholar (An Immortals of Indriell Series Companion) | Volunteer (An Immortals of Indriell Short Story) | Captive (Book 3) |Assignment: An Immortals of Indriell Novella | Heir (Book 4) Betrayal (Book 5) | Runaway (Book 6) | Proving (Book 7)

Queens of the Fae Series

Fae's Deception (Book 1)

Fae's Defiance (Book 2)

Fae's Destruction (Book 3)

Crimes of the Fae Series

Fae's Prisoner (Book 1)

Fae's Power (Book 2)

Fae's Promise (Book 3)

About Melissa A. Craven

Melissa A. Craven (the "A" stands for Ann—in case you were wondering) writes Young Adult Fantasy with crossover appeal to other genres and audiences of all ages. She believes in stories that make you think and she loves twisty plots, and playing with foreshadowing, leaving clues and hints for the careful reader. She draws inspiration from her background in architecture and interior design to help her with the small details in world building and scene settings. Melissa is also the indie manager and a staff reviewer at YABooksCentral.com. You can follow her reviews and her contributions to the YABC blog at the link below. And if you love Sweet Romance and Contemporary Fiction, you can find Melissa's books in those genres under her pen name, Ann Maree Craven.

Join Melissa's Facebook Group, Fantasy Book Warriors

Follow Melissa at Melissaacraven.com

- facebook.com/MelissaACravenAuthor
- twitter.com/melissaacraven
- instagram.com/melissaacraven
- bookbub.com/authors/melissa-a-craven
- amazon.com/Melissa-A-Craven/e/B00VSPF86W

ACKNOWLEDGMENTS

This book is dedicated to all my patient readers who have waited eagerly for Runaway. Through several delays and multiple rescheduled released dates, I've lost track of how late this book is.

To those who have been waiting, wondering and emailing, thank you for loving this series as much as you do!

I also have to thank my amazing editor, Caitlin Haines who isn't my regular editor for the Immortals of Indriell Series. After a scheduling mishap, Caitlin stepped up and saved my life, and she's the only reason Runaway is happening right now.

Another huge thank you to my sister, Angela for putting up with another round of "Let me just finish this book and then I'll do (insert whatever task Melissa has been putting off), I promise." This happens with every book.

And to Michelle Lynn, my author bestie and co-writer for always being there for venting, crying and freaking out—and most recently, for co-authoring a new fantasy series with me.

A big thank you to the city of Cleveland and to Kelleys Island especially. The island as it is portrayed in the book is purely fictional, but is based on the real Kelleys Island near Sandusky, Ohio.

Finally, I thank God for the constant reminder that I am doing what I'm supposed to be doing. Over the past years, circumstances *always* bring me back to writing—my favorite thing to do in the whole world.

www.ingramcontent.com/pod-product-compliance
Lightning Source LLC
Chambersburg PA
CBHW030525310726
48979CB00010B/1806/J

* 9 7 8 1 9 7 0 0 5 2 1 3 8 *